BEST
SCIENCE FICTION STORIES
OF THE YEAR
Eighth Annual Collection

About the Editor

Gardner Dozois was born and raised in Salem, Massachusetts, and has been writing and editing science fiction for over ten years. His short fiction has appeared in most of the leading SF magazines and anthologies, and he has been a Nebula Award finalist six times, a Hugo Award finalist four times, and a Jupiter Award finalist twice. He is the editor of a number of anthologies, among them *A Day in the Life, Future Power* (with Jack Dann), *Another World*, and *Beyond the Golden Age*. His most recent books are the Nebula Award finalist *Strangers*, a novel; *The Visible Man*, a collection of his short fiction; *Aliens!*, an anthology edited with Jack Dann; and *The Fiction of James Tiptree, Jr.*, a critical chapbook. He is also co-author, with George Alec Effinger, of the novel *Nightmare Blue* and is currently at work on another novel. He is a member of the Science Fiction Writers of America, the SFWA Speakers' Bureau, and the Professional Advisory Committee to the Special Collections Department of the Paley Library at Temple University. Mr. Dozois lives in Philadelphia.

BEST SCIENCE FICTION STORIES OF THE YEAR
Eighth Annual Collection

**Edited By
GARDNER DOZOIS**

E. P. Dutton | New York

For
Michael Swanwick

For information contact:
E.P. Dutton, 2 Park Avenue, New York, N.Y. 10016

Library of Congress Catalog Card Number: 77-190700

ISBN: 0-525-06497-4
Published simultaneously in Canada
by Clarke, Irwin & Company
Limited, Toronto and Vancouver

Designed by Nicola Mazzella

10 9 8 7 6 5 4 3 2 1

First Edition

Contents

Acknowledgments   vi

INTRODUCTION—Summation: 1978   vii

JOHN VARLEY—The Persistence of Vision   1

ISAAC ASIMOV—Found!   38

CHRISTOPHER PRIEST—Whores   50

BERNARD DEITCHMAN—Cousins   60

JOAN D. VINGE—View from a Height   90

THOMAS M. DISCH—Mutability   102

PHYLLIS EISENSTEIN—Lost and Found   117

MICHAEL BISHOP—Old Folks at Home   121

JAMES P. GIRARD—September Song   159

GREGORY BENFORD—In Alien Flesh   172

GENE WOLFE—Seven American Nights   192

Honorable Mentions—1978   232

Acknowledgments

The editor would like to thank the following people for their help and support:

Jim Frenkel, Lou Stathis, Jack Dann, Michael Swanwick, Susan Casper, Christopher Priest, Peter Weston, Virginia Kidd, Kirby McCauley, David G. Hartwell, John Douglas, Charles L. Grant, Geo. Proctor, Terry Carr, Pat LoBrutto, Art Saha, Victoria Schochet, John Silbersack, Ben Bova, Charles C. Ryan, James Baen, Ed Ferman, Meg Phillips, Darrell Schweitzer, George H. Scithers, Judy-Lynn del Rey, Jonathan Ostrowsky-Lantz, John M. Landsberg, Tom Purdom, Michael Bishop, Gregory Benford, Sheila Gilbert, Don and Grace Lundry, Fred Fisher of the Hourglass SF Book Store in Philadelphia, and special thanks to my own editor, Jo Alford.

Thanks are also due to Charles N. Brown, whose excellent newszine *Locus* (P. O. Box 3938, San Francisco, CA 94119—$13.50 for twelve issues) was used as a reference source throughout the Summation. Also used as reference sources were *Science Fiction Review*, edited by Richard E. Geis (P. O. Box 11408, Portland, OR 97211—$7.50 for one year, six issues), and *The Bulletin of the Science Fiction Writers of America*, edited by John F. Carr (10512 Yarmouth Ave., Granada Hills, CA 91344).

INTRODUCTION

Summation: 1978

The Big SF Boom of the late seventies kept right on booming in 1978. Despite the warnings of conservative critics, the boom did *not* bust this year, the predicted collapse and disastrous retrenchment of the genre did not occur, and though all but the most avid boosters will still admit to the uneasy fear that the field may indeed be in the process of overextending itself, SF as a commercial category continues to expand with no ceiling yet in sight.

The last few years have brought almost unbelievable changes to SF, changes that have—for better or worse—altered the very nature of the SF world, perhaps irrevocably. When I took charge of this series early in 1976, the SF magazine market was moribund, stagnant, obviously on its way to extinction—there were only five American SF magazines left, three of them on their last legs, and of them all only *Analog* boasted a circulation of 100,000 copies or more per issue. In 1978, there were at least thirteen SF and fantasy magazines available (one could easily get that figure up to twenty by counting the most marginal of the semiprozines), all but three of them (the same ailing three as in 1976, by the way) in at least reasonable health.

For the first time in history, an SF magazine, *Omni*, reached a circulation of 1 million copies per issue; *Starlog* and *Future*, two SF-related nonfiction magazines, claim a combined circulation of over 400,000 copies, and a readership near the million and a half mark; there are now two digest-size SF magazines with a circulation of 100,000 copies or greater, and other magazines are snapping at their heels. Prior to 1976, five-figure novel advances were almost unheard of; now, no year goes by without at least a half dozen high five-figure advances paid, and even a few six-figure advances. Robert Silverberg's new novel, *Lord Valentine's Castle*, sold to *hardcover* in 1978 for a reputed $127,500, and observers are already speculating that the paperback rights will go for half a million dollars or more. Similarly, rates of payment for fiction in the SF magazines have risen steadily in recent years. Prior to 1976, the top SF magazine fiction rate was five cents a word; in 1978, there were four magazines paying five cents a word as their *bottom* rate for short fiction, two paying ten cents a word for short fiction, one anthology series paying seven to eight cents a word, and one magazine paying the kind of really big money—$800 to $1,250 per short story—formerly reserved for top mainstream markets like *Playboy*.

More SF and fantasy books were published in 1978 than ever before, beating even last year's bumper crop. Charles N. Brown, of the SF newszine *Locus*, estimates that there were "well over a thousand" such books this year, and next year's total may well go up substantially. Dell has gone from eight titles a year in 1976 to twenty-eight titles in 1978, and will go up to forty-eight titles in 1979; Berkley has gone from two paperback titles a month and "an occasional hardcover" in 1976 to four paperbacks a month and fourteen hardcovers in 1978; Pocket Books has gone from two titles a month to three titles a month, and is "working toward four"; Del Rey Books has gone from three titles a month in 1976 to six titles a month and "an indeterminate number of hardcovers a year" in 1978; Ace Books, nearly moribund four years ago, now claims to be "the world's largest SF publisher, both in number of titles released and in volume of sales," having gone from four titles a month in 1976 to an incredible eight to ten titles a month, plus an additional six to nine "promotional titles" every other month, in 1978. And similar increases have taken place almost across the board.

Now, conventional wisdom tells us that the SF audience cannot possibly be sufficiently large to absorb such a vast outpouring of new books—that the market will become glutted and oversaturated, as happened during the postwar SF boom of the fifties, and that publishers will start losing money hand over fist: a bust, inevitably following—*caused by*—the boom.

To date, this has shown no sign of happening.

In fact, sales were *up* in 1978. Anne McCaffrey's *The White Dragon* (Del Rey Books) sold over 62,000 copies in a $10.95 hardcover edition, and many paperback titles sold over 100,000 copies, some a half million or more.

Has the SF audience suddenly grown—grown wide enough and various enough—*big* enough—to absorb all this? If not, then where is it all going? Has the SF audience been permanently expanded? If not, when will they stop buying?

No one knows.

It is quite possible to demonstrate, however, that SF and fantasy in all their related forms probably made more money in 1978 than ever before in history (I am tempted to say: more money in 1978 than in all of previous history *combined*, and even that statement might not be too far from the mark). According to Craig Miller, writing in *Asimov's SF Adventure Magazine, Star Wars* and *Close Encounters of the Third Kind* alone earned over $350 million in box-office receipts and rentals last year, plus an additional $150 million in spinoff paraphernalia: T-shirts, toys, games, books, records, and so forth. Add to that the profits of the year's other big-grossing SF and fantasy films—*Superman, The Wiz, Heaven Can Wait, The Lord of the Rings,* and so on—and the profits from *their* spinoff paraphernalia. Add the profits of SF and fantasy shows on television, and *their* spinoff paraphernalia. Add the perennially high-selling *Star Trek* paraphernalia, and a deluge of SF and fantasy-inspired calendars, postcards, paintings, jewelry, sculpture, glossy art books, coffee-table books, spoken-word records, puzzles, war games, and so on. Add the money earned by all the dealers in old manuscripts, fanzines, rare books, memorabilia. Add the profits of all the dozens—if not hundreds—of SF and fantasy conventions, film festivals, lectures, and seminars that now take place throughout the world. Add the profits earned by all of the books *about* SF: scholarly works, classic reprint series, biographies, bibliographies, checklists, histories, picture books, memoirs. Then add the money earned by the flood of hardcover and paperback novels, collections, and anthologies, and the massed profits of all the SF and fantasy magazines.

The total must be immense—certainly it breaks the billion-dollar mark.

Suddenly, we are no longer talking about a marginal, ghettoized literature with minimum profits and minimal expectations. Suddenly, we are talking about Big Business.

Not all of this forced-draft prosperity has been beneficial, by any means. This year we watched the producers of *Star Wars* and the producers of TV's *Battlestar Galactica* engage in a mutual exchange of multimillion-dollar lawsuits and countersuits to determine who was stealing concepts from whom—concepts which have been part of the common heritage of SF for more than fifty years, but which may soon be legally ceded to a large corporation, which will then have the right to defend them with unsmiling ferocity against future encroachments.

This is big business with teeth—and typical of the cold wind which is blowing some of that sweet smell of money into the genre. Attracted by SF's moneymaking potential, the creative end of the genre is in many places in danger of being taken over by corporate marketing specialists who have no intention of taking any risks, by people who care nothing about SF as an artform, by people who think of writers as sausage factories and regard the SF audience as just another cowlike group of consumers to be manipulated. The pressure increases to squeeze all the lush variety and scope of modern SF down into one narrow mold (if *Star Wars* sells best, then give them *nothing but Star Wars*, however shoddy the imitations become). In this year of big questions, the one that does not get asked is this: In a market suddenly and urgently (and rather condescendingly) aiming itself down to hit the audience it *thinks Star Wars* tapped, is there room anymore for the adult story of quality?

Many people I've talked to in the publishing world this year have told me: No, there is not.

It is ironic, in the face of all this booming, that the one SF magazine that consistently, year after year, maintains the highest overall level of literary quality is *The Magazine of Fantasy and Science-Fiction*, which is put together in Ed Ferman's living room on a shoestring budget and barely runs in the black, if it does—the very type of publication that would be immediately dropped by most conglomerate-owned publishers because it was only marginally profitable. And yet, if there comes a time when SF has no room for such labors of love, then we will have been killed by our success more surely than we ever were by failure.

Samuel Goldwyn's famous dictum "Nobody ever went broke underestimating the taste of the American public" applies just as well (perhaps better) to the SF reading public. Nevertheless, throughout the history of the genre an occasional naive or courageous editor has found—to everyone's surprise—that he did very well by treating his audience as if it were composed of intelligent adults of all ages; hopefully, a few editors will continue to act .on that unorthodox and possibly dangerous assumption even in years to come.

Again this year, most of the action was in the once-somnolent magazine market. And in that field, the success story of the year—if not the decade—was undoubtably Bob Guccione's *Omni*, which sold over a million copies of its premiere issue (at a steep $2 a copy), achieving, for the moment at least, by far the largest magazine circulation in SF history.

Omni is a large, slick, lavishly produced science fact-and-fiction magazine from the publishers of *Penthouse*—indeed, it is almost identical in look, layout, and packaging to *Penthouse*, except that *Omni* intersperses its fact articles with SF stories instead of pictures of naked women. With an enormous editorial budget, and the largest advertising budget in the history of the genre (used in part for a saturation campaign of very well done television commercials), *Omni* is attracting major advertisers like General Motors who have never slummed in SF before, and is paying the highest word rates for fiction of any publication calling itself an SF magazine (*Playboy* pays a bit more, but uses SF only occasionally). Indeed, due to *Omni*'s extensive and widespread advertising campaign, the chances are that if the average citizen on the street has ever heard of *any* SF magazine, *Omni* is the one.

In spite of all this, not everyone in the SF world is impressed with *Omni*, not by any means. Some object to the pseudoscientific articles (on astrology, the occult, ESP phenomenan, etc.) that fill a good percentage of every issue, or dislike the magazine's rather credulous stand on UFOs. Some think that too much space is devoted to photographic spreads and other graphics. Some feel that *Omni*'s fiction, aimed as it is at a wide, non-genre audience, is too watered down to be good SF. Others seem to be jealous of *Omni*'s commercial success, or even frightened by it. Some of these criticisms are justified, or at least partially justifiable. I would like to see more space and emphasis devoted to the fiction, and less to the articles and interviews (the SF writers are usually not even mentioned on the Contributors' Page, for instance), but I also realize that *Omni*'s publishers are unlikely to tamper with a winning formula. The magazine's rather calculated credulity toward UFOs and other faddish occult subjects annoys me as well, but the same comment applies—and if such stuff sells the magazine, I can live with it, as long as that attitude is kept out of the fiction. And while it's true that *Omni* has to date published some alarmingly poor fiction—considering that it's working with the top editorial budget in SF—it has also published some first-rate stuff by people like Isaac Asimov and Gregory Benford and Marc Laidlaw, and good work by Leigh Kennedy, Theodore Sturgeon, Harlan Ellison, and others; I also suspect that the influence of new fiction editor Ben Bova (formerly editor of *Analog*) has yet to make itself completely felt. What is really at question here, however, may go far beyond the excellence or lack of excellence of an individual magazine.

Right up until the end of the year, conservative observers were betting that the million-copy sellout of *Omni*'s first issue was a one-time fluke, a flash in the pan; that sales would drop off sharply on the second issue, perhaps by as much as half, or even two-thirds; that *Omni* would not last out the coming year.

But in a telephone interview just prior to the typing of a clean copy of this Summation, fiction editor Ben Bova told me that the second issue had sold "well over 800,000 copies" (plus a subscription list of 65,000) and mentioned that "major advertisers are now coming in for long-term commitments." *Omni* may eventually die (it took five years, after all, for *Penthouse*'s companion magazine *Viva* to finally give up the ghost), but unless sales plunge catastrophically in 1979, it's not going to happen soon.

If the conservative observers are wrong, if *Omni* is successful, then just by its existence and example it may change the face of SF publishing forever. Already, there are fairly well substantiated rumors that both *Playboy* and Time-Life are considering bringing out large, slick, high-paying SF magazines of their own, and there are less reliable rumors that say that at least two or three other major publishers are thinking of doing the same. If any of these other magazines do come out, and if they too are successful, then the SF magazine field could be nearly unrecognizable a couple of years from now. If so, then the proliferation of high-paying magazines like *Omni* may also reverse the long-standing tendency of SF writers to give up writing short fiction in favor of novels once they become moderately well known, simply by making short stories worth the time expended in writing them. And if even a portion of *Omni*'s huge audience can be converted into habitual SF readers, the gain to the genre could be enormous.

One thing that has been overshadowed by the gaudy publicity

surrounding *Omni* is the success (by pre-*Omni* standards) of that relative newcomer, *Isaac Asimov's Science Fiction Magazine*. Now appearing monthly, *IASFM* enjoys a circulation of about 108,000 copies an issue, divided more or less evenly between subscriptions and newsstand sales, making it the first digest-size SF magazine to outsell *Analog* in more than a decade. *IASFM* remains uneven in quality, and although many good stories did appear there this year—by Brian W. Aldiss, Randall Garrett, Tony Sarowitz, Hal Clement, Mildred Downey Broxon, and others—much of what the magazine publishes leaves me cold. Nevertheless, it cannot be denied that editor George H. Scithers has an uncanny grasp of what his own particular slice of the SF audience wants; in less than three years he has pushed his magazine to the sales leadership of the digest SF magazine field, and earned himself a Best Editor Hugo. Ironically, Scithers, three years ago the newest SF magazine editor, is today, due to upheavals within the magazine market, the most experienced editor of a digest-size magazine, excepting only Ed Ferman of *F & SF*.

IASFM's new companion magazine, *Asimov's SF Adventure Magazine*, a large-format magazine, has been much less successful—it is said to be breaking even at about 50,000 copies an issue, and its future is in doubt. Scithers has described *ASFA* as "an attempt to coax the reading-oriented end of the *Star Wars* audience—and the kids who are growing out of the SF comic books—into magazine SF," but the magazine doesn't seem entirely comfortable in practice with this policy; its practical (and unhappy) result has been a magazine clearly aimed at juveniles—and aimed rather condescendingly at that—that nowhere on the covers or in the copy advises the potential reader of that fact. Except for the first installment of Joe and Jack Haldeman's novel *Starschool*—again, clearly a juvenile novel in the Heinlein tradition, although it is not billed as such—*ASFA* has so far published little or nothing of value, although reportedly some more interesting and more adult material has been purchased for upcoming issues. Scithers might well do better to abandon the watered-down space opera slant of *ASFA* altogether and turn it into an adult fantasy/sword-and-sorcery magazine, something he certainly has the credentials to edit and with which he would probably feel more at home.

Shaken by internal reorganizations, outstripped in sales by younger magazines, suffering from slowly dwindling circulation, *Analog* this year was faced with its most serious crisis since the death of editor John W. Campbell, Jr., in 1971. *Analog*'s continued existence is probably not in doubt (it still has a circulation in the 100,000-copy range, after all), but, challenged for the leadership of the digest field on at least two fronts, it may not be flexible or adaptive enough to avoid a long, slow dwindling away into, in Richard Geis' words, "a respectable dotage." Lack of flexibility and an alleged "unwilling[ness] to put money into expanding their SF" were among the several policy disagreements that led to the resignation of longtime *Analog* editor Ben Bova this fall. (Bova subsequently became fiction editor of *Omni*.) Associate Editor Victoria Schochet also left *Analog* this year to become SF editor—along with John

Silbersack—of Berkley, replacing David G. Hartwell, who moved to Pocket Books.

Analog's new editor is Stanley Schmidt, a familiar name to *Analog* readers and a frequent contributor to the magazine under Bova's long regime. The question is: Can Schmidt breathe enough new life and excitement into *Analog* to enable it to compete successfully with *Omni*, or at least with *IASFM?* Bova's primary accomplishment as *Analog* editor was to open the magazine up to a number of writers who had been effectively barred from it during Campbell's editorship, among them Larry Niven, Roger Zelazny, Joe Haldeman, Gregory Benford, and George R. R. Martin; Bova is also to be praised for publishing—especially in the last couple of years—a moderately high percentage of stories that pushed hard at the limits of what is usually considered to be an "*Analog* story." If Schmidt is willing to keep pushing at those same limits, changing a formula that may have become overly familiar, then he might have a fighting chance of revitalizing the magazine; otherwise, *Analog*'s future may be, if not dim, at least dull.

As I mentioned above, *F & SF* was the most consistently excellent of all the SF magazines for yet another year, publishing first-rate material by John Varley, Christopher Priest, Brian W. Aldiss, Gregory Benford, Avram Davidson, Terry Carr, Thomas M. Disch, Stephen King, and many others. And certainly Ed Ferman—the unsung and unobtrusive editor of *F & SF*—is long, long overdue for a Best Editor Hugo; maybe next year. (For those of you who have difficulty finding *F & SF* on the newsstands—and it does have a limited distribution—the subscription address is: Mercury Press, Inc., Box 56, Cornwall CT 06753; $12.50 for one year.)

Although not in the rarefied realms we have been discussing, the success of *Galileo* has also been, relatively speaking, modestly spectacular. *Galileo* is now selling about 60,000 copies an issue—pretty damn good for a subscription-only magazine not generally available on newsstands. Although the overall quality of its fiction has not yet dependably reached the level of *F & SF* or *Analog*—or even that of the best of *IASFM—Galileo* has steadily improved over the last two years, and with its recently hiked word rate may begin to attract some really first-rate material. (*Galileo*'s subscription address is: 339 Newbury St., Dept. G, Boston MA 02115; $7.50 for six issues; $12 for 12 issues.) *UNEARTH*, another subscription-only magazine, also seems to have carved out a fairly steady audience of its own, although a much smaller one than *Galileo*'s. Perhaps more literarily ambitious than *Galileo*, and potentially wider in scope (*Galileo* is seriously hampered by an inane publisher's injunction against "downbeat stories" and "unhappy endings"), *UNEARTH* has also to date been more sporadic and uneven in quality. (*UNEARTH*'s subscription address is: 102 Charles St., #190, Boston MA 02114; $4 per year for four issues.) There are two other non-newsstand magazines worth mentioning: *Whispers*, edited by Stuart David Schiff, and *Shayol*, edited by Patricia Cadigan and Arnold Fenner. *Whispers*, the longer established of the two, specializes in the work of supernatural-horror-and-sword-and-sorcery writers like Manly Wade Wellman, Karl Edward Wagner, Avram Davidson, and Fritz Leiber. (*Whispers*: Box 1492W, Azalea St., Browns Mills, NJ 08015; $7 for a 4-issue subscription.) *Shayol* is probably the most handsomely produced fantasy magazine in America (the Roger Stine cover for *Shayol 1* gets my vote for most beautiful cover of the year) and features a crew of bright young talents working on the borderline of SF and fantasy—Lisa Tuttle, Howard Waldrop, Steven Utley, William Wallace, Pat Cadigan—as well as established writers like Harlan Ellison and the late Tom Reamy. (*Shayol*: 4324 Belleview, Apt. 3, Kansas City MO 64111; $3 a single copy, $10 for four issues.) The time is ripe for a major fantasy magazine, and either of these could expand to fill that ecological niche, given backing and professional distribution.

On the downhill side, J. J. Pierce resigned after less than a year as editor of *Galaxy*, stating that the publisher's alleged nonpayment of writers and artists made it impossible for him to continue. *Galaxy*'s new editor is writer Hank Stine, who announced a bizarre plan to pay off the magazine's alleged $18,000 in back debts by dropping *Galaxy*'s rate of payment from the old three cents a word to a flat one cent a word, the difference between the two rates being put toward payment of past contributors. Practically no short fiction of any merit appeared in *Galaxy* in 1978.

After years of skating on the brink of financial collapse, *Amazing* and *Fantastic* have finally died as original magazines; the titles, which were sold to a new publisher this fall, will be kept in existence as all-reprint magazines. Longtime editor Ted White is no longer connected with either magazine. Although I'll miss *Amazing* and *Fantastic*—Ted White often did a remarkably good job of making bricks entirely without straw—it is almost a relief to see the poor shambling, exhausted, half-dead things finally put out of their misery.

Things were also altering—although not necessarily for the better—in the original anthology market, with a few long-established anthology series lost here, a few new series added there. In 1976 there were eight anthology series—of these, in 1978, *Orbit* and the *Clarion* series are dead, the future of *New Dimensions* is in doubt, and the *Science Fiction Discoveries* series never produced another issue; some promised series, like Edward Bryant's *Entropy*, have never appeared at all.

Of these, the most grievous loss was the death of Damon Knight's *Orbit*, which was dropped by Harper & Row in 1977 and failed to find another publisher this year. Established in 1966, *Orbit* was the longest-running anthology series in SF history. At one time the spearhead of the avant-garde movement in American SF, *Orbit* published the bulk of Kate Wilhelm's short fiction, much of Gene Wolfe's best work, and stories by Joanna Russ, Thomas M. Disch, Richard McKenna, Carol Emshwiller, Avram Davidson, Ursula K. Le Guin, Brian W. Aldiss, and R. A. Lafferty that might otherwise have had difficulty finding a home. *Orbit* was also instrumental in introducing the work of newer authors such as Edward Bryant, George Alec Effinger, Jack Dann, Robert Thurston,

Joan D. Vinge, Charles L. Grant, Vonda N. McIntyre, Gardner Dozois, and many others. In later years, *Orbit* went into a slump (*Orbit 16* and *Orbit 17* have the most lackluster reputation) that was probably partially responsible—along with the continuing inability of the series to attract a paperback publisher (there has been no *Orbit* in paperback since *Orbit 13*)—for the series' subsequent demise. Ironically, *Orbit* had been recovering from its doldrums in the last few years—*Orbit 20*, for instance, features a superlative novella by Gene Wolfe, another first-rate novella by Kate Wilhelm, and good work by Pamela Sargent and R. A. Lafferty. Harper & Row has one further *Orbit* in production; tentatively scheduled to appear in 1980.

The two other oldest and most-prestigious anthology series are Terry Carr's *Universe* and Robert Silverberg's *New Dimensions*, and of the two only *Universe* seems to be on fairly secure economic ground. Harper & Row is reportedly thinking about dropping *New Dimensions*; a proposed paperback deal has fallen through, and it's anyone's guess as to whether the series will survive. At one time *New Dimensions* was probably the best anthology series in SF, and in spite of the relative weakness of the last few volumes, the series abundantly deserves another chance at life. *New Dimensions 8* is up a good deal in quality from last year's somewhat bland volume, although again the book is so uneven that it seems to split almost in half—one half contains excellent work by Jack Dann and Christopher Priest, and good work by Michael Bishop, Craig Strete, Greg Bear, and Robert R. Olsen; the other half is filled with stories that range from uninspired to unreadable. Carr's *Universe* was once again the best in overall quality of all the anthology series—*Universe 8* contains a fine novella by Michael Bishop, and good stuff by Gregory Benford, Michael Cassutt, Greg Bear, R. A. Lafferty, and Cynthia Felice.

If *New Dimensions* follows *Orbit* into oblivion, *Universe* and *F & SF* will be about the only remaining refuges of the "literary" or "experimental" story, a sobering thought in a period when many editors seem to be shooting for the lowest common denominator and taking fewer and fewer risks. Although the recent economic shakiness of *Orbit* and *ND* has been blamed on their being too "highbrow" for the new audience brought into SF by *Star Wars* (a rather snobbish and condescending thought in itself), I give a good deal more weight to the fact that they are both hardback originals with increasingly more prohibitive cover prices. Most of the other existing anthology series are paperback originals, and although none of them can as yet compete in overall literary quality with the "Big Three" hardcover series discussed above, it may also be that the hardcover series can no longer compete in the economic marketplace with the paperback anthology series.

Best of this year's paperback original series was Peter Weston's *Andromeda 3* (Futura Publications); up strongly from last year's disappointing slump, it featured good work by Christopher Priest and Larry Niven, and a powerful novelette by Fritz Leiber. Judy-Lynn del Rey's *Stellar 4* was also stronger than last year's edition, containing good stories by James Tiptree Jr. and Ben Bova, and quirky but interesting material by James P. Hogan and Stephen R. Donaldson. On the other hand, Roy Torgeson's *Chrysalis 2*(Zebra) was even more disappointing than last year's *Chrysalis*—a few decent minor stories here, but no really good ones, and a good deal of marginal stuff that probably shouldn't have been printed at all. Ben Bova's *Analog Yearbook* (Baronet—the reincarnation of 1977's *Analog Annual*) was a good deal more competent than *Chrysalis 2*, but still rather bland, and overpriced in an $8.95 trade paperback edition.

Two new anthology series were launched this year: James Baen's *Destinies* (Ace) and Charles L. Grant's *Shadows* (Doubleday). *Destinies*, billed as a "bookzine" or "magazine in book form," got off to a promising start, the first issue resembling nothing so much as it does an issue of Baen's *Galaxy*, complete with a Spider Robinson book review column, and a science article by Jerry Pournelle—interesting stuff here by Roger Zelazny, Gregory Benford, and Dean Ing. If Baen can keep up the quality—and he does have a large editorial budget to work with—this may be an important series. *Shadows*, an anthology featuring quiet but *scary* supernatural horror stories, was probably the best new series of the year—an excellent novella here by Stephen King, and good stuff by Avram Davidson, John Crowley, R. A. Lafferty, and Thomas Monteleone; I hope they find a paperback publisher as soon as possible.

There were fewer one-shot original anthologies this year, but on the whole they far outshone last year's lackluster crop. The best one-shot anthology of the year was Christopher Priest's *Anticipations* (Scribner's), a literate and speculatively exciting book that has unfortunately received little or no attention in the genre press; the kingpiece here is Brian W. Aldiss's long and brilliant novella "A Chinese Perspective," backed up by excellent short work by Thomas M. Disch, Ian Watson, Robert Scheckley, and Priest himself. Not far behind was Jack Dann's excellent anthology *Immortal* (Harper & Row), a novella collection featuring elegant and absorbing long work by Pamela Sargent, Gene Wolfe, and Thomas M. Disch. A very good short novel by Ursula K. Le Guin is the major asset of Virginia Kidd's *Millennial Women* (Delacorte); most people will buy the anthology on the strength of the Le Guin piece alone, but the book also contains a poignant novelette by Joan D. Vinge, and interesting work by Elizabeth A. Lynn and Cynthia Felice. The only real disappointment of the lot was Alice Laurance's *Cassandra Rising* (Doubleday), an anthology packed with a great many very short and very minor stories, none of which rise anywhere near the top range of any of the authors involved.

Among the reprint anthologies, unusually good buys were Ben Bova's *The Best of Analog* (Baronet), Ed Ferman's *The Best from F & SF, 22nd Series* (Ace), Robert Silverberg's *Alpha 9* (Berkley), and Terry Carr's *Classic Science Fiction: The First Golden Age* (Harper & Row).

Although 1978 produced no novels as strong, tightly plotted, and rigorous as last year's best (Frederik Pohl's *Gateway*, Gregory Benford's *In the Ocean of Night*, and Algis Budrys' *Michaelmas*), it did produce a number of well-crafted novels that relied heavily on mood, characterization, philosophy, "color," and elegantly written prose. Vonda N. McIntyre's *Dreamsnake* (Dell) was probably the most popular and critically acclaimed novel of 1978; its merits include some very good and very perceptive characterization, some excellent "color," and smoothly evocative prose, but for all that, it is rather pedestrianly—and episodically—plotted, and suffers from a weak ending. Similarly, James Tiptree Jr's long-awaited first novel, *Up the Walls of the World* (Berkley), is packed with fascinating ideas and characters, and with bravura prose pyrotechnics, but suffers from an overcomplicated plot that wanders on for at least two chapters after the book should already be over. Joanna Russ' *The Two of Them* (Berkley) starts out as a sophisticated, witty, and darkly elegant novel, but ultimately bogs down in its own polemic. Ian Watson's two novels—*Alien Embassy* (Ace) and *Miracle Visitors* (Ace)—on the other hand, are somewhat crudely crafted and show many signs of hurried writing, but are jampacked with new technical/philosophical/cosmological ideas. Some of these ideas are fascinating, some disturbing, many merely silly, but they make reading the Watson novels an intellectually stimulating and frequently outrageous experience. Also often outrageous (a million years indeed, Mr. Aldiss!) is Brian W. Aldiss's *Enemies of the System* (Harper & Row), a sly and acidulous combination of fable and political satire that unfortunately makes up into a *very* slender $7.95 hardcover (especially as, as far as I can tell, the complete text appeared as a novella in the June *F & SF*)—this, however, is the publisher's mistake, not the author's. Tom Reamy's posthumous novel *Blind Voices* (Berkley) is an insightful, well-crafted, and often moving rural fantasy reminiscent of vintage Bradbury. C. J. Cherryh's *The Faded Sun: Kesrith* (DAW) and George R. R. Martin's *The Dying of the Light* (Pocket Books) are excellent in their portrayal of alien folkways and psychology. Sleeper of the year, however, is Christopher Priest's *The Perfect Lover* (Dell), a first-rate novel that has received no attention whatsoever, although it balances literary craftsmanship with intriguing sociological speculation in a more even-handed and successful way than many of the more acclaimed novels mentioned above.

Also interesting were Poul Anderson's *The Avatar* (Berkley/Putnam), Gregory Benford's *The Stars in Shroud* (Berkley/Putnam), Ben Bova's *Colony* (Pocket Books), Marta Randall's *Journey* (Pocket Books), Barry Malzberg's *Chorale* (Doubleday), and a flock of promising first novels: Elizabeth A. Lynn's *A Different Light* (Berkley), Cynthia Felice's *Godsfire* (Pocket Books), Bruce Sterling's *Involution Ocean* (Jove), Robert Thurston's *Alicia II* (Berkley/Putnam), Joan D. Vinge's *The Outcasts of Heaven Belt* (NAL), and Scott Baker's *Symbiote's Crown* (Berkley).

1978 was also a good year for short story collections. Best of the lot was John Varley's first collection, *The Persistence of Vision* (Dell), a memorable book that may someday come to be ranked among such seminal collections as Cordwainer Smith's *Space Lords*, Samuel R. Delany's *Driftglass*, and James Tiptree Jr.'s *Ten Thousand Light-Years from Home*. Kate Wilhelm's *Somerset Dreams and Other Stories* (Harper & Row) and James Tiptree Jr's *Star-Songs of an Old Primate* (Del Rey

Books) are eloquent, passionate, and strange, the Tiptree in particular peopled with bizarre and wonderful characters, the Wilhelm full of spooky and oddly beautiful Jungian overtones that resonate long after the last page is turned. Algis Budrys has been writing again in recent years, after a dismayingly long silence, and some of the best of both Old and New Budrys are to be found in *Blood and Burning* (Berkley), which features mysteries and a sea story, as well as the expected SF. Also first-rate was Joe Haldeman's first collection, *Infinite Dreams* (St. Martin's Press)—although Haldeman does his best work at novel length, his short fiction is never less than entertaining and professionally crafted, often ingenious, occasionally funny, and sometimes very powerful indeed. Two other long-overdue collections, by two underrated and shamefully ignored writers, also saw print this year: Avram Davidson's *The Redward Edward Papers* (Doubleday) and Edgar Pangborn's posthumous collection *Still I Persist in Wondering* (Dell), both highly recommended to anyone who enjoys intelligent, literate, and thoughtful (and, in Davidson's case, wildly funny) fantasy and SF.

Also worthwhile were Harlan Ellison's *Strange Wine* (Harper & Row), Poul Anderson's *The EarthBook of Stormgate* (Berkley/Putnam), George Alec Effinger's *Dirty Tricks* (Doubleday), Phyllis Eisenstein's *Born to Exile* (Arkham House), and a paperback reprint of Robert Silverberg's *Unfamiliar Territory* (Berkley). The year's other good collections were all from Del Rey Books: *The Best of L. Sprague De Camp*; *The Best of Leigh Brackett*; *The Best of Murry Leinster*; *The Best of Jack Williamson*; *The Best of Lester del Rey*; *The Best of Eric Frank Russell*; and *The Best of Raymond Z. Gallun*.

The best SF-oriented nonfiction book of the year was Frederik Pohl's autobiography *The Way the Future Was* (Del Rey Books). Pohl's memoirs are perhaps less nakedly frank and self-revealing than Damon Knight's autobiography in *Hell's Cartographers*, but they are witty, acute, and absorbing, full of fascinating anecdotes and inside information about the giants of the field, one of whom is Pohl himself; this is recommended reading for anyone who is interested in the history of the genre, and should be (along with *Hell's Cartographers*, Knight's *The Futurians*, and the Doubleday restrospective *Early* collections like *The Early Asimov*) required reading for anyone attempting to write critically about it. The best SF reference book of the year (and quite probably the best of the decade) is Gregg Press's enormous *Index to Science Fiction Anthologies and Collections* compiled by William Contento, edited by L. W. Currey and David G. Hartwell; at $28.00 the *Index* may be too expensive for the casual reader, but it will prove invaluable to the scholar, anthologist, critic and collector. Much less impressive was *Science Fiction: Contemporary Mythology* (Harper & Row), edited by Martin Harry Greenberg, Joseph D. Olander, and Patricia Warrick, a well-intentioned but dry, mixed anthology of fiction and scholarly critical essays that contained far too many familiar and overanthologized stories to justify its high cover price. Samuel R. Delany's *The American Shore* (Dragon Press) is a dense, painstaking, 243-page sentence-by-sentence analysis of a single short story by Thomas M. Disch; although occasionally fascinating, this book is almost exclusively for the real scholar or specialist. On the other hand, Colin Lester's *SF Yearbook* (Quick Fox Books) is intended to be a guide for the general public to everything happening in the SF world, but it is so confusingly set up that I never did figure out how to find my way around its masses of data, in spite of a lengthy How-to-Use key in the front.

Among the flood of SF and fantasy art books this year, the best values were Brian Froud and Alan Lee's *Faeries* (Harry N. Abrams, Inc.), Ian Summers' *Tomorrow and Beyond* (Workman), and Harry Harrison's *Mechanismo* (Reed Books).

On the theatrical front, the expected wave of *Star Wars* imitations did not hit with full force in this country this year, although there were dozens of them in Europe and Japan, and more are in production, including *Flash Gordon*, a movie version of *Star Trek*, and *Star Wars II* itself. Television's *Battlestar Galactica*—a show so insipid, moronic, and vile that it makes *Star Wars* seem like a masterpiece by comparison—has been sinking slowly down the ratings list all year in spite of a multimillion-dollar advertising budget, and with any luck will have foundered completely by the time this book sees print. Unexpectedly, 1978 turned out to be the year of the big-budget light-fantasy movie instead, movies like *Superman*, *The Wiz*, *Heaven Can Wait*, and *Invasion of the Body Snatchers* doing big box-office business.

Of perhaps more immediate interest to the readers of this volume, 1978 also marked the return to prominence of the full-length animated feature (viable again for the first time since Disney-style animation became prohibitively expensive), and the use of animation to bring two classic fantasies to the screen.

I went to *Watership Down* prepared to scoff—talking rabbits?—but came away with the realization that it is unquestionably the finest fantasy film of 1978; in fact, *Watership Down* is the best fantasy movie I've seen in years, and only cynics and self-conscious sophisticates will have trouble suspending their disbelief enough to enjoy it. Intelligently scripted, featuring exquisite (and not at all Disneyfied) animation and excellent voice characterizations, *Watership Down* is as suspenseful as a good war movie, and often moving. Ralph Bakshi's *Lord of the Rings* is much more disappointing, although it wasn't as bad as I had feared it might be—after Bakshi's last film, *Wizards*, a monumental exercise in stupidity and poor taste that Bakshi had proclaimed was a dry-run for *LOTR*, I was fully prepared to see *LOTR* turned into a similar camp underground epic, perhaps retitled *Fritz the Hobbit*. However, while I doubt that *LOTR* will totally satisfy any Tolkien fan, it is at least a decent technical solution to an extremely difficult aesthetic problem; I would give it a C-plus, anyway. Not that the film doesn't make more than its share of aesthetic missteps: Galadrial looks like an airline stewardess, for instance, and Treebeard like a walking carrot. More seriously, Bakshi's rotoscoping technique (animating over live film footage) severely cramps both action and atmosphere in several places by limiting the animated characters to only those movements their live-action counterparts were physically capable of making. The film may also confuse (if not bewilder) those not already familiar with Tolkien's work, and ends with one of the most enormous (unannounced) cliff-hanging anticlimaxes anyone has ever had the nerve to foist on the viewing public.

The 36th World Science Fiction Convention, IguanaCon, was held in Phoenix, Arizona, over the Labor Day weekend and had the largest attendance (more than 4,700 people) of any worldcon in history. The 1977 Hugo Awards, presented at IguanaCon, were: Best Novel—*Gateway*, by Frederik Pohl; Best Novella—"Stardance," by Spider and Jeanne Robinson; Best Novelette—"Eyes of Amber," by Joan D. Vinge; Best Short Story—"Jeffty Is Five," by Harlan Ellison; Best Editor—George H. Scithers; Best Professional Artist—Rick Sternbach; Best Dramatic Presentation—*Star Wars*; Best Fan Artist—Phil Foglio; Best Fan Writer—Richard E. Geis; Best Fanzine—*Locus*; plus the John W. Campbell, Jr., Award to Orson Scott Card; the Gandalf Award for Best Fantasy Novel to *The Silmarillion* by J.R.R. Tolkien; and the Grandmaster of Fantasy Award to Poul Anderson.
The 1977 Nebula Awards were: Best Novel—*Gateway*, by Frederik Pohl; Best Novella—"Stardance," by Spider and Jeanne Robinson; Best Novelette—"The Screwfly Solution," by Raccoona Sheldon; Best Short Story—"Jeffty Is Five," by Harlan Ellison.
The Fourth Annual World Fantasy Awards were: Best Novel—*Our Lady of Darkness*, by Fritz Leiber; Best Collection—*Murgunstrumm and Others*, by Hugh B. Cave; Best Short Fiction—"The Chimney," by Ramsey Campbell; Best Artist—Lee Brown Coye; Special Award (professional)—E. F. Bleiler; Special Award (nonprofessional)—Robert Weinberg; plus a Life Achievement Award to Frank Belknap Long.
The Jupiter Awards for 1977 were: Best Novel—*A Heritage of Stars*, by Clifford Simak; Best Novella—"In the Hall of the Martian Kings," John Varley; Best Novelette—"Time Storm," by Gordon R. Dickson; Best Short Story—"Jeffty Is Five," by Harlan Ellison.

The SF world lost one of its most beloved figures this year with the death of writer Leigh Brackett. Born in 1915, she rose to prominence in the pulp SF magazines of the forties and fifties—particularly *Planet Stories*—where her lush, colorful, and fast-moving tales of planetary adventure outdid Edgar Rice Burroughs at his own game—unlike Burroughs, Brackett was not only a fine stylist but also a poet who knew her way very well around the human heart. Her best novel is usually considered to be *The Long Tomorrow* (Ballantine), but her series of novels about interplanetary swordsman Eric John Stark—*The People of the Talisman* (Ace), *The Secret of Sineheart* (Ace), and the more recent *Skaith* trilogy (Ballantine)—also have their avid supporters, as does her novel *The Sword of Rhiannon* (Ace). Brackett also worked for Hollywood throughout her long career; her credits as a screenwriter include the scripts for *The Big Sleep* and *Rio Lobo*, and the script for *Star Wars II*, completed just prior to her death. She lived long enough to see the release of *The Best of Leigh Brackett* (Del Rey Books), edited by her husband (now also deceased), writer Edmond Hamilton.

Dead at seventy-five, Ward Moore was best known in the SF world for his 1953 novel *Bring the Jubilee* (Avon), certainly one of the four or five best "alternate worlds" novels ever written, ranking with L. Sprague De Camp's *Lest Darkness Fall*, Keith Roberts' *Pavane*, and Philip K. Dick's *The Man in the High Castle*. Moore's other novels include *Joyleg* (Ace), a literate and funny collaboration with Avram Davidson, *Greener Than You Think, Breathe the Air Again* (both out of print), and *Caduceus Wild* (Pinnacle).

Eric Frank Russell, dead at seventy-three, was best known for his Fortean novel *Sinister Barrier*, for the short pieces "Dear Devil," "And Then There Were None," and the Hugo-winning "Allamagoosa," but my favorite Russell novel has always been *Wasp*, a witty, suspenseful, and intelligent book that is probably the ultimate political "dirty tricks" novel. As far as I can tell, all of Russell's books are out of print except for *The Best of Eric Frank Russell* (Del Rey Books), which was published this year.

Also dead in 1978 were J. Francis McComas, co-founder of *F & SF* (with Anthony Boucher) and co-editor of the classic anthology *Adventures in Time and Space* (with Raymond J. Healy); Mort Weisinger, one-time editor of *Thrilling Wonder Stories* and *Startling Stories*; and Donald B. Day, editor of the *Index to the Science Fiction Magazines*.

John Varley is a writer who attracts superlatives like sugar attracts flies; so many enthusiastic editors have described him in such complimentary terms that it's becoming hard for subsequent editors to find anything new to say in praise of him. Should I mention once again that he is "the hottest new talent to enter SF since Zelazny?" Should I mention his "explosive debut in 1975" or discuss his "meteoric rise to prominence"? Should I call him "the most exciting and most influential new writer of the decade," or settle for that old reliable workhorse of a phrase, "a bright new star in the SF firmament"?

Fortunately, it doesn't really matter which nice thing we choose to say about Varley, because they're all true.

I'm sure that by now most of you already know that Varley's stories have been multiple Hugo and Nebula award finalists; that he appears regularly in all the "Best of the Year" anthologies; that his new novel Titan *(Berkley/Putnam) is likely to be as talked about and controversial as was his first novel,* Ophiuchi Hotline *(Dell); that his new book,* The Persistence of Vision *(Dial Press), is being widely hailed as the best short story collection of the year.*

If you think you know all there is to know about John Varley, though, read the story that follows—Varley's single best piece of fiction to date and the winner of this year's Nebula—a powerful and evocative exploration of the subtle differences between those who are blind and those who will not see.

JOHN VARLEY
The Persistence of Vision

It was the year of the fourth non-depression. I had recently joined the ranks of the unemployed. The President had told me that I had nothing to fear but fear itself. I took him at his word, for once, and set out to backpack to California.

I was not the only one. The world's economy had been writhing like a snake on a hot griddle for the last twenty years, since the early seventies. We were in a boom-and-bust cycle that seemed to have no end. It had wiped out the sense of security the nation had so painfully won in the golden years after the thirties. People were accustomed to the fact that they could be rich one year and on the breadlines the next. I was on the breadlines in '81, and again in '88. This time I decided to use my freedom from the time clock to see the world. I had ideas of stowing away to Japan. I was forty-seven years old and might not get another chance to be irresponsible.

This was in late summer of the year. Sticking out my thumb along the interstate, I could easily forget that there were food riots back in Chicago. I slept at night on top of my bedroll and saw stars and listened to crickets.

I must have walked most of the way from Chicago to Des Moines. My feet toughened up after a few days of awful blisters. The rides were scarce, partly competition from other hitchhikers and partly the times we were living in. The locals were none too anxious to give rides to city people, who they had heard were mostly a bunch of hunger-crazed potential mass murderers. I got roughed up once and told never to return to Sheffield, Illinois.

But I gradually learned the knack of living on the road. I had started with a small supply of canned goods from the welfare and by the time they ran out, I had found that it was possible to work for a meal at many of the farmhouses along the way.

Some of it was hard work, some of it was only a token from people with a deeply ingrained sense that nothing should come for free. A few meals were gratis, at the family table, with grandchildren sitting around while grandpa or grandma told oft-repeated tales of what it had been like in the Big One back in '29, when people had not been afraid to help a fellow out when he was down on his luck. I found that the older the person, the more likely I was to get a sympathetic ear. One of the many tricks you learn. And most older people will give you anything if you'll only sit and listen to them. I got very good at it.

The rides began to pick up west of Des Moines, then got bad again as I neared the refugee camps bordering the China Strip. This was only five years after the disaster, remember, when the Omaha nuclear reactor melted down and a hot mass of uranium and plutonium began eating its way into the earth, headed for China, spreading a band of radioactivity six hundred kilometers downwind. Most of Kansas City, Missouri, was still living in plywood and sheet-metal shantytowns till the city was rendered habitable again.

The refugees were a tragic group. The initial solidarity people show after a great disaster had long since faded into the lethargy and disillusionment of the displaced person. Many of them would be in and out of hospitals for the rest of their lives. To make it worse, the local people hated them, feared them, would not associate with them. They were modern pariahs, unclean. Their children were shunned. Each camp had only a number to identify it, but the local populace called them all Geigertowns.

I made a long detour to Little Rock to avoid crossing the Strip, though it was safe now as long as you didn't linger. I was issued a pariah's badge by the National Guard—a dosimeter—and wandered from one Geigertown to the next. The people were pitifully friendly once I made the first move, and I always slept indoors. The food was free at the community messes.

Once at Little Rock, I found that the aversion to picking up strangers—who might be tainted with "radiation disease"—dropped off, and I quickly moved across Arkansas, Oklahoma, and Texas. I worked a little here and there, but many of the rides were long. What I saw of Texas was through a car window.

I was a little tired of that by the time I reached New Mexico. I decided to do some more walking. By then I was less interested in California than in the trip itself.

I left the roads and went cross-country where there were no fences to stop me. I found that it wasn't easy, even in New Mexico, to get far from signs of civilization.

Taos was the center, back in the sixties, of cultural experiments in alternative living. Many communes and cooperatives were set up in the surrounding hills during that time. Most of them fell apart in a few months or years, but a few survived. In later years, any group with a new theory of living and a yen to try it out seemed to gravitate to that part of New Mexico. As a result, the land was dotted with ramshackle windmills, solar heating panels, geodesic domes, group marriages, nudists, philosophers, theoreticians, messiahs, hermits, and more than a few just plain nuts.

Taos was great. I could drop into most of the communes and stay for a day or a week, eating organic rice and beans and drinking goat's milk. When I got tired of one, a few hours' walk in any direction would bring me to another. There, I might be offered a night of prayer and chanting or a ritualistic orgy. Some of the groups had spotless barns with automatic milkers for the herds of cows. Others didn't even have latrines; they just squatted. In some, the members dressed like nuns, or Quakers in early Pennsylvania. Elsewhere, they went nude and shaved all their body hair and painted themselves purple. There were all-male and all-female groups. I was urged to stay at most of the former; at the latter, the responses ranged from a bed for the night and good conversation to being met at a barbed-wire fence with a shotgun.

I tried not to make judgments. These people were doing something important, all of them. They were testing ways whereby people didn't have to live in Chicago. That was a wonder to me. I had thought Chicago was inevitable, like diarrhea.

This is not to say they were all successful. Some made Chicago look like Shangri-La. There was one group who seemed to feel that getting back to nature consisted of sleeping in pigshit and eating food a buzzard wouldn't touch. Many were obviously doomed. They would leave behind a group of empty hovels and the memory of cholera.

So the place wasn't paradise, not by a long way. But there were successes. One or two had been there since '63 or '64 and were raising their third generation. I was disappointed to see that most of these were the ones that departed least from established norms of behavior, though some of the differences could be startling. I suppose the most radical experiments are the least likely to bear fruit.

I stayed through the winter. No one was surprised to see me a second time. It seems that many people came to Taos and shopped around. I seldom stayed more than three weeks at any one place, and always pulled my weight. I made many friends and picked up skills that would serve me if I stayed off the roads. I toyed with the idea of staying at one of them forever. When I couldn't make up my mind, I was advised that there was no hurry. I could go to California and return. They seemed sure I would.

So when spring came I headed west over the hills. I stayed off the roads and slept in the open. Many nights I would stay at another commune, until they finally began to get farther apart, then tapered off entirely. The country was not as pretty as before.

Then, three days' leisurely walking from the last commune, I came to a wall.

In 1964, in the United States, there was an epidemic of German Measles, or rubella. Rubella is one of the mildest of infectious diseases. The only time it's a problem is when a woman contracts it in the first four months of her pregnancy. It is passed to the fetus, which usually develops complications. These complications include deafness, blindness, and damage to the brain.

In 1964, in the old days before abortion became readily available, there was nothing to be done about it. Many pregnant women caught rubella and went to term. Five thousand deaf-blind children were born in one year. The normal yearly incidence of deaf-blind children in the United States is one hundred and forty.

In 1970 these five thousand potential Helen Kellers were all six years-old. It was quickly seen that there was a shortage of Anne Sullivans. Previously, deaf-blind children could be sent to a small number of special institutions.

It was a problem. Not just anyone can cope with a blind-deaf child. You can't tell them to shut up when they moan; you can't reason with them, tell them that the moaning is driving you crazy. Some parents were driven to nervous breakdowns when they tried to keep their children at home.

Many of the five thousand were badly retarded and virtually impossible to reach, even if anyone had been trying. These ended up, for the most part, warehoused in the hundreds of anonymous nursing homes and institutes for "special" children. They were put into beds, cleaned up once a day by a few overworked nurses, and generally allowed the full blessings of liberty: they were allowed to rot freely in their own dark, quiet, private universes. Who can say if it was bad for them? None of them were heard to complain.

Many children with undamaged brains were shuffled in among the retarded because they were unable to tell anyone that they were in there behind the sightless eyes. They failed the batteries of tactile tests, unaware that their fates hung in the balance when they were asked to fit round pegs into round holes to the ticking of a clock they could not see or hear. As a result, they spent the rest of their lives in bed, and none of them complained, either. To protest, one must be aware of the possibility of something better. It helps to have a language, too.

Several hundred of the children were found to have IQs within the normal range. There were news stories about them as they approached puberty and it was revealed that there were not enough good people to properly handle them. Money was spent, teachers were trained. The education expenditures would go on for a specified period of time, until the children were grown, then things would go back to normal and everyone could congratulate themselves on having dealt successfully with a tough problem.

And indeed, it did work fairly well. There are ways to reach and teach such children. They involve patience, love, and dedication, and the teachers brought all that to their jobs. All the graduates of the special schools left knowing how to speak with their hands. Some could talk. A few could write. Most of them left the institutions to live with parents or relatives, or, if neither was possible, received counseling and help in fitting themselves into society. The options were limited, but people can live rewarding lives under the most severe handicaps. Not everyone, but most of the graduates, were as happy with their lot as could reasonably be expected. Some achieved the almost saintly peace of their role model, Helen Keller. Others became bitter and withdrawn. A few had to be put in asylums, where they became indistinguishable from the others of their group who had spent the last twenty years there. But for the most part, they did well.

But among the group, as in any group, were some misfits. They tended to be among the brightest, the top ten percent in the IQ scores. This was not a reliable rule. Some had unremarkable test scores and were still infected with the hunger to do something, to change things, to rock the boat. With a group of five thousand, there were certain to be a few geniuses, a few artists, a few dreamers, hell-raisers, individualists, movers and shapers: a few glorious maniacs.

There was one among them who might have been President but for the fact that she was blind, deaf, and a woman. She was smart, but not one of the geniuses. She was a dreamer, a creative force, an innovator. It was she who dreamed of freedom. But she was not a builder of fairy castles. Having dreamed it, she had to make it come true.

The wall was made of carefully fitted stone and was about five feet high. It was completely out of context with anything I had seen in New Mexico, though it was built of native rock. You just don't build that kind of wall out there. You use barbed wire if something needs fencing in, but many people still made use of the free range and brands. Somehow it seemed transplanted from New England.

It was substantial enough that I felt it would be unwise to crawl over it. I had crossed many wire fences in my travels and had not gotten in trouble for it yet, though I had some talks with some ranchers. Mostly they told me to keep moving, but didn't seem upset about it. This was different. I set out to walk around it. From the lay of the land, I couldn't tell how far it might reach, but I had time.

At the top of the next rise I saw that I didn't have far to go. The wall made a right-angle turn just ahead. I looked over it and could see some buildings. They were mostly domes, the ubiquitous structure thrown up by communes because of the combination of ease of construction and durability. There were sheep behind the wall, and a few cows. They grazed on grass so green I wanted to go over and roll in it. The wall enclosed a rectangle of green. Outside, where I stood, it was all scrub and sage. These people had access to Rio Grande irrigation water.

I rounded the corner and followed the wall west again.

I saw a man on horseback about the same time he spotted me. He was south of me, outside the wall, and he turned and rode in my direction.

He was a dark man with thick features, dressed in denim and boots with a gray battered stetson. Navaho, maybe. I don't know much about Indians, but I'd heard they were out here.

"Hello," I said when he'd stopped. He was looking me over. "Am I on your land?"

"Tribal land," he said. "Yeah, you're on it."

"I didn't see any signs."

He shrugged.

"It's okay, bud. You don't look like you out to rustle cattle." He grinned at me. His teeth were large and stained with tobacco. "You be camping out tonight?"

"Yes. How much farther does the, uh, tribal land go? Maybe I'll be out of it before tonight?"

He shook his head gravely. "Nah. You won't be off it tomorrow. 'S all right. You make a fire, you be careful, huh?" He grinned again and started to ride off.

"Hey, what is this place?" I gestured to the wall and he pulled his horse up and turned around again. It raised a lot of dust.

"Why you asking?" He looked a little suspicious.

"I dunno. Just curious. It doesn't look like the other places I've been to. This wall . . ."

He scowled. "Damn wall." Then he shrugged. I thought that was all he was going to say. Then he went on.

"These people, we look out for 'em, you hear? Maybe we don't go for what they're doin'. But they got it rough, you know?" He looked at me, expecting something. I never did get the knack of talking to these laconic Westerners. I always felt that I was making my sentences too long. They use a shorthand of grunts and shrugs and omitted parts of speech, and I always felt like a dude when I talked to them.

"Do they welcome guests?" I asked. "I thought I might see if I could spend the night."

He shrugged again, and it was a whole different gesture.

"Maybe. They all deaf and blind, you know?" And that was all the conversation he could take for the day. He made a clucking sound and galloped away.

I continued down the wall until I came to a dirt road that wound up the arroyo and entered the wall. There was a wooden gate, but it stood open. I wondered why they took all the trouble with the wall only to leave the gate like that. Then I noticed a circle of narrow-gauge train tracks that came out of the gate, looped around outside it, and rejoined itself. There was a small siding that ran along the outer wall for a few yards.

I stood there a few moments. I don't know what entered into my decision. I think I was a little tired of sleeping out, and I was hungry for a home-cooked meal. The sun was getting closer to the horizon. The land to the west looked like more of the same. If the highway had been visible, I might have headed that way and hitched a ride. But I turned the other way and went through the gate.

I walked down the middle of the tracks. There was a wooden fence on each side of the road, built of horizontal planks, like a corral. Sheep grazed on one side of me. There was a Shetland sheepdog with them, and she raised her ears and followed me with her eyes as I passed, but did not come when I whistled.

It was about half a mile to the cluster of buildings ahead. There were four or five domes made of something translucent, like greenhouses, and several conventional square buildings. There were two windmills turning lazily in the breeze. There were several banks of solar water heaters. These are flat constructions of glass and wood, held off the ground so they can tilt to follow the sun. They were almost vertical now, intercepting the oblique rays of sunset. There were a few trees, what might have been an orchard.

About halfway there I passed under a wooden footbridge. It arched over the road, giving access from the east pasture to the west pasture. I wondered, What was wrong with a simple gate?

Then I saw something coming down the road in my direction. It was traveling on the tracks and it was very quiet. I stopped and waited.

It was a sort of converted mining engine, the sort that pulls loads of coal up from the bottom of shafts. It was battery-powered, and it had gotten quite close before I heard it. A small man was driving it. He was pulling a car behind him and singing as loud as he could with absolutely no sense of pitch.

He got closer and closer, moving about five miles per hour, one hand held out as if he was signaling a left turn. Suddenly I realized what was happening, as he was bearing down on me. He wasn't going to stop. He was counting fenceposts with his hand. I scrambled up the fence just in time. There wasn't more than six inches of clearance between the train and the fence on either side. His palm touched my leg as I squeezed close to the fence, and he stopped abruptly.

He leaped from the car and grabbed me and I thought I was in trouble. But he looked concerned, not angry, and felt me all over, trying to discover if I was hurt. I was embarrassed. Not from the examination; because I had been foolish. The Indian had said they were all deaf and blind but I guess I hadn't quite believed him.

He was flooded with relief when I managed to convey to him that I was all right. With eloquent gestures he made me understand that I was not to stay on the road. He indicated that I should climb over the fence and continue through the fields. He repeated himself several times to be sure I understood, then held on to me as I climbed over to assure himself that I was out of the way. He reached over the fence and held my shoulders, smiling at me. He pointed to the road and shook his head, then pointed to the buildings and nodded. He touched my head and smiled when I nodded. He climbed back onto the engine and started up, all the time nodding and pointing where he wanted me to go. Then he was off again.

I debated what to do. Most of me said to turn around, go back to the wall by way of the pasture and head back into the hills. These people probably wouldn't want me around. I doubted that I'd be able to talk to them, and they might even resent me. On the other hand, I was fascinated, as who wouldn't be? I wanted to see how they managed it. I still didn't believe that they were *all* deaf and blind. It didn't seem possible.

The Sheltie was sniffing at my pants. I looked down at her and she backed away, then daintily approached me as I held out my open hand. She sniffed, then licked me. I patted her on the head, and she hustled back to her sheep.

I turned toward the buildings.

The first order of business was money.

None of the students knew much about it from experience, but the library was full of Braille books. They started reading.

One of the first things that became apparent was that when money was mentioned, lawyers were not far away. The students wrote letters. From the replies, they selected a lawyer and retained him.

They were in a school in Pennsylvania at the time. The original pupils of the special schools, five hundred in number, had been narrowed down to about seventy as people left to live with relatives or found other solutions to their special problems. Of those seventy, some had places to go but didn't want to go there; others had few alternatives. Their parents were either dead or not interested in living with them. So the seventy had been gathered from the schools around the country into this one, while ways to deal with them were worked out. The authorities had plans, but the students beat them to it.

Each of them had been entitled to a guaranteed annual income since 1980. They had been under the care of the government, so they had not received it. They sent their lawyer to court. He came back with a ruling that they could not collect. They appealed, and won. The money was paid retroactively, with interest, and came to a healthy sum. They thanked their lawyer and retained a real estate agent. Meanwhile, they read.

They read about communes in New Mexico, and instructed their agent to look for something out there. He made a deal for a tract to be leased in perpetuity from the Navaho nation. They read about the land, found that it would need a lot of water to be productive in the way they wanted it to be.

They divided into groups to research what they would need to be self-sufficient.

Water could be obtained by tapping into the canals that carried it from the reservoirs on the Rio Grande into the reclaimed land in the south. Federal money was available for the project through a labyrinthine scheme involving HEW, the Agriculture Department, and the Bureau of Indian Affairs. They ended up paying little for their pipeline.

The land was arid. It would need fertilizer to be of use in raising sheep without resorting to open range techniques. The cost of fertilizer could be subsidized through the Rural Resettlement Program. After that, planting clover would enrich the soil with all the nitrates they could want.

There were techniques available to farm ecologically, without worrying about fertilizers or pesticides. Everything was recycled. Essentially, you put sunlight and water into one end and harvested wool, fish, vegetables, apples, honey, and eggs at the other end. You used nothing but the land, and replaced even that as you recycled your waste products back into the soil. They were not interested in agribusiness with huge combine harvesters and crop dusters. They didn't even want to turn a profit. They merely wanted sufficiency.

The details multiplied. Their leader, the one who had had the original idea and the drive to put it into action in the face of overwhelming obstacles, was a dynamo named Janet Reilly. Knowing nothing about the techniques generals and executives employ to achieve large objectives, she invented them herself and adapted them to the peculiar needs and limitations of her group. She assigned task forces to look into solutions of each aspect of their project: law, science, social planning, design, buying, logistics, construction. At any one time, she was the only person who knew everything about what was happening. She kept it all in her head, without notes of any kind.

It was in the area of social planning that she showed herself to be a visionary and not just a superb organizer. Her idea was not to make a place where they could lead a life that was a sightless, soundless imitation of their unafflicted peers. She wanted a whole new start, a way of living that was by and for the blind-deaf, a way of living that accepted no convention just because that was the way it had always been done. She examined every human cultural institution from marriage to indecent exposure to see how it related to her needs and the needs of her friends. She was aware of the peril of this approach, but was undeterred. Her Social Task Force read about every variant group that had ever tried to make it on its own anywhere, and brought her reports about how and why they had failed or succeeded. She filtered this information through her own experiences to see how it would work for her unusual group with its own set of needs and goals.

The details were endless. They hired an architect to put their ideas into Braille blueprints. Gradually the plans evolved. They spent more money. The construction began, supervised on the site by their architect, who by now was so fascinated by the scheme that she donated her services. It was an important break, for they needed someone there whom they could trust. There is only so much that can be accomplished at such a distance.

When things were ready for them to move, they ran into bureaucratic trouble. They had anticipated it, but it was a setback. Social agencies charged with overseeing their welfare doubted the wisdom of the project. When it became apparent that no amount of reasoning was going to stop it, wheels were set in motion that resulted in a restraining order, issued for their own protection, preventing them from leaving the school. They were twenty-one years old by then, all of them, but were judged mentally incompetent to manage their own affairs. A hearing was scheduled.

Luckily, they still had access to their lawyer. He also had become infected with the crazy vision, and put on a great battle for them. He succeeded in getting a ruling concerning the rights of institutionalized persons, later upheld by the Supreme Court, which eventually had severe repercussions in state and county hospitals. Realizing the trouble they were already in regarding the thousands of patients in inadequate facilities across the country, the agencies gave in.

By then, it was the spring of 1986, one year after their target date. Some of their fertilizer had washed away already for lack of erosion-preventing clover. It was getting late to start crops, and they were running short of money. Nevertheless, they moved to New Mexico and began the backbreaking job of getting everything started. There were fifty-five of them, with nine children aged three months to six years.

I don't know what I expected. I remember that everything was a surprise, either because it was so normal or because it was so different. None of my idiot surmises about what such a place might be like proved to be true. And of course I didn't know the history of the place; I learned that later, picked up in bits and pieces.

I was surprised to see lights in some of the buildings. The first thing I had assumed was that they would have no need of them. That's an example of something so normal that it surprised me.

As to the differences, the first thing that caught my attention was the fence around the rail line. I had a personal interest in it, having almost been injured by it. I struggled to understand, as I must if I was to stay even for a night.

The wood fences that enclosed the rails on their way to the gate continued up to a barn, where the rails looped back on themselves in the same way they did outside the wall. The entire line was enclosed by the fence. The only access was a loading platform by the barn, and the gate to the outside. It made sense. The only way a deaf-blind person could operate a conveyance like that would be with assurances that there was no one on the track. These people would *never* go on the tracks; there was no way they could be warned of an approaching train.

There were people moving around me in the twilight as I made my way into the group of buildings. They took no notice of me, as I had expected. They moved fast; some of them were actually running. I stood still, eyes searching all around me so no one would come crashing into me. I had to figure out how they kept from crashing into each other before I got bolder.

I bent to the ground and examined it. The light was getting bad, but I saw immediately that there were concrete sidewalks crisscrossing the area. Each of the walks was etched with a different sort of pattern in grooves that had been made before the stuff set—lines, waves, depressions, patches of rough and smooth. I quickly saw that the people who were in a hurry moved only on those walkways, and they were all barefoot. It was no trick to see that it was some sort of traffic pattern read with the feet. I stood up. I didn't need to know how it worked. It was sufficient to know what it was and stay off the paths.

The people were unremarkable. Some of them were not dressed, but I was used to that by now. They came in all shapes and sizes, but all seemed to be about the same age except for the children. Except for the fact that they did not stop and talk or even wave as they approached each other, I would never have guessed they were blind. I watched them come to intersections in the pathways—I didn't know how they knew they were there, but could think of several ways—and slow down as they crossed. It was a marvelous system.

I began to think of approaching someone. I had been there for almost half an hour, an intruder. I guess I had a false sense of these people's vulnerability; I felt like a burglar.

I walked along beside a woman for a minute. She was very purposeful in her eyes-ahead stride, or seemed to be. She sensed something, maybe my footsteps. She slowed a little, and I touched her on the shoulder, not knowing what else to do. She stopped instantly and turned toward me. Her eyes were open but vacant. Her hands were all over me, lightly touching my face, my chest, my hands, fingering my clothing. There was no doubt in my mind that she knew me for a stranger, probably from the first tap on the shoulder. But she smiled warmly at me, and hugged me. Her hands were very delicate and warm. That's funny, because they were calloused from hard work. But they felt sensitive.

She made me to understand—by pointing to the building, making eating motions with an imaginary spoon, and touching a number on her watch—that supper was served in an hour, and that I was invited. I nodded and smiled beneath her hands; she kissed me on the cheek and hurried off.

Well. It hadn't been so bad. I had worried about my ability to communicate. Later I found out she learned a great deal more about me than I had told.

I put off going into the mess hall or whatever it was. I strolled around in the gathering darkness looking at their layout. I saw the little Sheltie bringing the sheep back to the fold for the night. She herded them expertly through the open gate without any instructions, and one of the residents closed it and locked them in. The man bent and scratched the dog on the head and got his hand licked. Her chores done for the night, the dog hurried over to me and sniffed my pant leg. She followed me around the rest of the evening.

Everyone seemed so busy that I was surprised to see one woman sitting on a rail fence, doing nothing. I went over to her.

Closer, I saw that she was younger than I had thought. She was thirteen, I learned later. She wasn't wearing any clothes. I touched her on the shoulder, and she jumped down from the fence and went through the same routine as the other woman had, touching me all over with no reserve. She took my hand and I felt her fingers moving rapidly in my palm. I couldn't understand it, but knew what it was. I shrugged, and tried out other gestures to indicate that I didn't speak hand talk. She nodded, still feeling my face with her hands.

She asked me if I was staying to dinner. I assured her that I was. She asked me if I was from a university. And if you think that's easy to ask with only body movements, try it. But she was so graceful and supple in her movements, so deft at getting her meaning across. It was beautiful to watch her. It was speech and ballet at the same time.

I told her I wasn't from a university, and launched into an attempt to tell her a little about what I was doing and how I got there. She listened to me with her hands, scratching her head graphically when I failed to make my meanings clear. All the time the smile on her face got broader and broader, and she would laugh silently at my antics. All this while standing very close to me, touching me. At last she put her hands on her hips.

"I guess you need the practice," she said, "but if it's all the same to you, could we talk mouthtalk for now? You're cracking me up."

I jumped as if stung by a bee. The touching, while something I could ignore for a deaf-blind girl, suddenly seemed out of place. I stepped back a little, but her hands returned to me. She looked puzzled, then read the problem with her hands.

"I'm sorry," she said. "You thought I was deaf and blind. If I'd known I would have told you right off."

"I thought everyone here was."

"Just the parents. I'm one of the children. We all hear and see quite well. Don't be so nervous. If you can't stand touching, you're not going to like it here. Relax, I won't hurt you." And she kept her hands moving over me, mostly my face. I didn't understand it at the time, but it didn't seem sexual. Turned out I was wrong, but it wasn't blatant.

"You'll need me to show you the ropes," she said, and started for the domes. She held my hand and walked close to me. Her other hand kept moving to my face every time I talked.

"Number one, stay off the concrete paths. That's where—"

"I already figured that out."

"You did? How long have you been here?" Her hands searched my face with renewed interest. It was quite dark.

"Less than an hour. I was almost run over by your train."

She laughed, then apologized and said she knew it wasn't funny to me.

I told her it *was* funny to me now, though it hadn't been at the time. She said there was a warning sign on the gate, but I had been unlucky enough to come when the gate was open—they opened it by remote control before a train started up—and I hadn't seen it.

"What's your name?" I asked her, as we neared the soft yellow lights coming from the dining room.

Her hand worked reflexively in mine, then stopped. "Oh, I don't know. I *have* one; several, in fact. But they're in bodytalk. I'm . . . Pink. It translates as Pink, I guess."

There was a story behind it. She had been the first child born to the school students. They knew that babies were described as being pink, so they called her that. She felt pink to them. As we entered the hall, I could see that her name was visually inaccurate. One of her parents had been black. She was dark, with blue eyes and curly hair lighter than her skin. She had a broad nose, but small lips.

She didn't ask my name, so I didn't offer it. No one asked my name, in speech, the entire time I was there. They called me many things in bodytalk, and when the children called me it was "Hey, you!" They weren't big on spoken words.

The dining hall was in a rectangular building made of brick. It connected to one of the large domes. It was dimly lighted. I later learned that the lights were for me alone. The children didn't need them for anything but reading. I held Pink's hand, glad to have a guide. I kept my eyes and ears open.

"We're informal," Pink said. Her voice was embarrassingly loud in the large room. No one else was talking at all; there were just the sounds of movement and breathing. Several of the children looked up. "I won't introduce you around now. Just feel like part of the family. People will feel you later, and you can talk to them. You can take your clothes off here at the door."

I had no trouble with that. Everyone else was nude, and I could easily adjust to household customs by that time. You take your shoes off in Japan, you take your clothes off in Taos. What's the difference?

Well, quite a bit, actually. There was all the touching that went on. Everybody touched everybody else, as routinely as glancing. Everyone touched my face first, then went on with what seemed like total innocence to touch me everywhere else. As usual, it was not quite what it seemed. It was *not* innocent, and it was not the usual treatment they gave others in their group. They touched each other's genitals a lot *more* than they touched mine. They were holding back with me so I wouldn't be frightened. They were very polite with strangers.

There was a long, low table, with everyone sitting on the floor around it. Pink led me to it.

"See the bare strips on the floor? Stay out of them. Don't leave anything in them. That's where people walk. Don't *ever* move anything. Furniture, I mean. That has to be decided at full meetings, so we'll all know where everything is. Small things, too. If you pick up something, put it back exactly where you found it."

"I understand."

People were bringing bowls and platters of food from the adjoining kitchen. They set them on the table, and the diners began feeling them. They ate with their fingers, without plates, and they did it slowly and lovingly. They smelled things for a long time before they took a bite. Eating was very sensual to these people.

They were *terrific* cooks. I have never, before or since, eaten as well as I did at Keller. (That's my name for it, in speech, though their bodytalk name was something very like that. When I called it Keller, everyone knew what I was talking about.) They started off with good, fresh produce, something that's hard enough to find in the cities, and went at the cooking with artistry and imagination. It wasn't like any national style I've eaten. They improvised, and seldom cooked the same thing the same way twice.

I sat between Pink and the fellow who had almost run me down earlier. I stuffed myself disgracefully. It was too far removed from beef jerky and the organic dry cardboard I had been eating for me to be able to resist. I lingered over it, but still finished long before anyone else. I watched them as I sat back carefully and wondered if I'd be sick. (I wasn't, thank God.) They fed themselves and each other, sometimes getting up and going clear around the table to offer a choice morsel to a friend on the other side. I was fed in this way by all too many of them, and nearly popped until I learned a pidgin phrase in handtalk, saying I was full to the brim. I learned from Pink that a friendlier way to refuse was to offer something myself.

Eventually I had nothing to do but feed Pink and look at the others. I began to be more observant. I had thought they were eating in solitude, but soon saw that lively conversation was flowing around the table. Hands were busy, moving almost too fast to see. They were spelling into each other's palms, shoulders, legs, arms, bellies; any part of the body. I watched in amazement as a ripple of laughter spread like falling dominoes from one end of the table to the other as some witticism was passed along the line. It was *fast*. Looking carefully, I could see the thoughts moving, reaching one person, passed on while a reply went in the other direction and was in turn passed on, other replies originating all along the line and bouncing back and forth. They were a wave form, like water.

It was messy. Let's face it; eating with your fingers and talking with your hands is going to get you smeared with food. But no one minded. *I* certainly didn't. I was too busy feeling left out. Pink talked to me, but I knew I was finding out what it's like to be deaf. These people were friendly and seemed to like me, but could do nothing about it. We couldn't communicate.

Afterwards, we all trooped outside, except the cleanup crew, and took a shower beneath a set of faucets that gave out very cold water. I told Pink I'd like to help with the dishes, but she said I'd just be in the way. I couldn't do anything around Keller until I learned their very specific ways of doing things. She seemed to be assuming already that I'd be around that long.

Back into the building to dry off, which they did with their usual puppy-dog friendliness, making a game and a gift of toweling each other, and then we went into the dome.

It was warm inside, warm and dark. Light entered from the passage to the dining room, but it wasn't enough to blot out the stars through the lattice of triangular panes overhead. It was almost like being out in the open.

Pink quickly pointed out the positional etiquette within the dome. It wasn't hard to follow, but I still tended to keep my arms and legs pulled in close so I wouldn't trip someone by sprawling into a walk space.

My misconceptions got me again. There was no sound but the soft whisper of flesh against flesh, so I thought I was in the middle of an orgy. I had been at them before, in other communes, and they looked pretty much like this. I quickly saw that I was wrong, and only later found out I had been right. In a sense.

What threw my evaluations out of whack was the simple fact that group conversation among these people *had* to look like an orgy. The much subtler observation that I made later was that with a hundred naked bodies sliding, rubbing, kissing, caressing, all at the same time, what was the point in making a distinction? There was no distinction.

I have to say that I use the noun "orgy" only to get across a general idea of many people in close contact. I don't like the word, it is too ripe with connotations. But I had these connotations myself at the time, so I was relieved to see that it was not an orgy. The ones I had been to had been tedious and impersonal, and I had hoped for better from these people.

Many wormed their way through the crush to get to me and meet me. Never more than one at a time; they were constantly aware of what was going on and were waiting their turn to talk to me. Naturally, I didn't know it then. Pink sat with me to interpret the hard thoughts. I eventually used her words less and less, getting into the spirit of tactile seeing and understanding. No one felt they really knew me until they had touched every part of my body, so there were hands on me all the time. I timidly did the same.

What with all the touching, I quickly got an erection, which embarrassed me quite a bit. I was berating myself for being unable to keep sexual responses out of it, for not being able to operate on the same intellectual plane I thought they were on, when I realized with some shock that the couple next to me was making love. They had been doing it for the last ten minutes, actually, and it had seemed such a natural part of what was happening that I had known it and not known it at the same time.

No sooner had I realized it than I suddenly wondered if I was right. *Were they?* It was very slow and the light was bad. But her legs were up, and he was on top of her, that much I was sure of. It was foolish of me, but I really had to know. I had to find out *what the hell I was in.* How could I give the proper social responses if I didn't know the situation?

I was very sensitive to polite behavior after my months at the various communes. I had become adept at saying prayers before supper in one place, chanting Hare Krishna at another, and going happily nudist at still another. It's called "when in Rome," and if you can't adapt to it you shouldn't go visiting. I would kneel to Mecca, burp after my meals, toast anything that was proposed, eat organic rice and compliment the cook; but to do it right, you have to know the customs. I had thought I knew them, but had changed my mind three times in as many minutes.

They *were* making love, in the sense that he was penetrating her. They were also deeply involved with each other. Their hands fluttered like butterflies all over each other, filled with meanings I couldn't see or feel. But they were being touched by and were touching many other people around them. They were talking to all these people, even if the message was as simple as a pat on the forehead or arm.

Pink noticed where my attention was. She was sort of wound around me, without really doing anything I would have thought of as provocative. I just couldn't *decide*. It seemed so innocent, and yet it wasn't.

"That's (--) and (--)," she said, the parentheses indicating a series of hand motions against my palm. I never learned a sound word as a name for any of them but Pink, and I can't reproduce the bodytalk names they had. Pink reached over, touched the woman with her foot, and did some complicated business with her toes. The woman smiled and grabbed Pink's foot, her fingers moving.

"(--) would like to talk with you later," Pink told me. "Right after she's through talking to (--). You met her earlier, remember? She says she likes your hands."

Now this is going to sound crazy, I know. It sounded pretty crazy to me when I thought of it. It dawned on me with a sort of revelation that her word for talk and mine were miles apart. Talk, to her, meant a complex interchange involving all parts of the body. She could read words or emotions in every twitch of my muscles, like a lie detector. Sound, to her, was only a minor part of communication. It was something she used to speak to outsiders. Pink talked with her whole being.

I didn't have the half of it, even then, but it was enough to turn my head entirely around in relation to these people. They talked with their bodies. It wasn't all hands, as I'd thought. Any part of the body in contact with any other was communication, sometimes a very simple and basic sort—think of McLuhan's light bulb as the basic medium of information—perhaps saying no more than "I am here." But talk was talk, and if conversation evolved to the point where you needed to talk to another with your genitals, it was still a part of the conversation. What I wanted to know was *what were they saying*? I knew, even at that dim moment of realization, that it was much more than I could grasp. Sure, you're saying. You know about talking to your lover with your body as you make love. That's not such a new idea. Of course it isn't, but think how wonderful that talk is even when you're not primarily tactile-oriented. Can you carry the thought from there, or are you doomed to be an earthworm thinking about sunsets?

While this was happening to me, there was a woman getting acquainted with my body. Her hands were on me, in my lap, when I felt myself ejaculating. It was a big surprise to me, but to no one else. I had been telling everyone around me for many minutes, through signs they could feel with their hands, that it was going to happen. Instantly, hands were all over my body. I could almost understand them as they spelled tender thoughts to me. I got the gist, anyway, if not the words. I was terribly embarrassed for only a moment, then it passed away in the face of the easy acceptance. It was very intense. For a long time I couldn't get my breath.

The woman who had been the cause of it touched my lips with her fingers. She moved them slowly, but meaningfully I was sure. Then she melted back into the group.

"What did she say?" I asked Pink.

She smiled at me. "You know, of course. If you'd only cut loose from your verbalizing. But, generally, she meant 'How nice for you.' It also translates as 'How nice for me.' And 'me,' in this sense, means all of us. The organism."

I knew I had to stay and learn to speak.

The commune had its ups and downs. They had expected them, in general, but had not known what shape they might take.

Winter killed many of their fruit trees. They replaced them with hybrid strains. They lost more fertilizer and soil in windstorms because the clover had not had time to anchor it down. Their schedule had been thrown off by the court actions, and they didn't really get things settled in a groove for more than a year.

Their fish all died. They used the bodies for fertilizer and looked into what might have gone wrong. They were using a three-stage ecology of the type pioneered by the New Alchemists in the seventies. It consisted of three domed ponds: one containing fish, another with crushed shells and bacteria in one section and algae in another, and a third full of daphnids. The water containing fish waste from the first pond was pumped through the shells and bacteria, which detoxified it and converted the ammonia it contained into fertilizer for the algae. The algae water was pumped into the third pond to feed the daphnids. Then daphnids and algae were pumped to the fish pond as food and the enriched water was used to fertilize greenhouse plants in all of the domes.

They tested the water and the soil and found that chemicals were being leached from impurities in the shells and concentrated down the food chain. After a thorough cleanup, they restarted and all went well. But they had lost their first cash crop.

They never went hungry. Nor were they cold; there was plenty of sunlight year-round to power the pumps and the food cycle and to heat their living quarters. They had built their buildings half-buried with an eye to the heating and cooling powers of convective currents. But they had to spend some of their capital. The first year they showed a loss.

One of their buildings caught fire during the first winter. Two men and a small girl were killed when a sprinkler system malfunctioned. This was a shock to them. They had thought things would operate as advertised. None of them knew much about the building trades, about estimates as opposed to realities. They found that several of their installations were not up to specifications, and instituted a program of periodic checks on everything. They learned to strip down and repair anything on the farm. If something contained electronics too complex for them to cope with, they tore it out and installed something simpler.

Socially, their progress had been much more encouraging. Janet had wisely decided that there would be only two hard and fast objectives in the realm of their relationships. The first was that she refused to be their president, chairwoman, chief, or supreme commander. She had seen from the start that a driving personality was needed to get the planning done and the land bought and a sense of purpose fostered from their formless desire for an alternative. But once at the promised land, she abdicated. From that point they would operate as a democratic communism. If that failed, they would adopt a new approach. Anything but a dictatorship with her at the head. She wanted no part of that.

The second principle was to accept nothing. There had never been a blind-deaf community operating on its own. They had no expectations to satisfy, they did not need to live as the sighted did. They were alone. There was no one to tell them not to do something simply because it was not done.

They had no clearer idea of what their society would be than anyone else. They had been forced into a mold that was not relevant to their needs, but beyond that they didn't know. They would search out the behavior that made sense, the moral things for blind-deaf people to do. They understood the basic principles of morals: that nothing is moral always, and anything is moral under the right circumstances. It all had to do with social context. They were starting from a blank slate, with no' models to follow.

By the end of the second year they had their context. They continually modified it, but the basic pattern was set. They knew themselves and what they were as they had never been able to do at the school. They defined themselves in their own terms.

I spent my first day at Keller in school. It was the obvious and necessary step. I had to learn handtalk.

Pink was kind and very patient. I learned the basic alphabet and practiced hard at it. By the afternoon she was refusing to talk to me, forcing me to speak with my hands. She would speak only when pressed hard, and eventually not at all, I scarcely spoke a single word after the third day.

This is not to say that I was suddenly fluent. Not at all. At the end of the first day I knew the alphabet and could laboriously make myself understood. I was not so good at reading words spelled into my own palm. For a long time I had to look at the hand to see what was spelled. But like any language, eventually you think in it. I speak fluent French, and I can recall my amazement when I finally reached the point where I wasn't translating my thoughts before I spoke. I reached it at Keller in about two weeks.

I remember one of the last things I asked Pink in speech. It was something that was worrying me.

"Pink, am I welcome here?"

"You've been here three days. Do you feel rejected?"

"No, it's not that. I guess I just need to hear your policy about outsiders. How *long* am I welcome?"

She wrinkled her brow. It was evidently a new question.

"Well, practically speaking, until a majority of us decide we want you to go. But that's never happened. No one's stayed here much longer than a few days. We've never had to evolve a policy about what to do, for instance, if someone who sees and hears wants to join us. No one has, so far, but I guess it could happen. My guess is that they wouldn't accept it. They're very independent and jealous of their freedom, though you might not have noticed it. I don't think you could ever be one of them. But as long as you're willing to think of yourself as a guest, you could probably stay for twenty years."

"You said 'they.' Don't you include yourself in the group?"

For the first time she looked a little uneasy. I wish I had been better at reading body language at the time. I think my hands could have told me volumes about what she was thinking.

"Sure," she said. "The children are part of the group. We like it. I sure wouldn't want to be anywhere else, from what I know of the outside."

"I don't blame you." There were things left unsaid here, but I didn't know enough to ask the right questions. "But it's never a problem, being able to see when none of your parents can? They don't . . . resent you in any way?"

This time she laughed. "Oh, no. Never that. They're much too independent for that. You've seen it. They don't *need* us for anything they can't do themselves. We're part of the family. We do exactly the same things they do. And it really doesn't matter. Sight, I mean. Hearing, either. Just look around you. Do I have any special advantages because I can see where I'm going?"

I had to admit that she didn't. But there was still the hint of something she wasn't saying to me.

"I know what's bothering you. About staying here." She had to draw me back to my original question; I had been wandering.

"What's that?"

"You don't feel a part of the daily life. You're not doing your share of the chores. You're very conscientious and you want to do your part. I can tell."

She read me right, as usual, and I admitted it.

"And you won't be able to until you can talk to everybody. So let's get back to your lessons. Your fingers are still very sloppy."

There was a lot of work to be done. The first thing I had to learn was to slow down. They were slow and methodical workers, made few mistakes, and didn't care if a job took all day so long as it was done well. When I was working by myself I didn't have to worry about it: sweeping, picking apples, weeding in the gardens. But when I was on a job that required teamwork I had to learn a whole new pace. Eyesight enables a person to do many aspects of a job at once with a few quick glances. A blind person will take each aspect of the job in turn if the job is spread out. Everything has to be verified by touch. At a bench job, though, they could be much faster than I. They could make me feel as though I was working with my toes instead of fingers.

I never suggested that I could make anything quicker by virtue of my sight or hearing. They quite rightly would have told me to mind my own business. Accepting sighted help was the first step to dependence, and after all, they would still be here with the same jobs to do after I was gone.

And that got me to thinking about the children again. I began to be positive that there was an undercurrent of resentment, maybe unconscious, between the parents and children. It was obvious that there was a great deal of love between them, but how could the children fail to resent the rejection of their talent? So my reasoning went, anyway.

I quickly fit myself into the routine. I was treated no better or worse than anyone else, which gratified me. Though I would never become part of the group, even if I should desire it, there was absolutely no indication that I was anything but a full member. That's just how they treated guests: as they would one of their own number.

Life was fulfilling out there in a way it had never been in the cities. It wasn't unique to Keller, this pastoral peace, but the people there had it in generous helpings. The earth beneath your bare feet is something you can never feel in a city park.

Daily life was busy and satisfying. There were chickens and hogs to feed, bees and sheep to care for, fish to harvest, and cows to milk. Everybody worked: men, women, and children. It all seemed to fit together without any apparent effort. Everybody seemed to know what to do when it needed doing. You could think of it as a well-oiled machine, but I never liked that metaphor, especially for people. I thought of it as an organism. Any social group is, but this one *worked*. Most of the other communes I'd visited had glaring flaws. Things would not get done because everyone was too stoned or couldn't be bothered or didn't see the necessity of doing it in the first place. That sort of ignorance leads to typhus and soil erosion and people freezing to death and invasions of social workers who take your children away. I'd seen it happen.

Not here. They had a good picture of the world as it is, not the rosy misconceptions so many other utopians labor under. They did the jobs that needed doing.

I could never detail all the nuts and bolts (there's that machine metaphor again) of how the place worked. The fish-cycle ponds alone were complicated enough to overawe me. I killed a spider in one of the greenhouses, then found out it had been put there to eat a specific set of plant predators. Same for the frogs. There were insects in the water to kill other insects; it got to a point where I was afraid to swat a mayfly without prior okay.

As the days went by I was told some of the history of the place. Mistakes had been made, though surprisingly few. One had been in the area of defense. They had made no provision for it at first, not knowing much about the brutality and random violence that reaches even to the out-of-the-way corners. Guns were the logical and preferred choice out here, but were beyond their capabilities.

One night a carload of men who had had too much to drink showed up. They had heard of the place in town. They stayed for two days, cutting the phone lines and raping many of the women.

The people discussed all the options after the invasion was over, and settled on the organic one. They bought five German shepherds. Not the psychotic wretches that are marketed under the description of "attack dogs," but specially trained ones from a firm recommended by the Albuquerque police. They were trained as both Seeing Eye and police dogs. They were perfectly harmless until an outsider showed overt aggression, then they were trained, not to disarm, but to go for the throat.

It worked, like most of their solutions. The second invasion resulted in two dead and three badly injured, all on the other side. As a backup in case of a concerted attack, they hired an ex-marine to teach them the fundamentals of close-in dirty fighting. These were not dewy-eyed flower children.

There were three superb meals a day. And there was leisure time, too. It was not all work. There was time to take a friend out and sit in the grass under a tree, usually around sunset, just before the big dinner. There was time for someone to stop working for a few minutes, to share some special treasure. I remember being taken by the hand by one woman—whom I must call Tall-one-with-the-green-eyes—to a spot where mushrooms were growing in the cool crawl space beneath the barn. We wriggled under until our faces were buried in the patch, picked a few, and smelled them. She showed me how to smell. I would have thought a few weeks before that we had ruined their beauty, but after all it was only visual. I was already beginning to discount that sense, which is so removed from the essence of an object. She showed me that they were still beautiful to touch and smell after we had apparently destroyed them. Then she was off to the kitchen with the pick of the bunch in her apron. They tasted all the better that night.

And a man—I will call him Baldy—who brought me a plank he and one of the women had been planing in the woodshop. I touched its smoothness and smelled it and agreed with him how good it was.

And after the evening meal, the Together.

During my third week there I had an indication of my status with the group. It was the first real test of whether I meant anything to them. Anything special, I mean. I wanted to see them as my friends, and I suppose I was a little upset to think that just anyone who wandered in here would be treated the way I was. It was childish and unfair to them, and I wasn't even aware of the discontent until later.

I had been hauling water in a bucket into the field where a seedling tree was being planted. There was a hose for that purpose, but it was in use on the other side of the village. This tree was not in reach of the automatic sprinklers and it was drying out. I had been carrying water to it until another solution was found.

It was hot, around noon. I got the water from a standing spigot near the forge. I set the bucket down on the ground behind me and leaned my head into the flow of water. I was wearing a shirt made of cotton, unbuttoned in the front. The water felt good running through my hair and soaking into the shirt. I let it go on for almost a minute.

There was a crash behind me and I bumped my head when I raised it up too quickly under the faucet. I turned and saw a woman sprawled on her face in the dust. She was turning over slowly, holding her knee. I realized with a sinking feeling that she had tripped over the bucket I had carelessly left on the concrete express lane. Think of it: ambling along on ground that you trust to be free of all obstruction, suddenly you're sitting on the ground. Their system would only work with trust, and it had to be total; everybody had to be responsible all the time. I had been accepted into that trust and I had blown it. I felt sick.

She had a nasty scrape on her left knee that was oozing blood. She felt it with her hands, sitting there on the ground, and she began to howl. It was weird, painful. Tears came from her eyes, then she pounded her fists on the ground, going "Hunnnh, hunnnh, *hunnnh!*" with each blow. She was angry, and she had every right to be.

She found the pail as I hesitantly reached out for her. She grabbed my hand and followed it up to my face. She felt my face, crying all the time, then wiped her nose and got up. She started off for one of the buildings. She limped slightly.

I sat down and felt miserable. I didn't know what to do.

One of the men came out to get me. It was Big Man. I called him that because he was the tallest person at Keller. He wasn't any sort of policeman, I found out later; he was just the first one the injured woman had met. He took my hand and felt my face. I saw tears start when he felt the emotions there. He asked me to come inside with him.

An impromptu panel had been convened. Call it a jury. It was made up of anyone who was handy, including a few children. There were ten or twelve of them. Everyone looked very sad. The woman I had hurt was there, being consoled by three or four people. I'll call her Scar, for the prominent mark on her upper arm.

Everybody kept telling me—in handtalk, you understand—how sorry they were for me. They petted and stroked me, trying to draw some of the misery away.

Pink came racing in. She had been sent for to act as a translator if needed. Since this was a formal proceeding it was necessary that they be sure I understood everything that happened. She went to Scar and cried with her for a bit, then came to me and embraced me fiercely, telling me with her hands how sorry she was that this had happened. I was already figuratively packing my bags. Nothing seemed to be left but the formality of expelling me.

Then we all sat together on the floor. We were close, touching on all sides. The hearing began.

Most of it was in handtalk, with Pink throwing in a few words here and there. I seldom knew who said what, but that was appropriate. It was the group speaking as one. No statement reached me without already having become a consensus.

"You are accused of having violated the rules," said the group, "and of having been the cause of an injury to (the one I called Scar). Do you dispute this? Is there any fact that we should know?"

"No," I told them. "I was responsible. It was my carelessness."

"We understand. We sympathize with you in your remorse, which is evident to all of us. But carelessness is a violation. Do you understand this? This is the offense for which you are (----)." It was a set of signals in shorthand.

"What was that?" I asked Pink.

"Uh . . . 'brought before us'? 'Standing trial'?" She shrugged, not happy with either interpretation.

"Yes, I understand."

"The facts not being in question, it is agreed that you are guilty." (" 'Responsible' " Pink whispered in my ear.) "Withdraw from us a moment while we come to a decision."

I got up and stood by the wall, not wanting to look at them as the debate went back and forth through the joined hands. There was a burning lump in my throat that I could not swallow. Then I was asked to rejoin the circle.

"The penalty for your offense is set by custom. If it were not so, we would wish we could rule otherwise. You now have the choice of accepting the punishment designated and having the offense wiped away, or of refusing our jurisdiction and withdrawing your body from our land. What is your choice?"

I had Pink repeat this to me, because it was so important that I know what was being offered. When I was sure I had read it right, I accepted their punishment without hesitation. I was very grateful to have been given an alternative.

"Very well. You have elected to be treated as we would treat one of our own who had done the same act. Come to us."

Everyone drew in closer. I was not told what was going to happen. I was drawn in and nudged gently from all directions.

Scar was sitting with her legs crossed more or less in the center of the group. She was crying again, and so was I, I think. It's hard to remember. I ended up face down across her lap. She spanked me.

I never once thought of it as improbable or strange. It flowed naturally out of the situation. Everyone was holding on to me and caressing me, spelling assurances into my palms and legs and neck and cheeks. We were all crying. It was a difficult thing that had to be faced by the whole group. Others drifted in and joined us. I understood that this punishment came from everyone there, but only the offended person, Scar, did the actual spanking. That was one of the ways I had wronged her, beyond the fact of giving her a scraped knee. I had laid on her the obligation of disciplining me and that was why she had sobbed so loudly, not from the pain of her injury, but from the pain of knowing she would have to hurt me.

Pink later told me that Scar had been the staunchest advocate of giving me the option to stay. Some had wanted to expel me outright, but she paid me the compliment of thinking I was a good enough person to be worth putting herself and me through the ordeal. If you can't understand that, you haven't grasped the feeling of community I felt among these people.

It went on for a long time. It was very painful, but not cruel. Nor was it primarily humiliating. There was some of that, of course. But it was essentially a practical lesson taught in the most direct terms. Each of them had undergone it during the first months, but none recently. You *learned* from it, believe me.

I did a lot of thinking about it afterward. I tried to think of what else they might have done. Spanking grown people is really unheard of, you know, though that didn't occur to me until long after it had happened. It seemed so natural when it was going on that the thought couldn't even enter my mind that this was a weird situation to be in.

They did something like this with the children, but not as long or as hard. Responsibility was lighter for the younger ones. The adults were willing to put up with an occasional bruise or scraped knee while the children learned.

But when you reached what they thought of as adulthood—which was whenever a majority of the adults thought you had or when you assumed the privilege yourself—that's when the spanking really got serious.

They had a harsher punishment, reserved for repeated or malicious offenses. They had not had to invoke it often. It consisted of being sent to Coventry. No one would touch you for a specified period of time. By the time I heard of it, it sounded like a very tough penalty. I didn't need it explained to me.

I don't know how to explain it, but the spanking was administered in such a loving way that I didn't feel violated. *This hurts me as much as it hurts you. I'm doing this for your own good. I love you, that's why I'm spanking you.* They made me understand those old clichés by their actions.

When it was over, we all cried together. But it soon turned to happiness. I embraced Scar and we told each other how sorry we were that it had happened. We talked to each other—made love if you like—and I kissed her knee and helped her dress it.

We spent the rest of the day together, easing the pain.

As I became more fluent in handtalk, "the scales fell from my eyes." Daily, I would discover a new layer of meaning that had eluded me before; it was like peeling the skin of an onion to find a new skin beneath it. Each time I thought I was at the core, only to find that there was another layer I could not yet see.

I had thought that learning handtalk was the key to communication with them. Not so. Handtalk was baby talk. For a long time I was a baby who could not even say goo-goo clearly. Imagine my surprise when, having learned to say it, I found that there were syntax, conjunctions, parts of speech, nouns, verbs, tense, agreement, and the subjunctive mood. I was wading in a tide pool at the edge of the Pacific Ocean.

By handtalk I mean the International Manual Alphabet. Anyone can learn it in a few hours or days. But when you talk to someone in speech, do you spell each word? Do you read each letter as you read this? No, you grasp words as entities, hear groups of sounds and see groups of letters as a gestalt full of meaning.

Everyone at Keller had an absorbing interest in language. They each knew several languages—spoken languages—and could read and spell them fluently.

While still children they had understood the fact that handtalk was a way for blind-deaf people to talk to *outsiders.* Among themselves it was much too cumbersome. It was like Morse Code: useful when you're limited to on-off modes of information transmission, but not the preferred mode. Their ways of speaking to each other were much closer to our type of written or verbal communication, and—dare I say it?—better.

I discovered this slowly, first by seeing that though I could spell rapidly with my hands, it took *much* longer for me to say something than it took anyone else. It could not be explained by differences in dexterity. So I asked to be taught their shorthand speech. I plunged in, this time taught by everyone, not just Pink.

It was hard. They could say any word in any language with no more than two moving hand positions. I knew this was a project for years, not days. You learn the alphabet and you have all the tools you need to spell any word that exists. That's the great advantage in having your written and spoken speech based on the same set of symbols. Shorthand was not like that at all. It partook of none of the linearity or commonality of handtalk; it was not code for English or any other language; it did not share construction or vocabulary with any other language. It was wholly constructed by the Kellerites according to their needs. Each word was something I had to learn and memorize separately from the hand-talk spelling.

For months I sat in the Togethers after dinner saying things like "Me love Scar much much well," while waves of conversation ebbed and flowed and circled around me, touching me only at the edges. But I kept at it, and the children were endlessly patient with me. I improved gradually. Understand that the rest of the conversations I will relate took place in either handtalk or shorthand, limited to various degrees by my fluency. I did not speak nor was I spoken to orally from the day of my punishment.

I was having a lesson in bodytalk from Pink. Yes, we were making love. It had taken me a few weeks to see that she was a sexual being, that her caresses, which I had persisted in seeing as innocent—as I had defined it at the time—both were and weren't innocent. She understood it as perfectly natural that the result of her talking to my penis with her hands might be another sort of conversation. Though still in the middle flush of puberty, she was regarded by all as an adult and I accepted her as such. It was cultural conditioning that had blinded me to what she was saying.

So we talked a lot. With her, I understood the words and music of the body better than with anyone else. She sang a very uninhibited song with her hips and hands, free of guilt, open and fresh with discovery in every note she touched.

"You haven't told me much about yourself," she said. "What did you do on the outside?" I don't want to give the impression that this speech was in sentences, as I have presented it. We were bodytalking, sweating and smelling each other. The message came through from hands, feet, mouth.

I got as far as the sign for pronoun, first person singular, and was stopped.

How could I tell her of my life in Chicago? Should I speak of my early ambition to be a writer, and how that didn't work out? And why hadn't it? Lack of talent, or lack of drive? I could tell her about my profession, which was meaningless shuffling of papers when you got down to it, useless to anything but the Gross National Product. I could talk of the economic ups and downs that had brought me to Keller when nothing else could dislodge me from my easy sliding through life. Or the loneliness of being forty-seven years old and never having found someone worth loving, never having been loved in return. Of being a permanently displaced person in a stainless-steel society. One-night stands, drinking binges, nine-to-five, Chicago Transit Authority, dark movie houses, football games on television, sleeping pills, the John Hancock Tower where the windows won't open so you can't breathe the smog or jump out. That was me, wasn't it?

"I see," she said.

"I travel around," I said, and suddenly realized that it was the truth.

"I see," she repeated. It was a different sign for the same thing. Context was everything. She had heard and understood both parts of me, knew one to be what I had been, the other to be what I hoped I was.

She lay on top of me, one hand lightly on my face to catch the quick interplay of emotions as I thought about my life for the first time in years. And she laughed and nipped my ear playfully when my face told her that for the first time I could remember, I was happy about it. Not just telling myself I was happy, but truly happy. You cannot lie in bodytalk any more than your sweat glands can lie to a polygraph.

I noticed that the room was unusually empty. Asking around in my fumbling way, I learned that only the children were there.

"Where is everybody?" I asked.

"They are all out ***," she said. It was like that: three sharp slaps on the chest with the fingers spread. Along with the finger configuration for "verb form, gerund," it meant that they were all out ***ing. Needless to say, it didn't tell me much.

What did tell me something was her bodytalk as she said it. I read her better than I ever had. She was upset and sad. Her body said something like "Why can't I join them? Why can't I (smell-taste-touch-hear-see) *sense* with them?" That is exactly what she said. Again, I didn't trust my understanding enough to accept that interpretation. I was still trying to force my conceptions on the things I experienced there. I was determined that she and the other children be resentful of their parents in some way, because I was sure they had to be. They *must* feel superior in some way, they *must* feel held back.

I found the adults after a short search of the area, out in the north pasture. All the parents, none of the children. They were standing in a group with no apparent pattern. It wasn't a circle, but it was almost round. If there was any organization, it was in the fact that everybody was about the same distance from everybody else.

The German shepherds and the Sheltie were out there, sitting on the cool grass facing the group of people. Their ears were perked up, but they were not moving.

I started to go up to the people. I stopped when I became aware of the concentration. They were touching, but their hands were not moving. The silence of seeing all those permanently moving people standing that still was deafening to me.

I watched them for at least an hour. I sat with the dogs and scratched them behind the ears. They did that chop-licking thing that dogs do when they appreciate it, but their full attention was on the group.

It gradually dawned on me that the group was moving. It was very slow, just a step here and another there, over many minutes. It was expanding in such a way that the distance between any of the individuals was the same. Like the expanding universe, where all galaxies move away from all others. Their arms were extended now; they were touching only with fingertips, in a crystal lattice arrangement.

Finally they were not touching at all. I saw their fingers straining to cover distances that were too far to bridge. And still they expanded equilaterally. One of the shepherds began to whimper a little. I felt the hair on the back of my neck stand up. Chilly out here, I thought.

I closed my eyes, suddenly sleepy.

I opened them, shocked. Then I forced them shut. Crickets were chirping in the grass around me.

There was something in the darkness behind my eyeballs. I felt that if I could turn my eyes around I would see it easily, but it eluded me in a way that made peripheral vision seem like reading headlines. If there was ever anything impossible to pin down, much less describe, that was it. It tickled at me for a while as the dogs whimpered louder, but I could make nothing of it. The best analogy I could think of was the sensation a blind person might feel from the sun on a cloudy day.

I opened my eyes again.

Pink was standing there beside me. Her eyes were screwed shut, and she was covering her ears with her hands. Her mouth was open and working silently. Behind her were several of the older children. They were all doing the same thing.

Some quality of the night changed. The people in the group were about a foot away from each other now, and suddenly the pattern broke. They all swayed for a moment, then laughed in that eerie, unselfconscious noise deaf people use for laughter. They fell in the grass and held their bellies, rolled over and over and roared.

Pink was laughing, too. To my surprise, so was I. I laughed until my face and sides were hurting, like I remembered doing sometimes when I'd smoked grass.

And that was ***ing.

I can see that I've only given a surface view of Keller. And there are some things I should deal with, lest I foster an erroneous view.

Clothing, for instance. Most of them wore something most of the time. Pink was the only one who seemed temperamentally opposed to clothes. She never wore anything.

No one ever wore anything I'd call a pair of pants. Clothes were loose: robes, shirts, dresses, scarves and such. Lots of men wore things that would be called women's clothes. They were simply more comfortable.

Much of it wa, ragged. It tended to be made of silk or velvet or something else that felt good. The stereotyped Kellerite would be wearing a Japanese silk robe, hand-embroidered with dragons, with many gaping holes and loose threads and tea and tomato stains all over it while she sloshed through the pigpen with a bucket of slop. Wash it at the end of the day and don't worry about the colors running.

I also don't seem to have mentioned homosexuality. You can mark it down to my early conditioning that my two deepest relationships at Keller were with women: Pink and Scar. I haven't said anything about it simply because I don't know how to present it. I talked to men and women equally, on the same terms. I had surprisingly little trouble being affectionate with the men.

I could not think of the Kellerites as bisexual, though clinically they were. It was much deeper than that. They could not even recognize a concept as poisonous as a homosexuality taboo. It was one of the first things they learned. If you distinguish homosexuality from heterosexuality you are cutting yourself off from communication—*full* communication—with half the human race. They were pansexual; they could not separate sex from the rest of their lives. They didn't even have a word in shorthand that could translate directly into English as sex. They had words for male and female in infinite variation, and words for degrees and varieties of physical experience that would be impossible to express in English, but all those words included other parts of the world of experience also; none of them walled off what we call *sex* into its own discrete cubbyhole.

There's another question I haven't answered. It needs answering, because I wondered about it myself when I first arrived. It concerns the necessity for the commune in the first place. Did it really have to be like this? Would they have been better off adjusting themselves to our ways of living?

All was not a peaceful idyll. I've already spoken of the invasion and rape. It could happen again, especially if the roving gangs that operate around the cities start to really rove. A touring group of motorcyclists could wipe them out in a night.

There were also continuing legal hassles. About once a year the social workers descended on Keller and tried to take their children away. They had been accused of everything possible, from child abuse to contributing to delinquency. It hadn't worked so far, but it might someday.

And after all, there are sophisticated devices on the market that allow a blind and deaf person to see and hear a little. They might have been helped by some of those.

I met a blind-deaf woman living in Berkeley once. I'll vote for Keller. As to those machines . . .

In the library at Keller there is a seeing machine. It uses a television camera and a computer to vibrate a closely set series of metal pins. Using it, you can feel a moving picture of whatever the camera is pointed at. It's small and light, made to be carried with the pinpricker touching your back. It cost about thirty-five thousand dollars.

I found it in the corner of the library. I ran my finger over it and left a gleaming streak behind as the thick dust came away.

Other people came and went, and I stayed on.

Keller didn't get as many visitors as the other places I had been. It was out of the way.

One man showed up at noon, looked around, and left without a word.

Two girls, sixteen-year-old runaways from California, showed up one night. They undressed for dinner and were shocked when they found out I could see. Pink scared the hell out of them. Those poor kids had a lot of living to do before they approached Pink's level of sophistication. But then Pink might have been uneasy in California. They left the next day, unsure if they had been to an orgy or not. All that touching and no getting down to business, very strange.

There was a nice couple from Santa Fe who acted as a sort of liaison between Keller and their lawyer. They had a nine-year-old boy who chattered endlessly in handtalk to the other kids. They came up about every other week and stayed a few days, soaking up sunshine and participating in the Together every night. They spoke halting shorthand and did me the courtesy of not speaking to me in speech.

Some of the Indians came around at odd intervals. Their behavior was almost aggressively chauvinistic. They stayed dressed at all times in their Levis and boots. But it was evident that they had a respect for the people, though they thought them strange. They had business dealings with the commune. It was the Navahos who trucked away the produce that was taken to the gate every day, sold it, and took a percentage. They would sit and powwow in sign language spelled into hands. Pink said they were scrupulously honest in their dealings.

And about once a week all the parents went out in the field and ***ed.

I got better and better at shorthand and bodytalk. I had been breezing along for about five months and winter was in the offing. I had not examined my desires as yet, not really thought about what it was I wanted to do with the rest of my life. I guess the habit of letting myself drift was

too ingrained. I was there, and constitutionally unable to decide whether-
to go or to face up to the problem if I wanted to stay for a long, long time.

Then I got a push.

For a long time I thought it had something to do with the economic
situation outside. They were aware of the outside world at Keller. They
knew that isolation and ignoring problems that could easily be dismissed
as not relevant to them was a dangerous course, so they subscribed to the
Braille *New York Times* and most of them read it. They had a television
set that got plugged in about once a month. The kids would watch it and
translate for their parents.

So I was aware that the non-depression was moving slowly into a more
normal inflationary spiral. Jobs were opening up, money was flowing
again. When I found myself on the outside again shortly afterward, I
thought that was the reason.

The real reason was more complex. It had to do with peeling off the
onion layer of shorthand and discovering another layer beneath it.

I had learned handtalk in a few easy lessons. Then I became aware of
shorthand and bodytalk, and of how much harder they would be to learn.
Through five months of constant immersion, which is the only way to
learn a language, I had attained the equivalent level of a five- or six-year-
old in shorthand. I knew I could master it, given time. Bodytalk was
another matter. You couldn't measure progress as easily in bodytalk. It
was a variable and highly interpersonal language that evolved according
to the person, the time, the mood. But I was learning.

Then I became aware of Touch. That's the best I can describe it in a
single, unforced English noun. What *they* called this fourth-stage
language varied from day to day, as I will try to explain.

I first became aware of it when I tried to meet Janet Reilly. I now knew
the history of Keller, and she figured very prominently in all the stories. I
knew everyone at Keller, and I could find her nowhere. I knew everyone
by names like Scar, and She-with-the-missing-front-tooth, and Man-with-
wiry-hair. These were shorthand names that I had given them myself,
and they all accepted them without question. They had abolished their
outside names within the commune. They meant nothing to them; they
told nothing and described nothing.

At first I assumed that it was my imperfect command of shorthand that
made me unable to clearly ask the right question about Janet Reilly. Then
I saw that they were not telling me on purpose. I saw why, and I
approved, and thought no more about it. The name Janet Reilly described
what she had been *on the outside*, and one of her conditions for pushing
the whole thing through in the first place had been that she be no one
special on the inside. She melted into the group and disappeared. She
didn't want to be found. All right.

But in the course of pursuing the question I became aware that each of
the members of the commune had no specific name at all. That is, Pink,
for instance, had no less than one hundred and fifteen names, one from
each of the commune members. Each was a contextual name that told the
story of Pink's relationship to a particular person. My simple names, based

on physical descriptions, were accepted as the names a child would apply to people. The children had not yet learned to go beneath the outer layers and use names that told of themselves, their lives, and their relationships to others.

What is even more confusing, the names evolved from day to day. It was my first glimpse of Touch, and it frightened me. It was a question of permutations. Just the first simple expansion of the problem meant there were no less than thirteen thousand names in use, and they wouldn't stay still so I could memorize them. If Pink spoke to me of Baldy, for instance, she would use her Touch name for him, modified by the fact that she was speaking to me and not Short-chubby-man.

Then the depths of what I had been missing opened beneath me and I was suddenly breathless with fear of heights.

Touch was what they spoke to each other. It was an incredible blend of all three other modes I had learned, and the essence of it was that it never stayed the same. I could listen to them speak to me in shorthand, which was the real basis for Touch, and be aware of the currents of Touch flowing just beneath the surface.

It was a language of inventing languages. Everyone spoke their own dialect because everyone spoke with a different instrument: a different body and set of life experiences. It was modified by everything. *It would not stand still.*

They would sit at the Together and invent an entire body of Touch responses in a night; idiomatic, personal, totally naked in its honesty. And they used it only as a building block for the next night's language.

I didn't know if I wanted to be that naked. I had looked into myself a little recently and had not been satisfied with what I found. The realization that every one of them knew more about it than I, because my honest body had told what my frightened mind had not wanted to reveal, was shattering. I was naked under a spotlight in Carnegie Hall, and all the no-pants nightmares I had ever had came out to haunt me. The fact that they all loved me with all my warts was suddenly not enough. I wanted to curl up in a dark closet with my ingrown ego and let it fester.

I might have come through this fear. Pink was certainly trying to help me. She told me that it would only hurt for a while, that I would quickly adjust to living my life with my darkest emotions written in fire across my forehead. She said Touch was not as hard as it looked at first, either. Once I learned shorthand and bodytalk, Touch would flow naturally from it like sap rising in a tree. It would be unavoidable, something that would happen to me without much effort at all.

I almost believed her. But she betrayed herself. No, no, no. Not that, but the things in her concerning ***ing convinced me that if I went through this I would only bang my head hard against the next step up the ladder.

   ***

I had a little better definition now. Not one that I can easily translate into English, and even that attempt will only convey my hazy concept of what it was.

"It is the mode of touching without touching," Pink said, her body going like crazy in an attempt to reach me with her own imperfect concept of what it was, handicapped by my illiteracy. Her body denied the truth of her shorthand definition, and at the same time admitted to me that she did not know what it was herself.

"It is the gift whereby one can expand oneself from the eternal quiet and dark into something else." And again her body denied it. She beat on the floor in exasperation.

"It is an attribute of being in the quiet and dark all the time, touching others. All I know for sure is that vision and hearing preclude it or obscure it. I can make it as quiet and dark as I possibly can and be aware of the edges of it, but the visual orientation of the mind persists. That door is closed to me, and to all the children."

Her verb "to touch" in the first part of that was a Touch amalgam, one that reached back into her memories of me and what I had told her of my experiences. It implied and called up the smell and feel of broken mushrooms in soft earth under the barn with Tall-one-with-green-eyes, she who taught me to feel the essence of an object. It also contained references to our bodytalking while I was penetrating into the dark and wet of her, and her running account to me of what it was like to receive me into herself. This was all one word.

I brooded on that for a long time. What was the point of suffering through the nakedness of Touch, only to reach the level of frustrated blindness enjoyed by Pink?

What was it that kept pushing me away from the one place in my life where I had been happiest?

One thing was the realization, quite late in coming, that can be summed up as "What the hell am I *doing* here?" The question that should have answered that question was "What the hell would I do if I *left*?"

I was the only visitor, the only one in *seven years* to stay at Keller for longer than a few days. I brooded on that. I was not strong enough or confident enough in my opinion of myself to see it as anything but a flaw in *me*, not in those others. I was obviously too easily satisfied, too complacent to see the flaws that those others had seen.

It didn't have to be flaws in the people of Keller, or in their system. No, I loved and respected them too much to think that. What they had going certainly came as near as anyone ever has in this imperfect world to a sane, rational way for people to exist without warfare and with a minimum of politics. In the end, those two old dinosaurs are the only ways humans have yet discovered to be social animals. Yes, I do see war as a way of living with another; by imposing your will on another in terms so unmistakable that the opponent has to either knuckle under to you, die, or beat your brains out. And if that's a solution to anything, I'd rather live without solutions. Politics is not much better. The only thing going for it is that it occasionally succeeds in substituting talk for fists.

Keller *was* an organism. It was a new way of relating, and it seemed to work. I'm not pushing it as a solution for the world's problems. It's possible that it could only work for a group with a common self-interest as binding and rare as deafness and blindness. I can't think of another group whose needs are so interdependent.

The cells of the organism cooperated beautifully. The organism was strong, flourishing, and possessed of all the attributes I've ever heard used in defining life except the ability to reproduce. That might have been its fatal flaw, if any. I certainly saw the seeds of something developing in the children.

The strength of the organism was communication. There's no way around it. Without the elaborate and impossible-to-falsify mechanisms for communication built into Keller, it would have eaten itself in pettiness, jealousy, possessiveness, and any dozen other "innate" human defects.

The nightly Together was the basis of the organism. Here, from after dinner till it was time to fall asleep, everyone talked in a language that was incapable of falsehood. If there was a problem brewing, it presented itself and was solved almost automatically. Jealousy? Resentment? Some little festering wrong that you're nursing? You couldn't conceal it at the Together, and soon everyone was clustered around you and loving the sickness away. It acted like white corpuscles, clustering around a sick cell, not to destroy it, but to heal it. There seemed to be no problem that couldn't be solved if it was attacked early enough, and with Touch, your neighbors knew about it before you did and were already laboring to correct the wrong, heal the wound, to make you feel better so you could laugh about it. There was a lot of laughter at the Togethers.

I thought for a while that I was feeling possessive about Pink. I know I had done so a little at first. Pink was my special friend, the one who had helped me out from the first, who for several days was the only one I could talk to. It was her hands that had taught me handtalk. I know I felt stirrings of territoriality the first time she lay in my lap while another man made love to her. But if there was any signal the Kellerites were adept at reading, it was that one. If went off like an alarm bell in Pink, the man, and the women and men around me. They soothed me, coddled me, told me in every language that it was all right, not to feel ashamed. Then the man in question began loving *me*. Not Pink, but the man. An observational anthropologist would have had subject matter for a whole thesis. Have you seen the films of baboons' social behavior? Dogs do it, too. Many male mammals do it. When males get into dominance battles, the weaker can defuse the aggression by submitting, by turning tail and surrendering. I have never felt so defused as when that man surrendered the object of our clash of wills—Pink—and turned his attention to me. What could I do? What I did was laugh, and he laughed, and soon we were all laughing, and that was the end of territoriality.

That's the essence of how they solved most "human nature" problems at Keller. Sort of like an oriental martial art; you yield, roll with the blow so that your attacker takes a pratfall with the force of the aggression. You do that until the attacker sees that the initial push wasn't worth the effort, that it was a pretty silly thing to do when no one was resisting you. Pretty soon he's not Tarzan of the Apes, but Charlie Chaplin. And he's laughing.

So it wasn't Pink and her lovely body and my realization that she could never be all mine to lock away in my cave and defend with a gnawed-off thighbone. If I'd persisted in that frame of mind she would have found me about as attractive as an Amazonian leech, and that was a great incentive to confound the behaviorists and overcome it.

So I was back to those people who had visited and left, and what did they see that I didn't see?

Well, there was something pretty glaring. I was not part of the organism, no matter how nice the organism was to me. I had no hopes of ever becoming a part, either. Pink had said it in the first week. She felt it herself, to a lesser degree. She could not ***, though that fact was not going to drive her away from Keller. She had told me that many times in shorthand and confirmed it in bodytalk. If I left, it would be without her.

Trying to stand outside and look at it, I felt pretty miserable. What was I trying to *do*, anyway? Was my goal in life *really* to become a part of a blind-deaf commune? I was feeling so low by that time that I actually thought of that as denigrating, in the face of all the evidence to the contrary. I should be out in the real world where the real people lived, not these freakish cripples.

I backed off from that thought very quickly. I was not totally out of my mind, just on the lunatic edges. These people were the best friends I'd ever had, maybe the only ones. That I was confused enough to think that of them even for a second worried me more than anything else. It's possible that it's what pushed me finally into a decision. I saw a future of growing disillusion and unfulfilled hopes. Unless I was willing to put out my eyes and ears, I would always be on the outside. *I* would be the blind and deaf one. I would be the freak. I didn't want to be a freak.

They knew I had decided to leave before I did. My last few days turned into a long goodbye, with a loving farewell implicit in every word touched to me. I was not really sad, and neither were they. It was nice, like everything they did. They said goodbye with just the right mix of wistfulness and life-must-go-on, and hope-to-touch-you-again.

Awareness of Touch scratched on the edges of my mind. It was not bad, just as Pink had said. In a year or two I could have mastered it.

But I was set now. I was back in the life groove that I had followed for so long. Why is it that once having decided what I must do, I'm afraid to reexamine my decision? Maybe because the original decision cost me so much that I didn't want to go through it again.

I left quietly in the night for the highway and California. They were out in the fields, standing in that circle again. Their fingertips were farther apart than ever before. The dogs and children hung around the edges like beggars at a banquet. It was hard to tell which looked more hungry and puzzled.

The experiences at Keller did not fail to leave their mark on me. I was unable to live as I had before. For a while I thought I could not live at all, but I did. I was too used to living to take the decisive step of ending my life. I would wait. Life had brought one pleasant thing to me; maybe it would bring another.

I became a writer. I found I now had a better gift for communicating than I had before. Or maybe I had it now for the first time. At any rate, my writing came together and I sold. I wrote what I wanted to write, and was not afraid of going hungry. I took things as they came.

I weathered the non-depression of '97, when unemployment reached twenty percent and the government once more ignored it as a temporary downturn. It eventually upturned, leaving the jobless rate slightly higher than it had been the time before, and the time before that. Another million useless persons had been created with nothing better to do than shamble through the streets looking for beatings in progress, car smashups, heart attacks, murders, shootings, arson, bombings, and riots: the endlessly inventive street theater. It never got dull.

I didn't become rich, but I was usually comfortable. That is a social disease, the symptoms of which are the ability to ignore the fact that your society is developing weeping pustules and having its brains eaten out by radioactive maggots. I had a nice apartment in Marin County, out of sight of the machine-gun turrets. I had a car, at a time when they were beginning to be luxuries.

I had concluded that my life was not destined to be all I would like it to be. We all make some sort of compromise, I reasoned, and if you set your expectations too high you are doomed to disappointment. It did oc-cur to me that I was settling for something far from "high," but I didn't know what to do about it. I carried on with a mixture of cynicism and optimism that seemed about the right mix for me. It kept my motor running, anyway.

I even made it to Japan, as I had intended in the first place.

I didn't find someone to share my life. There was only Pink for that, Pink and all her family, and we were separated by a gulf I didn't dare cross. I didn't even dare think about her too much. It would have been very dangerous to my equilibrium. I lived with it, and told myself that it was the way I was. Lonely.

The years rolled on like a caterpillar tractor at Dachau, up to the penultimate day of the millennium.

San Francisco was having a big bash to celebrate the year 2000. Who gives a shit that the city is slowly falling apart, that civilization is disintegrating into hysteria? Let's have a party!

I stood on the Golden Gate Dam on the last day of 1999. The sun was setting in the Pacific, on Japan, which had turned out to be more of the same but squared and cubed with neo-samurai. Behind me the first bomb-shells of a firework celebration of holocaust tricked up to look like festivity competed with the flare of burning buildings as the social and economic basket cases celebrated the occasion in their own way. The city quivered under the weight of misery, anxious to slide off along the fracture lines of some subcortical San Andreas Fault. Orbiting atomic bombs twinkled in my mind, up there somewhere, ready to plant mushrooms when we'd ex-hausted all the other possibilities.

I thought of Pink.

I found myself speeding through the Nevada desert, sweating, gripping the steering wheel. I was crying aloud but without sound, as I had learned to do at Keller.

Can you go back?

I slammed the citicar over the potholes in the dirt road. The car was falling apart. It was not built for this kind of travel. The sky was getting light in the east. It was the dawn of a new millennium. I stepped harder on the gas pedal and the car bucked savagely. I didn't care. I was not driving back down that road, not ever. One way or another, I was here to stay.

I reached the wall and sobbed my relief. The last hundred miles had been a nightmare of wondering if it had been a dream. I touched the cold reality of the wall and it calmed me. Light snow had drifted over everything, gray in the early dawn.

I saw them in the distance. All of them, out in the field where I had left them. No, I was wrong. It was only the children. Why had it seemed like so many at first?

Pink was there. I knew her immediately, though I had never seen her in winter clothes. She was taller, filled out. She would be nineteen years old. There was a small child playing in the snow at her feet, and she cradled an infant in her arms. I went to her and talked to her hand.

She turned to me, her face radiant with welcome, her eyes staring in a way I had never seen. Her hands flitted over me and her eyes did not move.

"I touch you, I welcome you," her hands said. "I wish you could have been here just a few minutes ago. Why did you go away, darling? Why did you stay away so long?" Her eyes were stones in her head. She was blind. She was deaf.

All the children were. No, Pink's child sitting at my feet looked up at me with a smile.

"Where is everybody?" I asked when I got my breath. "Scar? Baldy? Green-eyes? And what's happened? What's happened to you?" I was tottering on the edge of a heart attack or nervous collapse or something. My reality felt in danger of dissolving.

"They've gone," she said. The word eluded me, but the context put it with the *Mary Celeste* and Roanoke, Virginia. It was complex, the way she used the word *gone*. It was like something she had said before: unattainable, a source of frustration like the one that had sent me running from Keller. But now her word told of something that was not hers yet, but was within her grasp. There was no sadness in it.

"Gone?"

"Yes. I don't know where. They're happy. They ***ed. It was glorious. We could only touch a part of it."

I felt my heart hammering to the sound of the last train pulling away from the station. My feet were pounding along the ties as it faded into the fog. Where are the Brigadoons of yesterday? I've never yet heard of a fairy tale where you can go back to the land of enchantment. You wake up, you find that your chance is gone. You threw it away. *Fool!* You only get one chance; that's the moral, isn't it?

Pink's hands laughed along my face.

"Hold this part-of-me-who-speaks-mouth-to-nipple," she said, and handed me her infant daughter. "I will give you a gift."

She reached up and lightly touched my ears with her cold fingers. The sound of the wind was shut out, and when her hands came away it never came back. She touched my eyes, shut out all the light, and I saw no more.

We live in the lovely quiet and dark.

At one time, if you stopped the average man on the street and asked him to name an SF writer, the chances were good that—if he could name one at all—he would name Ray Bradbury.

Today, I'm willing to bet that that same man on the street (or his present reincarnation) would name Isaac Asimov instead.

A good case could be made for the proposition that Asimov is the most famous SF writer alive, outstripping even such darlings of the literary establishment as Kurt Vonnegut Jr.: Asimov is the author of more than two hundred books, including some of the best-known novels in the genre—novels like The Caves of Steel, I, Robot, *and the* Foundation *trilogy; he has written an enormous number of nonfiction books on a bewilderingly large range of topics, making him perhaps the best-known scientific popularizer of our time; he is the only SF writer ever to have an SF magazine named after him (Isaac Asimov's Science Fiction Magazine); he appears frequently on most of the late-night and daytime talk shows; he does television commercials; he even pops up in TV Guide.*

Some years ago, at the height of the New Wave revolution of the late sixties, Asimov wondered in print if he and the other members of his generation weren't "over the hill," unable to compete successfully with the aggressive Young Turks who were pushing their way into the field. Now, two Nebulas and two Hugos (and at least one fiction best-seller) later, that question seems fairly well settled, at least where Asimov is concerned. If any more proof is needed, consider the incisive and imaginative story that follows, a story that contains the only really new idea of the year—and a frightening idea it is, too.

ISAAC ASIMOV
Found!

Computer Two, like the other three that chased each other's tails in orbit round the Earth, was much larger than it had to be.

It might have been one-tenth its diameter and still contained all the volume it needed to store the accumulated and accumulating data to control all space flight.

They needed the extra space, however, so that Joe and I could get inside, if we had to. And we had to.

Computer Two was perfectly capable of taking care of itself. Ordinarily, that is. It was redundant. It worked everything out three times in parallel and all three programs had to mesh perfectly; all three answers had to match. If they did not, the answer was delayed for nanoseconds while Computer Two checked itself, found the malfunctioning part and replaced it.

There was no sure way in which ordinary people would know how many times it caught itself. Perhaps never. Perhaps twice a day. Only Computer Central could measure the time-delay induced by error and only Computer Central knew how many of the component spares had been used as replacements. And Computer Central never talked about it. The only good public image is perfection.

And it's *been* perfection. Until now, there was never any call for Joe and me.

We're the troubleshooters. We go up there when something really goes wrong; when Computer Two or one of the others can't correct itself. It's never happened in the five years we've been on the job. It did happen now and again in the early days, but that was before our time.

We keep in practice. Don't get me wrong. There isn't a computer made that Joe and I can't diagnose. Show us the error and we'll show you the malfunction. Or Joe will, anyway. I'm not the kind who sings one's own praises. The record speaks for itself.

Anyway, this time, neither of us could make the diagnosis.

The first thing that happened was that Computer Two lost internal pressure. That's not unprecedented and it's certainly not fatal. Computer Two can work in a vacuum after all. An internal atmosphere was established in the old days when it was expected there would be a steady flow of repairmen fiddling with it. And it's been kept up out of tradition. Who told you scientists aren't chained by tradition? In their spare time from being scientists, they're human, too.

From the rate of pressure loss, it was deduced that a gravel-sized meteoroid had hit Computer Two. Its exact radius, mass, and energy were reported by Computer Two itself, using that rate of pressure loss, and a few other irregularities, as data.

The second thing that happened was the break was not sealed and the atmosphere was not regenerated. After that came errors and they called us in.

It made no sense. Joe let a look of pain cross his homely face and said, "There must be a dozen things out of whack."

Someone at Computer Central said, "The hunk of gravel ricocheted very likely."

Joe said, "With that energy of entry, it would have passed right through the other side. No ricochets. Besides even with ricochets, I figure it would have had to take some very unlikely strikes."

"Well, then, what do we do?"

Joe looked uncomfortable. I think it was at this point he realized what was coming. He had made it sound peculiar enough to require the troubleshooters on the spot—and Joe had never been up in space. If he had told me once that his chief reason for taking the job was because it meant he would never have to go up in space, he had told it to me 2^x times, with x a pretty high number.

So I said it for him. I said, "We'll have to go up there."

Joe's only way out would have been to say he didn't think he could handle the job, and I watched his pride slowly come out ahead of his cowardice. Not by much, you understand—by a nose, let's say.

To those of you who haven't been on a spaceship in the last fifteen years—and I suppose Joe can't be the only one—let me emphasize that initial acceleration is the only troublesome thing. You can't get away from it, of course.

After that it's nothing, unless you want to count possible boredom. You're just a spectator. The whole thing is automated and computerized. The old romantic days of space pilots are gone totally. I imagine they'll return briefly when our space settlements make the shift to the asteroid belt as they constantly threaten to do—but then only until additional computers are placed in orbit to set up the necessary additional capacity.

Joe held his breath through acceleration, or at least he seemed to. (I must admit I wasn't very comfortable myself. It was only my third trip. I've taken a couple of vacations on Settlement Rho with my husband, but I'm not exactly a seasoned hand.) After that, he was relieved for a while, but only for a while. He got despondent.

"I hope this thing knows where it's going," he said pettishly.

I extended my arms forward, palms up, and felt the rest of me sway backward a bit in the zero-gravity field. "You," I said, "are a computer specialist. Don't you *know* it knows?"

"Sure, but Computer Two is off."

"We're not hooked into Computer Two," I said. "There are three others. And even if only one were left functional, it could handle all the space flights undertaken on an average day."

"All four might go off. If Computer Two is wrong, what's to stop the rest?"

"Then we'll run this thing manually."

"You'll do it, I suppose? You know how—I think not."

"So they'll talk me in."

"For the love of Eniac," he groaned.

There was no problem, actually. We moved out to Computer Two as smooth as vacuum and less than two days after takeoff, we were placed into a parking orbit not ten meters behind it.

What was not so smooth was that, about twenty hours out, we got the news from Earth that Computer Three was losing internal pressure. Whatever had hit Computer Two was going to get the rest, and when all four were out, space flight would grind to a halt. It could be reorganized on a manual basis, surely, but that would take months at a minimum, possibly years, and there would be serious economic dislocation on Earth. Worse yet, several thousand people now out in space would surely die.

It wouldn't bear thinking of and neither Joe nor I talked about it, but it didn't make Joe's disposition sweeter and, let's face it, it didn't make me any happier.

Earth hung over 200,000 kilometers below us, but Joe wasn't bothered by that. He was concentrating on his tether and checking the cartridge in his reaction-gun. He wanted to make sure he could get to Computer Two and back again.

You'd be surprised—if you've never tried it—how you can get your space-legs if you absolutely have to. I wouldn't say there was nothing to it, and we did waste half the fuel we used, but we finally reached Computer Two. We hardly made any bump at all when we struck Computer Two. (You hear it, of course, even in vacuum, because the vibration travels through the metalloid fabric of your spacesuits—but there was hardly any bump, just a whisper.)

Of course, our contact and the addition of our momentum altered the orbit of Computer Two slightly, but tiny expenditures of fuel compensated for that and we didn't have to worry about it. Computer Two took care of it, for nothing had gone wrong with it, as far as we could tell, that affected any of its external workings.

We went over the outside first, naturally. The chances were pretty overwhelming that a small piece of gravel had whizzed through Computer Two and left an unmistakable hole. Two of them in all probability; one going in and one coming out.

The chances of that happening are one in two million on any given day—even money that it will happen at least once in six thousand years. It's not likely, but it can, you know. The chances are one in not more than ten billion that, on any one day, it will be struck by a meteoroid large enough to demolish it.

I didn't mention that because Joe might realize that we were exposed to similar odds ourselves. In fact, any given strike on us would do far more damage to our soft and tender bodies than to the stoical and much-enduring machinery of the computer, and I didn't want Joe more nervous than he was.

The thing is, though, it wasn't a meteoroid.

"What's this?" said Joe, finally.

It was a small cylinder stuck to the outer wall of Computer Two, the first abnormality we had found in its outward appearance. It was about half a centimeter in diameter and perhaps six centimeters long. Just about cigarette-size for any of you who've been caught up in the antique fad of smoking.

We brought out our small flashlights.

I said, "That's not one of the external components."

"It sure isn't," muttered Joe.

There was a faint spiral marking running round the cylinder from one end to the other. Nothing else. For the rest, it was clearly metal, but of an odd, grainy texture—at least to the eye.

Joe said, "It's not tight."

He touched it gently with a fat and gauntleted finger and it gave. Where it had made contact with the surface of Computer Two it lifted, and our flashes shone down on a visible gap.

"There's the reason gas pressure inside declined to zero," I said.

Joe grunted. He pushed a little harder and the cylinder popped away and began to drift. We managed to snare it after a little trouble. Left behind was a perfectly round hole in the skin of Computer Two, half a centimeter across.

Joe said, "This thing, whatever it is, isn't much more than foil."

It gave easily under his fingers, thin but springy. A little extra pressure and it dented. He put it inside his pouch, which he snapped shut and said, "Go over the outside and see if there are any other items like that on it. I'll go inside."

It didn't take me very long. Then I went in. "It's clean," I said. "That's the only thing there is. The only hole."

"One is enough," said Joe gloomily. He looked at the smooth aluminum of the wall and, in the light of the flash, the perfect circle of black was beautifully evident.

It wasn't difficult to place a seal over the hole. It was a little more difficult to reconstitute the atmosphere. Computer Two's reserve gas-forming supplies were low and the controls required manual adjustment. The solar generator was limping but we managed to get the lights on.

Eventually, we removed our gauntlets and helmet, but Joe carefully placed the gauntlets inside his helmet and secured them both to one of his suit loops.

"I want these handy if the air pressure begins to drop," he said sourly.

So I did the same.

There was a mark on the wall just next to the hole. I had noted it in the light of my flash when I was adjusting the seal. When the lights came on, it was obvious.

"You notice that, Joe?" I said.

"I notice."

There was a slight, narrow depression in the wall, not very noticeable at all, but there beyond a doubt if you ran your finger over it. It could be noticed for nearly a meter. It was as though someone had scooped out a very shallow sampling of the metal so that the surface was distinctly less smooth than elsewhere.

I said, "We'd better call Computer Central downstairs."

"If you mean back on Earth, say so," said Joe. "I hate the phony space-talk. In fact, I hate everything about space. That's why I took an Earth-side job—I mean a job on Earth—or what was supposed to be one."

I said patiently, "We'd better call Computer Central back on Earth."

"What for?"

"To tell them we've found the trouble."

"Oh? What did we find?"

"The hole. Remember?"

"Oddly enough, I do. And what caused the hole? It wasn't a meteoroid. I never saw one that would leave a perfectly circular hole with no signs of buckling or melting. And I never saw one that left a cylinder behind." He took the cylinder out of his suit pocket and smoothed the dent out of its thin metal, thoughtfully. "Well, what caused the hole?"

I didn't hesitate. I said, "I don't know."

"If we report to Computer Central, they'll ask the question and we'll say we don't know and what will we have gained? Except hassle?"

"They'll call us, Joe, if we don't call them."

"Sure. And we won't answer, will we?"

"They'll assume something killed us, Joe, and they'll send up a relief party."

"You know Computer Central. It will take them two days to decide on that. We'll have something before then and once we have something, we'll call them."

The internal structure of Computer Two was not *really* designed for human occupancy. What was foreseen was the occasional and temporary presence of troubleshooters. That meant there needed to be room for maneuvering, and there were tools and supplies.

There weren't any armchairs, though. For that matter, there was no gravitational field, either, or any centrifugal imitation of one.

We both floated in mid-air, drifting slowly this way or that. Occasionally, one of us touched the wall and gently rebounded. Or else part of one of us overlapped part of the other.

"Keep your foot out of my mouth," said Joe, and pushed it away violently. It was a mistake because we both began to turn. Of course, that's not how it looked to us. To us, it was the interior of Computer Two that was turning, which was most unpleasant, and it took us a while to get relatively motionless again.

We had the theory perfectly worked out in our planetside training, but we were short on practice. A lot short.

By the time we had steadied ourselves, I felt unpleasantly nauseated. You can call it nausea, or astronausea, or space-sickness, but whatever you call it, it's the heaves and it's worse in space than anywhere else, because there's nothing to pull the stuff down. It floats around in a cloud of globules and you don't want to be floating around with it. So I held it back; so did Joe.

I said, "Joe, it's clearly the computer that's at fault. Let's get at its insides." Anything to get my mind off *my* insides and let them quiet down. Besides, things weren't moving fast enough. I kept thinking of Computer Three on its way down the tube; maybe Computer One and Four by now, too; and thousands of people in space with their lives hanging on what we did.

Joe looked a little greenish, too, but he said, "First I've got to think. Something got in. It wasn't a meteoroid, because whatever it was chewed a neat hole out of the hull. It wasn't cut out because I didn't find a circle of metal anywhere inside. Did you?"

"No. But I hadn't thought to look."

"*I* looked, and it's nowhere in here."

"It may have fallen outside."

"With the cylinder covering the hole till I pulled it away? A likely thing. Did you see anything come flying out?"

"No."

Joe said, "We may still find it in here, of course, but I doubt it. It was somehow dissolved and something got in."

"What something? Whose is it?"

Joe's grin was remarkably ill-natured. "Why do you bother asking questions to which there are no answers? If this was last century, I'd say the Russians had somehow stuck that device onto the outside of Computer Two—no offense. If it was last century, you'd say it was the Americans."

I decided to be offended. I said coldly, "We're trying to say something that makes sense *this* century, Yosif" giving it an exaggerated Russian pronunciation.

"We'll have to assume some dissident group."

"If so," I said, "we'll have to assume one with a capacity for space flight and with the ability to come up with an unusual device."

Joe said, "Space flight presents no difficulties, if you can tap into the orbiting computers illegally—which has been done. As for the cylinder, that may make more sense when it is analyzed back on Earth—downstairs, as you space buffs would say."

"It doesn't make sense," I said. "Where's the point in trying to disable Computer Two?"

"As part of a program to cripple space flight."

"Then everyone suffers. The dissidents, too."

"But it gets everyone's attention, doesn't it, and suddenly the cause of whatever-it-is makes news. Or the plan is to just knock out Computer Two and then threaten to knock out the other three. No real damage, but lots of potential, and lots of publicity."

He was studying all parts of the interior closely, edging over it square centimeter by square centimeter. "I *might* suppose the thing was of nonhuman origin."

"Don't be silly."

"You want me to make the case? The cylinder made contact, after which something inside ate away a circle of metal and entered Computer Two. It crawled over the inside wall eating away a thin layer of metal for some reason. Does that sound like anything of human construction?"

"Not that I know of, but I don't know everything. Even you don't know everything."

Joe ignored that. "So the question is, how did it—whatever it is—get into the computer, which is, after all, reasonably well sealed. It did so quickly, since it knocked out the resealing and air-regeneration capacities almost at once."

"Is *that* what you're looking for?" I said, pointing.

He tried to stop too quickly and somersaulted backward, crying, "That's it!"

In his excitement, he was thrashing his arms and legs, which got him nowhere, of course. I grabbed him and, for a while, we were both trying to exert pushes in uncoordinated directions, which got us nowhere either. Joe called me a few names, but I called him some back and there I had the advantage. I understand English perfectly, better than he does in fact; but his knowledge of Russian is—well, fragmentary would be a kind way of putting it. Bad language in an ununderstood language always sounds very dramatic.

"Here it is," he said, when we finally had sorted ourselves out.

Where the computer-shielding met the wall, a small circular hole appeared when Joe brushed aside a small cylinder. It was just like the one on the outer hull, but it seemed even thinner. In fact, it seemed to disintegrate when Joe touched it.

"We'd better get into the computer," said Joe.

The computer was a shambles.

Not obviously. I don't mean to say it was like a beam of wood that had been riddled by termites.

In fact, if you looked at the computer casually, you might swear it was intact.

Look closely, though, and some of the chips would be gone. The more closely you looked, the more you realized were gone. Worse, the stores that Computer Two used in self-repair had dwindled to almost nothing. We kept looking and would discover something else missing.

Joe took the cylinder out of his pouch again and turned it end for end. He said, "I suspect it's after high-grade silicon in particular. I can't say for sure, of course, but my guess is that the sides are mostly aluminum and the flat end is mostly silicon."

I said, "Do you mean the thing is a solar battery?"

"Part of it is. That's how it gets its energy in space; energy to get to Computer Two, energy to eat a hole into it, energy to—to—I don't know how else to put it. Energy to stay alive."

"You call it alive?"

"Why not? Look, Computer Two can repair itself. It can reject faulty bits of equipment and replace it with working ones, but it needs a supply of spares to work with. Given enough spares of all kinds, it could build a computer just like itself, when properly programmed—but it needs the supply, so we don't think of it as alive. This object that entered Computer Two is apparently collecting its own supplies. That's suspiciously lifelike."

"What you're saying," I said, "is that we have here a microcomputer advanced enough to be considered alive."

"I don't honestly know what I'm saying."

"Who on Earth could make such a thing?"

"Who on *Earth*?"

I made the next discovery. It looked like a stubby pen drifting through the air. I just caught it out of the corner of my eye and it registered as a pen.

In zero-gravity, things will drift out of pockets and float off. There's no way of keeping anything in place unless it is physically confined. You expect pens and coins and anything else that finds an opening to drift wherever the air currents and inertia lead it.

So my mind registered "Pen" and I groped for it absently and, of course, my fingers didn't close on it. Just reaching for something sets up an air current that pushes it away. You have to reach over and sneak behind it with one hand, and then reach for it with the other. Picking up any small object in mid-air is a two-hand operation.

I turned to look at the object and pay a little more attention to retrieval, then realized that my pen was safely in its pouch. I felt for it and it was there.

"Did you lose a pen, Joe?" I called out.

"No."

"Anything like that? Key? Cigarette?"

"I don't smoke. You know that."

A stupid answer. "Anything?" I said in exasperation. "I'm seeing things here."

"No one ever said you were stable."

"Look, Joe. Over there. Over there."

He lunged for it. I could have told him it would do no good.

By now, though, our poking around in the computer seemed to have stirred things up. We were seeing them wherever we looked. They were floating in the air currents.

I stopped one at last. Or, rather, it stopped itself for it was on the elbow of Joe's suit. I snatched it off and shouted. Joe jumped in terror and nearly knocked it out of my hand.

I said, "Look!"

There was a shiny circle on Joe's suit, where I had taken the thing off. It had begun to eat its way through.

"Give it to me," said Joe. He took it gingerly and put it against the wall to hold it steady. Then he shelled it, gently lifting the paper-thin metal.

There was something inside that looked like a line of cigarette ash. It caught the light and glinted, though, like lightly woven metal.

There was a moistness about it, too. It wriggled slowly, one end seeming to seek blindly.

The end made contact with the wall and stuck. Joe's finger pushed it away. It seemed to require a small effort to do so. Joe rubbed his finger and thumb and said, "Feels oily."

The metal worm—I don't know what else to call it—seemed limp now after Joe had touched it. It didn't move again.

I was twisting and turning, trying to look at myself.

"Joe," I said, "for heaven's sake, have I got one of them on me anywhere?"

"I don't see one," he said.

"Well, *look* at me. You've got to watch me, Joe, and I'll watch you. If our suits are wrecked we might not be able to get back to the ship."

Joe said, "Keep moving, then."

It was a grisly feeling, being surrounded by things hungry to dissolve your suit wherever they could touch it. When any showed up, we tried to catch them and stay out of their way at the same time, which made things almost impossible. A rather long one drifted close to my leg and I kicked at it, which was stupid, for if I had hit it, it might have stuck. As it was, the air current I set up brought it against the wall, where it stayed.

Joe reached hastily for it—too hastily. The rest of his body rebounded as he somersaulted, one booted foot struck the wall near the cylinder lightly. When he finally righted himself, it was still there.

"I didn't smash it, did I?"

"No, you didn't," I said. "You missed it by a decimeter. It won't get away."

I had a hand on either side of it. It was twice as long as the other cylinder had been. In fact, it was like two cylinders stuck together longways, with a constriction at the point of joining.

"Act of reproducing," said Joe as he peeled away the metal. This time what was inside was a line of dust. Two lines. One on either side of the constriction.

"It doesn't take much to kill them," said Joe. He relaxed visibly. "I think we're safe."

"They do seem alive," I said reluctantly.

"I think they seem more than that. They're viruses—or the equivalent."

"What are you talking about?"

Joe said, "Granted I'm a computer technologist and not a virologist—but it's my understanding that viruses on Earth, or 'downstairs' as you would say, consist of a nucleic acid molecule coated in a protein shell.

"When a virus invades a cell, it manages to dissolve a hole in the cell wall or membrane by the use of some appropriate enzyme and the nucleic acid slips inside, leaving the protein coat outside. Inside the cell it finds the material to make a new protein coat for itself. In fact, it manages to form replicas of itself and produces a new protein coat for each replica. Once it has stripped the cell of all it has, the cell dissolves and in place of the one invading virus there are several hundred daughter viruses. Sound familiar?"

"Yes. Very familiar. It's what's happening here. But where did it come from, Joe?"

"Not from Earth, obviously, or any Earth settlement. From somewhere else, I suppose. They drift through space till they find something appropriate in which they can multiply. They look for sizable objects ready-made of metal. I don't imagine they can smelt ores."

"But large metal objects with pure silicon components and a few other succulent matters like that are the products of intelligent life only," I said.

"Right," said Joe, "which means we have the best evidence yet that intelligent life is common in the universe, since objects like the one we're on must be quite common or it couldn't support these viruses. And it means that intelligent life is old, too, perhaps ten billion years old—long enough for a kind of metal evolution, forming a metal/silicon/oil life as we have formed a nucleic/protein/water life. Time to evolve a parasite on space-age artifacts."

I said, "You make it sound that every time some intelligent life-form develops a space-culture, it is subjected before long to parasitic infestation."

"Right. And it must be controlled. Fortunately, these things are easy to kill, especially now when they're forming. Later on, when ready to burrow out of Computer Two, I suppose they will grow, thicken their shells, stabilize their interior and prepare, as the equivalent of spores, to drift a million years before they find another home. They might not be so easy to kill then."

"How are you going to kill them?"

"I already have. I just touched that first one when it instinctively sought out metal to begin manufacturing a new shell after I had broken open the first one—and that touch finished it. I didn't touch the second, but I kicked the wall near it and the sound vibration in the metal shook its interior apart into metal dust. So they can't get us—or any more of the computer—if we just shake them apart, now!"

He didn't have to explain further—or as much. He put on his gauntlets slowly, and banged at the wall with one. It pushed him away and he kicked at the wall where he next approached it.

"You do the same," he shouted.

I tried to, and for a while we both kept at it. You don't know how hard it is to hit a wall at zero-gravity; at least on purpose; and do it hard enough to make it clang. We missed as often as not or just struck a glancing blow that sent us whirling but made virtually no sound. We were panting with effort and aggravation in no time.

But we had acclimated ourselves. We kept it up and eventually gathered up more of the viruses. There was nothing inside but dust in every case. They were clearly adapted to empty, automated space objects which, like modern computers, were vibration-free. That's what made it possible, I suppose, to build up the exceedingly rickety-complex metallic structures that possessed sufficient instability to produce the properties of simple life.

I said, "Do you think we got them all?"

"How can I say? If there's one left, it will cannibalize the others for metal supplies and start all over. Let's bang around some more."

We did until we were sufficiently worn out not to care whether one was still left alive.

"Of course," I said, panting, "the Planetary Association for the Advancement of Science isn't going to be pleased with our killing them all."

Joe's suggestion as to what the P.A.A.S. could do with itself was forceful, but impractical. He said, "Look, our mission is to save Computer Two, a few thousand lives and, as it turned out, our own lives, too. Now they can decide whether to renovate this computer or rebuild it from scratch. It's their baby.

"The P.A.A.S. can get what they can out of these dead objects and that should be something. If they want live ones, I suspect they'll find them floating about in these regions."

I said, "All right. My suggestion is we tell Computer Central we're going to jerry-rig this computer and get it doing some work anyway, and we'll stay till a relief is up for main repairs or whatever in order to prevent any reinfestation. Meanwhile, they'd better get to each of the other computers and set up a system that can set it to vibrating strongly as soon as the internal atmosphere shows a pressure drop."

"Simple enough," said Joe sardonically.

"It's lucky we found them when we did."

"Wait a while," said Joe, and the look in his eye was one of deep trouble. "We didn't find them. *They* found *us*. If metal-life has developed, do you suppose it's likely that this is the only form it takes?

"What if such life-forms communicate somehow and, across the vastness of space, others are now converging on us for the picking? Other species, too; all of them after the lush new fodder of an as-yet untouched space culture. *Other* species! Some that are sturdy enough to withstand vibration. Some that are large enough to be more versatile in their reactions to danger. Some that are equipped to invade our settlements in orbit. Some, for the sake of Univac, that may be able to invade the Earth for the metals of its cities.

"What I'm going to report, what I must report, is that we've been *found!*"

Although critics and insiders generally agree that Christopher Priest is the best new English SF author to come along since Keith Roberts, he has to date been shamefully ignored in this country. His fine novels The Space Machine *(Popular Library),* Darkening Island *(Manor Books),* The Inverted World *(Popular Library), and* Indoctrinaire *(Popular Library) have all received enthusiastic notices and won large audiences in Europe and Great Britain, but on this side of the Atlantic they often get lost behind the glaring publicity accorded to inferior but more aggressively-hyped books.*

Priest, however, may finally be on the verge of getting some of the recognition that he deserves. His anthology Anticipations *(Scribner's) was my choice for best one-shot original anthology of 1978, his subtle and brilliantly executed novel* The Perfect Lover *(Dell) was my own personal favorite this year, and his F & SF story "The Watched" was certainly one of the year's five best novellas. Also helping Priest along this year to well-deserved recognition as one of SF's major new talents is the cool, disturbing, and oddly beautiful story that follows, one of a marvelous series of stories Priest has been writing about the Dream Archipelago, to be released soon as the collection* An Infinite Summer *(Dell).*

CHRISTOPHER PRIEST
Whores

I left the war behind me and traveled to the tropical northern coast of the continent. Fifty days' sick leave stretched ahead of me, and my trouser pocket was heavy on my buttock with the wad of high-denomination notes I had received as back pay. It should have been a time for recuperation after the long spell in the military hospital, but I was still affected by the enemy synesthetic gas I had inhaled and my perception was disturbed.

As the train had clattered through the devastated towns and country-side, I seemed to taste the music of pain, feel the gay dancing colors of sound.

Waiting in the main port for the ferry across to the Dream Archipelago, I tried to rationalize my delusions as the medical orderlies had trained me. The brick houses, which between my perceptual lapses I saw glowed brown from the local sandstone, became synesthetic monstrosities: cynical laughter, a deep throbbing sound, cold like tempered steel to the touch. The fishing boats in the harbor were less unpleasant to perceive: they were a gentle humming sound, barely audible. The army hostel where I stayed overnight was a warren of associative flavors and smells: the corridors tasted to me of coal dust, the walls were papered with hyacinth, the bed linen enfolded me like a rancid mouth. I slept poorly, waking several times from vivid dreams. One recurred especially: I dreamed I was still with my unit in the front line of the war, advancing and retreating, setting up the monitoring complex then dismantling it, repeatedly, endlessly.

In the morning my synesthesia seemed to have receded again; in the last weeks I had sometimes passed a whole day without a relapse, and when I was discharged it was because they said I was cured.

I left the hostel and walked down to the harbor, soon finding the quay where the ferry berthed. There was an hour and a half to wait, and so I strolled pleasurably through the streets surrounding the harbor, noting that the town was a major center for the importation of military and civilian supplies; I was allowed into one warehouse and was shown large stacks of crates containing hallucinogenic grenades and neural dissociation gases.

The day was hot and sultry; the sky was clouded. I stood with about a hundred other people on the quay, waiting to board the ferry. This was an old diesel-powered boat, apparently top-heavy, riding high in the water. As I stepped down onto the deck, I experienced a wholly natural kind of synesthetic response: the smell of hot diesel oil, salt-stiff ropes, and sun-dried deck planks summoned a vivid nostalgic memory of a childhood voyage along the coast of my own country. The experience of the enemy gas had taught me how to recognize the response, and in moments I was able to recall, in explicit detail, my thoughts, actions, and ambitions of that time.

There was a delay and an argument when I came to pay my fare. The army money was acceptable, but the notes were too high in value. Change had to be found, and the disgruntled ferryman made me wait for it. By the time I was free to explore the ancient boat, we were a long way out to sea, and the warring continent I had left was a black outline on the southern horizon.

I was returning, at last, to the Dream Archipelago. In the days of mental torment in the military hospital, when food had seemed to shout abuse at me and light sang discordant melodies for my eyes, and my mouth would only utter pain and hurt, my consolation lay in the Dream Archipelago. I had been there once, before I went to war, and I urged—and was urged—to return.

"Visit the island of Salay," a rehabilitation orderly had said, over and over. "In Salay the food is the most exotic in the world. Or Muriseay. Or Paneron. Do you remember the women of Paneron?"

(I remembered nothing, then; only the agonies of twenty-five years of life, transmuted insanely to colors and smells and pain.)

I remembered the women of Paneron while I sat on the deck of the ferry, but they did not attract me. Nor did any woman so easily accessible. There was a woman sitting near me, a young woman. I had been idly appraising her, and she noticed, and my stare was returned forthrightly. It had been a long time since I had had a woman, and she was the first I had noticed. I turned away from her, wanting to choose, not to accept the first woman who stared back at me.

I was returning at last to the Dream Archipelago . . . and I knew where I'd go. Not to Paneron, although I had been there and tried the women, nor to Salay, nor to any other of the islands that the troops most often visited. I did not count myself above the others, nor was I seeking an esoteric experience for its own sake; but I was walking again on the path of a long-forgotten memory, one which had returned to me by the insane medium of my illness.

On the island of Winho there was a girl who spoke like musk, who laughed with the texture of spring water, and who loved in deep vermilion. . . .

It was five years since I had been to Winho. I had visited the archipelago on my way to war, and the boat had put in to Winho Town for overnight repairs. That evening I had taken a whore, had bid for her against a local man, and with my soldier's pay had bought her for twice the usual rate.

I had remembered the hour with her for a time, but since then there had been many whores and I did not think of her much. In my illness, though, I had remembered her again, the memory made more alluring by the associative images of the synesthesia.

On Winho, in the Dream Archipelago, I would find that girl. Her name was Slenje, and I wanted her again.

But Slenje was dead.

Winho Town had been occupied by enemy troops for several months when they opened a new front in the archipelago. It had been liberated with the other islands, but as our troops had blasted their way back into Winho, Slenje had died.

I was obsessed with her for two days, pacing the streets of the town, inquiring after her with many of the people, even though the answer was always the same. Slenje was dead, was dead.

On the second day, I had another attack of synesthesia, and the white-painted cottages and the lush vegetation and the streets of dried mud became a nightmare of beguiling smells and flavors, terrifying sounds, and bizarre textures. I stood for an hour in the central street of the town, convinced that Slenje had been swallowed: the houses ached like decaying teeth, the road was soft and hairy like the surface of a tongue, the tropical flowers and trees were like half-chewed food, and the warm wind that came in from the sea was like fetid breath.

When the attack was finished, I drank two beers in a local café, then went to the garrison and found an officer of my own rank.

"You'll suffer from it all your life," the officer said.

"The synesthesia?"

"You ought to be invalided out permanently."

"I'm on sick leave now," I explained.

We were walking through the courtyard of the castle where the soldiers were garrisoned. It was suffocatingly hot in the sun, for no breath of wind could reach the deep yard. The castle battlements were being patrolled by young soldiers in dark blue uniforms, who paced slowly to and fro, ever alert for a return of the enemy. These guards wore full battle gear, including the heavy gas-proof black hoods that covered their heads and faces.

"I'm trying to find a woman," I said.

"There are plenty in the town."

"A particular woman," I said. "A whore. The locals say she was killed."

"Then find another. Or use one of ours. We've twenty whores in the garrison. Keep away from the local women."

"Disease?" I said.

"In a sense. They're off-limits to us. No loss."

"Tell me about it."

The officer said, "We're fighting a war. The town is full of enemy infiltrators."

I looked at him carefully, and noticed that his face was expressionless as he said this.

"That's official army policy," I said. "What's the truth?"

"No different."

We continued to walk around the courtyard, and I decided not to leave until I heard a fuller explanation. The officer talked of his part in the archipelago campaign, and I listened with simulated interest. He told me that Winho Town had been occupied by enemy troops for nearly two hundred days, and he detailed some of the outrages they had perpetrated. I listened with real interest.

"The enemy performed . . . experiments here," the officer said. "Not with the synesthetics, something else. Their laboratories have been dismantled."

"By you?"

"By army staff officers."

"And what happened to the women?"

"The local people have been infiltrated," the officer said, and although we paced about the sun-hot courtyard for another hour, I learned no more. As I left the castle, one of the black-hooded guards on the battlements fainted from the heat. He was allowed to lie where he had fallen, and within moments had been replaced.

Night was falling when I returned to the town, and many of the people were walking slowly through the streets. Now that my quest for Slenje was over I was able to see with a new clarity and observe the town more objectively than before. The tropical evening was still and close, and the breeze had gone, but the oppressive heat could not by itself account for the way the people moved about. Everyone I saw walked slowly and painfully, shuffling along as if lamed. The hot night seemed to amplify sounds, but apart from occasional voices, and melancholy music coming from one of the restaurants, the only noise was that of the painful footsteps.

While I waited in the street, standing in the same spot as before, I reflected that in this stage of my recovery I was no longer frightened of the synesthesia. It didn't seem odd to me that certain kinds of music should be visualized as strands of colored lights; that I should be capable of imagining the circuitry of the army monitoring equipment in terms of geometric shapes; that words should have palpable textures, such as fabriclike, or metallic; that strangers should exude emotional coloration or hostility without even glancing my way.

A small boy ran across the street and darted behind a tree. He stared toward me from behind it. A tiny stranger: he exuded not the nervousness his manner indicated, but curiosity and playfulness.

At last he walked toward me, staring at the ground.

"Are you the man who was asking about Slenje?" he said and scratched his groin.

"Yes," I said . . . and instantly the child ran away. He was the only quick movement in the street.

A few minutes passed, and I continued to wait. I saw the boy again, running back across the street, zigzagging through the shuffling people. He ran toward a house, then vanished inside.

A little while later two girls came slowly down the street, their arms linked. They walked directly to where I stood. Neither of them was Slenje . . . but then I had not hoped. I knew she was dead.

One of the girls, with long dark hair, said, "It will cost you fifty."

"That's all right."

As she spoke I had caught a glimpse of her teeth. Several of them appeared to be broken, giving her a sinister, demoniac appearance. She was plumper than the other, and her hair seemed unwashed. I looked at the second girl, who was short, with pale brown hair.

"I'll take you," I said to her.

"It's still fifty," said the first girl.

"I know."

The girl with the broken teeth kissed the other on both cheeks, then shuffled away.

I followed the second girl as she headed down the street toward the tiny harbor.

I said, "What's your name?"

"Does it matter?" It was the first thing she had said to me.

"No, it doesn't matter," I said. "Did you know Slenje?"

"Of course."

We turned into a narrow side street that ran up the face of one of the hills surrounding the harbor. No wheeled vehicles ever used this way, for every so ofter there were shallow steps. The girl climbed slowly, pausing at each of the steps. She was breathing heavily in the humid air. I offered to take her arm, but she snatched it away from my hand; she was not hostile, though, but proud, for she gave me a quick smile a moment later. As we stopped at the door of an old house, she said, "My name is Elva."

She opened the door and stepped inside. I was about to follow her when I noticed that a number had been painted on the door: 14. It caught my attention because ever since my illness I had had strong color associations with numbers. 14 had an emphatic association with blueness . . . but this number had been painted in white. I found it disconcerting, because as I looked at it, the number seemed to change from white to blue, to white again. I knew then that another synesthetic attack was beginning and, anticipating the worst, I felt a deep mood of depression. I started forward and closed the door behind me, as if shutting the number away from my sight would forestall the attack.

As the girl switched on a light, my mind cleared and the synesthetic attack faded. I recoiled from the disturbing images of the lapses, but they were now a part of me. I followed the girl up a flight of stairs (she went slowly, placing one foot beside the other on each step), and I remembered Slenje's vermilion lovemaking. I tried perversely to will the attack to return, as if the distraction of the sickness would add an extra sensation to the act of sex.

We came to a small bedroom by the top of the stairs, which, although close and airless in the heat, was clean and tidy. It was lit by a single light bulb, which glared harshly against the white-painted walls.

Elva, the girl, said, "I'd like the fifty now."

It was the first time she had faced me as she spoke, and in doing so revealed the inside of her mouth. Like those of the dark-haired girl, Elva's teeth were broken and jagged. I recoiled mentally from her, this sudden fastidiousness of mine making me uncertain of what I had been expecting. Elva must have noticed my reaction, for she smiled at me with her lips lifted away from her teeth: then I saw that they were not broken by decay or neglect, but that every single tooth, upper and lower, had had a piece broken away from it in a clean line, as if with a surgical instrument.

I said nothing, remembering that the enemy had occupied the town. I reached into my pocket and took out the money.

"I only have a hundred," I said, and slipped one of the notes from the wad, returning the rest to my pocket.

She took the note.

"I have change," she said, and opened a drawer. For a few seconds she searched through it, and while her back was turned I stared appraisingly at her body. In spite of her physical affliction, which gave her the movements of an old woman, she was very youthful, and I felt pity for her, mingling with the sexual desire which was even now asserting itself.

At last she turned, and showed me five silver ten-piece coins. She placed them in a neat pile on top of the dresser.

I said to her, "Elva . . . please keep the money. I must leave."

I was shamed by her degraded state, shamed by my use of her.

Her only reply was to lean down by the side of the bed, and turn the switch of a power-point. An electric fan whirred round, sending a welcome draft through the stuffy room. As she straightened, I saw that behind the thin fabric of her blouse her nipples were erect.

She began to undo the buttons of the blouse.

"Elva, I cannot stay with you."

She paused then to look at me. "You regret your choice?"

Before I could answer, before I had to answer, we both heard a sudden cry coming from nearby. Elva turned away from me immediately and went to a door on the opposite side of the room. She opened this and went through, leaving it open behind her.

I saw that beyond the door there was another room, small and dark, filled with the sound of whining insects, and in it was a tiny bed. A child had fallen from it and lay on the floor, crying. Elva picked up the naked child—it was a little boy, no more than a year old—and held him to her, trying to soothe him. For a few minutes, the boy was inconsolable, tears running down his bright pink face, saliva glossing his chin. Elva kissed him.

I saw that the little boy, in falling from the bed, had landed on his hand, for when Elva took the hand in hers he screamed with pain. Elva kissed the hand.

She kissed the fingers, and she kissed the palm . . . and she kissed the tiny, puffy wrist.

Elva opened her mouth, and some trick of the bright light in the main bedroom made her white chipped teeth shine momentarily. She brought the little boy's hand up to her lips . . . and then she took the fingers into her mouth, sucking and working her lips forward, until at last the entire hand was inside her mouth. All the while she caressed his arm, making tender, soothing noises in her throat.

At last the little boy stopped crying, and his eyes closed. She laid him on the bed, drew the covers over him and tucked them under the mattress . . . then came back to where I waited for her.

Elva took off her clothes, and so I undressed, too. We climbed into the bed, and in a while we made love. Elva kissed me passionately as we roused, and with my tongue I explored her mouth, feeling how each of her teeth had been fined to sharp edges. She bit my tongue and lips gently, as she had bitten the hand of the little boy, and there was a great tenderness to her.

She sobbed when we had finished, lying in the bed with her back toward me, and I stroked her hair and shoulders, thinking I should leave. Our union had been brief, but for me, after months of enforced celibacy, memorable. There had not been Slenje's vermilion passion, for the synesthetics had let me alone, but Elva had been expert and seemingly affectionate. I lay with my eyes closed, wondering if I should ever return to her.

From the next room there came a quiet whimpering noise, and at once Elva left the bed and opened the interconnecting door. She peered at the child within, but seemed satisfied and closed the door again. She came back to the bed, where I was already sitting up, preparing to dress.

"Don't leave," she said.

"I've had my time," I said, my thoughts at variance with my words.

"You are not here for time," she said and pushed me down across the bed again.

She straddled me, kissing my neck and chest, letting her damaged teeth run tiny harmless scratches across my skin.

I roused again and tried to roll her over on to the bed beside me, but she stayed above me, continuing to kiss and suck at my skin.

And it seemed to me, as her mouth found my rigid organ and took it deep inside, that there was a sudden sense of lemon pleasure, and the liquid sounds of her mouth became as a hot pool of stagnant voices, endlessly circling. . . .

I became aware of my own identity, and it took the shape of the capital letter *I*. It was surrounded by whiteness and stood out clear and black against it. My eyes were wide open, staring at the ceiling of the dingy room, but my actual vision was subordinated to the inner perception of myself. The letter *I* became larger and thicker; the lower crossline vanished, the upper one became a solid triangle with rounded corners.

I pulsed rhythmically.

I was surrounded by knives, flickering in light from an unseen source. I pulsed toward them, shrank away. The blades of the knives glinted irregularly, for their cutting edges were not evenly honed. One knife moved toward *I*, its jagged edge shining, and *I* shrank away. The knife withdrew.

Then there was the white, stagnant pool, radiating warmth. The voices sucked *I* in; identity was lost, as one with the rest.

Then the kaleidoscope of colored pleasure: bursting from below, spinning so fast that the colors blended optically to a creaming white.

But no vermilion.

I said, when I had dressed, "Take a hundred."

"Fifty, we agreed."

"Not for that."

She was still lying on the bed, face down, and her hair was blowing in the cool stream from the electric fan. I noticed that the skin on the back of her legs had been damaged in some way: there was a pattern of barely detectable scars high on each thigh.

I looked at the five silver coins lying on the top of the dresser. "I'll leave them there anyway. Buy something for the boy."

She sat up and came slowly over to me, her pale skin blotched with red where she had lain. She took the five coins and slipped them determinedly into the breast pocket of my shirt.

"Fifty."

That was the end of it.

From the next room I heard the sound of her child again, who was waking. He was muttering quietly to himself. Elva heard him too, for she looked briefly in that direction.

"You have a husband?" I said, and she nodded. "Where is he?"

"The whores took him."

"Whores?"

"The enemy. They took him when they left, the bitches."

There had been sixteen hundred female troops in Winho Town during the occupation, and every man had been held in captivity. When the town was relieved by our troops, the men had been taken away as the enemy withdrew. Only the very old or very young had been left behind.

"Is he still alive?" I said, when she had finished speaking.

"I suppose so . . . how do I know?"

She was sitting, naked still, on the edge of the bed. I expected her to cry again, but her eyes were dry.

"Do you want me to stay?" I said.

"No . . . please go."

"Shall I come again?"

"If you want to."

The little boy in the next room was beginning to cry. I opened the door, went down the stairs, and a moment later was outside the house.

The following day I discovered that a ferry would be calling in the afternoon, and I decided to leave Winho. While I was waiting I walked slowly through the narrow streets of the town, wondering if I would see Elva.

The day was humid, and I undid the buttons at the front of my shirt to let my skin breathe more easily. It was then I noticed that a tracery of fine scratches had appeared across my chest, and I remembered Elva's sharpened teeth, delicately teasing at my neck and chest. I touched one of the longer scratches with my finger, but there was no painful sensation.

The town, languid in the heat, seemed to be moist and soft, and the air which surrounded me was like the embrace of fur. It was only when I reached the harbor, and stood on the pier waiting for the ferry, that I realized I was suffering yet another synesthetic attack. It seemed to be a mild one, and I tried to disregard it.

I paced up and down the pier, trying to feel the real substance of the concrete surface through the rubbery, cushioned texture my sensations lent it. My mouth and thoat were sore, tasting synesthetically scarlet, and my genital organs were hurting as if trapped in a vise.

Glancing down, I saw that several of the scratches had opened, for blood was smearing where my shirt flapped against me.

At last the ferry arrived, and I went along to its berth with the other waiting passengers. Knowing I should have to pay the fare again, I reached for the wad of notes in my back pocket . . . but then remembered the difficulty I had had with the high-denomination notes on the outward journey. I still had the five silver coins that Elva had given me, and I reached into the breast pocket of my shirt.

Something soft and warm wrapped itself about my two searching fingers, and I withdrew them at once.

I found a hand gripping my fingers!

It was a small, perfect hand, a child's hand. It was pink in the bright daylight, severed at the wrist.

I stepped back, shaking my hand in wild horror.

The child's hand gripped me more tightly.

I let out a cry of fright and swung my arm frantically, trying to throw off the little hand, but when I looked again it was still there. I turned away from the bustle of the other passengers on the quayside, and took hold of it with my free hand and tried to wrench it away. I pulled and pulled, perspiring with horror and tension . . . but nothing I could do would make it relax its hold. I could see the effect on itself of the grip: a whiteness around the knuckles and beneath the tiny nails.

No one on the quayside was taking any notice of me, for there was much movement to and fro of other passengers. I stared round in anguish, feeling I should never be released from the nightmare of the severed hand.

I made one more attempt to free myself by pulling with my other hand: then, in desperation, I put my trapped fingers on the concrete surface of the quay and pressed down on top of it with my boot. I leaned forward, putting as much weight on my hand as I could bear. The child's hand relaxed a little, and I pulled my fingers away. Suddenly I was free, and I jumped back.

The child's hand lay on the quay, still tightly clenched.

The fingers opened, and the hand began to crawl toward me like a bloated pink spider.

I stepped forward and brought my boot down on it with all my weight. I stamped again, and then again, and again. . . .

There was another argument on the boat, and to avoid it I let the ferryman keep the banknote without paying me change. I was in no condition to argue with him: I was shaking convulsively, and the pain I had noticed earlier in my mouth and chest and in my genitals was growing worse with every minute. When the business of the fare had been settled I went to the back of the boat and sat alone, trembling and frightened. The sea was clean; calm and blue in the windless heat.

My shirt was now stained with blood in several places, and I took if off. I felt on the outside of the breast pocket to see if the coins were still there. I could not bring myself to feel inside with my fingers again. At last I held the pocket open upside-down above the deck, but nothing fell out.

As the boat moved out to sea, and the island of Winho became distant behind us, I sat bare-chested in the sun, watching one scratch after another ooze blood down my body. I dared not try to speak to anyone, for my mouth was an open pit of pain.

The boat went from one island in the archipelago to the next, but I did not leave it until nightfall. By then we were at the island of Salay, and I went ashore. That night I slept in the local garrison, having to share a large room with sixteen other officers and men. My dreams were rich and textured with agony and lurid colors, and an uncontrollable and unfulfilled sexual desire. In the morning, the sheets of the bed were stiff with the blood from my wounds.

We owe our existence to battles fought before the dawn of history; all that we have gained—and, perhaps, without our knowing, lost—has come from a million unsung victories and unlamented defeats, from a million faceless individuals who have struggled against the blind grinding engines of death and fate, snatching tiny incremental gains from a hostile world before they were ground down into darkness, providing the footholds upon which future generations would climb.

Here new writer Bernard Deitchman provides a vivid portrait of a forgotten war waged in a prehistoric world to determine just what sort of creature would survive ultimately to write the history books. . . .

BERNARD DEITCHMAN
Cousins

I

The rain stopped.

Stonebreaker squatted in the long grass and looked at the sky. The clouds were breaking and lifting. Daylight grew stronger, and Stonebreaker had to shield his eyes while they adjusted to it. Were the rains over? He looked toward the distant outcrop of rock, at the pinnacle that rose above the rest of the outcrop. He looked at the low trees, the only things other than the outcrop that broke the even horizon of the plains. There was not much cover for him, if the rain did not come back. But if the season was about to turn he might not need stone from the outcrop. He might be able to wait out the flood in the South Lake that covered his usual supply of stone. He might be able to turn back to the forest.

But if the season had not turned? He pulled the animal skin pouches on his shoulder forward and looked in them. They held nothing but rock dust and splinters. He could not trust the weather to give him stone, but he had hoped it would give him protection, that it would hide him from the Longheads while he ran to the outcrop. Now he felt as if his best weapon had been torn from him.

He looked back at the forest, and whined. He threw the pouches back across his shoulder, and stood up and searched the plains for movement. There was none. Encouraged, he ran for the outcrop, his spear ready. The pouches and his other spear bounced on his back.

He came to a narrow stream. Unable to swim, he waded across carefully, probing the bed of the stream in front of him with the butt of his spear. At the other side he found a plains cat asleep in the grass beyond the bank.

The cat was larger than the tree cats he knew, and its markings were of a different pattern and a duller color, but otherwise it was much like them. Stonebreaker began to sneak off through the grass, and the cat woke. It stood up, its legs stiff, and backed away, hissing as it went.

Stonebreaker waited to see if the cat would stalk him. It did not, and he went on, happy—and surprised—that the cat feared him so.

He was soon running among scattered boulders and short piles of rock that were deeply weathered and streaked with moss. He would find nothing he could use here. He ran on to the pinnacle, where there would be fresh rock falls, and a better choice of stone.

He prowled all sides of the pinnacle, searching for danger. On its north side he found a thing that frightened him. A wide, twisting path led up the north face. He went up the path a few steps, but, after the long rain, there was no mark or scent to tell him what animal had made it. He looked out across the plains. Even a short way up the path, his view of the plains was much better than it had been on the ground. He saw a herd of animals he had not been able to see from below, distant specks too small to name. The sight of so much meat made his stomach rumble. The tribe could not find that much meat in the forest in many seasons of hunting. Even if there was no scent, he knew now what animal had made the path he stood on. The pinnacle was made for hunters, for Longheads.

He wanted to run. He choked back a whine and looked up the path. He saw no cave or overhang that would give hunters shelter from the rain. The Longheads must live here only in the dry season, he thought. He hoped so.

He began to search for stone, and gradually worked his way up the path. The best, hardest stone was still buried in the pinnacle itself. He could make a crude tool and chip off what he wanted, but he would make much noise doing it. Longheads anywhere near would know that a man was on the plains, and come to kill him. He forgot about making a tool, and looked among the fallen rocks for chunks not too weathered to be reliable, or pieces only partly weathered from which he could save something.

Once he saw a plains cat going south past the pinnacle, and he wondered if it was the cat he had met at the stream. He had just lost sight of the cat when he smelled a strange scent. He ran down the path and crouched in the grass, but no animal came after the scent. The scent was quickly gone from the wind, and after a walk around the pinnacle showed nothing dangerous near, he went back up the path to work. He tested the damp, shifting wind often after that, ready to run again. He would not have gone back at all, expect that only one pouch was filled with stone, and that was not enough. And the plains were new to Stonebreaker. The animals here would not smell like the animals in the forest. The strange scent he had smelled could have been from an animal the cat had been stalking. It did not have to be the scent of a Longhead.

His other pouch was nearly filled when the scent came again. He searched the plains, and saw no animals close. He stared up the path, which went on much higher than he had climbed. He saw nothing there.

He decided he had enough stone. He started down the path carefully, as the weight of the stone in his pouches affected his balance. The scent grew stronger, and then he heard something move above him. He did not look back. He dropped his pouches and his other spear, and ran. He heard something leaping after him.

He hit the ground and rolled on to his back. He raised his spear before him as he rolled, to catch anything that might try to land on him. He saw the Longhead for the first time as it made its final leap down the pinnacle, and he was frightened at its speed, and surprised to see how much it was like a man. It leaped at him and did not try to dodge his spear, its arms out before it aimed for his throat. It caught itself on the spear, and the point went deep in its chest. Stonebreaker screamed as its fingers touched his skin and its scent poured over him, and then he felt strange in his chest and neck, and blackness fell over him.

Stonebreaker woke to the sound of eating. Though he felt no pain, he thought that the Longhead was still alive even though he had speared it, and was getting its strength back eating his flesh. So he must be dead. Only that would explain why he felt no pain. Then he smelled fresh meat, and his stomach rumbled. Can the dead smell, and be hungry? Stonebreaker opened his eyes.

He saw only the sky. He turned his head, and saw that the Longhead was not still alive. It had become a plains cat's meal. He, Stonebreaker, had killed a Longhead!

The cat was only a few spear-lengths away. His mouth watered at the sight of fresh meat, but Stonebreaker had to lie quietly and wait for the cat to have its fill, and hope that it would not try to eat him. He wanted to kill the cat as he saw it rip the guts from the Longhead—from *his* Longhead!—but he knew better than to try. One wet length of gut got wrapped around his spear, and the cat pulled at it and the whole body turned over in the dirt. Seen this way, the Longhead was just another animal, prey to spears and fangs. Why did men fear them so much? He thought of the blackness that had taken his senses from him when the Longhead touched him. Had the Longhead done that, even as it was dying? That would be a thing to fear.

The cat left the body. It stretched, and licked its mouth. Its claws dug long scars in the soft ground. It cleaned its face, and yawned, and then looked at Stonebreaker.

Its eyes met his before he could close them, and the cat hissed. He did not move, and the cat began to walk slowly toward him. Terrified, Stonebreaker rolled into a crouch and searched the bare ground for a rock. He found one and waited for the cat to leap.

But the cat did not leap. It stopped and snarled at him, and then it backed away, as the other cat had done, and ran off into the grass. Stonebreaker's fear left him and he let out a long sob and ran to pull his spear from the dead Longhead.

The cat feared him because he was so much like a Longhead. It must be so. It would eat a dead Longhead, but would not attack a live one. The Longheads were a thing to be feared, if cats ran from them.

Stonebreaker waited, and the cat did not come back. He ripped what meat he could find from the Longhead, and his stomach growled for more. The meat tasted like a man's flesh, but was not as hard to chew. He broke a rib loose and chewed at one end of it and set to work to get his trophy, the head, free from the body.

It was hard to do. His hands were strong from working stone, and they broke the backbone easily, but the tough string within the backbone would not break when he twisted it. He spat out the rib and ripped at what was left of the throat. He reached the backbone, pulled the head as far from the body as he could, and got his teeth on the string. He bit hard. Instead of the sweet taste he knew from the brains and backbones of other animals, he got a sour, foul juice that burned his mouth, and he jerked back. He spat, and snarled at the torn face, and drove a fist into it. The head snapped free and bounced along the ground. His bite had broken the string, though it fouled his mouth.

He went after the head, picked it up, and went to get his pouches of stone and his other spear. He tied the head between the pouches with a piece of gut from the Longhead, and threw the whole thing over his shoulder with his other spear. He tore off more ribs to take with him to the forest, and while he was doing that he saw for the first time the tools lying near the Longhead.

He picked up one of them. It was a crude thing, no more than a small stone edged on one side. It might work for skinning or cutting, but it was not a thing to hunt with. He looked at the rest. None of them would be any more deadly than a plain stone. Stonebreaker grunted. The Longheads might be like men, but they made tools no better than he had made when he was a child, and they made no weapons at all.

But if they could take the senses from their prey, what else would the Longheads need but tools to cut and skin with? He thought of the blackness again, and he shivered. He stood up and threw the tool away, and set off for the forest. While he ran he planned how he would tell the tribe about his kill. He thought of Blue Eyes then, and his mood darkened. Blue Eyes would not be happy with him for going on the plains. But would he punish the hunter who brought home the head of a Longhead?

He saw clouds moving across the sky. The smell of rain was in the air again. The season had not turned, and he had enough stone to wait out the rains. Blue Eyes would see that he had done a good thing, a brave thing. Stonebreaker forgot the chance of punishment, and chewed happily on a Longhead rib.

II

Blue Eyes stared at the Longhead skull. He nibbled at it, and sniffed it. He said, "What is this? There is no scent left."

Stonebreaker touched the fat bulge at the back of the skull.

"Longhead," he said.

"No," Blue Eyes said. "It is too small to be from so big an animal."

"It is a Longhead. I killed it."

"No," Blue Eyes said. "Longheads are bigger than giants, and they have clubs and spears as tall as a man. Old men tell us that."

"The body was as big as a man's body. You see the head."

"Was it a cub?" Blue Eyes said.

"No, no. It attacked me. We fought, and I killed it. It stalked me, when I went for stone. We fought, a long fight. It broke my spear. I tore out its throat. I killed it."

"There are no marks on you."

Stonebreaker had no answer for that. He sat in his tree beside Blue Eyes and watched the rain drip from the branches above him, and he said nothing.

"Who killed this?" Blue Eyes said.

"I killed it."

"What weapons did it have?"

"It had. . . ."

"What weapons?" Blue Eyes said, and he put a hand on Stonebreaker's shoulder and shook him.

"No weapons. Its tools were small and weak, for cutting. It had no weapons."

"A Longhead with no weapons? Old men tell us . . . old men tell us what other old men told them," Blue Eyes said. "What old man ever saw a Longhead?"

"None."

Blue Eyes stared at the skull, and then he said, "If it is not a cub, and it had no weapons, why do men fear the Longheads?"

"It was not a cub. It attacked me."

"It had no weapons?"

Stonebreaker hesitated. He should not have told Blue Eyes that the Longhead had no weapons. He said, "It had stones."

"It fought you with stones, and you killed it."

"Yes."

"No hunter kills a Longhead," Blue Eyes said.

Stonebreaker puffed out his chest. Blue Eyes at last saw how great a thing he had done.

"You are not a hunter," Blue Eyes said.

"I—I hunt," Stonebreaker said, confused, and suddenly demoralized.

"You make tools. Others hunt, you make tools. What do you hunt? How can you kill a Longhead?"

"My spear killed it."

"No hunter kills a Longhead," Blue Eyes said.

"What hunter tries?" Stonebreaker said, angry that Blue Eyes would not call him a hunter. He was also angry that he had been for Blue Eyes against Shortlegs. Shortlegs would call him a hunter.

"It is stupid to try." Blue Eyes said, and he ran his tongue over the top of the skull. "Yet, if you killed a Longhead, a hunter could kill many

Longheads. Why do men fear them?"

Stonebreaker said nothing. To tell Blue Eyes of the blackness, he would have to tell him how the Longhead died. If he did that, he would be shamed.

Blue Eyes gave the skull to Stonebreaker. "Cut it open," he said. "We will eat the brains."

Stonebreaker cut out part of the top of the skull with one of his tools, and took out some of the brains. He tasted the light gray slippery stuff, and it was sweet. He gave some to Blue Eyes, who ate it and said, "Good."

Stonebreaker dug out more, and he and Blue Eyes ate together, and Stonebreaker's anger faded. They ate their way across the top of the brain, then into the center of it. There they found a tough, dark meat like the strange cord Stonebreaker had bit through in the backbone of the Longhead. One bite of this was enough to make Blue Eyes grimace and cram leaves in his mouth to kill the taste. He took the skull from Stonebreaker and groped inside it.

"Poison," he said, sniffing another section of the dark meat.

Stonebreaker cut open the back of the skull where the bone bulged to give the Longhead its name, and the meat there was light-colored and good to eat. Their hands and faces smeared with mashed brain, Stonebreaker and Blue Eyes cleaned out the skull, and found more good meat in the bottom. Mixed with it were strings of foul stuff that ran down to where the skull connected to the backbone.

When they were done, Blue Eyes said, "Give it to the ants."

Stonebreaker climbed down and dropped the skull near the roots of his tree. The ants that lived under the roots picked the skull clean quickly. They ate the dark parts the men had left, and were not harmed by them. Blue Eyes watched from the tree, and he said, "Not poison, but bad in the mouth."

Stonebreaker said nothing. He watched the ants prepare his trophy for hanging on his tree.

"The Longhead is not poison, and it had no weapons," Blue Eyes said. He was silent a while, then he said, "I have been on the plains."

Stonebreaker looked up at him, surprised.

"There is much meat on the plains," Blue Eyes said. "Men fear the Longheads, and do not hunt there."

"Yes," Stonebreaker said, uneasy to hear Blue Eyes talk about the plains and hunting.

"When Catkiller and the hunters are home," Blue Eyes said, "you will tell them how you killed the Longhead, and I will tell them that we will all kill a Longhead, and men will hunt on the plains."

Stonebreaker shivered. He had to tell Blue Eyes about the blackness now. It was better to be shamed now than dead later when the hunters learned of the blackness for themselves.

"No."

"What?" Blue Eyes said.

"There is a weapon."

Blue Eyes leaped on him, and knocked him down with his feet. Stonebreaker rolled backward and tried to stand, but Blue Eyes was on him, hitting him with his fists. Stonebreaker cowered behind his arms, and when Blue Eyes had spent his anger he lay on the ground and rubbed his bruises.

"Tell me," Blue Eyes said, and Stonebreaker told him. When he was done Blue Eyes said, "How does a Longhead bring blackness?"

"Who can say?"

"Was it the Longhead, or was the blackness from fear?"

"Not fear," Stonebreaker said.

Blue Eyes was quiet then. He picked up the Longhead skull and stared at it, and he looked at Stonebreaker. At last he said, "You will tell the hunters how you killed the Longhead, and I will tell them that we will hunt on the plains."

"Will I tell them about the blackness?"

"No." Blue Eyes said, and he dropped the skull and walked away toward the center of the camp.

Stonebreaker stood up. He picked up the Longhead skull and saw that it had mud on it. He wiped it clean, and then looked up at his tree for a place to put it.

He was still looking when Longhair and one of his tame chewers came by. Longhair said, "Killed a Longhead, you? Talk killed a Longhead. Here? Where?"

Stonebreaker gave him the skull. Longhair sniffed it while his tame chewer sat down in the rain among some bushes and dug for roots to eat.

"How do you know about the Longhead?" Stonebreaker said.

"Blue Eyes tells Onethumb. Kill it? How?"

"With my spear."

"Great thing," Longhair said. "No hunter does a great thing so."

"None."

"Not Catkiller."

"Not Catkiller."

"Keep it?" Longhair said, holding it by a finger thrust through an eye hole. Stonebreaker did not answer. What else would a man do with such a trophy, but keep it?

"Give food for it," Longhair said. "Season."

"No. I don't want chewer food. I get meat for my tools."

"Chewers get fruit. Chewers climb good, get best fruit.'"

"Apes get the best fruit," Stonebreaker said. "Chewers get roots and bark."

Longhair had no answer for that, though Stonebreaker knew he was trying to find one. Neither man spoke for several breaths, while Longhair stared at the skull. Then he gave it back to Stonebreaker. "Food for season," he said.

"No."

"More."

"No," Stonebreaker said, and Longhair started to walk away. Longhair said something to the chewer, and it stood up, a piece of root in its mouth.

"Chewer food," Stonebreaker said, as Longhair turned to speak. "No."

Stonebreaker watched them walk away. From behind, it was hard to see which was man, which was chewer. Both had short legs and long arms. Both had small heads, and both had bodies covered with thick fur. Stonebreaker had heard men say that Longhair's mother had been a chewer, but he did not think Longhair looked enough like a chewer for that. He knew that Longhair himself mated with his female chewers, and none of the cubs the chewers had ever looked part-human, even human like Longhair.

Longhair was strange, but he was a man. He was awkward, but he did not waddle—like a water bird on land—when he walked, the way chewers did. When he ran, he ran like a man, and his knuckles did not touch the ground. It was hard for him to think of things, and he had trouble following even simple talk sometimes, but he could speak human words and put them together well enough to be understood, though he liked the simple chewer language better than human. He was the only man who knew the chewer language. He could not hunt, or make tools, but he could speak to the chewers and they worked for him and brought in so much food that Longhair had a place in the tribe as safe as Stonebreaker's. If it were not for the chewers, Longhair would have been sent out to live with the other males the tribe did not need, the males who were bad hunters and who could find no other place for themselves in the tribe. Longhair had found a place.

Stonebreaker set the Longhead skull on one of the lower branches of his tree. He stood back and looked at it, and then at the other skulls on the tree. There were the skulls of apes and chewers and men on his tree, and one skull from a giant. The giant skull had been the one that Stonebreaker liked the best until now. It came from the first giant anyone in the tribe had seen in Stonebreaker's lifetime. No tree in the camp had as many skulls on it as Stonebreaker's. Hunters kept some human skulls if they marked fights with other tribes worth remembering from one season to the next, but even these might end up as toys for children. Stonebreaker had not taken any of his trophies himself—except for the Longhead!—but he liked to pretend that he had. He liked to sit in his tree and look at them, and pretend that he was a hunter and had killed them all.

He got to know his skulls well. He knew the differences in shape and size, in teeth and jaws and eye holes among men and apes and chewers and giant. He saw that a man's skulltop was smooth, while a ridge of bone went from front to back along the top of chewer and giant and ape skulls. He saw that the eye holes of chewer and giant and ape were close together, and a man's were wide apart. He saw that men shared a thing with apes but not with chewers or giants, a space between the second and third teeth on each side of the upper line of teeth.

Stonebreaker noticed that the teeth of men did not change much in size from the front to the back of the jaw, while in chewers and giants the back teeth were bigger than the front, and in apes the front were bigger than the back. Stonebreaker saw that in all but men the front of the skull was mostly face, but in men the top of the skull rose to make a forehead.

How did the Longhead look next to the skulls on his tree? He picked it off the branch and held it face-upward in his hands.

The eye holes were wide apart, and the top of the skull was smooth and rose as high as the top of a man's skull.

The jaw was light and thin, like a man's jaw, and the teeth—he climbed into his tree and pulled off a human skull to hold beside the Longhead—the teeth were human, except that there were no spaces between the second and third teeth on either side of the upper row.

It was much like the skull of a man, except for the fat bulge at the back. It was strange to find an animal with a skull so human. Were the Longheads another tribe of men? Stonebreaker thought of the sour meat in the Longhead's brains then, and he thought of the blackness. What man could bring blackness, though? None. The Longheads were animals, he thought, and the plains were theirs and they kept men in the forest, but now Blue Eyes was talking about killing them. Stonebreaker did not like the plan. Blue Eyes might make him go along when the hunters went on the plains. He looked at his Longhead skull and wondered if he should have left it on the plains.

The hunters were home late the next day, with meat from a few small animals. Blue Eyes called in most of the sentries and gathered them with the hunters in the center of the camp. Stonebreaker told his story and said nothing of the blackness, and was much praised while the Longhead skull was passed around as proof of what he had done.

Shortlegs, once the leader of the tribe and now old and slow and a sentry, said, "A great fight. An old man is proud to hear it," and a prickling chill ran up the skin of Stonebreaker's back, and he forgot that the Longhead had not died in the fight he described and that one of his listeners knew it as well as he did.

Then Blue Eyes told them of his plan.

The older men were frightened. "The Longheads are great hunters," Shortlegs said.

"They have no weapons," Blue Eyes said.

The hunters made sounds of surprise, and Blue Eyes had Stonebreaker tell them about the tools he had found with the Longhead.

"They have no weapons," Blue Eyes said. "And they do not come in the forest."

"They do not need to come in the forest," Shortlegs said. "They have meat."

"They fear the forest," Blue Eyes said. "They fear death from the trees, the tree cats and the tree snakes that will fall on them, and they have no weapons. We have weapons."

Shortlegs said, "All our fathers—"

"We are better than our fathers. We have fought the cats and the chewers and the snakes. We have grown strong in the forest, and the Longheads are weak. A man who is no hunter goes out alone and kills a Longhead!"

The hunters liked the plan. Stonebreaker listened while they decided, and he heard the hunger in them. Only Catkiller was quiet, as though he were thinking of a plan of his own. A tall, thick-armed man whose beard was not yet full and not yet dark, Catkiller looked long at the skull and then he said to Blue Eyes, "It is small."

"The Longheads are weak," Blue Eyes said.

"Is it a cub?" Catkiller said to Stonebreaker.

"No, it fought me."

"Something bothers me," Catkiller said.

"The Longheads are weak," Blue Eyes said.

"Men have always feared the Longheads," Catkiller said, "but there is meat on the plains, and none in the forest. I will go to the plains, if this one goes with us," and he pointed to Stonebreaker.

"He will go," Blue Eyes said.

The next morning Stonebreaker woke to find the rain gone, and he was fearful to think what waited for the hunters on the plains. But, though the sky was clear and many animals were on the plains, the men reached the pinnacle without seeing a Longhead, and when Blue Eyes and Stonebreaker climbed the pinnacle and found the nest of the Longhead that Stonebreaker had killed, the nest was empty.

The nest was far out on one side of the pinnacle. A line of handholds led to it, and Blue Eyes sent Stonebreaker to see what he could find in the small hollow filled with branches and grass. Stonebreaker started along the handholds, but had to stop at the third one, his feet braced on a narrow ledge. The Longhead, he saw, had not used its feet to get to the nest, because below the rest of the handholds there was nothing he could see to stand on. A man could not reach the nest, even a man like Stonebreaker, who spent much of his life in trees, who was a good climber and not afraid of heights. An ape could have done it, with its long arms and short legs, with its hands for feet, but the Longhead was not an ape. It was strange, he thought, that the Longhead climbed like an ape.

Blue Eyes tried, but he could not reach the nest either. They climbed to the top of the pinnacle, and Blue Eyes said, "The rain stopped in the night, and there is no scent. No Longhead here since the night?"

"Or since I killed the one I found here."

"Where are they?" Blue Eyes said. He looked out across the plains and grew excited at the many animals he could see. He watched a long time, and looked in all directions that did not lead back to the forest. "How far can we go?" he said. "How far to fight a Longhead?"

"We do not have to go," Stonebreaker said. "They will come back. Will they leave this place?"

"We will find them, and I will see how it is to kill a Longhead."

They went down to the hunters, and Blue Eyes told Catkiller to get meat. Catkiller said, "There are no Longheads?"

"Not here. It may be that you will see them."

"This one—"

"He will stay with me and we will watch from the rock," Blue Eyes said.

"He says the Longhead had no weapons," Catkiller said. "Hunters have weapons."

"If the Longhead had weapons, how could one like this kill it?" Blue Eyes said. "Go, and hunt."

The sun was far in the west before all the hunters were back at the pinnacle. They had killed many kinds of animal, and they carried more meat than Stonebreaker had ever seen at one time. Though there was much blood on them, they were hungry. They talked about the feast they would have in the forest, and they praised Blue Eyes for taking them where there was so much meat. Stonebreaker listened, and he felt uneasy.

They started for home. Catkiller walked with Blue Eyes, and Stonebreaker came behind them. Catkiller said that the hunters had seen no Longheads, but that the animals they had stalked had run at the sight of them, and a pack of dogs had followed them to get the parts of their kills they left behind.

"They knew us as hunters before they saw us kill," Catkiller said, "yet they did not fear our spears until I killed one of them."

"Men do not hunt here," Blue Eyes said. "The animals do not know your spears."

"They knew us as hunters," Catkiller said. "It bothers me."

"The dogs did not know you. Men do not hunt here."

"The dogs knew us."

Blue Eyes came up close beside Catkiller, so that his head was hidden by the meat across Catkiller's shoulders, and he said something that Stonebreaker could not hear. Then he moved away from Catkiller, and they walked the rest of the way to the forest and talked no more about dogs.

The season changed. The hunters went to the plains every day for several days. They went no farther from the forest than they had the first day, and they saw no Longheads. Stonebreaker wondered where the Longheads were, and he thought of the blackness sometimes, but he never went back to the plains. The hunters used up many spears and cutting tools now, and he was busy making new ones, and he sent his helper Crosseyes to the pinnacle for stone. At the end of the day he would see Blue Eyes and Catkiller standing apart from the other men, talking, and he would fear what they were planning. His fear was not mistaken. One sunset Blue Eyes split the hunters into two groups, one to stay with the women and children and hunt for them, and another, of the youngest and fastest hunters, to hunt for Longheads. Blue Eyes told Stonebreaker, "Crosseyes will make tools for the hunters of meat. You will come with the hunters of Longhead."

III

They started with the first light, and Blue Eyes led them to the plains a new way. They went north, toward the territory of their neighbors, the Irkw, and stayed in the forest until half the day was gone, and then they

went on the plains. The country here was much like the country to the
south, except that no rocks broke the grass. The trees that grew here were
like the ones around the pinnacle, strange and low-limbed, with branches
that curved toward the ground in the shape of roots, so that the trees
looked upside-down. They were scattered widely across the plains, and
did nothing to comfort Stonebreaker as he watched the forest shrink
behind him.

Blue Eyes said that taking a new way might bring them to Longheads,
but they walked east the rest of the day and saw none. They hunted when
the sun was low, and while they ate the kill one of the hunters said,
"Where will we sleep?"

Stonebreaker had been wondering the same thing all day, so the
question did not surprise him, but he saw that it surprised the other
hunters. They looked around the plains for shelter and did not like what
they saw. They were no happier when Blue Eyes led them to the largest of
the upside-down trees and said they would sleep there. The hunters
grumbled, but it was too far to walk back to the forest before dark and
so they climbed into the tree after Blue Eyes and Catkiller. Stonebreaker climbed with them and wondered if the hunters would go on in
the morning.

The night was full of terror. Great roars came from the north, sounds of
fury that ended in terrible coughing noises. Answering roars came from
the east, and soon Stonebreaker caught a scent on the wind like cat, but
strange. Could a cat make so fearsome a noise?

Then it was quiet for a time, and Stonebreaker moved his head back
and forth to hear what sounds the small night wind might bring. He
heard steps in the grass.

The hunters also heard the steps. They moved on the branches to face
the sound. The wind came stronger and brought the scent of chewer, and
then the steps came closer, and stopped.

"Hunters? Longhair is," came a voice from below.

"What?" Blue Eyes said.

"Longhair is. And chewers. Dark. Come up?"

"You are stupid," Blue Eyes said. "Come up. Be quiet."

Longhair and his chewers settled on the branch below Stonebreaker.

"Hunters far. Chewers slow. Dark."

"Be quiet," Blue Eyes said.

The men listened, and breathed the wind. Nothing followed Longhair
to the tree. The men relaxed, and Stonebreaker heard sounds of sleep. He
fell asleep himself only when the wind died, and woke when it was fresh.
Once he woke to the smell of Longhead.

He listened to the wind. The Longhead smell came stronger and then
he heard quick steps in the grass. An animal cried out, and the sound was
followed by the noise of many animals running and snorting. The sound
of their hooves faded to the north.

Stonebreaker smelled blood. Longheads hunted at night.

The men were awake around him, and Blue Eyes whispered so quietly
that Stonebreaker barely heard him over the wind, "Longhead?"

"Yes."

Stonebreaker did not hear anyone sleep after that, even when the smell of blood and Longhead was gone.

In the morning the hunters wanted to go back to the forest, and Blue Eyes said, "Go. Tell Shortlegs you were afraid. Catkiller and the Stonebreaker and I will kill Longheads."

One of the hunters said, "You shame us. Any man would go back from here. There are great cats. The trees are small. You did not say the Longheads hunted in the night."

"I did not know how they hunted," Blue Eyes said. "If they hunt in the night, they sleep in the day. We will find where they sleep. If a man sees what he needs, he takes it. The Stonebreaker has killed a Longhead and we hunt where it hunted. Other Longheads will come to hunt there and we will go back to hunt in the forest if we are afraid to kill them. A man sees what he needs, and goes on."

The hunters said, "We will wait for the Longheads to come back, and then we will kill them."

"Go. Wait. Tell Shortlegs you were afraid."

The hunters did not move or speak, and Longhair said, "I come."

Blue Eyes said to him, "What do you want with Longheads?"

"Hunters get meat. Leave chewer food. I come."

"Shortlegs will keep you," Blue Eyes said.

"I come."

"What?" Blue Eyes said. "Will you mate with a Longhead?"

"Might," Longhair said.

Blue Eyes hissed and showed his teeth. He said to the hunters, "Longhair will come with us, and he does not hunt. Longhair shames you," and then he walked away. Catkiller and Longhair went after him, and the chewers walked awkwardly after Longhair. Stonebreaker wanted to stay with the hunters, but he feared Blue Eyes too much to try. He left the hunters and caught up with Longhair. He looked back once, and saw the hunters going home.

Blue Eyes followed the scent of the Longhead to the place where it had killed. He squatted by the crushed, bloody grass and sniffed the ground. Whatever the Longhead had killed was gone, the parts it had left dragged away by dogs that left their scent on the blood. Blue Eyes stood up and looked north, the direction the Longhead had gone, and Stonebreaker saw that his face was still happy.

Catkiller said, "What will they tell Shortlegs?"

"Who can say?" Blue Eyes said.

"Will they tell him we are dead?" Catkiller said.

"Who can say? I am not dead, and I will not die."

"One day you will die," Catkiller said.

"I will kill a Longhead and come back to the forest. Much is in front of us, and the hunters do not see it. They are stupid, and they will be shamed when we come back."

"Do you not fear the Longheads, and the blackness?" Catkiller said.

"I will live, and the Longheads will die. Much is in front of us."

"A Longhead is in front of us," Catkiller said.

"No more?"

"I am a hunter. I see a Longhead."

"Will you go with the hunters?"

"No," Catkiller said. "Hunters will go where there is meat. If you say we must kill the Longheads to hunt on the plains, then I will do it."

"Good."

They followed the scent north and east. Often it was crossed by the cat scent that Stonebreaker had smelled in the night. Then they kept close to trees, ready to run for them if they saw the animals that roared with such fury.

They lost the scent by a small lake. The ground near the lake was muddy, and many kinds of animal had left tracks in it. Birds walked in the shallow parts of the lake, and the strong smell of their droppings made Stonebreaker's eyes water. Men and chewers went carefully around the lake, because the grass was thick and high there, and their noses were filled with strange scents, but even so they walked into a pack of great cats.

These were the biggest cats Stonebreaker had ever seen. They lay in the grass and their fur was hard to see against it. Only the black on their muzzles and on the tips of their tails and ears stood out sharply. Their eyes were yellow.

The cats were slow to move, as they had full bellies, and men and chewers all reached the nearest tree unharmed. The cats followed. Longhair walked out on a branch above them, and let water. The cats sniffed at the water, and moved away from the tree. Longhair made stupid noises at the cats, and the other men hissed at him. At last the cats went back to their nest, and the men and chewers left the tree. They found the Longhead scent again east of the lake, going north. They followed it the rest of the day, and the country changed from what they had known so far. The grass grew higher and stiffer than before, and its tips were as sharp as thorns. More trees grew, and other kinds besides the upside-down tree. There were short trees with blue-gray leaves as sharp and stiff as the grass, and tall straight trees with leaves like feathers. These feather trees looked like better shelter than the upside-down trees, and at sunset the men killed a small animal and climbed into one and ate while the sky darkened.

They had found no place where the Longhead had slept or hunted. Catkiller said, "The Longhead came far in one night."

"Far and more," Blue Eyes said. "Why does it run so far? There is meat everywhere. Why does it run?"

"Who can say?" Stonebreaker said. "The other had a nest."

"The other had a nest, and this one runs," Blue Eyes said. "Does it stop at dawn? Does it run in the day?"

No one answered. Below them, where Longhair and his chewers were, there was grunting and sighing, and the sound of feet on bark. Longhair was trying to mate with one of the female chewers, but the up-growing limbs of the feather tree did not give him much room to move. Stonebreaker felt lust rise in him, though he had no desire for chewers. He thought of the women of the tribe, now far away. He thought more about them, and then he said, "It runs to mate."

"What?" Blue Eyes said.

"When the rains stop, animals mate," Stonebreaker said. "There was no female with the Longhead I killed. The females are far away. It runs to mate."

"It runs to mate," Blue Eyes said. "Good. Other Longheads will run to mate, and if we do not catch this Longhead there will be more."

Cats roared that night, but the wind brought no smell of Longhead. Nothing bothered them in their tree, and in the morning they set out again on the trail. The sun was not yet high when they came to a feather tree where the Longhead had slept. Near the tree were droppings like those of a man, and Blue Eyes and Catkiller decided that the Longhead had left them. Later they found signs that the Longhead had killed.

They followed the scent all morning, and the land changed more. It rose to the east and north, and it grew greener than any country they had seen since they had left the forest. There were many small trees, and small animals that lived in them. The animals saw them as Longheads and feared them, as all animals they had seen on their hunt had done, except for the great cats. The great cats were so big and fierce that nothing frightened them, Stonebreaker thought, not even Longheads or men who looked like Longheads.

Late in the morning they met another pack of these cats, this time a pack with bellies loose and empty. Stonebreaker and Blue Eyes and Catkiller and Longhair were fast enough to reach the closest feather tree, but the chewers were not. The cats caught them and killed them and stripped their bones bare, and then came to the tree the men were in, and stared up at them.

Longhair screamed at the cats. He broke limbs from the tree and threw them at the cats. He wet himself in his fury, and threw his droppings at the cats. The cats snarled, and did not move away until a herd of small grazing animals caught their noses.

The men waited until they were out of sight, and then got away. They passed the bones of the chewers, and Longhair made sad noises. He was angry when he saw birds picking at the bones, and he ran at them and threw stones. He sat down and nibbled at a bone. Catkiller and Blue Eyes did not notice him. Longhair might have been left behind if Stonebreaker had not called to him. Longhair licked at the bone and left it, and ran to catch up.

The land went higher, and Stonebreaker's legs began to ache. They came at last to a down slope that led to a wide stream. The stream moved fast, and the Longhead scent ran toward the only place Stonebreaker could see where the stream could be crossed. Across the stream the land rose again, going on and on toward brown hills. Here the land was green, and the sound of the stream made Stonebreaker thirsty.

They found many Longhead scents on the slope. Some were fresh, and all pointed toward the stream crossing.

"They run in the day," Catkiller said.

"It is mating season," Blue Eyes said.

The crossing was a place where many large rocks stuck out of the stream close together. Blue Eyes led them across, jumping from one rock to the next. On the other side there was only one Longhead trail going away from the stream, toward the north.

"A Longhead will come," Blue Eyes said, "and we will see how it dies."

Stonebreaker and Catkiller hid in the grass on one side of the trail, and Blue Eyes and Longhair on the other. They waited, and a Longhead came. They leaped out as it passed them, and surrounded it.

The Longhead crouched in the circle of men, and then it leaped for the space between Longhair and Catkiller. It moved faster then any animal Stonebreaker knew, except a cat. Longhair pushed his spear at it awkwardly. There was fear on his face, but he did not fall back, and his spear went into the Longhead's side. The Longhead retreated into the circle. At the sight of blood Longhair lost his fear, and he came at the Longhead. Catkiller moved with him.

"I will kill it," Blue Eyes said, and the other men stopped where they were.

The Longhead looked at its side, and then it looked at the spear Blue Eyes held as he came toward it. The Longhead's hands were empty, and much bigger than a man's hands. Stonebreaker looked at its eyes and wondered at them. The Longhead's eyes were not like the eyes of other hunting animals. They were nothing like the eyes of the great cats. No strength or courage showed in their darkness, only fear.

The Longhead moved, first to one side and then the other, too quickly for Blue Eyes to follow with his spear. It leaped at him, past his spear, and got its hands on his throat. His back and legs stiffened, and then he fell. Catkiller was on the Longhead as it let go of Blue Eyes and his spear went deep in its back. It fell on Blue Eyes while Stonebreaker and Longhair put their spears into it, and it died.

Catkiller dragged the body off Blue Eyes, who lay on his back with his eyes open. Only white showed in his eyes. Catkiller said, "When will he wake?"

"Soon," Stonebreaker said.

They pulled their spears from the body, and rolled the body over so it lay next to Blue Eyes. They looked at what they had killed.

It was thinner than Blue Eyes, and its legs were longer than his legs, but otherwise it was much like him. Stonebreaker knelt beside it, and sniffed. When the Longhead had touched Blue Eyes, Stonebreaker had smelled a strange thing, the smell that lightning makes. Now he smelled it again, but much weaker, and he found that it came from the Longhead's hands.

"What?" Catkiller said, and knelt beside him.

Stonebreaker held one of the dead hands palm upward in his. The skin was hard and dark and had large pores in it rather than the fine lines of a man's palm. It was damp, and Stonebreaker licked it and the taste was sour. He let the hand fall back to the ground. The Longhead was a strange animal, he thought, to be so much like a man.

The Longhead wore a pouch of animal skin around its waist, and Stonebreaker opened it and found tools as simple as the tools of the first Longhead he had killed.

"Not a man's tools," he said, and gave them to Catkiller.

"But it is much like a man," Catkiller said.

"It hunts like an animal. Its tools are like a chewer's tools. Chewers are stupid, and this is like a chewer, but it eats meat."

"It is more like a man than a chewer," Catkiller said.

"It is an animal. I will show you," Stonebreaker said, and he took out his tools and cut open the Longhead's skull. He showed Catkiller the dark, sour meat in the brain of the Longhead. Catkiller tasted it and said, "It is strange."

"No man has such meat in him," Stonebreaker said.

They shared the good brain meat with Longhair, and cut up the rest of the body. They ate the heart, and saved the liver for Blue Eyes. Stonebreaker found more of the sour meat leading from the backbone down the arms to the hands.

When Blue Eyes woke he went to the stream and drank. He put his face in the water, and pressed his hands to his forehead. He felt weak, he said.

He ate the liver and other meat, and he said he felt better. He went to look at the Longhead. He said nothing about the way it had died, but told them to throw it in the stream, and after they had done that he sent Catkiller and Longhair to kill an animal to leave in its place.

"Longheads will come in the night," he said. "If they find a dead Longhead they will come to find what killed it, and I do not want to fight them at night."

Stonebreaker sat with him while the others hunted. Blue Eyes sat with his feet in the stream, and Stonebreaker thought he slept at times.

The sun had almost set when Catkiller and Longhair came back with their kill, a large brown animal with long twisting horns on its head. They put it where the Longhead had died, and cut it up and spread blood on the ground around it. They ate some of the meat, and then Blue Eyes led them to the stream, and into it up to their knees. They walked south in the water until Blue Eyes decided they were far enough from the Longhead trail for safety, and he led them up the bank to look for a tree.

The sun had set, but the sky was still light. They walked east, into the wind. Strange scents came on the wind, as always in this country, and Stonebreaker gave no thought to them. Then Blue Eyes stopped, and pointed at something for Catkiller to see. Stonebreaker came up beside them and tried to see what they were looking at. Sticking up from the grass ahead were things he thought were tree stumps. There was not enough light to see the stumps clearly. Then one of them moved, and Blue Eyes said, "Giants."

Stonebreaker was afraid. He had seen the dead giant the skull on his tree had been taken from, but he did not think it had been anything like the animals he saw now. He thought these must be twice the height of a man, with chests and shoulders as wide and powerful as an ape's. He could not see their teeth, but he knew what they were like.

"Do giants eat meat?" he said.

"Who can say?" Blue Eyes said.

Blue Eyes turned south. Stonebreaker and Catkiller went with him, but Longhair stayed behind and watched the giants. Blue Eyes called softly to him, and he did not move.

Blue Eyes went to get him. Stonebreaker was sure that the giants turned their heads to watch Blue Eyes, but they did not follow when all the men went on south together.

Blue Eyes said, "He sees them as big chewers."

Longhair looked back at the giants while he walked, and when they were lost from sight he whined and tried to go back. Blue Eyes dragged him along. When he turned him loose to climb into a feather tree, Longhair ran off.

IV

Longhair did not come back that night, and in the morning they went to look for him. Blue Eyes had his strength back. While they walked he said, "A man will not kill a Longhead alone in the open, unless he is lucky like the Stonebreaker."

"No," Catkiller said.

"We know how to kill the Longheads," Blue Eyes said. "We will find the mating ground, and the next mating season we will go there before the Longheads, and we will kill them all as they come."

Catkiller said nothing for a few heartbeats, then, "This is a great plan."

"I saw it in the night, as I slept," Blue Eyes said. "All the Longheads will die."

"It is a great plan," Catkiller said again, and even Stonebreaker was excited, though he knew there were many risks in the plan. To kill all the Longheads! Had there ever been such a plan?

Blue Eyes showed his teeth. He was pleased with himself and with Catkiller's praise. He punched Catkiller lightly on the chest, and then Stonebreaker. Stonebreaker was surprised by the touch. It was a gesture hunters used among themselves, and never before had Blue Eyes treated him like a hunter, not even when he killed the Longhead. The touch pleased Stonebreaker greatly, and it showed him how happy Blue Eyes was with his plan.

Longhair's trail was short, and not hard to follow, as Longhair had wet himself many times along the way. They found him with the giants at the banks of the stream. The giants were feeding on water plants. They ripped the tough stalks open with their teeth, and ate the soft inner parts. They pulled up roots as thick as a man's arm and ate them as easily as a man would eat a soft fruit. They ate much, and they ate fast, and they left behind a wide muddy trail scattered with the remains of plants.

The giants were not fully twice as big as a man, as Stonebreaker had thought the day before, but they were still much bigger than he was. His head came no higher than their bellies. Their faces were apelike, but with jaws wider and longer, and teeth much bigger, than an ape's. He tried to look unafraid as he walked toward them, but it was not easy.

Longhair sat with some males, and Stonebreaker thought they were talking, but he could make no sense of the noises they made. One of the other giants saw the men approaching, and called out. Others stopped eating and came to challenge the men. Each one carried a rock as big as a man's head, and swung it in its hand as easily as Stonebreaker would carry a cutting tool. This was how they lived on the plains without spears, Stonebreaker thought. Many of them throwing such rocks at once could kill any hunting animal he knew. Some of the giants raised their rocks as if to throw, and Blue Eyes stopped. He called to Longhair, and Longhair came over to him.

"Come with us," Blue Eyes said.

"Good here," Longhair said. He looked back at the giants.

"They are not chewers," Blue Eyes said. "Giants. Come with us."

"Big chewers. Good here," Longhair said. He showed his teeth. "Stay. You stay."

"No," Blue Eyes said. "We hunt the Longheads."

"Stay. Big chewers good. Men good."

"Come with us."

"Mate big chewers," Longhair said, and he walked back to the giants. He sat down with them and began making noises with them again. Stonebreaker thought that Blue Eyes would be angry, but Blue Eyes said, "Longhair is a strange man," and led them away from the giants. Blue Eyes was too pleased with his plan, Stonebreaker thought, to be angry with Longhair.

They went east, and then north, and found the Longhead trail. There were no fresh scents on it. All the Longheads had gone to mate.

The trail led north along the stream. The country was green, and they found fruit to eat and did not have to hunt. The brown hills east ran alongside them as they walked, and ahead they saw more hills just as brown, yet strange, because above them the sky itself was brown. The trail and the stream turned northeast, toward the place where the two lines of hills met, and Stonebreaker watched the sky. He wondered what made the sky the color of the hills. He saw no dust blowing across the hills, not to the north or the east. He thought of fire, and was afraid, but nothing grew on the hills that might burn, and his fear went away. Neither dust nor fire made the sky brown. It was strange country.

The day passed, and the two lines of hills came together. Where they met was a valley with a lake in it. The lake was fed by a waterfall in the northern hills, and from the lake ran the stream the Longhead trail followed. There were caves in the northern hills where they came nearest the lake, and Stonebreaker saw Longheads in the caves, and many more Longheads below the caves on the lake shore. They had found the mating ground.

They climbed a small hill at the mouth of the valley to watch the Longheads. The brown soil of the hill was soft and fine, finer than sand,

and it tired them to walk in it. Their feet raised dust that dried their throats and stung their eyes. The dust settled on them, and when they lay down at the crest to watch the Longheads their skins were the color of the hill beneath them. The Longheads would not see them.

The Longheads in the caves, Stonebreaker saw, were females and their young. He looked at the Longheads below the caves, and he saw no mating. Were all the ones outside the caves males? He looked carefully, and found this was so, except for one group of females farther down the shore and well away from the males.

They watched, and soon a female left its group by the lake and walked toward the nearest males. Two males came forward to meet the female. Then several females and young came down from the caves and stood near the two males.

The females sat down in the grass, and the two males began a dance. The female watched as they leaped across a patch of bare ground worn in the grass. Stonebreaker thought that many males had danced there. He saw stains on the soil that he thought were blood, and he waited for the males to fight.

But the males did not fight. They leaped at each other, and away, then back at each other and away again, round and round, while the females and young from the caves made a ring around them. The dance ended when each male leaped for the other's throat, and both fell stunned to the ground.

The Longheads waited. There had been some noise from the other males while the two danced, but now all were silent. At last one of the two stood up, and walked toward the female who sat in the grass, and did not look at the one that still slept. That Longhead was killed by the females and young. They cut its throat with their tools before it could wake, and it bled to death while the male it had danced with and the female it had danced for climbed to one of the caves together. Then Stonebreaker could no longer see them. He knew they had gone to mate.

The dead Longhead was cut up, and its parts were taken to the caves. Before long, two more males danced for another female, then two more, and two more after them, for other females, and there was more fresh meat. Then the females that were still by the lake went into the caves, and none of the males followed. The meat was not for them, Stonebreaker thought, only for the females and their young. They had enough meat for the day, and so they would not mate again until they were hungry. Stonebreaker shivered. He was happy that he was not one of the Longhead males who had to wait for a chance to mate or die.

The males went to the far end of the lake. They drank, and they waded. They found things to eat in the water. Stonebreaker wondered if they ate plants or caught fish. Did the Longhead weapon work in water? He thought how hungry they must be to eat fish or water plants, and not leave the valley to hunt. If the females did not have enough meat, they would come out of the caves, and any male that left to hunt would miss a chance to mate. Stonebreaker thought that he would go to hunt and never come back, if he were a Longhead male.

Blue Eyes said, "The Longheads are not like men."

"They are animals," Stonebreaker said.

"They are animals, and a female can kill as quickly as a male," Blue Eyes said. "The females live here. They need the males to mate, and they do not need them to hunt."

Catkiller and Stonebreaker said nothing. Blue Eyes said, "They eat the males. Something bothers me."

What bothered Blue Eyes also bothered Stonebreaker, but he knew what it was. It was fear at the power that the females had over the males among the Longheads. Had Blue Eyes never felt fear before?

"The females live here, and the males live on the plains and come here to mate," Blue Eyes said. "We will not kill the males. We will kill the females and young after the mating season. There will be no more Longheads."

"It is a great plan," Catkiller said.

Blue Eyes said, "If the hunters were here. . . ."

Stonebreaker and Catkiller waited for him to say more, to hear what he would do if the hunters were with them, but when he spoke again he said, "The Longheads are not like men."

Stonebreaker thought that something more than fear bothered Blue Eyes, and he said, "They are animals. They have no tools, and they do not hunt together."

And then he saw what bothered Blue Eyes. He said, "There is no leader of the Longheads."

Blue Eyes looked at him. Stonebreaker said, "The Longheads are stupid, like chewers. They have no leader, and they make no plans."

"Yes," Blue Eyes said, and he showed his teeth. "The Longheads have no leader." He looked at Catkiller and said, "The Stonebreaker knows Longheads."

"Yes," Catkiller said, and Stonebreaker felt good.

"They make no plans," Blue Eyes said. "I will make a plan, and kill them. If the hunters were here. . . ."

"The hunters will come," Catkiller said. "We will tell them about the Longheads."

"I will make a plan without them," Blue Eyes said. "We will kill the females when the males are gone."

"What?" Catkiller said. "You and I and the Stonebreaker?"

"I will make a plan," Blue Eyes said, and Stonebreaker did not feel good any more. He was sorry that he had said anything about leaders and plans at all.

The day was near its end. They went down the hill to the grasslands and drank at the stream and found fruit. Stonebreaker took his fruit to the stream and waded in the water to cool his legs while he ate. Blue Eyes and Catkiller came in after him.

They ate and belched and threw water on themselves. They stayed at the stream until the sun was down, and then found a feather tree to sleep in.

Stonebreaker could not sleep. He worried about what Blue Eyes had said. He waited and hoped for sleep, but his eyes came open often, and he watched the sky.

The sun was long set, but he did not see many stars. He waited, and the sky got no darker. Finally he moved to the end of his branch and looked around the horizon as best he could. To the northeast, where the sky had been brown in the day, there was a bright yellow mist. It spread across the sky, and he could see no stars in the north or east. He was terrified, and all he could think of was fire. If there was fire in the sky, it could spread over all the land, and kill everything it touched. He whined, and a whisper answered him, "Be quiet. Blue Eyes sleeps."

Stonebreaker said, "The fire—"

"Be quiet," Catkiller said. "I see no fire."

"There is fire in the sky."

"How can there be fire in the sky? There is light. Do you see fire?"

Stonebreaker looked northeast. He saw no fire, but he could think of nothing else that could make light there. The moon was not up. He said, "What is the light?"

"Who can say? I see no fire."

Later, Blue Eyes woke, and he took the light for dawn. Catkiller told him it was not, and no one tried to sleep after that, though Stonebreaker napped at times despite his fear. When dawn came the strange light faded, and they saw below the place it had been a great mountain. As the sun came up, the mountain was hidden by mists that rose from the plains, but not before Stonebreaker saw the smoke that came from the mountain's top. Then the mists and smoke came together and made the sky the way it had been the day before.

"There is no fire in the sky," Stonebreaker said, his fear replaced by curiosity, "but somehow a mountain burns."

"How will a mountain burn?" Blue Eyes said.

"There is smoke on the mountain," Stonebreaker said. "Something there burns."

Blue Eyes looked a while longer at the brown sky, and then he led Stonebreaker and Catkiller back to the hilltop overlooking the Longhead mating ground. Blue Eyes did not forget the burning mountain. Many times that day, as they watched the Longheads, he talked about it, and Stonebreaker grew tired of saying "Who can say?" to his questions.

It was the middle of the day before any females came out of the caves. Blue Eyes said he wanted to see how many females there were to be killed, but fewer than the men had first seen the day before came down to the lake. Stonebreaker watched the females and thought that only the ones that had not mated, and the ones that came with their young to kill males, had left the caves. Blue Eyes was unhappy.

The next day fewer females again left the caves, and fewer the day after that, until the mating was done. That left many males still unmated, and these walked quickly from the valley. Stonebreaker wondered if they were happy that they had not danced for a mate. The day after that the males in the caves began to leave, and that night Longheads hunted on the plains, near the tree the men slept in.

The next morning Blue Eyes said, "The Longheads hunt again. They will find us here in the dark, but no animals live in the hills, and no animals hunt in the hills."

"Yes," Catkiller said, and Stonebreaker shivered. He thought he knew what Blue Eyes was going to say, and he had never slept on the ground one night of his life.

"We will sleep in the hills," Blue Eyes said.

That day more Longhead males left the valley, and only a few females and young came out of the caves. Well before sunset the men went to the plains to eat and drink, and then they climbed a hill higher than the one they watched the valley from, and tried to sleep.

It was quiet in the hills, but for a small wind and the sound the soft land made whenever Stonebreaker moved. The land was strange against his skin, and formed itself closely to his body. He itched. There was not enough air around him. He did not like the sound the land made when he moved. He waited and hoped for sleep, but his eyes often came open and he watched the light in the sky. Sometime before dawn he slept.

The next day a few more males left the valley, and a few left every day for several days after that. Each day Blue Eyes and Stonebreaker and Catkiller came to watch, and each night they slept in the hills. It was easier after the first night, though Stonebreaker was tired of Longheads, and he missed the forest. Blue Eyes said nothing about the forest. He talked about killing the females, and at night he watched the light in the sky and asked questions Stonebreaker could not answer. Stonebreaker thought of the forest much of the time.

One morning they went to the plains for fruit and saw giants by the stream, and with the giants was Longhair. The giants were walking upstream toward the Longhead valley and did not feed.

Longhair saw them and came running over, happy. As he ran he made noises to the giants, and they stopped and watched the men, but none raised a rock in threat.

Longhair carried an armload of strange brown things that Stonebreaker thought were large nuts. He said, "Good, good, good," and gave each man one of the nuts.

Blue Eyes said, "You are good to us, Longhair."

"Happy. See you."

"Do the big chewers know there are Longheads there?" Blue Eyes said, and he pointed toward the valley.

"Yes. Not go."

"What will they do?" Blue Eyes said.

"Other place. Show great thing. You come. Great thing."

"What?" Blue Eyes said.

"You come. Great thing."

Stonebreaker looked at the thing Longhair had given him. He tried to bite it and found it was as hard as dry wood.

"Will a giant eat this?" Stonebreaker said.

"Good. Eat good. You come. Show great thing."

Blue Eyes said to Catkiller, "Will we see this great thing?"

"It is for you to say. We have seen the Longheads many days."

"We will go with you," Blue Eyes said to Longhair.

"Good, good, good," Longhair said, and he took them to where the giants waited. The giants carried the same kind of nuts as Longhair. Those giants that did not carry a rock in one hand carried two armloads of the nuts. The giants stared at the men, and their eyes frightened Stonebreaker, but then Longhair made noises at them and pointed at the men, and the giants looked away.

The giants went up the stream to a place where the water was shallow, and they crossed to the north bank. They went upstream again, to a line of grass that was still deep green even though everywhere else on the plains the grass was drying and yellowing. The green line led north to the hills, and the giants walked along it. Soon the ground was soft and damp, and then the hills were around them and they were in a small valley.

White mist rose from cracks in the hills, and water trickled out of caves. The valley floor grew thick green grass, and strange plants with pulpy limbs. The giants walked through the valley and went into a cave. Though Longhair went with them, Blue Eyes stopped outside.

The hillside was wet. Mist came from the cave, and out of a crack in the hill above it.

"The ground is warm," Stonebreaker said.

"Is there fire?" Blue Eyes said. "The mountain that burns is beyond these hills."

"This is mist," Stonebreaker said. "It is not smoke."

Longhair came out of the cave and said, "Come. Show great thing," and they went cautiously into the cave with him.

Light came through the crack in the top. The ground grew warmer as they walked. Near the end of the cave was a pool of water, and the giants were gathered around it. The water bubbled, and mist rose from it. Stonebreaker saw that the giants had thrown the nuts they carried into the pool, and the nuts bobbed and danced in the bubbles.

Water ran into the pool from the back of the cave. Stonebreaker went to look closer at the place where it came from, and when the mist rising there blew past his chest and face, the pain of the heat made him cry out and jump back.

"What?" Blue Eyes said.

"Hot," Stonebreaker said, and he stood under the draft from the crack in the roof and let it cool him.

Blue Eyes went cautiously to look at the mist hissing out of the rock behind the pool. He pushed the butt of his spear into a hole in the rock. He worked a few stones loose, and they fell into the pool. Water splashed on him, and he yelped and rubbed his skin where the water had hit.

Stonebreaker saw that the butt of Blue Eyes' spear was smoking and had been blackened by the heat. He showed it to Blue Eyes.

"The rocks are like fire," Blue Eyes said, and he watched the spear butt until the smoke died.

There was excitement among the giants, and the men turned to look at them. The giants were taking the nuts from the pool. Each giant had kept one nut from its armload and was now using it to pull others from the water and flip them about until they cooled. Longhair brought a nut that was ready to eat to Blue Eyes, who tasted it and said, "Good." Longhair hissed, and gave some of the nut to Catkiller and Stonebreaker. The nut was easy to chew now, and it *was* good, with a taste almost like meat.

"It is a great thing," Stonebreaker said, and Longhair said, "Eat. Take more."

They ate all that Longhair gave them. When the water was empty the giants threw in the nuts they had used as tools. When these were ready to eat Longhair gathered them to one side of the pool with his spear and flipped them out with the point.

The giants left the cave after all the food was gone, and Longhair said to Blue Eyes, "You come. Big chewers good."

"No. We fight the Longheads."

"Big chewers good."

"They are good," Blue Eyes said, "and we will see you another time." Longhair's face was sad. He touched each of them, and then he ran after the giants.

Blue Eyes put the point of his spear into the pool near the place the mist came from, and he dragged out a stone. Catkiller and Stonebreaker moved to help him, but he said, "Go, and get grass and wood."

"What?" Stonebreaker said, suddenly afraid.

"Get grass. If the stones make fire, we will burn the Longheads."

The grass they brought from the valley would not burn, and they could find no trees to get wood from, only the soft plants. Blue Eyes sent them to the plains, and when they came back with yellow grass and dead wood, Blue Eyes had several stones in a pile on the cave floor. He took some of the grass and threw it on the stones, and the grass began to smoke.

Stonebreaker watched the grass and hoped that it would not burn, but Blue Eyes pressed it down against the rocks with a stick and flame burst up. Blue Eyes showed his teeth, and he threw more grass on the stones, and then some wood.

"We will kill the Longheads," Blue Eyes said. Stonebreaker looked at the fire. It frightened him, but he could not look away. Blue Eyes built it higher, and used up all the grass and wood, and only when the last spark had died did he leave the cave.

V

It was Blue Eyes' plan to set fire to the grass between the Longhead caves and the lake. The fire would spread to the grass and bushes on the slopes below the caves and then to the caves themselves, where there would be nests to burn. "The Longhead the Stonebreaker killed had a nest of grass," Blue Eyes said, "and there will be nests in the caves."

Stonebreaker saw that Catkiller did not like the plan, and neither did he, for he feared greatly to run into the Longhead valley, even with fire in his hand—for he feared the fire as much as he feared the Longheads.

Catkiller said, "If there are no nests in the caves?"

"Will the Longheads sleep on rocks?" Blue Eyes said. "There are nests."

"Will the fire reach them?" Catkiller said. "The grass on the slopes is thin."

"There are bushes, and the bones the Longheads throw."

"Will bones burn?" Catkiller said.

"Yes."

Stonebreaker wondered how Blue Eyes could know that bones would burn, and then he thought that Blue Eyes did not know, any more than he or Catkiller knew. But Stonebreaker did not dare to challenge him. Catkiller said, "We are not many. The mating season is gone, and the males are on the plains. If all of us live, the way to the forest will be hard. If one man dies, or two, will any of us live?"

"We will not die," Blue Eyes said.

"Who can say?" Catkiller said. "If you die, will the Stonebreaker and I live?"

Blue Eyes said, "We have not come far east. If I am dead, you will live. Two days will take you to the forest. If you sleep the night in the northern hills, you will not see the Longheads."

"We have come far north," Catkiller said. "There are not many of us."

"We will not die," Blue Eyes said. "The Longheads will die."

"The things you see in front of us are strange," Catkiller said. "No hunter makes his weapons from fire."

"I see death in front of us," Blue Eyes said. "The death of men, or the death of Longheads. Will you leave me? I will set the fire myself."

"Has any man ever seen much things?" Catkiller said. "Nothing is like it was before the Stonebreaker killed a Longhead."

"I will stay."

On the day the last male left the Longhead caves, the females came down to the lake at sunset. There were many more of them than Stonebreaker had thought there would be, and most of them had young. The females waded in the lake, and their young ran in the shallows, and Stonebreaker could see no Longheads left in the caves.

The next morning, when the Longheads were back in their caves, Blue Eyes and Catkiller and Stonebreaker went to the fire cave. As they walked they gathered dry wood and grass. The grass, and some of the wood, they took with them to the cave. The rest of the wood they left in small piles along the way to the Longhead valley.

In the fire cave they pulled many stones from the place the hot mist came from and piled them up and threw grass on them, and soon had a fire. Blue Eyes threw twigs, and then larger sticks, on the fire until only three pieces of wood were left. Each man held one of these pieces on the fire, and when the wood was burning strongly Blue Eyes led them from the cave.

Stonebreaker carried his fire fearfully, and long before they reached the first pile of wood he had let it go out. Blue Eyes was angry, and when

Stonebreaker had new fire he said, "Do not fear it."

"No," Stonebreaker said, and before they reached the next pile of wood he had let the new fire also go out. It was not until they were on their way to the last pile, the one that waited at the mouth of the Longhead valley, that he did not let his fire go out. Blue Eyes was pleased, and Stonebreaker was proud of himself.

They thrust their fire into the last pile of wood, and when it was burning they each took a new fire from it and ran on to the valley. The way into the valley was wide enough for the stream and the Longhead trail and no more. The smell of Longhead was strong. Stonebreaker's fear of fire was lost in his fear of Longheads. It was near the middle of the day, yet Stonebreaker worried that some of the Longheads would be awake and see them.

They came out of the hills. Stonebreaker looked across the valley, and there were no Longheads by the lake, and nothing moved in the caves.

They ran along the stream toward the caves. The wind was behind them, and now Stonebreaker worried that their scent and the smell of fire would carry to the caves. He thought this worried Blue Eyes too, because Blue Eyes ran faster and Stonebreaker had trouble keeping his fire from going out.

They stopped once and watched the caves. There was nothing to see but darkness, and they ran on. When they stopped again, there were Longheads in the mouth of one cave, and Stonebreaker felt their eyes on him.

"They smell the fire," Catkiller said.

"Yes," Blue Eyes said, "and we are not to the place I wanted. We will do it here."

He pointed the way they had been running and said to Catkiller, "Go that way. When you see my fire, set your fire."

"Yes," Catkiller said, and he left.

Blue Eyes pointed toward the grass between the caves and the mouth of the valley and said, "That way, and when you see Catkiller's fire, set your fire."

Stonebreaker ran. At first he tried to crouch below the grass, but his fire threatened to catch on the dry stalks. He stood up and ran, and watched the Longheads. There were many awake now. They did not come out of the caves to attack the men, though, and Stonebreaker thought they were frightened of the smell of fire.

Then he heard their voices. He looked around and saw smoke rising before the caves. Blue Eyes had set his fire, and soon Stonebreaker could hear it over the noise of the Longheads. He waited. The wind blew smoke toward the caves, and some Longheads started down the slope. Stonebreaker watched them, and then the fire, and he waited, his legs aching to run, for Catkiller's fire.

There was more smoke, and it seemed to be all around him. Had the wind changed? The crackling of the fire was closer. He tried, but the could not tell how many fires were burning, but then he saw Longheads running toward him, looking for a way past Blue Eyes' fire, and he threw his fire into the grass, and started back toward the stream.

The grass caught, and smoke rose. Stonebreaker heard cries from the Longheads. He stopped and watched his fire spread, and he showed his teeth. He felt good. He ran on, and smoke was everywhere. He looked back and saw flames taller than a giant, and he was not frightened, but so excited that he was shouting. These flames were his and Blue Eyes' and Catkiller's! He shouted at the fury of smoke and flames, and ran on, looking for the other men.

He found Catkiller at the stream. Catkiller's hair and beard had been burned in places. His arms had been touched by the fire, and he held them in the stream to cool them. His eyes watered. He was out of breath.

"Fire is fast," he said.

"Where is Blue Eyes?"

Catkiller pointed toward the fire. Then he put his head in the stream and threw water up on his shoulders and back. When he stood up the water ran down his body and he rubbed it over his skin.

Small animals came out of the grass. Some passed close to the men and gathered beside them on the stream bank. Others jumped into the stream. Some of these got to the other side, and some were carried away with the current. The fire burned closer, and Stonebreaker's excitement was overtaken by fear. Where was Blue Eyes?

The wind blew around Stonebreaker. It came hot from the flames and carried ashes and sparks. Soon fire was leaping up on the other side of the stream. All the valley was going to burn. Where was Blue Eyes?

"If he is dead?" Stonebreaker said.

Catkiller looked around at the fury they had started. His face was unhappy, but not afraid. "If he is dead, he has killed himself," he said. "We will wait. If the fire comes we will go in the water."

But Blue Eyes came before the fire did. The fire had touched him, and what was left of his hair and beard still smoked, though he beat at it with one hand. In the other hand he carried his spear, and the head of a Longhead. He stuck his spear in the ground and swung the head by its hair for them to see. He said, "It found a way past the fire, and I killed it."

"A great thing," Stonebreaker said, and he saw how happy Blue Eyes was. Catkiller did not look at the trophy. He said, "Will we leave?"

"No. The fire is close. We will go into the water," Blue Eyes said, and he stuck his trophy on the point of his spear and walked into the stream. Stonebreaker and Catkiller went after him.

The fire on the far side of the stream had reached the bank, and the air grew foul. Smoke and ash burned Stonebreaker's eyes. Then fire reached the bank the men had left, and the stream was filled with small animals. Some tried to climb on the heads of the men, who knocked them away and watched them float down the stream.

With fire all around, the hot wind carried no life. The men gasped in it, and Stonebreaker's throat ached. Only when the fire on the far bank burned out did a fresh wind blow along the stream. It fed the fire on the near bank and lifted the smoke from the stream. Stonebreaker breathed again without pain.

The wind blew the flames high and the fire on the near bank burned out. They walked from the stream up the blackened bank and looked across the valley. Fire burned to the east and south, and smoke was everywhere.

They waited while the wind blew the smoke east, and then they could see the Longhead caves. Fresh smoke came out of them. The fire had reached the caves, though Stonebreaker could not tell if the bones below them had burned.

"We have killed the Longheads," Blue Eyes said.

"Not all," Catkiller said. "Look."

There were Longheads on the bank upstream. As the smoke cleared, more of them came in sight along the lake shore. Altogether there were not many, and they moved about like the frightened animals that had gathered with the men at the stream. Some came near, and Blue Eyes pulled his spear from his trophy and the men faced the Longheads, ready to fight.

The Longheads stopped when they saw the men. They stared, but their eyes were empty of any threat.

"They are animals," Stonebreaker said. "The fire has taken the fight from them."

"The fight will come back to them," Catkiller said, "Will we leave?"

"Wait," Blue Eyes said. The Longheads had not moved. Blue Eyes picked up his trophy by the hair and threw it at them. It landed at their feet and they looked at it and backed away. Blue Eyes hissed. He said, "We will come back with the hunters and we will kill them all."

The Longheads backed farther away, and Blue Eyes followed them and got his trophy. The Longheads turned and ran and were lost among others upstream.

"This is a great thing," Blue Eyes said, and he looked around the valley. Where the fire had passed the ground was black, and where the fire still burned smoke hid the hills and the sky.

"A great thing," Blue Eyes said, and he started downstream toward the plains. Stonebreaker looked once at the Longheads, then started after Blue Eyes, happy that he had seen the last of the fire.

They went as Blue Eyes had said to Catkiller. They walked the plains the rest of that day, and slept in the hills that night. They smelled Longhead on the plains, but they did not follow the scent. The only danger they faced was from the great cats, but there were feather trees for safety. The next day they came to the end of the hills.

They hunted, and ate, and slept in the hills, and the next day they started west with the first light. They walked fast across the plains, though Stonebreaker thought the day went faster, and they saw nothing of the forest. Stonebreaker began to worry as the sun passed the top of the sky. Blue Eyes was happy. He looked at the animals on the plains and he said, "When the Longheads are all dead, we will come and live on the plains, and sleep in the big trees. Other tribes can live in the forest."

"What tribe lives here in the forest?" Catkiller said.

"Gti live at the North Lake," Blue Eyes said. "I was with Shortlegs once at the North Lake, and I know them."

"If we are north of the North Lake?" Catkiller said.

"We will go south on the plains and find the Gti."

They saw the dark line of the forest on the horizon well before dark. Blue Eyes stopped. He said, "We will take meat to the Gti."

They killed one of the horned animals of the plains, and cut it up. They went on, and Catkiller and Stonebreaker carried the meat, and Blue Eyes walked behind them and watched for danger.

The forest was close. Stonebreaker's worry turned to excitement. They had great stories to tell to the Gti, and anyone else they met on the way home. Stonebreaker thought of the North Lake, and hoped he would see it. Old men said that it was so big that a man could not see across it, that a man would take many days to walk around it. He thought more about the North Lake, and then he thought of the things he had already seen since he had gone with Blue Eyes to hunt the Longheads. When he thought of the giants, he thought of Longhair, and missed him, though he knew that Longhair was happy with the giants. The food Longhair got from chewers was no longer needed by the tribe, but he had found a new place with the giants.

Giants. Longheads. Fire. They had much to tell, and Stonebreaker was happy.

There were men in the forest. Blue Eyes shouted words at them that Stonebreaker did not know. The men answered, and Blue Eyes said, "They are Gti."

Then Stonebreaker smelled the forest. He showed his teeth, and looked at Blue Eyes and saw that Blue Eyes too smelled home and was happy.

"We have done many great things," Blue Eyes said. "Men will talk about them for many seasons," and Stonebreaker felt a chill run up his back, as when Shortlegs had praised him for killing the first Longhead.

"We have done many great things," Blue Eyes said again, "and we will do many more."

The shade of the first trees crossed Stonebreaker's face. Deeper in the forest, where the trees were thick, the Gti waited, and Blue Eyes held his spear straight up in greeting. The Gti stared at Blue Eyes, and Stonebreaker knew they were looking at the burns on his skin, and the places where his hair was gone, and the skull he carried that looked like a man's. Then they looked at the meat that Stonebreaker and Catkiller carried, and they raised their spears in welcome.

Joan D. Vinge is another talented new writer who is on her way up fast.
*Unknown only a few years ago, she has already won a Hugo Award, for
her novelette "Eyes of Amber." Her first novel,* The Outcasts of Heaven
Belt *(NAL), was generally well received; a book of novellas,* Fireship, *is
out from Dell; and she has sold another novel,* The Snow Queen, *to Dell
for a five-figure advance.*

*In the tale that follows, she tells a moving story about the varieties of
solitude and the bittersweet nature of hope.*

JOAN D. VINGE
View From a Height

Saturday, The 7th

I want to know why those pages were missing! How am I supposed to
keep up with my research if they leave out pages—?

(*Long sighing noise.*)

Listen to yourself, Emmylou: You're listening to the sound of fear. It
was an oversight, you know that. Nobody did it to you on purpose. Relax,
you're getting Fortnight Fever. Tomorrow you'll get the pages, and an
apology too, if Harvey Weems knows what's good for him.

But still, five whole pages; and the table of contents. How could you
miss *five* pages? And the table of contents.

How do I know there hasn't been a coup? The Northwest's finally taken
over completely and they're censoring the media—And like the Man
without a Country, everything they send me from now on is going to have
holes cut in it.

In *Science*?

Or maybe Weems has decided to drive me insane—?

Oh, my God . . . it would be a short trip. Look at me. I don't have any
fingernails left.

("*Arrwk. Hello, beautiful. Hello? Hello?*")

("Ozymandias! Get out of my hair, you devil." *Laughter.* "Polly want a
cracker? Here . . . gently! That's a boy.")

It's beautiful when he flies. I never get tired of watching him, or looking at him, even after twenty years. Twenty years . . . . What did the
psittacidae do, to win the right to wear a rainbow as their plumage?
Although the way we've hunted them for it, you could say it was a mixed
blessing.' Like some other things.

Twenty years. How strange it sounds to hear those words, and know
they're true. There are gray hairs when I look in the mirror. Wrinkles
starting. And Weems is bald! Bald as an egg, and all squinty behind his
spectacles. How did we get that way, without noticing it? Time is both
longer and shorter than you think, and usually all at once.

Twelve days is a long time to wait for somebody to return your call.
Twenty years is a long time gone. But I feel somehow as though it was only last week that I left home. I keep the circuits clean, going over them
and over them, showing those mental home movies until I could almost
step across, sometimes, into that other reality. But then I always look
down, and there's that tremendous abyss full of space and time, and I
realize I can't, again. You can't go home again.

Especially when you're almost one thousand astronomical units out in
space. Almost there, the first rung of the ladder. Next Thursday is the day.
Oh, that bottle of champagne that's been waiting for so long. Oh, the
parallax view! I have the equal of the best astronomical equipment in all
of near-Earth space at my command, and a view of the universe that no
one has ever had before; and using them has made me the only
astrophysicist ever to win a PhD in deep space. Talk about your field
work.

Strange to think that if the Forward Observatory had massed less than
its thousand-plus tons, I would have been replaced by a machine. But
because the installation is so large, I in my infinite human flexibility, even
with my infinite human appetite, become the most efficient legal tender.
And the farther out I get the more important my own ability to judge
what happens, and respond to it, becomes. The first—and maybe the
last—manned interstellar probe, on a one-way journey into infinity . . .
into a universe unobscured by our own system's gases and dust . . .
equipped with eyes that see everything from gamma to ultra-long
wavelengths, and ears that listen to the music of the spheres.

And Emmylou Stewart, the captive audience. Adrift on a star . . . if
you hold with the idea that all the bits of inert junk drifting through
space, no matter how small, have star potential. Dark stars, with
brilliance in their secret hearts, only kept back from letting it shine by
Fate, which denied them the critical mass to reach their kindling point.

Speaking of kindling: the laser beam just arrived to give me my daily
boost, moving me a little faster, so I'll reach a little deeper into the
universe. Blue sky at bedtime; I always was a night person. I'm sure they
didn't design the solar sail to filter light like the sky . . .·but I'm glad it
happened to work out that way. Sky-blue was always my passion—the
color, texture, fluid purity of it. This color isn't exactly right; but it
doesn't matter, because I can't remember how any more. This sky is a sun-
catcher. A big blue parasol. But so was the original, from where I used to

stand. The sky is a blue parasol . . . did anyone ever say that before, I wonder. If anyone knows, speak up—

Is anyone even listening. Will anyone ever be?

("Who cares, anyway? Come on, Ozzie—climb aboard. Let's drop down to the observation porch while I do my meditation, and try to remember what days were like.")

Weems, damn it, I want satisfaction!

Sunday, the 8th

That idiot. That intolerable moron—how could he do that to me? After all this time, wouldn't you think he'd know me better than that? To keep me waiting for twelve days, wondering and afraid: twelve days of all the possible stupid paranoias I could weave with my idle hands and mind, making myself miserable, asking for trouble—

And then giving it to me. God, he must be some kind of sadist! If I could only reach him, and hurt him the way I've hurt these past hours—

Except that I know the news wasn't his fault, and that he didn't mean to hurt me . . . and so I can't even ease my pain by projecting it onto him.

I don't know what I would have done if his image hadn't been six days stale when it got here. What would I have done, if he'd been in earshot when I was listening; what would I have said? Maybe no more than I did say.

What can you say, when you realize you've thrown your whole life away?

He sat there behind his faded blotter, twiddling his pen, picking up his souvenir moon rocks and laying them down—looking for all the world like a man with a time bomb in his desk drawer—and said, "Now, don't worry, Emmylou. There's no problem . . ." Went on saying it, one way or another, for five minutes; until I was shouting, "What's *wrong*, damn it?"

"I thought you'd never even notice the few pages . . ." with that sidling smile of his. And while I'm muttering, "I may have been in solitary confinement for twenty years, Harvey, but it hasn't turned my brain to mush," he said.

"So maybe I'd better explain, first—" and the look on his face; oh, the look on his face. "There's been a biomed breakthrough. If you were here on Earth, you . . . well, your body's immune responses could be . . . made normal . . ." And then he looked down, as though he could really see the look on my own face.

Made normal. Made normal. It's all I can hear. I was born with no natural immunities. No defense against disease. No help for it. No. *No, no, no;* that's all I ever heard, all my life on Earth. Through the plastic walls of my sealed room; through the helmet of my sealed suit . . . And now it's all changed. They could cure me. But I can't go home. I knew this could happen; I knew it had to happen someday. But I chose to ignore that fact, and now it's too late to do anything about it.

Then why can't I forget that I could have been f-free. . . .

. . . I didn't answer Weems today. Screw Weems. There's nothing to say. Nothing at all.

I'm so tired.

Monday, *the 9th*

Couldn't sleep. It kept playing over and over in my mind. . . . Finally took some pills. Slept all day, feel like hell. Stupid. And it didn't go away. It was waiting for me, still waiting, when I woke up.

It isn't fair—!

I don't feel like talking about it.

Tuesday, *the 10th*

Tuesday, already. I haven't done a thing for two days. I haven't even started to check out the relay beacon, and that damn thing has to be dropped off this week. I don't have any strength; I can't seem to move, I just sit. But I have to get back to work. Have to . . .

Instead I read the printout of the article today. Hoping I'd find a flaw! If that isn't the greatest irony of my entire life. For two decades I prayed that somebody would find a cure for me. And for two more decades I didn't care. Am I going to spend the next two decades hating it, now that it's been found?

No . . . hating myself. I could have been free, they could have cured me; if only I'd stayed on Earth. If only I'd been patient. But now it's too late . . . by twenty *years.*

I want to go home. I want to go home. . . . But you can't go home again. Did I really say that, so blithely, so recently? *You* can't: You, Emmylou Stewart. You are in prison, just like you have always been in prison.

It's all come back to me so strongly. Why me? Why must I be the ultimate victim— In all my life I've never smelled the sea wind, or plucked berries from a bush and eaten them, right there! Or felt my parents' kisses against my skin, or a man's body. . . . Because to me they were all deadly things.

I remember when I was a little girl, and we still lived in Victoria—I was just three or four, just at the brink of understanding that I was the only prisoner in my world. I remember watching my father sit polishing his shoes in the morning, before he left for the museum. And me smiling, so deviously, "Daddy . . . I'll help you do that, if you let me come out—"

And he came to the wall of my bubble and put his arms into the hugging gloves, and said, so gently, "No." And then he began to cry. And I began to cry too, because I didn't know why I'd made him unhappy. . . .

And all the children at school, with their "spaceman" jokes, pointing at the freak; all the years of insensitive people asking the same stupid questions every time I tried to go out anywhere . . . worst of all, the ones who weren't stupid, or insensitive. Like Jeffrey . . . no, I will not think about Jeffrey! I couldn't let myself think about him then. I could never afford to get close to a man, because I'd never be able to touch him. . . .

And now it's too late. Was I controlling my fate, when I volunteered for this one-way trip? Or was I just running away from a life where I was always helpless; helpless to escape the things I hated, helpless to embrace the things I loved.

I pretended this was different, and important . . . but was that really what I believed? No! I just wanted to crawl into a hole I couldn't get out of, because I was so afraid.

So afraid that one day I would unseal my plastic walls, or take off my helmet and my suit; walk out freely to breathe the air, or wade in a stream, or touch flesh against flesh . . . and die of it.

So now I've walled myself into this hermetically sealed tomb for a living death. A perfectly sterile environment, in which my body will not even decay when I die. Never having really lived, I shall never really die, dust to dust. A perfectly sterile environment; in every sense of the word.

I often stand looking at my body in the mirror after I take a shower. Hazel eyes, brown hair in thick waves with hardly any gray . . . and a good figure; not exactly stacked, but not unattractive. And no one has ever seen it that way but me. Last night I had the Dream again . . . I haven't had it for such a long time . . . this time I was sitting on a carved wooden beast in the park beside the Provincial Museum in Victoria; but not as a child in my suit. As a college girl, in white shorts and a bright cotton shirt, feeling the sun on my shoulders, and—Jeffrey's arms around my waist. . . . We stroll along the bayside hand in hand, under the Victortorian lamp posts with their bright hanging flower baskets, and everything I do is fresh and spontaneous and full of the moment. But always, always, just when he holds me in his arms at last, just as I'm about to . . . I wake up.

When we die, do we wake out of reality at last, and all our dreams come true? When I die . . . I will be carried on and on into the timeless depths of uncharted space in this computerized tomb, unmourned and unremembered. In time all the atmosphere will seep away; and my fair corpse, lying like Snow White's in inviolate sleep, will be sucked dry of moisture, until it is nothing but a mummified parchment of shriveled leather and bulging bones. . . .

("*Hello? Hello, baby? Good night. Yes, no, maybe.* . . . *Awk. Food time!*")

("Oh, Ozymandias! Yes, yes, I know . . . I haven't fed you, I'm sorry. I know, I know . . .")

(*Clinks and rattles.*)

Why am I so selfish? Just because I can't eat, I expect him to fast, too. . . . No. I just forgot.

He doesn't understand, but he knows something's wrong; he climbs the lamp pole like some tripodal bem, using both feet and his beak, and stares at me with that glass-beady bird's eye, stares and stares and mumbles things. Like a lunatic! Until I can hardly stand not to shut him in a cupboard, or something. But then he sidles along my shoulder and kisses me—such a tender caress against my cheek, with that hooked prehensile beak that could crush a walnut like a grape—to let me know that he's worried, and he cares. And I stroke his feathers to thank him, and tell him that it's all right . . . but it's not. And he knows it.

Does he ever resent his life? Would he, if he could? Stolen away from his own kind, raised in a sterile bubble to be a caged bird for a caged human. . . .

I'm only a bird in a gilded cage. I want to go home.

Wednesday, the 11th

Why am I keeping this journal? Do I really believe that sometime some alien being will find this, or some starship from Earth's glorious future will catch up to me . . . glorious future, hell. Stupid, selfish, short-sighted fools. They ripped the guts out of the space program after they sent me away, no one will ever follow me now. I'll be lucky if they don't declare me dead and forget about me.

As if anyone would care what a woman all alone on a lumbering space probe thought about day after day for decades, anyway. What monstrous conceit.

I did lubricate the bearings on the big scope today. I did that much. I did it so that I could turn it back toward Earth . . . toward the sun . . . toward the whole damn system. Because I can't even see it, all crammed into the space of two moon diameters, even Pluto; and too dim and small and faraway below me for my naked eyes, anyway. Even the sun is no more than a gaudy star that doesn't even make me squint. So I looked for them with the scope. . . .

Isn't it funny how when you're a child you see all those drawings and models of the solar system with big, lumpy planets and golden wakes streaming around the sun. Somehow you never get over expecting it to look that way in person. And here I am, one thousand astronomical units north of the solar pole, gazing down from a great height . . . and it doesn't look that way at all. It doesn't look like anything; even through the scope. One great blot of light, and all the pale tiny diamond chips of planets and moons around it, barely distinguishable from half a hundred undistinguished stars trapped in the same arc of blackness. So meaningless, so insignificant . . . so disappointing.

Five hours I spent, today, listening to my journal, looking back and trying to find—something, I don't know, something I suddenly don't have anymore.

I had it at the start. I was disgusting; Pollyanna Grad-student skipping and singing through the rooms of my very own observatory. It seemed like heaven, and a lifetime spent in it couldn't possibly be long enough for all that I was going to accomplish, and discover. I'd never be bored, no, not me. . . .

And there was so much to learn about the potential of this place, before I got out to where it supposedly would matter, and there would be new things to turn my wonderful extended senses toward . . . while I could still communicate easily with my dear mentor Dr. Weems, and the world. (Who'd ever have thought, when the lecherous old goat was my thesis advisor at Harvard, and making jokes to his other grad students about "the lengths some women will go to to protect their virginity," that we would have to spend a lifetime together.)

There was Ozymandias's first word . . . and my first birthday in space, and my first anniversary . . . and my doctoral degree at last, printed out by the computer with scrolls made of little x's and taped up on the wall. . . .

Then day and night and day and night, beating me black and blue with blue and black . . . my fifth anniversary, my eighth, my decade. I crossed the magnetopause, to become truly the first voyager in interstellar space . . . but by then there was no one left to *talk* to anymore, to really share the experience with. Even the radio and television broadcasts drifting out from Earth were diffuse and rare; there were fewer and fewer contacts with the reality outside. The plodding routines, the stupifying boredom—until sometimes I stood screaming down the halls just for something new; listening to the echoes that no one else would ever hear, and pretending they'd come to call; trying so hard to believe there was something to hear that wasn't *my* voice, *my* echo, or Ozymandias making a mockery of it.

("*Hello, beautiful. That's a crock. Hello, hello?*")

("Ozymandias, get *away* from me—")

But always I had that underlying belief in my mission: that I was here for a purpose, for more than my own selfish reasons, or NASA's (or whatever the hell they call it now), but for Humanity, and Science. Through meditation I learned the real value of inner silence, and thought that by creating an inner peace I had reached equilibrium with the outer silences. I thought that meditiation had disciplined me, I was in touch with my self and with the soul of the cosmos. . . . But I haven't been able to meditate since—it happened. The inner silence fills up with my own anger screaming at me, until I can't remember what peace sounds like.

And what have I really discovered, so far? Almost nothing. Nothing worth wasting my analysis or all my fine theories—or my freedom—on. Space is even emptier than anyone dreamed, you could count on both hands the bits of cold dust or worldlet I've passed in all this time, lost souls falling helplessly through near-perfect vacuum . . . all of us together. With my absurdly long astronomical tape measure I have fixed precisely the distance to NGC 2419 and a few other features, and from that made new estimates about a few more distant ones. But I have not detected a miniature black hole insatiably vacuuming up the vacuum; I have not pierced the invisible clouds that shroud the ultra-long wavelengths like fog; I have not discovered that life exists beyond the Earth in even the most tentative way. Looking back at the solar system I see nothing to show definitively that we even exist, anymore. All I hear anymore when I scan is electromagnetic noise, no coherent thought. Only Weems every twelfth night, like the last man alive. . . . Christ, I still haven't answered him.

Why bother? Let him sweat. Why bother with any of it. Why waste my precious time.

Oh, my precious time. . . . Half a lifetime left that could have been mine, on Earth.

Twenty years—I came through them all all right. I thought I was safe.

And after twenty years, my facade of discipline and self-control falls apart at a touch. What a self-deluded hypocrite I've been. Do you know that I said the sky was like a blue parasol eighteen years ago? And probably said it again fifteen years ago, and ten, and five—

Tomorrow I pass 1000 AUs.

Thursday, the 12th

I burned out the scope. I burned out the scope. I left it pointing toward the Earth, and when the laser came on for the night it shown right down the scope's throat and burned it out. I'm so ashamed. . . . Did I do it on purpose, subconsciously?

("*Goodnight starlight. Arrk. Good night. Good . . .*")

("Damn it. I want to hear another human voice—!")

(*Echoing, "voice, voice, voice, voice . . ."*)

When I found out what I'd done I ran away. I ran and ran through the halls. . . . But I only ran in a circle: This observatory, my prison, myself . . . I can't escape. I'll always come back in the end, to this green-walled room with its desk and its terminals, its cupboards crammed with a hundred thousand dozens of everything, toilet paper and magnetic tape and oxygen tanks. . . . And I can tell you exactly how many steps it is to my bedroom or how long it took me to crochet the afghan on the bed . . . how long I've sat in the dark and silence, setting up an exposure program or listening for the feeble pulse of a radio galaxy two billion light-years away. There will never be anything different, or anything more.

When I finally came back here, there was a message waiting. Weems, grinning out at me half-bombed from the screen—"Congratulations," he cried, "on this historic occasion! Emmylou, we're having a little celebration here at the lab; mind if we join you in yours, one thousand astronomical units from home—?" I've never seen him drunk. They really must have meant to do something nice for me, planning it all six days ahead. . . .

To celebrate I shouted obscenities I didn't even know I knew at him, until my voice was broken and my throat was raw.

Then I sat at my desk for a long time with my jackknife lying open in my hand. Not wanting to die—I've always been too afraid of death for that—but wanting to hurt myself. I wanted to make a fresh hurt, to take my attention off the terrible thing that is sucking me into myself like an imploding star. Or maybe just to punish myself, I don't know. But I considered the possibility of actually cutting myself quite calmly; while some separate part of me looked on in horror. I even pressed the knife against my flesh . . . and then I stopped and put it away. It hurts too much.

I can't go on like this. I have duties, obligations, and I can't face them. What would I do without the emergency automechs? . . . But it's the rest of my life, and they can't go on doing my job for me forever—

Later.

I just had a visitor. Strange as that sounds. Stranger yet—it was Donald Duck. I picked up half of a children's cartoon show today, the first coherent piece of nondirectional, unbeamed television broadcast I've recorded in months. And I don't think I've ever been happier to see anyone in my life. What a nice surprise, so glad you could drop by. . . . Ozymandias loves him; he hangs upside down from his swing under the cabinet with a cracker in one foot, cackling away and saying, "Give us a kiss, *smack-smack-smack*". . . . We watched it three times. I even smiled, for a while; until I remembered myself. It helps. Maybe I'll watch it again until bedtime.

Friday, the 13th
Friday the Thirteenth. Amusing. Poor Friday the Thirteenth, what did it ever do to deserve its reputation? Even if it had any power to make my life miserable, it couldn't hold a candle to the rest of this week. It seems like an eternity since last weekend.

I repaired the scope today; replaced the burnt-out parts. Had to suit up and go outside for part of the work . . . I haven't done any outside maintenance for quite a while. Odd how both exhilarating and terrifying it always is when I first step out of the airlock, utterly alone, into space. You're entirely on your own, so far away from any possibility of help, so far away from anything at all. And at that moment you doubt yourself, suddenly, terribly . . . just for a moment.

But then you drag your umbilical out behind you and clank along the hull in your magnetized boots that feel so reassuringly like lead ballast. You turn on the lights and look for the trouble, find it and get to work; it doesn't bother you anymore. . . . When your life seems to have torn loose and be drifting free, it creates a kind of sea anchor to work with your hands; whether it's doing some mindless routine chore or the most intricate or repairs.

There was a moment of panic, when I actually saw charred wires and melted metal, when I imagined the damage was so bad that I couldn't repair it again. It looked so final, so—masterful. I clung there by my feet and whimpered and clenched my hands inside my gloves, like a great shining baby, for a while. But then I pulled myself down and began to pry here and unscrew there and twist a component free . . . and little by little I replaced everything. One step at a time; the way we get through life.

By the time I'd finished I felt quite calm, for the first time in days; the thing that's been trying to choke me to death this past week seemed to falter a little at my demonstration of competence. I've been breathing easier since then; but I still don't have much strength. I used up all I had just overcoming my own inertia.

But I shut off the lights and hiked around the hill for a while, afterwards—I just couldn't face going back inside just then: Looking at the black convex dish of the solar sail I'm embedded in, up at the radio antenna's smaller dish occluding stars as the observatory's cylinder wheels endlessly at the hub of the spinning parasol. . . .

That made me dizzy, and so I looked out into the starfields that lie on every side. Even with my own poor, unaugmented senses there's so much more to see out here, unimpeded by atmosphere or dust, undominated by any sun's glare. The brilliance of the Milky Way, the depths of star and nebula and farthest galaxy breathlessly suspended . . . as I am. The realization that I'm lost for eternity in an uncharted sea.

Strangely, although that thought aroused a very powerful emotion when it struck me, it wasn't a negative one at all: it was from another scale of values entirely; like the universe itself. It was as if the universe itself stretched out its finger to touch me. And in touching me, singling me out, it only heightened my awareness of my own insignificance.

That was somehow very comforting. When you confront the absolute indifference of magnitudes and vistas so overwhelming, the swollen ego of your self-important suffering is diminished. . . .

And I remembered one of the things that was always so important to me about space—that here *any*one has to put on a spacesuit before they step outside. We're all aliens, no one better equipped to survive than another. I am as normal as anyone else, out here.

I must hold onto that thought.

Saturday, The 14th
There is a reason for my being here. There is a reason.

I was able to meditate earlier today. Not in the old way, the usual way, by emptying my mind. Rather by letting the questions fill up the space, not fighting them; letting them merge with my memories of all that's gone before. I put on music, that great mnemonic stimulator; letting the images that each tape evoked free-associate and interact.

And in the end I could believe again that my being here was the result of a free choice. No one forced me into this. My motives for volunteering were entirely my own. And I was given this position because NASA believed that I was more likely to be successful in it than anyone else they could have chosen.

It doesn't matter that some of my motives happened to be unresolved fear or wanting to escape from things I couldn't cope with. It really doesn't matter. Sometimes retreat is the only alternative to destruction, and only a madman can't recognize the truth of that. Only a madman.
. . . Is there anyone "sane" on Earth who isn't secretly a fugitive from something unbearable somewhere in their life? And yet they function normally.

If they ran, they ran toward something, too, not just away. And so did I. I had already chosen a career as an astrophysicist before I ever dreamed of being a part of this project. I could have become a medical researcher instead, worked on my own to find a cure for my condition. I could have grown up hating the whole idea of space and "spacemen," stumbling through life in my damned ugly sterile suit. . . .

But I remember when I was six years old, the first time I saw a film of suited astronauts at work in space . . . they looked just like me! And no one was laughing. How could I help but love space, then?

(And how could I help but love Jeffrey, with his night-black hair, and his blue flightsuit with the starry patch on the shoulder. Poor Jeffrey, poor Jeffrey, who never even realized his own dream of space before they cut the program out from under him. . . . I will not talk about Jeffrey. I will not.)

Yes, I could have stayed on Earth, and waited for a cure! I knew even then there would have to be one, someday. It was both easier and harder to choose space, instead of staying.

And I think the thing that really decided me was that those people had faith enough in me and my abilities to believe that I could run this observatory and my own life smoothly for as long as I lived. Billions of dollars and a thousand tons of equipment resting on me; like Atlas holding up his world.

Even Atlas tried to get rid of his burden; because no matter how vital his function was, the responsibility was still a burden to him. But he took his burden back again too, didn't he; for better or worse. . . .

I worked today. I worked my butt off getting caught up on a week's worth of data processing and maintenance, and I'm still not finished. Discovered while I was at it that Ozymandias had used those missing five pages just like the daily news: crapped all over them. My sentiments exactly! I laughed and laughed.

I think I may live.

Sunday, The 15th

The clouds have parted.

That's not rhetorical—among my fresh processed data is a series of photo reconstructions in the ultra-long wavelengths. And there's a gap in the obscuring gas up ahead of me, a break in the clouds that extends thirty or forty light-years. Maybe fifty! Fantastic. What a view. What a view I have from here of everything, with my infinitely extended vision: of the way ahead, of the passing scene—or looking back toward Earth.

Looking back. I'll never stop looking back, and wishing it could have been different. That at least there could have been two of me, one to be here, one who could have been normal, back on Earth; so that I wouldn't have to be forever torn in two by regrets—

(*"Hello. What's up, doc? Avast!"*)

(*"Hey, watch it! If you drink, don't fly."*)

Damn bird. . . . If I'm getting maudlin, it's because I had a party today. Drank a whole bottle of champagne. Yes, I had *the* party . . . we did, Ozymandias and I. Our private 1000 AU clebration. Better late than never, I guess. At least we did have something concrete to celebrate—the photos. And if the celebration wasn't quite as merry as it could have been, still I guess it will probably seem like it was when I look back on it from the next one, at 2000 AUs. They'll be coming faster now, the celebrations. I may even live to celebrate 8000. What the hell, I'll shoot for 10,000—

After we finished the champagne . . . Ozymandias thinks '98 was a great year, thank God he can't drink as fast as I can . . . I put on my Strauss waltzes, and the *Barcarolle*: oh, the Berliner Philharmonic; their touch is what a lover's kiss must be. I threw the view outside onto the big screen, a ballroom of stars, and danced with my shadow. And part of the time I wasn't dancing above the abyss in a jumpsuit and headphones, but waltzing in yards of satin and lace across a ballroom floor in nineteenth-century Vienna. What I wouldn't give to be *there* for a moment out of time. Not for a lifetime, or even a year, but just for an evening; just for one waltz.

Another thing I shall never do. There are so many things we can't do, any of us, for whatever the reasons— time, talent, life's callous whims. We're all on a one-way trip into infinity. If we're lucky we're given some life's work we care about, or some person. Or both, if we're very lucky.

And I do have Weems. Sometimes I see us like an old married couple, who have grown to a tolerant understanding over the years. We've never been soul mates, God knows, but we're comfortable with each other's silences. . . .

I guess it's about time I answered him.

Thomas M. Disch is what is known as a writer's writer, the expert so coolly adroit that he solves the most difficult technical problems without fuss, pyrotechnics, noticeable effort, or excessively loud breathing. One of the best stylists in SF, Disch also moves easily back and forth across genre boundaries and has achieved an impressive reputation both as a mainstream novelist and as a poet. His books include 334 *(Avon),* Camp Concentration *(Avon),* Getting into Death *(Knopf),* Fun with Your New Head *(Signet), a poetry collection,* The Right Way to Figure Plumbing *(Basilisk Press), and the forthcoming novel* On Wings of Song *(St. Martin's Press).*

Here—in one of a series of stories he has been writing about a future in which a strange plague has rendered the majority of humanity immortal—Disch examines the implications of a new kind of generation gap: the aching, unbridgeable distance between those who will not die and those who must return to the soil, between the chosen and those who are constantly reminded that they have not been called, between the haves and the newest kind of have-nots.

THOMAS M. DISCH
Mutability

Tübingen, 2 July 2097: Veronica Quin
The free university city of Tübingen (alt. 315m; population 2,090,140,400) is situated on the banks of the Neckar thirty-five kilometres south of Stuttgart. It is chiefly renowned in modern times for its university, founded in 1477 by Count Eberhard im Bart of Wurtemberg. Melancthon lectured at the Bursa from 1514 to 1518. In 1536 Duke Ulrich founded the Protestant seminary, where Kepler later studied under the astronomer Mästlin. Kepler's first work, the Mysterium cosmographicum, *was published in Tübingen by the Gruppenbach Press. During the 19th Century the university regained the high reputation it had lost during the devastations of the Thirty Years War. Hegel, Schelling, Hölderlin, Uhland, and Mörike (all identified with the Swabian "renaissance") studied and taught at the seminary, which was also, a few decades later, the centre of the critical movement in Protestant theology, exemplified by Baur and Strauss. Inevitably the long decline of Protestantism during the unification and expansion of the German Reich under Bismarck and Hitler affected the stature of the university, but it once again came into prominence in the*

*first decades of this century when its faculty and students spearheaded
the Pan-Germanic Anarchist movement. In 2024 it became the capital
of the independent state of Baden-Schwaben, and in 2039 the United
Nations granted its petition for free-city status. In 2096 the university
enrolled 21,300 students in its graduate faculties (approximately half
of this number receiving stipends) and 243 undergraduates. In recent
years the faculty of history (enrolling more than 8,000 students) has
won world-wide recognition for its achievements, and the "bifurcating
bibliographies" of the Tübingen school have revolutionized modern
historical methodology. This faculty was the first at the university to
abolish voluntarily, in 2019, the increasingly meaningless distinction
between the teaching staff and the body of graduate students. Despite
the controversy that still attaches to its uniquely democratic government, Tübingen attracts eminent scholars from all fields and from all
countries. No university in Europe and only California in America can
boast an alumni of equal distinction.*

from Baedecker's The German States,
2097 edition

1 p.m.
Antennae either, the ant seeks its fellows on the hinderside of her
hand. She turns her hand palm up. With *Angst* the ant considers the index
fingers, then veers off along the lifeline. The middle finger, gilded with
nicotine, bends forward and crushes the ant, or pismire (from the Danish
myre, though long, long before the Danes there had been Myrmidons,
and before Myrmidons a plague.):
HCOOH.
Meanwhile they poured up out of the floorboards in their multitudes.
Avoiding the suitcases, the column followed the crack to the west wall,
ascending the wall as far as to the wainscoting that concealed the power
cable, and followed this traverse northwards and then, at the corner, to
the east. Where a doorway interrupted the wainscoting the ants once
again ascended. Against the age-dark wood of the beam they became invisible. Reaching the south wall they descended, slanting left, to the
counter where that morning Veronica had left the unwashed spoon, their
fleece of Golden Syrup.
A journey, she estimated, of fifty feet: an ideal itinerary would not have
exceeded seven. It was allegorical.
"Fools," Veronica said, not without affection.
Michael Divine, who'd lost interest in the ants half an hour ago, seemed
uncertain how to interpret this remark. He smiled faintly, faint wrinkles
forming about his eyes and mouth.
Aligning himself (she thought) *on the side of wisdom.*
She rubbed the smear of formic acid off on her T-shirt and returned to
her worktable, where a random compost of notes and artifacts, quanta of
history, confronted her: Doctor Emeritus Veronica Quin.
She inserted the tape of *12 August 1998, 7:30 p.m. E.S.T., N.B.C.,
"Beware, Babylon!"* and speeded through the first minutes, making a

monkey gibber of the opening hymn. She slowed at the first close-up of the blurred ghostly chiliast, who crackled portents of the Days to Come. His Leonardesque finger pointed to the handwriting on the wall. The audience was made to consider whether they were sheep or goats, grain or chaff. Then came the show-stopper, as he clawed away the numeral days from a giant calendar.

The estimates for that first show had been 22 million, and the ratings increased steadily until February of 2000, a month after the terminal date of the universe. In the interim months Reverend Delmont had been elected governor of the state of Nevada (where the Elect had been asked to assemble) and mayor of Los Angeles (where they'd been assembling already for eighty years). "Beware, Babylon!" was an essential datum in any consideration of millennialism.

She observed:

1. The *frisson* of the Apocalypse; hell's sex appeal.
2. The seduction of numerology. We are all Pythagoreans.
3. The secret suicidal wish (Freud, the Cold War, *et. al.*).

Beyond these partial causes there had been the memory of the Plague, of decimations, of landscapes more vivid than Bosch, providing both a portent and a model of the universal wrack. How much more satisfying to the moral sense than the nescient speculations of PhDs if this should be the *meaning* of the Plague—that all those million deaths had been accomplished as a word to the wise.

"Who is he?" Michael Divine asked.

She had forgotten, so seldom did she have visitors in the day, to localize the sound.

"Baptist Delmont, who promised us that time would stop. To his chagrin, it wouldn't. Inertia, I guess."

"Never heard of him. Was he important?"

So the lad would chatter. Then to oblige Joseph she would for a while chatter too. She touched a finger to HOLD, stopping time within the microcosm of the viewer. A plosive froze on Baptist Delmont's lips.

"He was representative. For my purposes that's better than being important. There were hundreds of Baptists in those days, big and little, and tens of millions of believers. Workers stopped working, the crime rate rose, and the market dropped."

"Oh. Is that what you had in mind when you said 'Fools'?" He caught exactly the tone she'd used.

"Can anything so big really be foolish?" (Though it *might* have been at the back of her mind. What was society, after all, but one vast formicary? Black ants waging war on red ants. Milking aphids. Building tunnels.) "You see, it wasn't just the zealots who felt the end was coming," she added. "The *fin de siècle* had begun a century before. Some of the best minds of the time were convinced the end was at hand. If not of the world, then of history, of the West, of us."

She touched, illustratively, the cast-bronze first edition of *Der Untergang des Abendlands* that weighted down a sedimentary heap of her primary sources. From such muck as this, compacted for years by the pressure of thought, the rocks of history are made.

Michael came up to the table and lifted the metal book in one hand. His movements were quick and crisp, but seen this close his flesh betrayed the cells' inexorable attrition. Small fulciform pouches had begun to form beneath his eyes. Eyes of hazel, that shifted into an improbable red when the sunlight caught them at an oblique angle.

"Well, in a way, wasn't he right?" Michael said. "A lot of that did come to an end."

"Every age, however, feels that it's a culmination, the tonic chord that resolves the imperfect progressions of the past." *I am doing this* (she thought) *for Joseph's sake. Only for him.*

"I don't feel that way. But maybe that's because I'm a fossil."

For the first time since Joseph had brought him round that morning Veronica regarded Michael Divine with some interest. His remark indicated a degree of intelligence, a quickness, that she never took for granted in a mortal. Or, for that matter, in any of Joseph's featherweight *liebhabers*.

"A fossil? In the Toynbeean sense, perhaps. On the other hand, most immortals feel much the same. The past has lost its hold on all of us. It may be from a sense that the larger historical process has stopped. The red armies and the black armies have declared a truce. There's no turnover in the personnel department. Kings don't die. Did you know that Charles IV is still alive? He works at an undersea development station off the Japanese coast. Once a year he comes back to Hampton Court and entertains. So much for History with a capital H."

"Well, it hasn't lost its hold on you, anyhow. Or on Joseph. He's obsessed with the past."

"That's because we both represent a kind of intermediate species. We were already adults before we begun to suspect we were immortal. For a long time it was only a small doubt. Agerasia was no proof of immortality; in fact, it remains to be proved. But after a century or so, the conviction takes root anyhow. People younger than us grew up with that conviction. For them the present is absolutely discontinuous with the past. Even for Joseph and me the past that interests us has been the past we've lived through ourselves. This man, for instance—I might have seen his debut on N.B.C. If my mother hadn't forbidden it."

"How old were you?"

"Nine."

(Was he tallying it up? 9 + 2 + 97. Old, old, old.)

· "And what is his interest now?" He pointed at the pouting face of Baptist Delmont.

"He's one of my facts. Paul and I are putting together a kind of sequel to *2000 +*. About the decline of religion since 1900 till now. When the world refused to end, there was some disillusionment."

"Which you shared?"

"Never completely, or I wouldn't have become an historian. It's a profession that still has more in common with theology than with science. It's so easy to make patterns. I tend to confuse my patterns with the world's facts. In that respect I probably preserve more illusions than you."

Michael blinked. In contrast with other movements of his face and body, there was a tiredness in this unconscious gesture that pointed to a possible retardation of the neural response. He was probably closer to forty than to thirty, which had been her first guess.

"That would be difficult," he said.

The tonic chord. Neither felt any need to say more. Michael crossed the room to stare at his face in the empty aquarium. Veronica reanimated Baptist Delmont, but first she noted on her shorthand pad the tidy simile of the rocks and the muck.

2 p.m.

Time was tangible in this room not simply in the absolute sense that this was a very old room, but also in the way that whole eras of geology can be encapsulated in a single conglomerate rock. The constituent pebbles (the books, the photographs, the tins of film, the rusted Spandau, shelves and boxes of kitsch and curios) were cemented together by a dross adhesive of the contemporary: empty tetrahedrons of Lowenbrau, vases of dried and moulting blooms, her own filth packets of wiring, cheeserinds, butts and ashes, Niobe's kitty litter, cast-off clothes, the polychrome debris of her typed and scribbled notes.

The world with metaphors. But dried up. Herself dried up, a sack of dust.

A memory: cleaning out the East 11th Street apartment, the half-empty box of Kotex in the cabinet underneath the sink in which the mice had made their comfy nest. She ought to have preserved that for her stock of souvenirs. It seemed unlikely that Oliver, to whom she'd mailed it in the same spirit she'd sent him cartoons clipped from magazines, would have saved it. (And if he had, how many light-years away would it be now?)

If Michael Divine *were* forty, he would still be too young, by twenty years, to have been the son she'd never had.

He was, distinctly, a handsome boy. A pleasure to look at. She looked at the small motions of enforced idleness, the restless flicker of his gaze, the quick snap of his wrist that made the face of his silver bracelet lie flat against the back of his hand.

She bent down to take his hand in hers. "What does it say?"

So wary of her he was: the young Adonis.

"Your bracelet," she explained. He let her lift his forearm to read the inscription. She laughed. She released him, and he leaned back in the chair, safe.

"Beer? Coffee? Tea?"

"No, thank you."

"You'll excuse me if I make some for myself." She went into the utility room, drew water from the tap, and lighted the Volkswagen. "A marvelously inconvenient place, this," she commented from the doorway. "No room. Draughty in winter. And Paul knocks himself silly at least once a week on the rafters. How tall are you, Michael?"

"Five foot eight."

"Then you're safe."

Let him think so anyway.

She held up two cups. "You're sure?"

"Well, if it's already made. . . ."

"Draughty and—" Turning back to the console. "Oh, a dreadful nuisance, but it is stone-old. That's its charm for a historian. The Gruppenbach Press used to be down on the ground floor, and the building goes back before even that."

She poured out the potion, gave him his cup.

"Really?" he said, without interest.

He took a sip, saw the stains all round the inside edge of the cup, grimaced. Veronica didn't take much trouble with the decorative side of cleanliness.

"Is it that bad?" she asked.

"Bad? No, it's delicious."

She laughed. "Not the coffee, Michael. Your life."

"Oh, that."

"Are you furious with Joseph?"

"I've no cause to be angry with him, only grateful. He must have told you how we met."

"No." (Or if he had, she'd forgotten.)

"Good. I won't either. It was nasty and a bit ridiculous, but the upshot of it was that Joseph pretty much saved my life. I was going under and he put me on my feet. I am on my feet, still. For that I'm grateful, still."

"And you do love him, still?"

"Do you?"

Unfair.

She shrugged off the question as though it were some bulky, unseasonable cardigan and sprawled on a pile of pillows on the floor. She could lose twenty pounds of her slipshod flesh in a month, if she made the effort. How long had it been since she was wholeheartedly physical?

"Do you?" he insisted.

"I was thinking. It's a difficult question. I guess I'd have to say no. We've had our moments, of course. Most of them a long time ago. Nearly a century's gone by since we met. I was his secretary at Freedom Mutual. He used to work in insurance then, you know, on the investment end."

"I know."

"I was twenty-one. Joseph was forty. He wasn't getting on with his wife. It was exactly the sort of thing one used to see all the time on teevee. Had it been anything else, I wouldn't have been able to follow the script. Life was so much simpler then. But you've probably heard the whole thing from Joseph already."

"Some of it, though never that much about you. About the wife."

"Hope?"

"No, the other one. Emma?"

An ant, or emmet, strayed across the cushion. Had she ever, in fact, met Emma? She remembered her eyes, a deep brown, solemn with accusation, but no actual confrontation.

"Emma. It was a tragic case. She killed herself, you know."

"How old was she?"

"Forty. Maybe forty-one."

"Premature," Michael said. 'I give myself much longer than that."

"I should hope you do." She squashed the ant, or emmet: HCOOH. "Are you going off with Joseph to London?"

"Is that where he's going? Then I'll go there. At this point, you know, I'm just holding on and hoping. What else did he say?"

"That your father is dying."

"Yes. He's always dying. He's fairly rich. He can afford doctors. He used to be quite rich, twenty years back, but geriatricians are expensive. I fairly hope he does die this time. I'd like there to be a little something left for me."

"How old is he?"

"Eighty-one."

"My mother held out till she was eighty-eight. For the last five, six years she watched teevee from a stuffed recliner. Her mind went, and every time she exhaled a breath she made a sort of whistling sound. Quite unnerving. One summer there was a power failure that lasted twelve hours. We thought she was going to die with the set blank. She got all fussed. But Joseph came up with the most wonderful idea. He took the insides out of the set, and we took turns the rest of the day talking to her from inside. It was enormous fun."

"Did she die?"

"Not then. A week later, during the Senate Committee hearings on contract labor. If you don't want to go off to London right away, you can stay on here for a while. We have room."

"Wouldn't Mr. Regnier mind?"

"Paul is very permissive. Besides, we have boxes of things that have to be catalogued, so you could pick up a bit of cash. Assuming you need some. It's interesting work."

"I'll consider it."

"And Joseph would probably be pleased. Not at being rid of you, mind. But to know you were in good hands." She smiled a sly, nose-wrinkling, rabbity smile.

And Michael (in his element again) leaned forward to take the taste of her mouth. She closed her eyes, and the waters of the past rippled over her lax flesh, the ghostly caresses of a hundred vanished lovers, mortal and immortal, men and women.

"In a month or so, I could lose twenty pounds."

"I like you better this way," he said. Then, as a machinist will begin as a matter of course to test the tolerances of a new piece of equipment, he added: "Sluttish."

"Ah!" It wasn't necessary to say what it was she found attractive in him. Even so, she framed an ambiguous compliment: "Have you always been a grasshopper, Michael?"

"How is that?"

"A grasshopper, as opposed to an ant."

"No one *wants* to be an ant."

Once on the wall of one of those characterless European rooms she'd taken after Joseph had left her the second time she'd made a chart or model to represent the structure of her own life. Wishfully, she had gerrymandered the contours until its form had approximated a crystal structure. SiO^2. That mural was now painted over, or the wall demolished, but the map had remained with her, to become encrusted with baroque embellishments or reduced to the cubical simplicity of copper according as her life seemed to her various or plain.

She rose to her feet, walked to the bookshelf, lifted the chunk of what she'd been told was Martian rock. "My valence is rising," she said. But these little mystifications were no longer enough to put Michael off his form.

"Because," he said, pursuing the previous metaphor, "they get squashed."

Observant too. She began to see why Joseph had let it drag on so long. "Michael, *zeig Er mir jetzt die Zunge!*"

Before he could obey, the phone rang. It was Joseph. She localized the sound and hunched in front of the screen to keep him to herself.

"What did he say?" Michael asked.

"He's on his way over."

They regarded each other closely. Already he'd sensed she was lying to him.

3 p.m.

Michael was in the alcove exploring a sonnet of drawers in a massy Teutonic catchall, emptiness rhyming to emptiness. ("You can see," Veronica said, "I have nothing to hide.") But the fifteenth drawer yielded a holly warping from a glorious garland of cloisonné and florentined gold.

"And this?" he asked.

A platoon of office workers in sad long-ago clothes arranged themselves in the (count them) three dimensions of a fluorescent space. This was to holography what tintypes were to photography—and conveyed by its stiffness a similar pathos.

"The nothing in question," she answered, and almost told him to put it back.

"Which is you?"

She pointed to two tiny blue eyes staring eighty-six years straight ahead at these hazel eyes that shifted to red. "I was in love then."

"That very moment? You don't look it." The comment and his inflection were mediate between cruelty and a finicking regard for the instant's inner truth, a tone he must have picked up from Joseph, who was an enthusiast of the abstracter virtues: honesty, clarity, *esprit*, and whatever else might be ranged against Duty.

Without quibbling, she took the holly from him and pressed it flat into its incongruously fine frame. Six of the twenty-six faces showed signs of age. Dorothy Jerrold, who'd been supervisor of the typing pool then, and Larry Noonan, who took over from Dorothy a few years later, and Mr.

Whewell, who read all the best-sellers, and Yolanda—or was it Eula?—Sloane. The names of the other two black women she'd forgotten. All six of them would be dead by now, and the building itself turned into some kind of dorm, or so she'd heard. The clouds roll by. She put the picture back where it belonged.

Meanwhile he was into another drawer, poking at a pretty jumble of electronic junk resembling a spilled bracelet or the shingle of a beach. "I love other people's souvenirs," he said, "much more than my own. What else is there?"

She told him about the Kotex box and the mice; then (he had discovered the motel ashtray) about her momentous weekend of adultery in the Florida Disneyland.

"He took *me* to Belgium," Michael said, not to be outdone.

"He would. He loves anything *wiederaufgebaut*, not to say fake. He's wild over what they've done to the Colosseum."

"Which is Greek for?"

She thought. "Latin, isn't it? For gigantic."

"No, before that, what he loves—Diderot's cow?" Sounding the *t*.

The latch began to lift and Michael's hand, from gesturing airily, fell into Veronica's lap.

Paul came in, and with him Niobe.

"Paul, this is Michael Divine."

Paul's psyche was borne, smiling, toward the sofa by his dowdy soma, rather as the Baptist's head might have been carried in to Herod by the axeman. Arriving, he bent down, lifted Michael's hand and kissed it. (He was French.) "I've heard so much about you."

"No, Niobe!" Veronica called out to the very *enceinte* cat, who was furtively making her way underneath the Volkswagen. Then, to Paul: "Michael and I are waiting for Joseph. We thought, as you came in, that *you* might be he."

This was ironic. It was their understanding, Paul's and Veronica's, that he and Joseph were opposites something along the lines of Mind and Matter: Paul having been the Pygmalion to her Galatea, while Joseph was the bull to her Europa. There was a further irony in that they both knew Joseph had already left Tübingen.

Michael's antennae were out, however. He'd understood what had passed between them as clearly as if it had come in on his own police radio. "He's left. Hasn't he?"

"Left?" Paul echoed. He was easily stared down. "Well, yes, he has. He was afraid, you see, that you might—as you'd followed him here—that you might follow him . . . away."

"Away where?"

"He didn't know. To a mountain perhaps. He wanted to unfuzzy his mind."

"He couldn't tell me himself?"

"Hasn't he been trying to?" Veronica asked, taking over for Paul, who had no talent for confrontations.

"So he just up and leaves all that here?"

"All that" was the two holly suitcases with their sunbursts of cheap glitter. It had been their presence in the corner all through the afternoon that had allowed Michael to feel that Joseph was still safely shackled to him. But really! Would anyone who identified with his own suitcases have bought two such sleazy specimens as these?"

"Did he want us to *keep* them for him?" she asked Paul. "He knows there isn't room, and the last time we had those awful boxes of his for two years. We never could figure out where that smell was coming from—remember?"

Paul waved the question aside. Michael, standing in the middle of the littered room, had begun to cry, and Paul studied this process with panicky fascination, as though, visiting a zoo, he'd suddenly encountered a beautiful tiger on the graveled path. Then, as if the tiger were calmly to walk back into its cage, Michael stopped.

"I think if we were to leave Michael alone for a minute—"

Paul was more than willing to be led away. He collapsed into his bed with his all-purpose curse. "Holy fucking moly!"

"You know what it is?" Veronica said soothingly.

"*Glänzende Götterlufte!*"

"It's their goddamned vulnerability. *They're* always so wide open, and they make *us* feel the same way."

"Oh, I don't blame him, poor thing. But they do take it out of you somehow. Look at the shape Joseph's in. One minute he's going to do this, the next moment it's something else, going on like a flittermouse. And all for what? For a boy."

"Michael is scarcely a boy."

Paul was too pleased with "flittermouse" to notice what she'd said. "I'll admit he's attractive in a rather *unheimlich* way. But even so, Joseph is old enough to know better."

"By the by, I've told Michael he can stay on here a while, so if he should—"

"It's not as though he even *cared* for boys. He doesn't, as a rule."

"Be *nice* to him."

Michael was standing in the doorway in his underwear. He knocked on the open door. "I feel dirty. Can I take a bath?"

Paul became Arabian in his courtesies. The apartment belonged to Michael. He could stay on a week or a month. He explained, twice, how the console worked, found a fresh bar of soap, and dug into the wardrobe for a fresh towel. As Michael accepted it Paul squinted at the writing on his bracelet, and laughed. "Oh, I like that! Did you see this, Ronny?"

"Yes, I saw it."

"*Your name.* That's precious."

Michael released the catch, and the bracelet glissaded down the folds of the towel. Paul tried to catch it, missed.

"You like it," Michael said, with a smile of stony insincerity, "it's yours."

"Oh but—"

Michael stepped round him, entered the bathroom, and locked

the door.

5 p.m.

Bursting with new kittens and well content, Niobe lay beside Michael on the rumpled bed. From time to time Veronica would reach across his knees to ruffle the fur of her throat and she would purr. People (she thought) should be more like cats.

Sleep had smoothed the grosser signs of age from his face, but gradually in the half-light of the hall she was able to decipher, in the pebbling of the skin, in the pulse of a vein, in a breath, the tragic implications wound into his genes. Was it worth it? Worth the pain of reading, always more clearly, the same portents? Of growing every day a little guiltier until her heart was ripe to betray him? And for what? For love? She would not have called it that, but it was there, inside of her, by whatever name, the reason for it.

A hollowness. As though some creature, intelligent yet inarticulate, compounded of volatile gases, were pushing and prodding at her inner organs, writhing in the oily machineries of her imperishable flesh. Not a child. (Of those regrets no particle remained.) An anti-child perhaps, which Michael's sperm, dying within her, might cause to die as well.

He woke at last, all fuzzy and mild from the sedation.

"You're in my bed. You'll be all right."

"Oh." Slowly his mind added it up; he grimaced at the sum. The worst of it seemed to be not that he'd failed but that it would be supposed he'd meant to fail. "Jesus. I'm sorry. I really didn't mean to—"

"You *did* mean to, I think," she reassured him. "You have your own good looks to blame. There's a hole in the wall near the flush mechanism. Paul was watching you every moment. When you blanked out we broke in. Five minutes, he said, would have done the trick. You made it quite deep enough."

He touched the bandage round his left wrist. "Who?"

"Paul. Ages and ages ago, when I was typing in that typing pool, Paul was a chirurgeon in Grenoble."

"I might as well have gone straight to the Emergency Ward to kill myself. Christ."

"Well, you weren't to know."

Niobe, moved either by suspicion or by appetite, was attempting delicately to take the bandage off his right wrist. He swatted her, and winced with pain.

"Niobe, no! *Bad* Niobe. Would you like something to eat? Paul said you should."

"Maybe later."

"What a flutter you put *him* in. Once he'd sewn you up, it was all I could do to get him not to call in the University's health service to cart you off. I said it would be better just to find you a nice pill that will see you through the next week or two. You *won't* try again, will you? You said before that forty-one was premature."

"I promise not to kill myself. Now would you make some soup or something? Or if you've got to stare at me, do it from another peep-hole. Okay?"

"Okay. But Michael?"

"What?"

"Nothing."

Was it only what he seemed to think—morbid curiosity? Wasn't it at least as much the case that she liked Michael? She balked at the word "love." But Joseph, evidently, had fallen in love with him. Why couldn't she, eventually?

She raised one partition and lowered another, turning the bathroom into the kitchen. As she rolled the Volkswagen to the tap, the bloody water sloshed about inside. She turned the faucet: not a drop. Recycling what was in the sac seemed tantamount to vampirism, but it was Michael's own fault for having taken two days' worth of water for his bath. Before she switched on the purifier she dipped a cup down into the water.

The transparent pink of a red balloon blown up almost to bursting. She could taste soap, but of his blood there was not a glimmer.

7 p.m.

"And where," Paul asked, blundering daintily in, "is our young Werther?" He put down a beribboned baggy on the Martian rock. Niobe came up to sniff at it.

"Gone. For good, I think."

"Oh damn. And I just made such an ass of myself with Marilyn insisting on *three* of these. Niobe, get off that."

"We can split the third one between us."

"And I meant to thank him for this." Jingling the bracelet. "Well, let's hope he hasn't gone and jumped into the Neckar. I wish, though, he had waited till he'd swallowed something to make him cheerful. Maybe you'd better swallow it."

"Me?"

"Life goes *on*, Ronny. Tomorrow and tomorrow and tomorrow. As you just said yourself, it's for the best. If he'd stayed you'd only have got entangled. You're well out of it. You know you are. Here, look." He snapped the ribbon, spread the yellow paper apart like the crinkly petals of some November flower, to reveal three wedges of sacher torte. "You see. Even in the midst of affliction Earth pours forth her blessing. I don't suppose there are any clean forks?"

"Use your fingers."

He already was.

"Guess what he—Oh, these are delicious."

"Then remember to say so—" He sprayed crumbs across the desk. "—to Marilyn."

"Guess what he stole."

"All my notes."

"No, not as bad as that."

"All yours."

"That picture of Joseph—the one I've kept all this time, that his wife painted."

"Oh, the little shit. That enamel frame must be worth a year's rent. I *told* you to hide all those things away. The minute Joseph called to say they were coming, I said put *that* where they won't see it."

"I did. He found it. I'd fixed an old holly of me in the frame, but it had come halfway out. He must have noticed. I just wish I knew if it were the picture or the frame that he wanted. If it was the frame I could feel righteous."

"I'm glad now I *didn't* get to thank him for the bracelet."

"Otherwise it's my just dessert."

"*Our* dessert," he said primly, breaking the third wedge in half. He compared the pieces carefully and took the larger for himself.

"Because *I* stole it when Joseph had just thrown *me* over. With, as I recall, a perfectly clear conscience."

Paul shook his head. "Love."

"Joseph does that to people."

"Apparently. But I don't see how. He's rather thick, he has *no* discernible gifts, and he's that homely he's almost grotesque. An indifferent physique. A complexion like a Matisse."

"A nose like a Brancusi," Veronica added.

"It's all he has. A noble nose. That's it."

"He's irresistible."

"*Ihr Gewaltigen!* Does that mean you let him have it? The whole, overweening amount he asked for?"

"He always pays me back. With interest."

"How much this time, Ronny? How much?"

"Five thousand. He asked for ten."

"I throw up my arms," he said, though this was only a figure of speech, for his arms hung, as ever, lifelessly at his sides, "and ask no more. You are a fool for love."

11 p.m.

As he wound back the tape, Paul's hand brushed the acoustics control, and when the music began again the whole room resounded with the doctor's abrasive triumphings: "*Oh! meine Theorie! Oh mein Ruhm. Ich werde unsterblich! Unsterblich! Unsterblich!*" Immersed and unaware, he didn't notice that *Wozzeck* had spilled over into Veronica's part of the room until, at the start of Act Three, the phone rang, "Oh! Oh, I'm sorry." He pulled back the sound just as Veronica answered. "If that's Joseph," he said warningly.

The screen was blank, allowing her to hope that Paul had guessed right. A long silence and the screen still dead. Could it be Michael?

"Ronny? Hello?"

"Loren? Is that you, Loren?"

"Ronny, your screen is jammed. Can you hear me?"

"Loren?"

"I can't hear you, and there's no image."

"Loren, I think we have a bad connection. Why don't you"

"I'm going to hang up and"

"hang up dial again?"

"dial again."

She hung up and sat beside the phone waiting for it to ring. It didn't. This is what comes, she thought, of living in a country run by anarchists.

She checked to see if the phone was still tied on a line to the library. No. Then she located the problem: RECORD was on, and the tape had come to an end. As she removed it from the slot, half of the holly she'd put up front of Joseph's picture came out with it. Every face a little dimmer, every edge a little duller, as though Time had just taken a bite of her mind.

In ballpoint on the back of the holly someone—Michael—had written: "This is just to say 'Thanks for a lovely time!' and 'Till we meet again!' The tape is for Joseph. Please see that he gets it. Ever, Michael D."

She put the tape back in the phone (Loren, evidently, had given up), reversed it, and pushed REPLAY.

First the time—5:58—and date—2/7/97—flashed red on black as an operator chirruped: ". . . through your call to New York, sir." The screen was blank while the phone rang: an unlisted number.

Then, a clown's face. A most literal and traditional clown it was—with a bright red bulb of a nose, maniac eyes, a broad, foolish frown, and tonsured crimson hair sprouting vividly from chalk-white flesh. "Blessed be the holy name of Jesus," the clown piped in a piercing falsetto.

"Hi, Lulu," Michael said. (His own features unrecorded throughout the call.) "Is Cole there?"

"Michael! Michael Divine?" the clown shrilled. "Where *are* you?"

"Germany. Is *Cole* there?"

"Just a moment, Michael. Oh, Father Severson! Yoo-hoo, Father Severson! Michael, if you would hold the line just one minute I will see if I can find him. I think he may be hearing confession. Oo La La!" He rolled his eyes and tongue about in a parody of *voluptas*.

"I'll hold the line."

"I won't say who it is. I'll let you surprise him!" The clown's face moved out of the camera's eyes, revealing a few square feet of sandalwood wall and a severe, silver-on-teak crucifix.

Then—another phone, a smoother voice: "Sassahty of Jesus, Fathuh Severson speakin!" Before black drapes, Cole Severson, blond and blandly Byronic, regarded the screen of his own phone with a smile of cautious satisfaction.

"Hi, Cole."

"Wail, wail, wail. As ah live an' breathe! If it ain't my old frayend Michael Dee-vahn! Long tom, no see."

"Yeah."

"What *can* ah do for yahl? In a word."

"I guess you know."

Cole dropped his accent. "And I guess *you* can say."

"What you didn't do the last time."

"Through no fault of my own, dear child. You rather disappeared."

"I'm willing to come back now. On one condition."

"It isn't for you to be making conditions."

"On one condition."

"And what is that, Michael?"

"That you document the whole thing, as it happens, all the gory details. And that you send the installments to someone who—whose address I'll—I don't have it now but—"

"Oh-ho. It's like that, is it?"

"That's my condition."

"A pleasure to fulfill it, Michael. Tears? Are you crying real tears? Bless your soul. But you still haven't said, have you, just what it is you want me—the Society, rather—to do?"

"I want you to kill me."

"Gently, lad, gently. Even on telstar, you know, there are monitors. We don't live, like you Europeans, in a state of anarchy. We have a government, for which I daily give thanks to God."

"I want to join the Society of Jesus. Is that better?"

"You'll take the three vows?"

"However many you like."

Cole raised his voice: "Lulu!"

And the falsetto: "Father?"

"You may join us on the other line."

The screen divided: Cole on the right, Lulu on the left. His costume now included a little straw hat with a big floppy fuchsia daisy sticking up from it.

"Lulu, Michael will be coming to live with us at the rectory. He wishes to return to a religious life."

"Oh!" Lulu squealed. "How simply divine!"

"Why don't you sing a song for Michael—to welcome him home."

Lulu bowed his head submissively. Then, looking earnestly into the telephone, he broke into a florid, forlorn rendition of Schubert's *Ave Maria*. Tears rolled down from both his eyes, and, triggered by tweaks of his bulbous nose, his little straw hat lifted off his head each time he reached a particularly high note. The daisy wobbled on its wire stem.

Veronica turned it off.

Paul was standing beside her. "God," he said, "don't they break your heart?"

In The Borrowers, *one of the classic fantasy novels of our time, Mary Norton explained the frequent disappearance of household objects by postulating the existence of a race of tiny people who live by scavenging the leavings of our larger world: if pins, paperclips, pencil stubs disappear, if you* know *you put the scissors in that drawer and now you can't find them, if you put things down for a moment and they vanish forever the moment you turn your head . . . why, the borrowers have taken them.*

Here writer Phyllis Eisenstein—one of the brightest new talents in SF, author of Born to Exile *(Arkham House),* Sorcerer's Son *(Del Rey Books), and* Shadow of Earth *(Dell)—offers an alternative explanation for the same phenomenon, one equally plausible but much more unsettling.*

PHYLLIS EISENSTEIN
Lost and Found

It started one winter night when I couldn't find the screwdriver.

I told my roommate Cath, "I'm sure I left it on top of the refrigerator. I used it to put the light fixture back together, and then I laid it on top of the fridge while I made a snack. That wasn't more than three hours ago, and now it's gone."

"The roaches borrowed it," said Cath, who was washing the week's accumulation of dirty dishes. "You always say they'll walk off with the place someday."

"Be serious."

"Poltergeists, then."

I poked her shoulder. "Did you take it?"

"I was in the living room reading Freud. Do I need a screwdriver for that?"

"Well, what happened to it, then?"

"Honest to God, Jenny, I don't know. It'll turn up. What thief would climb three flights of stairs just to steal a lousy screwdriver?"

I wondered about that. For several minutes I'd felt that someone was standing behind me, watching me. Not Cath; someone else, someone I couldn't see. The suggestion of a burglar struck too close to my own suspicions. I resisted the impulse to peek into the broom closet, but I did check the back door; it was securely locked.

I shook off my uneasiness and returned to my room, determined to study through the rest of the evening. I'd been loafing a lot lately; with exams a week away, I played solitaire at my desk rather then review my chemistry notes. It helped dispel the tension. I sat down and picked up the deck. After half a dozen poor rounds, I promised myself I'd play only one more, and I dealt it out with vicious slaps. When the game turned sour, I began cheating, but no mater what I did, I couldn't win. No wonder: pawing through the cards, I realized that the ace of spades and the ten of clubs were missing. I peered under the desk; there was the ten, but no ace. I checked the drawers, the bookcase, the floor beneath the bed, the dart board. Nowhere. I'd won a game earlier in the day—how could I have done that without the ace of spades?

If Cath was playing a joke on me, I'd wring it out of her.

She must have heard me step into the living room, for she looked up from her book. "Jenny, you look terrible. What's the matter? You *can't* be studying too hard."

"Did you take a card from my desk?"

"Card? What kind of card?"

"A playing card."

"Today?"

"A little while ago."

"I haven't been in your room today."

"The ace of spades is gone."

Cath shut her book and shook her head. "That's terribly symbolic," she said. With her green pen, she added small horns to the portrait of Freud gracing the dust jacket. "I'd say you were getting absentminded, Jenny." She meditated a moment. "Knowing you, of course, you couldn't have used it as a bookmark."

I sat on the arm of the chair. "Cath," I said very seriously, "have you ever thought you might be a kleptomaniac?"

She looked me in the eye. "No, but I guess *you* have. Couldn't you use your time a little more constructively?"

Growling under my breath, I took the hint and stalked back to my room. I sat down at my desk, put my feet up, and let my eyes and mind roam. Something was odd about the bookshelf in front of me. My University mug was gone. My quartz paperweight was gone. My leatherbound copy of *Othello* was gone. I turned in my chair and looked at the rest of the room, wondering where I could have put the stuff. Was I sleepwalking? My tennis racket was missing from its peg above the bed; the stack of records on the floor had shrunk by half. I looked into the wastebasket, wondering if I had unconsciously thrown anything there, but it was empty. That wasn't right: hadn't I thrown away some old English papers this afternoon?

Where *was* everything?

Again, the creepy feeling of being secretly observed stole over me. Someone was staring at my back, perhaps waiting for me to leave so he could come in and get more. More what? None of my stuff was particularly valuable.

I heard a muffled shuffling noise behind me. I turned and looked at the closet door. I didn't have the nerve to open it.

I shouted, "Cath!"

Suddenly I felt naked and weaponless. What if it *was* a burglar? He was trapped in there, probably desperate, maybe armed. Even though there were two of us, it might be wiser to call the cops and let them handle it.

Cath came in. "What do you want?"

"The closet," I whispered.

"What?"

"I think there's someone inside."

We stood there a moment. I could feel my guts twisting. The last thing on earth I wanted to do was open that door. I wanted to run out of the room, out of the apartment, as fast as I could.

Cath shrugged, stepped forward, turned the doorknob, and yanked the closet door open.

My heart, and everything under it, suddenly pressed at the top of my throat.

There was nothing in the closet but clothing.

I had a mild case of jitters for the next couple of minutes. Cath clucked her tongue, then led me to the kitchen and poured me a cup of tea.

"Take it easy, Jenny," she said, forcing me into a chair by the table. "You can't crack up till after exams are over."

"I . . . I . . . thought . . . someone was in the closet." I gulped some tea; the cup clattered as I set it down in its saucer.

"We've been home all afternoon and evening. How could anyone have gotten in?"

I attempted a nonchalant shrug, but it turned into a shudder. "I don't know."

Cath pulled me into the living room after I finished my tea, and she handed me a paperback sex novel. "You sit in this nice soft chair and read something light, to relax. I'll sit over there and study."

I read, but I couldn't concentrate; I was too nervous to string the words and phrases together.

Then I heard something. A scuffling, rustling sound.

"Did you hear something?" I asked. "From my room?"

"Roaches," Cath said without looking up. "Or mice. Forget it."

I heard it again. "Cath!" I gasped hoarsely, springing across the room. She caught my arm as I passed her. "Maybe we'd better go to a movie."

Then there was another noise, louder this time.

"I hear something in your room," she said.

"Roaches," I whispered.

"Okay, let's see what it is. Wait here a minute." She went to the kitchen and returned with two long, sharp carving knives. She gave one to me.

"What do you think it is?" I murmured.

"Some nut trying to get in a third-floor window."

But when we stepped into my room, we saw that the window was closed and locked, as it had been for several months. Outside, silent snow fell vertically through the darkness; the thick, white frosting it had slathered on the windowsill remained velvet-smooth, undisturbed. The closet door, however, was slightly ajar, although Cath had shut it firmly just a little while ago.

"There can't be anyone in the closet," Cath said. "There simply can't be." Still, she went to the closet and threw open the door.

Someone was in the closet, all right. Two someones, both young and muscular, one male, one female. They were fair-haired and evenly tanned, and they wore only scanty metallic briefs and weblike sandals. We stared; they stared back.

"Are you Jennifer Erica Templeton?" the man demanded of Cath.

"Not me," said Cath. "Her." The tip of her knife wavered in my direction.

"Jennifer Erica Templeton?" he asked me. "Born June 3, 1958 in Chicago, to Albert and Sara Templeton; student at the University of Chicago from 1977 to 1985, BA, MA, PhD Anthropology?" He rattled off the data as if it were name rank and serial number, and then he paused expectantly.

His friend nudged him. "I told you this was only '79, dear. She doesn't have any degrees yet, and her field is still chemistry."

I found myself nodding.

The man lunged, grabbing at my head. As I elbowed him in the solar plexus, I heard a snipping sound behind my right ear, and then he reeled away, clutching a handful of my hair. "Authentic souvenir!" he croaked.

"All right, all right," the woman said, hauling him back into the oddly deep space of the closet. "Now that you've got one, too, let's go home!" She slammed the door, and for several seconds a rummaging noise sounded beyond it. Then there was silence.

Cath stared at me, her mouth agape. She reached out and very slowly and gingerly pulled open the door. The strangers had vanished; once again, the closet was shallow and inhabited only by my clothes.

"Jenny," Cath whispered, "what's going on?"

I looked at her for a minute, and then I looked at the closet. I fingered my scalp where the spray of stubble interrupted the smooth flow of hair. "I'm not sure," I replied, "but tomorrow I think I'm going to transfer to the Anthropology Department."

Other societies have venerated the aged, but in today's America they are worse than despised—they are ignored. Old people are expected to fade quietly away without fuss or muss or smell, expelled from a system that no longer has any use for them and would much rather never hear from or of them again. And so in every large city you can see the old folks sitting on their park-bench homes with their possessions in a paper bag, hoping that it won't snow that night, or that they'll at least be able to find a hot-air vent to sleep on.

In the brilliant story that follows—one of his UrNu *series about life in a domed Atlanta of the future—Bishop demonstrates once again that old folks are still* people, *capable of creativity, love, joy, sorrow, still able to grow even in the shadow of the grave.*

Michael Bishop—perhaps the best of all the new SF writers—has lost so many Hugo and Nebula awards by now that he has taken to referring to himself as "the Harold Stassen of Science Fiction." His books include Stolen Faces *(Dell),* A Little Knowledge *(Berkley),* A Funeral for the Eyes of Fire *(Ballantine),* Under the Shattered Moons *(DAW), and the forthcoming* Catacomb Years *(Berkley/Putnam), a collection of his* UrNu *stories.*

MICHAEL BISHOP
Old Folks at Home

1. *"sold down the river"*

At a stilly six o'clock in the morning Lannie sat looking at the face of her visicom console in their sleeper-cove, Concourse B-11, Door 47, Level 3. Nausea was doing its stuff somewhere down in her plumbing: bubbles and fizzes and musical flip-flops. And Sanders—Sanders, her blue-jowled lummox—he lay sprawled snoring on their bed; if Levels 1 and 2 fell in on them, he'd still sleep, and he didn't have to get up for another hour. But Lannie intended to fight it; she wasn't going to the bath booth yet, no matter how tickly sick she began to feel.

That would wake Zoe, and she wasn't ready for Zoe yet, maybe not for the rest of the day.

Putting her arms across her stomach, Lannie leaned over the glowing console and tapped into the *Journal/Constitution* newstapes. Day 13 of Winter, 2040, New Calendar designation. Front page, editorial, sports: peoplenews, advertisements, funnies.

Then, in among the police calls and obituaries, a boxed notice:

WANTED: Persons over sixty to take part in the second phase of a five-year old gerontological study funded by the URNU HUMAN DEVELOPMENT COMMISSION. Health and sex of applicants of no consequence; our selections will be based on a consideration of both need and the individual interest of each case. Remuneration for the families of those applicants who are selected. Contact DR. LELAND TANNER, or his representative, UrNu Human Development Tower.

Lannie, still clutching her robe to her middle, held this "page" on the console. After two or three read-throughs she sat back and gazed at the room's darkened ceiling. "Eureka," she whispered at the acoustical punctures up there. "Eureka."

Sanders, turning his mouth to the pillow, replied with a beluga-like whistling.

She wasn't deceived, Zoe wasn't. She read the newstapes, too, maybe even more closely than they did, and if Melanie and Sanders thought they could wool-eye her with this casual trip to the UrNu Human Development Tower, they needed to rethink their clunky thinking. I wasn't born yesterday, Zoe thought. Which was so ludicrous a musing that right there in the quadrangle, on the gravel path among the boxed begonias and day lilies, Sanders craning his head around like a thief and Melanie drawing circles in the gravel with the toe of her slipper, Zoe chuckled: *Clucka-clucka-cluck.*

"Mother, hush!"

"'Scuse me, Lannie, 'scuse me for living." Which was also reasonably funny. So she *clucka-clucked* again.

Sanders said, "What does he want to meet us out here for? How come he can't conduct this in a businesslike fashion?" Sanders was a freshman investment broker. He had had to take the afternoon off.

"Not everyone runs their business like you do," Melanie answered. She was a wardrobe model for Consolidated Rich's.

It was 2:10 in the afternoon, and the city's technicians had dialed up a summery 23° C. in spite of its being the month Winter. The grass in the quadrangle, as Zoe had already discovered by stepping off the path, was Astroturf; and for sky the young Nobles and Melanie's mother had the bright, distant geometry of Atlanta's geodesic dome. On every side, the white towers of that sector of the Human Development complex called the Geriatrics Hostel. Many of the rooms had balconies fronting on the garden, and at various levels, on every side but one (the intensive-care ward), curious faces atop attenuated or bloated bodies stared down on them, two or three residents precariously standing but many more seated in wheelchairs or aluminum rockers. Except for these faces, the Nobles and the old woman had the carefully landscaped inner court . to themselves.

"Home, sweet home," Zoe said, surveying her counterparts on the balconies. Then: "Sold down the river, sold down the river."

"Mother, for God's sake, stop it!"

"Call it what you want to, Lannie, I know what it is."

"Leland Tanner," a young man said, surprising them. It was as if he had been lying in wait for them behind a bend in the path, the concealing frond of a tub-rooted palm.

Leland Tanner smiled. More than two meters tall, he had a horsy face and wore a pair of blue-tinted glasses whose stems disappeared into shaggy gray hair. A pleasant-looking fellow. "You're Zoe Breedlove," he said to her. "And you're the Nobles. . . . I thought our discussion might be more comfortable out here in the courtyard." He led them to a ginkgo-shaded arbor on one of the pathways and motioned the family to a stone bench opposite the one he himself took up. Here, they were secure against the inquisitive eyes of the balcony-sitters.

"Zoe," the young man said, stretching out his long legs, "we're thinking of accepting you into our community."

"Dr. Tanner, we're very—" Melanie began.

"Which means I'm being sold down the river."

"Damn it, Mother!"

The young man's eyes, which she could see like clear drops of sapphire behind the colored lenses, turned toward her. "I don't know what your daughter and your son-in-law's motives are, Zoe, but it may be that—on down the Chattahoochee, so to speak—you'll find life a little better than it was on the old plantation. You may be freer here."

"She's as free as she wants to be with us," Sanders said, mounting his high horse. "And I don't think this plantation metaphor's a bit necessary." His foot always got caught in that wide, loose stirrup: his mouth.

Only the young doctor's eyes moved. "That may be true, Mr. Noble," he said. "In the Urban Nucleus everyone's freedoms are proscribed equally."

"The reason they're doing it," Zoe said, putting her hands on her papery knees (she was wearing a disposable gown with clip-on circlets of lace at sleeves and collar), "is 'cause Lannie's gone and got pregnant and they want me out of the cubicle. They're not gonna get off Level 3 anytime soon, and four rooms we've got. So they did this to get me out."

"Mother, we didn't *do it* to get you out."

"I don't know why we did it," Sanders said, staring at the gravel.

Zoe appealed to the intent, gracefully lounging young doctor. "It could sleep in my room, too, that's the shame of it: it could sleep in my room." Then, chuckling again, "And they may be sorry they didn't think of that before hauling me up here. Like two sneaky Simon Legreedies, Lannie and Sandy."

"Dr. Tanner," Melanie said, "we're doing this for her as much as for ourselves and the baby. The innuendoes about our motives are only—"

"Money," Zoe said, rubbing her fingers against her thumb like a usurer. "I read that box in the newstapes, you know. You're auditioning for old people, aren't you?"

"Sort of like that," Leland Tanner said, standing. "Anyway, Zoe, I've made up my mind about you." Under a canopy of ginkgo leaves he stared down at the group huddled before him, his eyes powerful surrogates for the myopic ones on the balconies.

"Don't take me," Zoe said, "it'll serve them right."

"From now on," the young man said, "we're going to be more interested in serving *you* right. And in permitting you to serve."

Sanders, her son-in-law, lifted his head and squinted through the rents in the foliage. "It's supposed to be Winter," he said. "I wish they'd make it rain." But an even, monochromatic afternoon light poured down, and it was 23° C.

2. *to marry with the phoenix*

She was alone with young Leland in a room opening onto the garden, and he had pulled the curtain back so that she could see out while they talked. A wingback chair for her, with muted floral-print upholstery. Her feet went down into a pepper-and-salt shag carpet. Tea things on a mahogany coffee table, all of the pieces a dainty robin's-egg blue except for the silver serving tray.

Melanie and Sanders had been gone thirty minutes, but she didn't miss them. It didn't even disturb her that it might be a long while—a good long while—before she saw them again. The ginkgo trees in the garden turned their curious oriental leaves for her examination, and the young man was looking at her like a lover, although a cautious one.

"This is a pretty room," she said.

"Well, actually," he said, "it's a kind of decompression chamber, or air-lock, no matter what the comfortable trappings suggest. Usually I'm not so candid in my explanation of its function; most prospective residents of the Geriatrics Hostel must be introduced into their new environment slowly, without even a hint that a change *is* occurring. But you, Zoe, not only realize from the outset what's going on, you've also got the wit to assimilate the change as if it were no more significant than putting on a new pair of socks."

"That's not so easy any more, either."

He tilted his head. "Your response illustrates what I'm saying. I judge you to be a resilient woman; that, along with my interview with your family, induces me to select you as a candidate for the second stage of our study. I can use a term like *air-lock* to describe this sitting room without flustering you. Because, Zoe, if you decide to stay with us, and to press your candidacy, you'll be very much like an astronaut going from the cramped interior of a capsule—via this room, your air-lock—into the alien, but very liberated realm of outer space."

"First a sold-down-the-river darkie. Now a spaceman." Zoe shook her head and looked at the damp ring her teacup had made on the knee of her gown. "Well, I'm old, Mr. Leland, but I'm still around. More than you can say for slaves and astronauts, thank goodness in the one case, too bad in the other."

Young Mr. Leland's violet eyes (he had taken those hideous glasses off) twinkled like St. Nick's, but he didn't laugh, not with his voice. Instead he said, "How old are you, Zoe?"

"Sixty-seven. Didn't *they* tell you?"

"They told me. I wanted to see if you would."

"Well, that's correct. I was born in 1973, before the domes ever was, and I came into Atlanta from Winder, Georgia, during the First Evacuation Lottery. Barely twenty-two, virgin and unmarried, though in those days you'd best not admit to the first condition any more than you had now. Met my husband, Rabon Breedlove, when the dome wasn't even a third finished. But a *third* of my life—my entire youth, really—I spent in the Open, not even realizing it was dangerous, the city politicians even said traitorous, to be out there." A few bitter, black leaves adhered to the robin's-egg blue china as she turned her empty cup.

"And how old is Melanie, then?"

"Twenty-eight or -nine. Let's see." She computed. "Born in 2011, a late child and an only one. Rabon and me had tried before, though. Four times I miscarried, and once I was delivered of a stillborn who went into the waste converters before we had a chance to put a name on it. Boy or girl, they didn't tell us. Then Melanie, a winter baby, when we thought we'd never have one. All the other times was forgotten, a pink and living tadpole we had then, Rabon and me."

"Your husband died when she was eight?"

"Embolism."

Young Mr. Leland stood up and went to the window drapes. She saw how the shag lapped over his work slippers, even though his feet were big: good and big. "The Geriatrics Hostel has two parts, Zoe, one a nursing home and hospital, the other an autonomous community run by the residents themselves. You don't need the first, but you can choose to be a candidate for the second."

"I got a choice, huh?"

"We coerce no one to stay here—but in the case of those committed to the hostel's nursing sector it's often impossible for the residents to indicate choice. Their families make the decisions for them, and we then do the best we can to restore their capacity for reasoned, self-willed choice."

"What does it mean, I'm a 'candidate'?"

"If you so decide, you'll go into one of our self-contained communities. Whether you remain with that group, however, is finally up to you and the members of the group themselves."

"S'pose the old fuddy-duddies don't like me?"

"I view that as unlikely. If so, we find you another family or permit you to form one of your own. No losers here, Zoe."

Very quietly she said, "Hot damn." Young Mr. Leland's eyebrows went up. "An expression of my daddy's."

And came down again into an expression amusingly earnest. "Your husband's been dead twenty years. How would you like to get married again?"

"You proposin'?"

Well, he *could* laugh. With his voice as well as his eyes. She was hearing him. "No, no," he said, "not for myself. For the first septigamic unit we want to introduce you to. Or for the six remaining members of it, that is. You'll have six mates instead of one, Zoe. Three husbands and three wives, if those terms mean anything at all in such a marriage covenant. The family name of the unit is Phoenix. And if you join them your legal name will be Zoe Breedlove-Phoenix, at least within the confines of the Geriatrics Hostel itself. Elsewhere, too, if things work out as we wish."

"Sounds like a bridge group that's one short for two tables."

"You'll be doing more than playing bridge with these people, Zoe. No false modesty, no societally dictated inhibitions. And the odd number is a purposive stipulation, not merely a capricious way of messing up card games. It prevents pairing, which can sometimes occur on an extremely arbitrary basis. The old NASA programmers recognized this when they assigned *three* men to the Apollo missions. The same principle guides us here."

"Well, that's fine, Mr. Leland. But even with those astronauts, you'll remember, only two of 'em went down honeymooning."

His horsy face went blank, then all his cheek- and jawbones and teeth worked together to split the horsiness with a naughty-boy grin. He scratched his unkempt hair: shag on top, shag around his shoes. "Maybe I ought to renege on the Phoenix offer and propose for myself, Mrs. Breedlove. All I can say to answer you is that honeymooning needn't be what tradition only decrees. For the most part, the septigamic covenant has worked pretty well these last five years at the hostel. And your own wit and resilience make me believe that you can bring off your candidacy and marry with the Phoenix. Do you wish to become a candidate, Zoe?"

Zoe put her cup on the silver serving tray. "You know, Mr. Leland, you shoulda been a comedy straight man." By which she didn't mean to imply that he was even half so humorless as Sanders Noble. No, sir. That Sanders could stay sour in a room full of laughing gas.

"Missed my calling. But do you want to?"

"Oh, I do," Zoe said, taking what he'd served up. "I do."

3. *helen, and the others*

Dr. Leland Tanner made a call on an intercom unit in the sitting room. Then, leaning over Zoe so that she could smell the sharp cologne on him, he kissed her on the forehead. "I'm going out now, Zoe. If you decide to stay, you'll see me only infrequently; your new family will occupy your time and your attention. There's no interdict, however, on associating with the culturally immature. If you like, you can see me or anyone else younger than yourself. Just let me know."

"Then I s'pose I shall, Mr. Leland."

"'Bye," and he strode through the whipping shag, saluted at the sliding glass doors, and went out into the quadrangle. In only a moment he was lost to Zoe on one of the foliage-sheltered paths, and the calm, curious ginkgo trees held her amazed interest until an inner door opened and a thin woman with close-cropped gray hair came in to her.

"Zoe Breedlove?" A Manila envelope clasped in front of her, the newcomer looked *toward* the wingback but not exactly *at* it. A handsome, frail woman with silverly opaque eyes and an off-center smile.

"That's me," Zoe said. The other's eyes focused on her then, and the smile firmed up. The woman navigated through waves of carpet to a chair opposite Zoe's, and they faced each other across the tea service.

"I'm Helen," the woman said. "Helen Phoenix. Parthena and Toodles wanted another man, I think, but I'm happy Leland found somebody who won't have to compete with our memories of Yuichan. That would have been unfair to you."

"Yui-chan?" The word sounded foreign, particularly to a dome-dwelling Georgia girl. Whereas Helen's accent marked her as no native to Atlanta. New York? Something cosmopolitan, anyhow: once.

"Yuichan Kurimoto-Phoenix. He was born in Kyoto, but he behaved like a raving Italian. Had execrable taste in everything; not a bit subtle. There's an unpainted plaster-of-Paris squirrel on the bole of one of the trees in the garden: Yuichan's doing." Helen lowered her head. "A lovely man; just lovely."

"Well, I hope the others don't think I'm even going to try to take Yoo-chi's place. I don't even know anything about China."

The woman's smile died at the corners of her mouth, then slowly grew back. "Nevertheless," she said, "you may be more like Yuichan than you know. Which is all to the good: a bonus for us. And the question of your competing with Yuichan's memory won't enter into our appreciation of you at all. I'm sure of that. Toodles only favored another man, I'm sure, because she's a voluptuary and thinks Paul and Luther inadequate for our servicing."

Servicing: that probably meant exactly what she thought it did. Zoe leaned over the coffee table. "Would you like some of this tea Mr. Leland left with me?"

"Please. And if you'll push the service to one side, Zoe—may I call you Zoe?—I'll introduce you to the others even before we go upstairs. That's an advantage you'll have over them, but probably the only one. We hardly begrudge it."

"Good. I could use an evener." And it was after pushing the tea service aside and while watching Helen take the photographs and printouts out of the Manila envelope that Zoe realized Helen was blind. The opaque eyes worked independently of her smile and her hands: the eyes were beautiful, somehow weightless ball bearings. Mechanical moving parts in a body that was all Siamese cat and animal silver. Without fumbling, Helen's small hands laid out the pictures and the data sheets. Reminiscently, Zoe touched one of the photographs.

"You can examine it all while I drink my tea, Zoe. I won't bother you."

The top sheet on the pile was neatly computer-typed. Zoe held it up and tilted it so that she could read it.

THE PHOENIX SEPTIGAMOKLAN

Covenant Ceremony:

Day 7 of Spring, 2035, New Calendar designation.

Septigamoklanners:

M. L. K. Battle (Luther). *Born July 11, 1968, Old Calendar designation. No surviving family. Last employer: McAlpine Construction and Demolition Company. Septigamoklan jack-o-trades and activity-planner. Ortho-Urbanist, lapsed, age-exempted. Black.*

Parthena Cawthorn. *Born November 4, 1964, o.c.; Madison, Georgia. A son Maynard, a daughter-in-law, and three grandchildren: enfranchised UrNu citizens. Last employer: Inner Earth Industries. Sgk artisan and folklorist. Ortho-Urbanist, semiactive. Black.*

Paul Erik Ferrand. *Born October 23, 1959, o.c.; Bakersfield, California. Family members (children, grandchildren, great-grandchildren) in the Urban Nuclei of Los Angeles and San Francisco. Last employer: (?). Unclassifiable Mystic, age-exempted. White.*

Yuichi Kurimoto (Yuichan). *Born May 27, 1968, o.c.; Kyoto, Japan. Children, grandchildren, great-grandchildren alive in Kyoto and Tokyo. Last employer: Visicomputer Enterprises, Atlanta branch. Sgk legislator. Neo-Buddhist, lapsed, nationality-exempted. Oriental.*

Joyce Malins (Toodles). *Born February 14, 1971, o.c.; Savannah, Georgia. No surviving family. Last employer: Malins Music, Voice, and Dance. Sgk musician. Ortho-Urbanist, lapsed, age-exempted. White.*

Helen Mitchell. *Born July 11, 1967, o.c.; Norfolk, Virginia. A son in the Washington UrNu, a daughter in the Philadelphia UrNu. Last employer: UrNu Civil Service, Atlanta branch. Sgk mediator. Ortho-Urbanist, semiactive. White.*

Jeremy Zitelman (Jerry). *Born December 9, 1970, o.c.; No surviving family. Last employer: University of Georgia, Urban Extension, Astronomy Department. Sgk historian. Recidivist Jew, age-exempted. White.*

A mixed lot, Zoe decided: a party assortment. Over the capsuled-biography of Yuichi Kurimoto the word DECEASED was stamped in large, double-line-red letters which did not conceal the information under them. Zoe looked at the photographs and tried to match them up with the résumés (they weren't very good photographs); she got them all matched up, but it was pretty apparent that some of the pictures had been taken years ago. For instance, Paul Erik Ferrand, supposedly just over eighty, was a rakish, lupine man wearing a style of cravat that hadn't been fashionable in two decades. Before their names and faces meant anything Zoe would have to meet these people: in the flesh.

"Is that what I'll be—a septigamoklanner—if y'all like me?"

"That's an institute word, Zoe, made up by someone who didn't know what to call a family like ours. Don't worry. None of us use it. You see, these information sheets contain only passed-upon, UrNu-validated 'facts': impersonal and bureaucratic. Jerry or I, either one, could have put a little pizzazz into the sketches. . . . Unfortunately, civil service sachems frown on pizzazz. . . ." Helen's voice trailed off.

"Well, that's encouraging—'cause I think I'd have a hard time thinking of myself as a . . . *septigamoklansperson*." A mouthful, that. "But in Yoo-chi's biography here, it says he was the family legislator. Does that mean, since I'm coming in for him, I have to put on his shoes and be a legislator?"

"No, no. On these official data sheets everyone's given a position, as if we were baseball players or chess pieces. Really, though, we do whatever we do best, and by defining ourselves in that way we become ourselves to the others. Later, someone will probably put a label on what you are. It won't be a Phoenix who does it, though."

"Mr. Leland?"

"Perhaps. A study is going on here, though we're mostly oblivious to it, and studies demand statistics and labels. A cosmic law, like gravitation and magnetism and whatnot."

"Well, if it was *age-exempted*, even an apple might not have to fall."

Helen's opaque eyes locked on her face. "An appropriate observation. But we do have a chance to do some naming of our own. Phoenix was our own choice, you know. Some of the other families in the Tower are Cherokee, Piedmont, O'Possum, and Sweetheart."

"Oh, those are good ones, too." They were, too; had what Helen would probably call pizzazz.

"Yes," Helen said, pleased. "Yes, they are."

4. *climbing jacob's ladder*

Zoe met them all at supper that evening. They ate in a room decorated with a quilted wall banner, and with several potted plants that Joyce Malins (Toodles) said she had bought from a slum-area florist in a place called the Kudzu Shop.

The Phoenix family had an entire suite of rooms, including a kitchen, on the Geriatrics Hostel's fourth floor, and this evening Luther, Toodles, and Paul had shared the cooking: corn bread, frozen vegetables, and pasta with a sauce of meat substitutes. Better than Lannie managed after two hours of sloozying around in new clothes for the lechers at Consolidated Rich's; better than Zoe usually did for herself, come to that. The table was round, and wooden, and big enough for seven people, a metal pitcher of cold, sweetened tea, and several china serving dishes. No attendants waited on them, Zoe noted, no nurses, no white-smocked young men with pursed lips. A biomonitor cabinet, to which they were all linked by means of pulse-cued silver bracelets, was the only alien presence in the dining room, and it kept quiet. (The people downstairs had a hookup to the monitor, though, she was sure of that.) Zoe self-consciously turned her own new bracelet, a handsome thing in spite of its being, also, a piece of medical equipment. Plugged in already she was, a rookie Phoenix.

Helen had introduced her. She was sitting between Helen and Jerry. Then clockwise beyond Helen: Parthena, Paul, Luther, and Toodles. Jerry was sitting in a wheelchair, a lap robe over his knees. The others, like Helen, looked pretty mobile—even the eighty-year-old Paul, whose eyes resembled a Weimaraner dog's and whose mouth still knew how to leer.

"How old are you, Zoe?" he asked, after the opening small talk had faded off into mumbles and spoon-rattling.

Helen said, "Paul!" Like Lannie shushing her, Zoe; only nicer.

"Bet she ain't as old as me. Three-to-one odds. Place your bets." He smacked his lips.

"No one's so old as that," Jerry said. Jerry's hair was a dandelion puff-ball: just that round, that gray, that delicate. His face was red.

"I'm sixty-seven," Zoe said. Second time today. But saying so didn't age you, just worrying about it.

"Young blood," the wide-faced black man said: Luther. His hair (she was comparing now) was the kind of white you see on a photograph negative, a darkness turned inside out. His hands, on either side of his plate, looked like the mallets on sledgehammers. "Hooooi! Old folks, we're being transfused, we're gettin' new blood."

"Toodles ain' the baby no mo'," Parthena said out of a tall, stern Zulu mask of a face. Plantation accent, Zoe noticed. Luther sounded more like Paul or Toodles than he did Parthena; except for that *Hooooi!* Except for that.

"How 'bout that, Toodles?" Paul said. "Puttin' your foot on the bottom rung of Jacob's ladder at last. I'm up the highest, but you've finally climbed on." Toodles, whose mouth was a red smear, a candy heart (even though no one wore lip ices or eye blacking any more), lowered a forkful of squash to reply, but crazy old Paul turned to Zoe again: "I'm up the highest, but I'm never gonna die. I was born in California."

"Which is your typical Ferrand-Phoenix *non sequitur*," Jerry said.

"I've never made an issue of being the youngest one here," Toodles interjected. "And I'm not disturbed by losing that position, either." Her jowly face swung toward Zoe. "Zoe, I bought that fuchsia and the coleus for your arrival today. Parthena and I walked into that jungle off New Peachtree and haggled with the little Eurasian shopkeeper over prices. Then we carried our purchases back, pots and all, no help from these noble gentlemen."

"Course," Parthena said, "that 'fo' she knew how old you was." Her Zulu mask smiled: perfect dentures. Taller than anyone else in the room, Parthena, even seated, loomed.

"Parthena, damn your black hide, you know that wouldn't've made any difference! It wouldn't've!" Toodles dropped her fork, her mouth silently working itself into a multiplex variety of lopsided O's.

"Joke," Parthena said. "Jes' funnin'."

"Well, what the hell's funny about my being younger than you old cadavers?" Her mascara, tear-moistened, was making crater holes out of her eyes. "What's so damn funny about that?!"

"What's she takin' on like this for?" Luther asked the table.

"Humor her," Jerry said, winking at Zoe from under his puffball. "She thinks she's in her period."

Which brought guffaws from Paul and Luther and pulled the roof down on everyone else. Rearing back as if bee-stung, Toodles knocked her chair over and stood glaring at each member of her family in turn. Not counting Zoe.

"Jackasses!" she managed. Then, more vehemently: "Limp ole noodles!" Her mouth had begun to look like a pattern on an oscilloscope. Zoe, in fact, saw that one of the miniature screens on the biomonitor cabinet was sending delicate, pale comets back and forth across its surface: Toodles pulsing into the hysterical.

In person, Toodles left off glaring and, without looking back, moved painfully, heavily, out of the dining room. A minute or two after her exit, the pale comets stopped whizzing. Not dead, Toodles wasn't; just out of range. Another cabinet would pick her up shortly.

"Silly biddy," Paul announced, chewing.

"Jerry's last remark was crude," Helen said. "A sort of crudity, Zoe, that he usually doesn't permit himself."

"Please believe that," the crimson-faced man said, wheeling himself back from the table. "Lately she's been upset. That she was on the verge, though, I didn't think. I'm sorry, I'm honestly sorry, you know." The chair powered him out the door.

"Hot damn," Zoe said. "Some debut."

"Ain' yo' fault," Parthena said. "She been eggcited. Las' two week, she knew we was gonna fine a 'placement for Yuichan, that's all."

"That's true," Helen said. "We argue like young married couples do sometimes, Zoe, but usually not before company and not very often. Ordinarily Toodles is a lovely woman. And the only explanations I can give for her behavior are the menfolk's bad manners and her excitement. Courting's always made her nervous; always."

"As for the sort of crudity you heard from *her*," Luther said, "that's her style. She don't mean nothin' by it, though, even when she's mad."

"Silly biddy," the time-blotched old Frenchman (or whatever he was) said. "Carry on like that, die before I will. . . . I ain't gonna die." He was the only one who finished eating what was on his plate. Once finished, long lips glistening, he let a red, translucent eyelid drop lasciviously over an amber eye: a wink. For Zoe.

5.   *rotational reminiscence*

Two hours later. The roof court of the UrNu Human Development

Tower, geriatrics wing. Temperature holding steady at 21° C. Night had risen as the city's fluorescent suns had been gradually dialed down.

The Phoenix had patched things up among themselves and now sat in a semicircle at a tower railing overlooking the Biomonitor Agency on West Peachtree and, ten floors down, a floodlit pedestrian park. All the Phoenix but that oddie, Paul: he still hadn't come up. Zoe put that old codger out of her mind, though. The rooftop was open and serene, and she had never seen such a pretty simulated twilight. Not much chance on Level 3, *under*. Now, winking on across the city's drying-into-the-violet skyscape, a thousand faint points of light. The breath sucked away just at the glory of it.

Jerry Zitelman-Phoenix maneuvered his wheelchair into position beside her. (Ramps and lift-tubes made it possible for him to go anywhere at all inside the complex.) "I want to apologize, Zoe, for my uncalled-for remark in your presence."

"I always try to apologize to the person who needs it."

"Me, too. Look, you can see she's back." And she was, Toodles: sitting with Luther, Parthena, and Helen and animatedly narrating another episode of her afternoon's shopping. "But you, too, need an apology for the disruption I made." Jerry said, "so to you also I say, 'Sorry.' "

Zoe accepted his apology, and Jerry began talking. He told her that on Thursday nights—alternate ones, anyhow, and it was Thursday night that night—the Phoenix clan had this screened section of the rooftop for whatever purpose they wished. He told her that tonight it was a game they called "rotational reminiscence" and that they were waiting for Paul, who never participated but who insisted on attending every session. The rules, Jerry said, were simple and would become clear once they started. Then, pointing to the darkened, concave hollow overhead, the honeycombed shell in which they all lived, he told her that in his youth he had been an astronomer.

"Even now," he said, "I can look up there at night and imagine the constellations rolling by. Oh, Zoe, it's just as plain as day—which is one more of your typical Ferrand *non sequiturs*, Zitelman version thereof. But it's true, I can. There's Cassiopeia, there's Ursa Major, there's Camelopardalis. . . . Oh, all of them I can see. The dome is no impediment to me, Zoe, but it's certainly no joyous boon either. That it isn't."

He went on. He told her that the only advantage the dome offered him was that he could just as easily imagine the constellations of the *Southern* Hemisphere passing in procession across its face. Sometimes he so imagined: Canis Minor, Hydra, Monoceros. There they all were, so dizzying in their splendor that he felt sure he would one day power his wheelchair right up into their diamond-dusted nets and connect the dots among them with the burning tip of a raunchy, green cigar. "Cigars I'm not allowed any more," he said. "Not even the neutered ones with no tobacco, no tar, and no taste. And stars . . . ?" He pointed at the dome. "Well," Zoe said, "we got three stars at least. And they move."

Jerry's puffball rolled back, his vein-blossomed cheeks shone with wan, reflected light. "Ah, yes. Girder-cars is what we've got there, Zoe. Torch-

light repairs on the dome. So they send out the magnetized girder-cars at
night and let us pretend, with these insulting sops to our memory, that the
sky hasn't been stolen. Pretty, though, I grant you." He was right. Artificial stars—only three—on a metal zodiac. How did the men inside
those topsy-turvy trolleys feel? What was that old song? She mentally
hummed a bit of it:

> *Would you like to ride on a star?*
> *Carry moonbeams home from afar?*

"Damn that old zombie!" Toodles suddenly said to them. "Let's go on
without Paul. He never contributes anyway."

"Yeah," Luther said. "Let's start."

Helen persuaded them to wait a few more minutes. OK with Zoe,
A-OK. She listened as Jerry related how he had been involved in a bone-
crushing, paralyzing automobile accident in 1989, when most of the old
"interstates" were falling into disuse: cracked pavements, weed-grown
shoulders, brambly medians. He hadn't walked since. "When it
happened, I'd never even had relations with a woman; impossible, after.
At night, sometimes, I'd cry. Just like that fellow in the Hemingway
book—except his legs, they weren't crushed; it was something else. So I
never got married until Dr. Tanner accepted me for the study here. Then
three wives at once I got. Now, in my old age, poor Yuichan dead, I'm
helping my spouses court a fourth one. Who can say it isn't a strange and
wizardly life, our pains and weaknesses notwithstanding?"

"Not me, Jerry," Zoe said. "Not me."

So Jerry went on and told her about how he had got his degree and then
moved into the dome and tried to teach astronomy by means of textbooks,
slide programs, and old films. He'd done it for almost twenty years, at
which point the city decided it was foolish to pay somebody to lecture
about a subject with so limited an application to modern society. "Fffft!"
Jerry said. "Fired. Me and others, too. A whole program, kaput!" He had
had to live on Teachers' Retirement and future-secure benefits in a Level 6
cubicle until—

"Howdy," Paul said. "Ain't you started yet?"

"Sit down," Luther said. "What have you been up to?"

Paul, running his fingers through tatters of thin hair, lowered himself
creakingly to the fore-edge of a chair between Parthena and Zoe.
"Fetched up some night things for our fiancée. She didn't bring
none with her." He looked at Zoe. And winked. "'Gainst my better
judgment, too."

"You mighty sweet," Parthena said. "Now let's get on with it."

They did. The rules were these: (1) Silence while the person whose turn
it was thought of a pre-Evacuation experience he wished to evoke for
himself or, better, himself and the others. (2) An evocation of that experience in one word, the settled-upon word to be spoken, very clearly,
only once. (3) An after-silence in which this word might resonate. (4) No
repetitions from previous games. (5) An automatic halt after each Phoenix

had had two turns. (6) In order to avoid a debilitating preoccupation with the past, no mention or replaying of any of the game's reminiscences before or after the sessions themselves.

Helen, a new Gardner-Crowell braille-writer in her hands, recorded the evening's twelve reminiscences and called down anyone who repeated any of the old shibboleths. As Zoe discovered, accusations of encroaching senility flew around the circle when this happened. No worries tonight, though. She had never played before, and there'd be no whistle-blowing no matter what words she spoke into the quiet ring of their anticipation.

"Three months," Toodles said. "It's been three months since we've done this. Back when Yuichan was ill."

"Go ahead, then," Helen said. "You start, Toodles."

The group's silence grew. The girder-cars above them slid in slow motion down the steeps of the dome. In three or four minutes Toodles dropped a word into the pooling dark, the well of their ancient breaths:

"*Fudgsicles*," she said.

Paul, Zoe noticed, had his head thrown all the way back over the top of his chair, his eyes all goggly and shiny. The old man's mouth was open, too. If he hadn't already moved his butt back into the chair, he would have fallen to the roof tiles.

It was Parthena's turn. Three or four minutes after Toodles' reminiscence, the tall black woman said,

"*Scup'nins.*" Scuppernongs, that meant. A kind of grape.

When the word had echoed in their heads for a while, Luther said, "Paul isn't going to say nothin', Zoe. You go ahead now. It's your turn." No, he wasn't going to say anything, Paul: he was still mouthing Parthena's word.

As for Zoe, she was ready. She had thought of it while Jerry was explaining the rules to her. But it wouldn't do to blurt it out, it wouldn't do to show she'd been thinking ahead of the game. (Surely, they all did it, though.) So she waited. Then, leaning forward to look into the pedestrian park below, she gave the word to her new family:

"*Fireflies. . . .*"

6.   *mount fujiyama and the orpianoogla*

In their suite on the fourth floor the Phoenix slept in a circular common room, their beds positioned around a hub where the self-locomoting biomonitor cabinet (the first of three on the floor) had already taken up its brooding watch. Each bed had a nightstand, an effects-bureau, and an easy chair in its vicinity, as well as plasti-cloth dividers that, at a finger's touch, would roll automatically into place. Since no one seemed to use these, Zoe, grateful to Paul for having fetched her a nightgown, got ready for bed in front of the others.

Like having six Rabons in the room with you. Well, five: Jerry had powered himself off somewhere. "Like some time to himself 'fo' turnin' in," Parthena said. But even five Rabons was plenty, even if they were decent enough not to devour you with their eyes. (Rabon never had been.)

Old Paul, of the five, excepted. Again.

Anyhow, it didn't take this creaky crew long to start plying the waters of Nod. No, sir. Everyone off, it seemed, but Zoe herself. She even heard Jerry come whirring back into the snore-ridden room and hoist himself out of the wheelchair onto his bed. In five or ten minutes he, too, was rowing himself under. Only Zoe had her head clear, her whole, fatigued body treading against the desire to be drowned in sleep. My sweet lord, what a day! Every bit of it passed in front of her eyes.

Then Zoe heard the sobs. For a long time she listened to them. It was Toodles, two beds away, heart-troubled Toodles.

Feeling for slippers that weren't there, Zoe got out of bed. She walked barefooted to the easy chair beside Toodles, sat down, and smoothed back the woman's moist, frizzly bangs. "Can you tell me what it is?"

Unnhuh; nope. Strangled, desperate noises.

"Is it about that supper-time business, Toodles? Hope not. Up against you I look like the . . . the Wicked Witch of the North." Which was a Glinda-the-Good lie if she'd ever told one: white lie, though.

Subsiding strangles—"It . . . isn't . . . that"—trailing off into hiccups. "Really . . . it . . . isn't . . . that." Apparently to prove this contention, Toodles pulled herself up to a sitting posture. Across her rumpled lap she reeled in, inch by hand-wrung inch, a dressing gown that had been spread out over her bedclothes. A corner of it went to her throat, and was held there. .

"What, then? Can you say?"

A modicum of control now. "Yuichan," Toodles said. "I was thinking of Yuichan. You see this robe, Zoe. . . . He gave me this robe." It was too dark to see well, but Toodles turned the robe toward her and displayed it anyway, an occasional hiccup unsteadying her hands. All Zoe got was a musty whiff of a familiar, kidneylike odor.

"Here," Zoe said, and punched on the reading light on Toodle's headboard. A circle of paleness undulated on the dressing gown. Execrable taste, Helen had said. And rightly: On one side of the robe, an embroidered, snow-covered peak; on the other (once Toodles had lifted the limp lapel so that she could see them), the words Mount Fujiyama. An ugly and smelly garment, no matter how you hemmed or whiffed it.

"Oh, I know it's not to everybody's taste," Toodles said. "But it reminds me of Yuichan. He mail-ordered it from San Francisco four years ago when he learned that there was a very sick Japanese woman in the nursing section of the hostel. That was just like Yuichan. He gave the robe to that poor woman. A coupla years later, when the woman died and her son threw away almost all of her effects, Yuichan brought the gown back and gave it to me. Oh, it was tight on me and it smelled like urine, all right, but I knew what spirit Yuichan gave it in and I had it washed and washed—till I was afraid it'd fall apart in the water." Toodles spread the dressing gown over her knees. "And tonight . . . tonight . . . it reminds me of him . . . of Yuichan . . . just ever so much." And propped her elbows on her shrouded knees and lowered her face into her hands.

The consolation Zoe gave Toodles was that of sitting beside her until the poor, blowsy woman, mascara long since washed away, fell into a sleep as mortally shallow as the crater holes of her eyes.

But the next afternoon, in the room they called the recreation center, Toodles sat at the battery-powered orpianoogla and led them all in a songfest: thin, strained vocal cords reaching for notes those cords couldn't remember. In fact, only Toodles had an unimpaired range, a bravura contralto that could soar like an undercourse glissador or tiptoe stealthily through a pianissimo lullaby. With one arm she led their singing, with her free hand she rippled the keys, punched buttons, flipped toggles, and mixed in the percussion. Nor did her heavy legs keep her from foot-pedaling like an unbeliever on burning coals. The whole suite of rooms reverberated with Toodles' music, and Zoe, clapping and croaking with the rest, wondered dimly if she had dreamed, only dreamed, the midnight despair of this boisterous Phoenix.

"Very good!" Toodles would shout at them between choruses. "Ain't you glad we're too old for them jackasses who passed the Retrenchment Edicts to come in here and shut us up?!"

Zoe was. Outlawed music they were souling on, outlawed lyrics and proscribed morals-corrupting rhythms. Old times. As they clapped and sang, Helen told Zoe that Toodles had once been a renaissance-wing headliner in a New Orleans hookah club. "Turn of the century and a few years after," Helen stage-whispered in her ear as they all clapped to the rumbling orpianoogla. "When she was forty she was doing a bushman, pop-op-rah review in D.C. Forty! Quite professional, the old newsfax say." Since '35, when the ward reps and urban councilmen panicked, those kinds of performances had been totally *nyetted*, at least in Atlanta. Who knew, these days, what other cities did?

"All right!" Toodles shouted. "This one's 'Ef Ya Gotta Zotta!' Way back to twenny-awht—tooo, evvverbodddy!"

So they all sang, the orpianoogla singlehandedly—literally singlehandedly—sounding like the entire defunct, blown-away, vinyl-scrutchy Benny Goodman Orchestra of a century ago. Or Glenn Miller's, maybe. This was the chorus:

> *Ef ya gotta zotta*
> *Thenna zotta wa me:*
> *Durnchur lay ya hodwah*
> *On tha furji Marie.*
> *Ef ya gotta zotta,*
> *Then ya gotta zotta wa me!*

My sweet lord! Zoe remembered the whole song, every kaporni word of all seven verses. She and Rabon had danced to that one; they'd done the buck-and-wing jitters in the remodeled Regency lobby ballroom. My sweet lord, she thought: "Ef Ya Gotta Zotta!"

But after the last sing-through of the chorus, Toodles barreled out of the renaissance-swing retrospective and into a hard, hard computer-augmented tour of late-twenties/early-thirties racked-and-riled terrorism. With the advent of this deliberate cacophony, old Paul stopped stomping and let his mouth fall open, just as it had during the rotational reminiscence. The others, like Zoe, irresistibly fell to swaying in their chairs.

Toodles sang the ominous lyrics, and sang them so certainly that you could look at her full, jowly face and see that despite the sags, and wens, and ludicrous, smeared lips, she was living every note, vivisecting every lurid word and dragging its guts out for the purpose of feeding her own and her listeners' irrational fears. (Which was fun: a musical horror movie.) Toodles sang, and sang, and sang. She sang "Walnut Shell Nightmare," "Tomb of the Pharaohs," "Crimson Clay Tidal Wave," and "Outside Sky." When the last note of the orpianoogla died away, a rain of bravos fell down on the (incredibly) beginning-to-blush Miz Joyce "Toodles" Malins-Phoenix. Even Paul joined in, though he stomped like a jackass rather than hallooed.

"Her first concert since Yuichan died," Helen whispered.

"Encore!" Jerry shouted. "That we wish more of!"

"Hooooi!" Luther said. "I ain't heard her sing or play so well since Year-end Week in '38."

"I'm in as fine a voice as I was thirty years ago," Toodles said, turning on her stool. "It's hard to believe and it sounds like bragging, but by God! it's the gospel truth."

"Damn straight," Luther said.

"You ain' done, though," Parthena said. "Finish out now like we awways do, 'fo' we have to go eat."

Toodles, turning back to the keyboard, honored this request. Ignoring the buttons, switches, and resonator pins on the console, she played with both hands: an old melody, two hundred years almost. Everyone sang, everyone harmonized. Zoe found that, just as with "Ef Ya Gotta Zotta," she remembered the words—every word, each one called to her lips from a time-before-time that had nothing to do with the Urban Nucleus, or with Sanders and Lannie, or with Mr. Leland and the Geriatrics Hostel. And it wasn't timesickness or nostalgia that fed her recollection of the lyrics (some things you don't ever want to go back to), but instead a celebration of the solidity of the present: this present: the moment itself. They all sang:

> 'Way down upon the Swanee River
> Far, far away,
> There's where my heart is turning ever,
> There's where the old folks stay.

They even sang the stanza about the old plantations and the plaintive line "Oh, darkies, how my heart grows weary," Luther and Parthena too, and none of what they sang distressed them. Stephen Foster somehow was and wasn't Stephen Foster when interpreted by an orpianoogla. Sticks and stones, Zoe thought, and names can never . . .

Why, only a week ago her own daughter had called her, during a moment of ill-concealed morning sickness, a mummified witch. Zoe had chuckled: *Clucka-clucka-cluck.* What else could she do? When you're two steps from the finish line, you laugh at the self-loathing insults of also-rans. You have to. Even in the melancholy performance of a nigh-on dead-and-gone work of a sure-enough dead-and-gone composer, Toodles' whole body laughed. Toodles was two steps from the finish line. They all were. And it certainly wasn't death they were running at, not as Zoe saw it. No, sir. Something else altogether; something else.

7. parthena

That evening, after the orpianoogla-assisted songfest, Parthena, Helen, and Jerry saw to the cooking of supper. And after supper Zoe helped these three clean up in the galley beside the dining room (whereas, downstairs, three levels under, Lannie and Sanders had only a kitchen board in their cubicle and no dining room at all). A beautiful day it had been, a zippity-doo-dah day if she'd ever lived one. Not since Rabon . . .

"You quilt?" Parthena asked her as they put the last of the china away. But Zoe's attention was momentarily elsewhere. Jerry, in his wheelchair, was handing the plates to Helen, and the blind woman was stacking them cleanly in the hanging plastic cabinet over the sink. Before beginning, Helen had produced a pair of miniature black goggles, or binoculars, from a dress pocket and snapped these on over her eyes with seemingly only a thin metal bridge-piece to support them. With these in place she moved as if sighted. And yet this was the first time she had worn the goggles in Zoe's presence.

"Hey, Zoe," Parthena said again. "You quilt?"

"You mean stitch squares together? Sew? Maybe. Things with my hands I could always bluff through. I'm a bluffer."

"Shoot, we ain' even axed you yet what you good at. Where you work 'fo' you got put on the Ole Folk Dole Role?"

"Photography," Zoe said. "I took pitchurs. Still ones and moving ones. And I was good, too, you know. If you want to know the truth, some of my still pitchurs are pretty moving."

They all laughed. Zoe told them how she and Rabon had been a team for both the *Journal/Constitution* combine and one of the visual-media affiliates; neither wrote copy ("I didn't have the schooling and Rabon hadn't put his to use that way"), but they could both wield cameras, video portables, and the instant-print-making varieties. She had been better than Rabon was, but from '01 to '09 she had been taken out of action four times by the onset of motherhood and he had got more commissions by virtue of his being insusceptible, as he put it, to pregnancy. But it had all been planned, and after Melanie was born the UrNu Sitter Mission Program had freed them both to pursue their careers. Sort of. They got docked an incredible number of earnies to have Lannie mission-sat for four hours a day, four days a week, she and Rabon splitting up the remaining hours and working less frequently as a team. But they'd done it, she and Rabon, and maybe it was only Lannie's having been their only child that had caused her to grow up a gimme girl and a sometimes-sweet, more-usually-petulant young woman. What lovely portraits Zoe had made of her when she was little, ole sweet-treat Lannie. In a telecom to her that morning Zoe had asked her daughter to bring from her sleeper-cove only the few clothes she had there and the photographs on the walls, and Melanie had said she would bring them: maybe Mr. Leland had them already.

"Well, if you can shoot pitchurs," Parthena said, "you can he'p us knock off that new wall banner what you seen on the quiltin' frame in the rec center. So you c'mon now, Zoe."

They were finished in the galley. Parthena led them out of there and down the corridor: seventy-six years old and as straight and skinny as a broom handle.

"Other work I got this evening," Jerry said. "If you all will excuse me." And he zoomed around them in his winged chair and disappeared into a room Zoe hadn't been in yet. A closetlike alcove between the rec center and the dining room.

Luther and Toodles were already at the quilting frame when they got there: a monstrous, plastic contraption over which the layer of sewn squares, the synthetic cotton batting, and the underlining had all been tautly spread and whipped down. Zoe had seen this thing—"a Wright brothers plane made of sewing scraps"—during their afternoon songfest, but it had been behind them and partially hidden by a moving screen and no one had volunteered to explain its purpose or its function to her.

Now the screen had been shoved back against the wall, and Toodles and Luther were sitting at opposite ends of the frame pushing and pulling their needles through the three layers of material. Helen, still wearing her goggles, sat down between them, and Parthena and Zoe took up chairs on the other side of the frame, which was tilted like an aileron. It was 1903, and they were Orville and Wilbur, crazy-quilt pilots at a Kitty Hawk where the sands of time had transmogrified into linoleum tile.

"Helen," Zoe blurted, "with those goggles on you look like you're gonna fly us right out of here—right up to the dome." Ooops. Was that the right thing to say to a blind person?

Helen raised her head and stared at Zoe. Straight on, the goggles—or glasses, or binoculars—gave her the look not of a biplane pilot but of an unfriendly outerspace critter. "Aren't they hideous?" Helen said. "I'd wear them all the time except for the way they look." And, expertly, she began plunging her own needle into the layers of cloth and forcing it back through.

Parthena showed Zoe how to do it, giving her a needle and thimble and making her watch her technique. "I taught us all how to quilt—but Paul he don' like it and use his weekend to think on keepin' himsef a-live for awways. Jerry he got real bidness to tend to. Otherwise, he 'most awways here. Now you keep yo' thumb in that thimble, gal, or that needle it gonna bite you. Look here—"

Well, Zoe had sewn before and she'd always been pretty handy anyway. Easy, take it easy, she told herself, and pretty soon she was dipping in and digging out as well as any of them, stitching those jaunty, colored squares—yellow, green, and floral-print blue in a steppin'-'round-the-mountain pattern—to batting and lining alike. Much concentration to begin with, like a pilot taking off; then, the hang of it acquired, free, relaxing flight. Nobody talked, not anyone.

When had she ever felt so serene and at peace? Serene and at peace, yes, but with a tingle of almost physical pleasure throwing off cool little sparks up and down her backbone. The quiet in the room was a part of this pleasure.

Then Parthena began to talk, but not so that it violated the silence they were working in: "I use to do this up in Bondville, when my son Maynard jes' a little flea and the dome ain' even half finished yet. Oh, the wind it blow then, it didn' have no dome to stop it, and we use these quilts to sleep unner, not to hang up on them ole broke-up plasser walls of ours. I still 'member how Maynard, when I was workin', would get himsef up unner the frame—a wooden un my husban' made—and walk back and fo'th like a sojer so that all you could see was the bump of his head goin' from one end of that frame to the other, up and down, till it seem he warn' ever gonna wear out. Laugh? Lord, I use to laugh him into a resentful meanness 'cause he didn' unnerstan' how funny his ole head look."

She laughed in a way that made Zoe join her. "Now he got three babies of his own—Georgia, Mack, and Moses—and a wife what can do this good as me; better maybe, she so spry."

They quilted for an hour. When they broke off, Parthena insisted that Zoe come back to the dormitory common room and see the "pitchurs of my gran'babies. Shoot, you like pitchurs and babies, don' you?" So Zoe went. She sat in the easy chair while Parthena, having lowered her bed to an accommodating height, sat like an ebony stork on its edge.

"This one my pert Georgie," Parthena said, handing her a picture of a handsome little black girl. "She twelve now and one sassy fas' chile. She gonna get out of Bondville all by hersef, jes' on charm and speed." The two boys were older and a little meaner-looking; they probably had to be. None of them were babies. "I jes' want you to see I had me a fam'ly 'fo' the Phoenix. I ain' like Luther and po' Toodles what suffer till they was pas' sixxy without finin' a real home. Now, though, they got us an' we got them—but they come a long road, Zoe, a long road. Jerry, too. Sometime I jes' lif' up a prayer for how lucky I been."

"I never did pray much," Zoe said, "but I know what the urge is like." Like loving somebody in a way that didn't permit you to tell them: Zoe remembered.

They talked while some of the others got ready for bed. Parthena showed Zoe a set of dentures that had been made for her in 2026; she even made Zoe take them in her hand and examine them as if they were the teeth of an australopithecine. "They clean," she said. "I ain' wore 'em since '29. The reason I show 'em to you is 'cause they made by Dr. Nettlinger."

"Who?"

"Gee-rard Nettlinger. You 'member, Zoe. He that fellow what shot

Carlo Bitler. Stood up in the middle of the Urban Council meetin' and shot that tough, holy man. The day I heard that, I took out them dentures and never put 'em in again. They shoddy-made, anyhow. Only keep 'em so Maynard can sell 'em one day. People go all greedy-crazy over doodads what b'long to 'sassins. People crazy."

"Yep," Zoe agreed. "My daddy said it was the new idolatry."

"It idle, awright. Don' make a mussell-shell worth o' sense."

Then, somehow, their conversation got around to why the original family members had chosen Phoenix—rather than something light like Sweetheart or O'Possum—as the group's surname. Zoe said she had supposed it was because Atlanta was sometimes called the Phoenix City, having risen again from its own ashes after the Civil War (which Zoe's grandfather, even in the 1980s, had insisted on calling the War Between the States—as if that made some kind of significant difference). And when the dome went up in that decade linking the old century with the new one, Atlanta had undergone still another incarnation. Were those part of the group's original reasons?

"They part of 'em awright," Parthena said. "But jes' part. Another one is, we all come out of our own ashes when we 'greed to the cov'nant. We all bone again, Zoe, like in Jesus."

"Well, I thought that, too, you know. That's what makes the name so good."

"Yeah. But Paul he like it 'cause the phoenix a 'Gyptian bird what was im-ortal, you see. It only *look like* it die, then it spurt back up jes' as feathery and fine as befo'. He a mean man on that pint, Paul is."

"He ought to be happy with the Ortho-Urban Church, then. It says the same sort of thing happens to *people* after they die."

"Ain' the same, though, Paul say. 'Cause people do die, no lookin'-like in it, and they don' get a body back at all. Paul he hung up on the body."

"You don't say? It's good to know he's not just a Dirty Old Man."

"Oh, he that, too, he sho' is." They chuckled together. "But it the other thing keep him thinkin' and rockin' and figgerin'. The Phoenix lucky. Mos' of us still got our mines. But Paul he eighty-some-odd and he been goin' ever since we marry. Mr. Leland awmos' didn' 'cept him in this program five year back, you see. Res' of us made him say yes. So Mr. Leland fine'ly 'cepted him, hopin' we could haul him back on the road. We done it, too. Pretty much."

"Did Paul suggest the name?"

"No. Maybe. I don' 'member zackly. What I do 'member is that the name fit, it fit fo' all kinds o' reasons. One other, and maybe the bes' un, was a story my gran'daddy tole that his own daddy tole him. It was 'bout a slave chile, a little gal, what was made to watch the two-year-ole baby of the boss man, the 'marster' as gran'daddy say his daddy say.

"Well, that little baby fell down the steps while the slave gal was watchin' it: she took her eye away a minute and it bumped down them ole steps and took on a-hollerin'. Scared, you know, but not kilt. Well, when the white mistresses in the house heard this, they took on a-cryin' and carryin' on terrible—jes' like that baby been murdered. They kep' on till the marster himsef come strollin' in and axed them what it was. When they tole him, he pick up a board and hit that little slave gal in the head. Kilt her. Then he gathered 'round him a bunch of niggers (my gran'daddy he tole it this way, now) and ordered 'em to thow the gal in the river. The gal's mama begged and prayed and axed him to spare the gal fo' buryin', but he paid her no mine and made 'em thow the chile in.

"Now this where the story get magical, Zoe. The little girl's name was Phoebe, and five slaves and the girl's mama went down to the river with her—the biggest nigger in front, carryin' little Phoebe with her bloody head hangin' down, mournful and cold. This big nigger he thew the gal in like the marster order him to, Phoebe's mama jes' moanin' and beatin' on hersef, and then he walk right in affer the girl and hole himsef unner water till he drown. The others they resolve to do the same. And they do it too, the mama goin' in las' and prayin' to God they all be taken up together.

"One night later, the white folks from the big house is walkin' by the river and all at once they see seven small, ugly birds fly up outa the water and go sailin' straight at the moon. The higher they get, the brighter and purtier and bigger they get too—till at las' they stop in the sky like stars and stay still over the big house where them white folks live. A new constellation they become, which evvyone on that plantation call the Phoenix—'cep' this constellation don' move like it s'posed to but jes' sit with its wings spread, wide and haughtylike, over the marster's house.

"And that the story, Zoe. Jerry he say he never heard of no constellation call the Phoenix. But with that dome up there who gonna 'member zackly how the sky look? Nobody; not nobody.

"An' I believe it still up there somewhere."

8. *flashforward: at the end of winter*

Almost three old-style months after entering the Geriatrics Hostel, not as patient or prisoner but as a genuine, come-and-go-as-you-please resident, Zoe sat on the roof one evening and recalled the steps of her slow immersion in the Phoenix clan. Supper was eaten: a calming warmth in her stomach and bowels.

Pretty soon the family would decide. When you're streaking toward either seventy or eighty—as well as that something else that isn't death—long courtships are as foolish as whirlwind ones. Three months is plenty to decide in, maybe too much. Anyhow, they were formally going to pass on her, and it might be that in giving her this hour of solitude, this retrospective moment on the darkening rooftop, they were already engaged in the process of their decision. Was it in doubt? And hadn't they been so engaged all along, every day that Zoe had lived among them sharing their lives?

One girder-car tonight, and a flight of pigeons wheeling together in great loops in front of a huge, neon Coca-Cola sign.

Look what had happened in these three old-style months: For one thing, she had found out that the septigamoklans in the Tower weren't living there as welfare recipients solely, as so many helpless mendicants on the Old Folk Dole Role. Most of them had spent their lives paying into the medicaid and future-secure programs of the city; since 2035, the year young Mr. Leland's study had begun, the quarterly benefits of all the people in the hostel had been pooled and invested. This was done with permission from the residents, only a scant number of whom denied the Ur-Nu Human Development Commission the legal administration of their estates. And against these holdouts, no penalty at all. In any event, the dividends on these pooled investments and the interest on several well-placed accounts financed the feeding and the sheltering of the residents and even provided them with personal funds to draw on. They also helped remunerate the surviving families of those who came into the study.

Each family had a budgeter: Helen was the Phoenix budgeter, and, wearing those little, black, vision-assisting binoculars, she kept books like a born-and-bred C.P.A. (which was C.U.A. now, Zoe remembered). Other times, she used her braille-writer. Anyhow, they weren't dole-riders, the people in the Tower—although Zoe had to admit that the hostel's system was dependent upon the good offices and business acumen of those who administered their benefits. This drawback was partially offset by the budgeter of each septigamoklan's having a seat on the Commission Board of Financial Planners, as well as by the judicious appeal to market-forecasting computers.

Down on Level 3 with Sanders and Melanie, Zoe's quarterly allotments—only a day or two after the future-secure printout chit arrived—had been eaten up like nutmeg-sprinkled oatmeal. The Nobles garnisheed the entire value of the chit, without even so much as a counter-signature, for granting Zoe the privilege of living with them. Only the coming of their child and the prospect of a lump-sum reward from the commission had induced them to hand Zoe over. Just like a prisoner-exchange, or the sale of a decrepit and recalcitrant slave. Yessir, Zoe thought: Sold down the river. But a river out of which it was possible to fly like a sleek bird, dripping light as if it were water. An old bird, Zoe was; a bird of fire being reborn in the Lethe of Sanders and Melanie's forgetfulness and neglect.

"A pox on self-pity," Zoe said aloud, surprising herself. Overhead, the torchlit girder-car had almost reached the acme of the dome.

Well, what else? What else? Lots of things. She had met members of other septigamoklans, the O'Possums and the Cadillacs and the Graypanthers and oh! all the others, too. There'd been a party one Saturday night in the garden, with food and music and silly paper decorations. Hostel attendants had closed the patio windows and pulled the acoustical draperies in the intensive-care rooms, and everyone else had gone to town. Young Mr. Leland, at their invitation, had been there, and nobody but Paul of all the Phoenix went to bed before 4 A.M. Sometime after midnight Toodles led everybody in a joyful, cacophonous version of "Ef Ya Gotta Zotta."

Then there were Sunday afternoons, alone with Paul or Luther or maybe, just maybe, one of the girls. During the week, field trips to the

Atlanta Museum of Arts ("Boring as hell," said Paul) and Consolidated Rich's and the pedestrian-park flea markets. Two different excursions to the new theatre-in-the-round opera house, where they had watched a couple of interesting, council-sanctioned hologramic movies. They were OK, sort of plotless and artsy, but OK. Back in their own fourth-floor suite, though, they could show old-fashioned, two-dimensional movies; and just since Zoe had been there, the Phoenix had held a Rock Hudson festival and a mock seminar in the "Aesthetic of Late Twentieth-century X-rated Cinema," during which Jerry had turned off the sound tracks and lectured to quite humorous effect with the aid of a stop-action button and a pointer.

After one such lecture, when the rooftop was theirs, Luther and Zoe had laid out a croquet course; and, except for Jerry, in 23° C. weather (the internal meteorologists had given them one or two cold days, though) they had all played without their clothes! Nude, as Helen said. And that had been one of those rare occasions *not* requiring meticulous attention to detail—quilting, putting away dishes, keeping books—when Helen wore her goggle-binoculars. And, not counting the pulse-cued bracelet, *only* the goggle-binoculars. The idea, lifted from an old book of short stories, had been Toodles', but Paul had given it a vigorous seconding. And so Zoe, like a girl going skinny-dipping in the before-the-dome countryside, shed her paper gown, her underthings, her inhibitions, and let the temperate air swaddle her sensitive flesh and her every self-conscious movement. Much merriment. And no repugnance for their blotched and lignifying bodies; instead, a strange tenderness bubbling under the surface merriment.

What, after all, did the bunions, and the varicosities, and the fleshy folds signify? Zoe could answer that: the onset of age and their emphatic peoplehood, male and female alike. Finally, that day, she forgot the sensuous stirrings of the dome winds, lost herself in the game, and became extremely angry when Parthena sent her ball careening off into an unplayable position. Yessir, that had been an all-fun day.

And what else? Well, the Phoenix had given her a still camera, and for the first time in ten or fifteen years she had begun taking pictures again. The camera was an old but still beautifully operable Double-utility Polaroid, and the first project Zoe undertook was the capturing in stark black and white of the faces of her new family. Posed photographs, candid ones, miniatures, darkroom enlargements: group portraits, singles, double-exposure collages, meditative semiabstracts. The best of these went up in the rec center. The Wall of the Phoenix, this gallery became, and it was framed on both sides by bright, quilted wall banners.

Paul and Toodles both grew quite vain about certain of these portraits and occasionally got caught staring at their favorites: teen-agers ogling themselves in a mirror. Vanity, vanity, saith somebody or other, Zoe remembered. But Helen never donned her little binoculars to look at her own photographed image, even though she had more justification than either Paul or Toodles. One day Zoe asked her why. "I haven't looked at my own face since I was thirty," she said, "because I am quite content with the self-deluding vision of my thirty-year-old one that still resides up here." She tapped her head. Then she showed Zoe an old photograph of herself, one that glinted in the common room's fluorescents and revealed a woman of disgusting, not-to-be-gainsaid beauty. "I can *feel* what I look like now," Helen said. "I don't have to *look*." Even so, Zoe's portraits of Helen did her no disservice; in fact, they launched a thousand tiresome accolades from the men, Paul in particular—when, that is, he wasn't mesmerized by his own amber-eyed, celluloidally distanced self. Well, why not? Zoe's pitchurs were damn good, if she did say so herself, just by way of echoing the others.

The month Spring was coming on. What else could she recall about Winter in the hostel? Visits by Melanie and Sanders. The prospect of a grandchild. This last excited her, tickled her like air on her naked body, and for it alone did she anticipate the biweekly drop-ins of her daughter and son-in-law. No, that wasn't true. Lannie she always had a hankering to see, whether a baby was growing in her womb or not. Her daughter Lannie was, her own flesh and that of dead Rabon: her daughter. Only fatuous Sanders did she have difficulty tolerating, and he had never once called her anything as brutal as a mummified witch, not ever in his life. So what did you do?

Zoe, for her part, never visited them in their Level 3 cubicle, and when they came to see her, thereby perfunctorily carrying out their filial duty, she always greeted them in the quadrangle where they had first put her on the block. That made Sanders uncomfortable: he scuffed his street slippers in the gravel and craned his neck around as if looking for the one mean old codger in the hostel who would use his balcony advantage to shoot him, Paul, with a blowgun or pellet rifle. Minor sport for Zoe, watching her son-in-law sidelong as she asked Melanie how she felt—if the morning sickness had gone away yet ("There are pills for that, Mother!")—what sex the Jastov-Hunter test had said the child would be—other things that Lannie was at last willing to talk about.

But she never used her freedom to visit them on Level 3, and they never extended her such an invitation. No, sir. Not once.

Zoe tilted her head back and saw that the girder-car she had been following was nowhere in sight. My sweet lord, hadn't she been up on the Tower roof a long time? And hadn't the time flown by? They were reaching a decision on her, the Phoenix were. That was it.

Was the outcome in doubt? Would Mr. Leland send her into another incomplete septigamoklan (if one existed) because of a single person's snide, blackballing veto? As Mr. Leland had explained it, they could easily do that, blackball her. How would she feel if they did? As far as that went, did she herself want to marry with the Phoenix, to join with them in a new covenant?

Well, the answer to that was an easy one. The answer was yes; yes, she wanted to marry with Luther, Parthena, Toodles, Paul, Helen, and Jerry. And her reason for wanting to was a simple one, too: she was in love.

9. *spending the afternoon with luther*

On her first Sunday among the Phoenix, Toodles told Zoe that although it was her, Toodles', turn to spend the afternoon with Luther, she would be happy to yield to Zoe. "I don't feel all that good," she explained, "and, besides, it's the only really hospitable way for me to behave, don't you think?" Propped up in bed, Yuichan's awful Fujiyama robe bundled about her shoulders, Toodles was eating a breakfast roll that a cartlike servo-mechanism had wheeled into the common room from the galley. A hairline smear of artificial-peach jelly rode Toodles' upper lip like a candied mustache, and Zoe wanted to take a tissue and daub it away.

"If you don't feel well, should you be eating jelly rolls?"

Toodles winked. "You know the ole saying: jelly rolls is medicine. But I'm having mine this morning and don't need a dose this afternoon."

"Does 'spend the afternoon' mean what the young drakes and duckies call 'bodyburning'?" Why was she asking? She already knew the answer. Parthena and Helen were off to an Ortho-Urban service somewhere on West Peachtree, Paul was asleep across the room from them, and Jerry and Luther had both got up early and gone down the hall toward the rec center. Zoe had declined an invitation to attend services with Parthena and Helen. Now she wished she were with them.

"You ain't slow, Zoe," Toodles said. "I'da been blunter, but it embarrasses Errol."

"Errol?"

Flipping up the bed linen and extending a heavy leg, Toodles put one bunion-afflicted foot on the tray of the servo-cart. "Errol," she reiterated. The cart hummed and backed up, but Toodles got her leg off the tray in time to avoid a nasty spill. A doughnut did drop to the floor, though. "Temperamental, Errol is. . . . You're not thinking of saving yourself for after the covenant ceremony, are you?"

"Well, if I am, I been saving myself so long that my interest's now a whole lot greater than my principles." That was the punch line of a joke Rabon used to tell. It didn't suit Zoe's mood, which was cautious and a bit skeptical, but it perfectly suited Toodles'—she was delighted. I always play to my audience, Zoe thought; can't seem to help it. Aloud, attempting to recover, "I never was one to kiss on the first date, Toodles; just not the sort."

"Oh, I always said that, too. Anyhow, you've already slept in the same room with the Phoenix, you know. It's not like you'd be sacking out with some bulgy-britches thugboy." And at last she wiped the peach-jelly mustache off her upper lip. "Please say yes. Luther's liable to be hurt." And with her little, gold remote-con box Toodles beckoned Errol (who, Zoe noted with some annoyance, was something of a whiner) closer to the bed so that she could pick up another breakfast pastry.

"OK," Zoe answered, almost as if it were someone else: not her.

So that afternoon she and Luther walked through the pedestrian courts outside the Geriatrics Hostel and stopped to eat lunch at a little restaurant that seemed to be made entirely of plate glass; it was nestled under the stone eaves of a much taller building, though, and had green, reed-woven window shades to keep out the glare of the dome's day lamps. Atmosphere, Rabon would have said the shades gave the place.

They sat in a simulated-leather booth with potted ferns on both sides of them to cut off their view to the front door and drank scotch and water while waiting for the steward to bring them their meal. A Sunday drink. Well, that was something the Retrenchment Edicts hadn't outlawed. You could get one right after your favorite Ortho-Urban services, which was what half the people in this place, it looked like, were doing. The other half were sharing table hookahs and letting the thin smoke coil away from them through the decorative ferns.

"Good food," Luther said. "They do know how to throw together good food here." He was a little nervous, Zoe could see. He kept putting his malletlike hands on the table, dropping them to his lap, taking a sip of his drink, then sticking those heavy, purplish hands back on the table. "You ain't disturbed that Toodles pushed you into this, are you now?" he said, his brow comically corrugating.

"Luther, my daughter and son-in-law *pushed* me into this, not Toodles. And they don't even know when they're doing me a favor."

That loosened him, more than the scotch even. He asked her questions about her family, he told her about himself. Their meal came—a vegetable dinner featuring hydroponically grown snapbeans, zucchini, tomatoes (stewed), and some sort of hybrid greens—and Luther, between bites, kept on talking. A warm rumble.

"I was born the same year Dr. King was assassinated," he said at one point. "That's how I got my name. The shame of it is, I lived to see that sort of business over and over before the cities went undercover—and then after the doming, too. I wasn't quite six when I saw a young man shoot Mrs. Martin Luther King, Sr., and several other people right in the old man's own church. My church, too. Then. More died after the dome was up. That young Bitler he was the last one, and it's been eleven years since we've had to walk our hungry-children miles to some good man's grave.

"You know, I was so sick I almost shot myself that year, I almost took a razor to my wrists. Back when you could breathe, when you could look up and see a sun or a moon, some men used to be born in the year a comet come through and wait their whole lives till it come back again so that they could die. That year, I was so down I knew it had been written that Luther Battle was supposed to come in and go out with another man's assassination.

"But I was in my thirty-second year with McAlpine Company in '29, and we had a lot of work that year. Bitler had done made a lot of people angry, he had got a lot of ole dead asses movin'. After he was shot, there was all kind of uproar to tear down the surfaceside slums and stick up some kind of halfway decent housing on top of the streets instead of under 'em. I was on McAlpine's demolition crews, not the construction ones. Sixty years old and I was workin' off my anger and grief by wreckin' ole tenements; it was the only way they let us make anything of our own. I bossed the demolition of fifteen buildings that year, workin' it all out so that walls come down clean and the guts got hauled off neat. Cranes, cats, tractors, trucks, all of 'em doin' this and doin' that 'cause of how I told 'em to go. Only thing that kep' me sane, Zoe: tearin' down another century's toilets and doin' it with that century's equipment. Then the uproar quieted off, the work contracts run out, and the Urban Council didn't do nothin' to start 'em up again. We still got some damn ghettos in Atlanta, no matter what the ward reps say. Bondville, one of the worst. Parthena's boy and her gran'chillun still live there. . . . But that bad year was over, and I had survived it, Zoe.

"Retired, then. Lived alone on 7, *under*, just like I had all the years I was with McAlpine. The company had been my family since all the way back to '97. My mama and daddy was lucky: they died before they had to see a dome go up over their heads. Me, I wasn't lucky: I had to sign on with McAlpine and help build that damn thing up there."

"You helped build the dome?" Zoe said. She'd never met anyone who had, not anybody who'd admit to it at least.

"I did. They was twelve different outfits, different companies, workin' to do it, everybody goin' from blueprints they had run off a computer somewhere up East or maybe in California. We were a year behind New York and Los Angeles, McAlpine told us, and we had to catch up. He was still sayin' this in '97, the year I come on, three after the dome Projec' started; and no one ever asked why the hell we had to catch up with this foolishness that New York and L.A. was pursuin'. Most of us hadn't had any kinds of jobs at all before the projec', so we shut up and did what all of a sudden the city was givin' us money to do. Yessir, Zoe. We started in a-buildin' a pyramid, a great ole tomb to seal ourselves into and never come out of again. Slaves in Egypt might have to work twenty years to build a House of the Dead for Pharaoh, but they didn't have to lie down in it themselves. We was more advanced. We done ours in ten and managed it so we could put the lid on ourselves from the *inside*. No Moses anywhere to say, 'Hey! wait a minute, you don't want to live in this place forever!' But we were pullin' down some decent cash, even if they was Ur-Nu dollars, and didn't think there'd ever be a day you couldn't see at least a little square of sky somewhere, at least enough blue to make denim for a workingman's britches. It was an adventure. Nobody thought he was just another one of Pharaoh's slavin' niggers. I didn't, anyhow. Even when I first come on with McAlpine, I felt like *I* was the chief mucketymuck myself."

"How come?"

"Well, we had to go up to the sections of the dome's gridwork that we'd completed, and we always went up in girder-cars, just like the ones you see comb-crawlin' along after dark with their torches alight. You worked on platforms or from harnesses on the girder-car, and you was always right out there over the whole damn state, you could see everything—even when the wind was streamin' by you like it wanted to shake all your hard labor into rubble and scrap. Stone Mountain. All kinds of lakes. The mountains up by Gainesville.

"And kudzu, Zoe, kudzu like you've never seen or can even remember. That ole madman vine ran itself over everything, telephone poles and broken-down barns and even some of them cheapjack townhouses and condo-minny-ums they hammered up all las' century. The whole world was green, dyin' maybe 'cause of that kudzu but so green it made your eyes ache. And up there above the whole world Luther Battle felt like Kheops himself, or King Tut, or whichever one of them mean bastards built the bigges' tomb. And I never did say, 'Hoooi! Luther, why are we doin' this?'"

After their meal, Zoe and Luther went back to the hostel and rode the Tower lift-tube up to the fourth floor. Although she hadn't let him do it in the pedestrian courts on the walk home, in the lift-tube she gave him her hand to hold. Ten years after retiring from the McAlpine Company, he still had calluses on his palm, or the scars of old calluses. In the lift-tube he didn't talk. He was embarrassed again, as if his talking at lunch had been a spiritual bleeding which had left him weak and uncertain of his ground. Well, she was embarrassed too. Only Luther had an advantage: a blush on him wasn't so all-fired conspicuous as it was on her.

In the common room, which was unoccupied by group design and agreement, Luther took her to his bed and made the automatic room dividers roll into place. Bodyburning, the young people called it now. That's what it was for her, too, though not in the way the term was supposed to suggest and not because Luther was a snorting dragon in the act. No, it had been a long time. Rabon was the last, of course, and this ready compliance to the rule of the Phoenix surprised her a little. For years she had been (what was Melanie's amusing vulgarity?) *mummifing,* and you couldn't expect to throw off the cerements, vaporize the balms and preservatives, and come back from your ages-long limbo in one afternoon.

So that afternoon Zoe experienced only the dull excitement of pain; that, and Luther's solicitude. But each Sunday—the next one with Paul, the one after with Luther, the following one with Paul, and so on, depending on inclination and a very loose schedule—it got better. Since she had never really been dead, it didn't take so long as might the hypothetical, attempted resurrection of a Pharaoh. Not anywhere near so long as that. For she was Zoe, Zoe Breedlove, and she no longer remembered her maiden name.

10. *jerry at his tricks*

What did Jerry do in that mysterious alcove between the rec center and the dining room? Zoe wondered because whenever Jerry had a moment of free time—after dinner, before bed, Sunday morning—his wheelchair, humming subsonically, circled about and went rolling off to that little room. And Jerry would be gone for fifteen minutes, or thirty, or maybe an hour, whatever he could spare. What provoked her curiosity was the midnight vision of his puffball hairdo and his sad hollow eyes floating out of the corridor's brightness and into the darkened common room after one of these recurrent disappearances.

On the Sunday night (more properly, the Monday morning) after her conversations, both social and carnal, with Luther, Zoe had this vision again and heard the crippled man unmindfully whistling to himself as he returned from that room: "Zippity-Doo-Dah," it sounded like. And up to his unmade bed Jerry rolled.

Jerry rolls in at night, Zoe thought, and jelly rolls in the afternoon. A muddled, word-fuzzy head she had. It all had something to do with Toodles. And Helen, Parthena, and Luther. Only Paul left out, to date anyway. But these members of the Phoenix were all sleeping.

Sitting up and lowering her feet to the floor, she said, "Jerry?"

"Who is it?" She couldn't see his eyes any more, but the macrocephalic helmet of his silhouette turned toward her, dubiously. "Is it Zoe?"

"Yep," she said. "It's me. Can't sleep." She pulled on her dressing gown (Sanders had brought most of her things to the hostel on Saturday afternoon, but had not come up to see her) and walked barefooted on the cold floor over to Jerry's territory.

The Phoenix could certainly saw wood. No danger of these buzz saws waking up; it was enough to make you wish for impaired hearing. Except that each one of the sounds was different, and interesting: an orchestra of snorers. There, a tin whistle. There, a snoogle-horn. Over there, a tubaphone. That one, a pair of castanets. And . . . .

Jerry grinned quizzically at her and scratched his nose with one finger. "Can't sleep, heh? Would you like to go to the galley for a drink? Maybe some wine. Wine's pretty good for insomnia."

"Wine's pretty good for lots of things," Zoe said. "What I wanted to ask was, what are you up to when you get all antisocial on us and shut yourself up in that closet out there?" She nodded toward the door.

"You're a nice lady. You get a multiple-choice test. (A) I'm concocting an eternal-youth elixir. (B) I'm perfecting an antigravity device which will spindizzy all of Atlanta out into the stars. (C) I'm performing unspeakable crimes of passion on old telescope housings and the jellies in Petri dishes. Or (D) I'm . . . I'm . . . My wit fails me, dear lady. Please choose."

"D," Zoe said.

"What?"

"I choose D. You said multiple-choice. That's what I choose."

As if struck with an illuminating insight (for instance, the key to developing an antigravity device), Jerry clapped his hands together and chuckled. "Ah. Even at this late hour, *your* wit doesn't fail *you*," he said. "I am bested."

"Not yet. You haven't given me a real answer yet, and I've been talking to you for almost two minutes."

"Oh ho! In that case, dear Zoe lady, come with me." Jerry Zitelman-Phoenix circled about in his subsonically humming chair and went rolling through the common room door. Zoe followed.

Down the corridor Jerry glided, Zoe now more conscious of the raw slapping of her feet than of his wheelchair's pleasant purr. Which stopped when he reached the mysterious room. "I would have preferred to wait for tomorrow, you know. But over the years I have learned to honor the moods of insomniac ladies. And, besides, what I have been working on is finished. It won't hurt for you to get a foreglimpse of the issue of my labors. It won't hurt *me*, anyway. *You*, on the other hand, may merely aggravate your sleepless condition."

At two in the morning, if it wasn't later than that, Jerry was a caution, a nonstop caution. Not much like Thursday night on the roof when he had talked about unseeable stars and his lifelong paralysis. Fiddle! Zoe knew better: he was just like he was Thursday night, if you were talking about the underneath part of him; the seeming change was only in his approach to the revelation of this self. Then, candor. Now, a camouflage that he stripteased momentarily aside, then quickly restored. Oh, it wasn't hard to undress this man's soul. You just had to warn yourself not to destroy him by letting him know that you could see him naked. Nope. Keep those pasties in place, wrap up the emotional overflow in an old G-string. And smile, smile, smile.

Because he was funny, Jerry was. In spite of his tricks.

They went into the little room, and he hit the light button. Zoe, standing just inside the door, saw a counter with some sort of duplicating machine on it, reams of paper, an IBM margin-justifying typer (they had had those in the offices of the *Journal/Constitution* combine), and a stack of bright yellow-orange booklets. There were little inset docks in the counter (put there by Luther) so that Jerry could maneuver his wheelchair into comfortable working positions.

Booklets. You didn't see booklets very often. One good reason: The Retrenchment Edicts of '35 had outlawed private duplicating machines. Everyone had a visicom console and better be glad he did. The Phoenix had two such consoles in the rec center, though Zoe couldn't recall seeing anyone use either of them. Why, since she'd been at the hostel, she hadn't tapped into one at all. And now she was seeing booklets: *booklets!*

"I always wondered where Atlanta's pamphleteers holed up," Zoe said. "You preachin' the overthrow of our Urban Charter?"

Jerry put a hand to his breast. "Zoe lady, the name is Zitelman, not Marx, and I am first—no, not first, but last and always—a Phoenix." He took a copy of one of the booklets from the counter and handed it to Zoe, who had moved deeper into his crowded little den of sedition. "This issue, which has been in preparation for three or four weeks now, nay, longer, is for you. Not just this copy, mind you, but the whole issue."

Zoe looked at the booklet's cover, where on the yellow-orange ground a stylized, pen-and-ink phoenix was rising from its own ashes. The title of the publication was set in tall, closely printed letters on the bottom left: *Jerry at His Tricks.* Beneath that: Volume VI, No. 1. "What is it?" she asked.

"It's our famzine," Jerry said. "All the septigamoklans have one. *Fam*ily maga*zine*, you see. Of which I am the editor and publisher. It is the True History and Record of the Phoenix Septigamoklan, along with various creative endeavors and pertinent remarks of our several spouses. One day, dear Zoe, you will be represented herein."

Leafing through the famzine, Zoe said, "Don't count your chickens . . ."

"Well, as an egghead who has already hatched his personal fondnesses, I am now seriously counting." He pointed a wicked, crooked finger at her. "One," he said in a burlesque, Transylvanian accent. "One chicken."

She laughed, patting him on top of his wiry puffball. But it was not until the next day, before breakfast, that she had a chance to read through the booklet—the advance copy—that Jerry had given her. In it she found artwork signed by Parthena, Helen, and Paul, and articles or poems by everyone in the family. Several of these were tributes, brief eulogies, to the dead Yuichan Kurimoto. The issue concluded with a free verse poem welcoming Zoe Breedlove as a candidate for marriage with the Phoenix. It was a flattering but fairly tastefully done poem. It was signed J. Z-Ph., and at the bottom of this last page was the one-word motto of the clan: *Dignity*.

It was all too ridiculously corny. How did they have the nerve to put that word there? Zoe had to wipe her eyes dry before going into the dining room for breakfast.

11. *in the sun that is young once only*

Of all of them Paul was the hardest to get to know. Parthena had spoken rightly when she said that part of the difficulty was that his mind was going, had been going for a long time. He seemed to have a spiritual umbilicus linking him to the previous century and the time before the domes. He had been nine years old at the time of the Apollo 11 moon landing, thirteen at the time of the final Apollo mission, and he remembered both of them.

"Watched 'em on TV," he said. "Every minute I could of the first one. Just enough of the last one to say I saw it."

And he talked considerably more lucidly about his boyhood in California than he did about everyday matters in the hostel. His other favorite subject was the prospect of attaining, not in a dubious and certainly vitiated afterlife, but in the flesh, immortality. His only real grounding in the present, in fact, was the unalloyed joy he took in Sunday afternoons, at which time he performed creditably and behaved like a mature human being. The leers and the winks, it seemed, were almost involuntary carry-overs from a misspent youth.

"He gone sklotik up here"—Parthena tapped her head—"from the life he led as much as from jes' gettin' ole." (*Sklotik*, Zoe figured out, was *sclerotic*.) "Drugs, likker, womens, card playin'. Brag on how he never had a real job, jes' gamble for his keep-me-up. Now Mr. Leland 'fraid to use on him them new medicines what might stop his brain cells a-dyin'. Easy to see, he done los' a bunch."

And with his washed-out, Weimaraner eyes and raw, long lips Paul sometimes seemed like his own ghost instead of a living man. But he could still move around pretty good; he drifted about as effortlessly as a ghost might. And one day, three weeks after Zoe's arrival, he drifted up to her after dinner in the rec center (she was making a photo-display board) and pulled a chair up next to hers. She turned her head to see his raw lips beginning to move.

"It's time for one of my services," he said. "You don't go to the Ortho-Urbanist ones with Helen and Parthena, so I expect you're a fit body for one of mine. This Sunday morning, right in here."

"What sort of services?"

"My sort." A wink, maybe involuntary. "The True Word. Once every quarter, once every new-style month, I preach it."

"The True Word on what? Everybody's got his own true word, you know."

"On how not to die, woman. The basis of every religion."

"No," Zoe said. "Not every one of them; just the ones that don't know exactly what to do with the here-and-now."

His long lips closed, his eyes dilated. She might just as well have slapped him. In eighty years no one had told him that an ontological system didn't have to direct its every tenet toward the question of "how not to die." Or if someone had, Paul had forgotten. Even so, he fought his way back from stupefaction. "The basis," he said archly, "of every *decent* religion."

Jerry, who had overheard, powered himself up to the work table. "Rubbish, Paul. And besides, if tomorrow we were all granted everylasting life, no better than struldbrugs would we be, anyhow."

Zoe raised her eyebrows: *struldbrugs?* Paul kept silent.

"That's someone," Jerry explained, "who can't die but who nevertheless continues to get older and more infirm. Two hundred years from now we'd all be hopelessly senile immortals. Spare me such a blessing."

That ended the conversation. A ghost impersonating a man, Paul got up and drifted out of the room.

On Sunday morning, though, Luther went down to the rec center and took a box of aluminum parts, the largest being a drumlike cylinder, out of the closet where they kept the dart boards, the croquet equipment, and the playing cards, and assembled these aluminum pieces into . . . a rocking horse, one big enough for a man.

It was a shiny rocking horse, and its head, between its painted eyes, bore the representation of a scarab beetle pushing the sun before it like a cosmic dung ball. Zoe, who was in the rec center with all the Phoenix but Paul, went up to the metal critter to examine it. The scarab emblem was so meticulously wrought that she had to lean over to see what this horse had crawling on its forehead. A blue bug. A red ball. Well, that was different: funny and mysterious at once. "What's this?," she asked Luther, who, mumbling to himself, was trying to wedge the cardboard box back into the closet.

"Pulpit," he said. He thought she meant the whole thing. No sense in trying to clarify herself, he was still shoving at the box. But *pulpit* was a damn funny synonym for *rocking horse*.

After wedging the parts box back into place, Luther dragged a tall metal bottle from the closet and carried it over to the biomonitor cabinet next to Toodles' orpianoogla. Then he set it down and came back to the ring of chairs in front of the rocking horse. A silly business, every bit of it. Zoe put a single finger on the horse's forehead, right on the blue bug, and pushed. The horse, so light that only its weighted rockers kept it from tipping, began to dip and rise, gently nodding. No one was talking. Zoe turned to the group and shrugged. It looked like you'd have to threaten them all with premature autopsy to get anyone to explain.

"Don't ask," Jerry said finally. "But since you're asking, it's to humor him. He asked for the horse the second month after our covenant ceremony in '35, and Dr. Tanner said OK, give it to him. Now, four times a year, he plays octogenarian cowboy and rides into the sunset of his own dreams right in front of everybody. It's not so much for us to listen to him, you know."

Zoe looked at the five of them sitting there afraid she wouldn't understand: five uncertain, old faces. She was put off. They had been dreading this morning because they didn't know how she would react to the living skeleton in their family closet: the *de*-ranged range-rider Paul Erik Ferrand-Phoenix. Well, she was put off. All somebody'd had to do was tell her, she was steamingly put off. "O ye of little faith," she wanted to say, "go roast your shriveled hearts on Yuichan's hibachi. All of it together wouldn't make a meal." But she didn't say anything, she sat down with the group and waited. Maybe they didn't think she had Yuichan's compassion, maybe they didn't think she was worthy to replace their dear departed Jap. . . .

Just then Paul came drifting in: an entrance. Except that he didn't seem to be at all aware of the impression he was making; he was oblivious of his own etiolated magnificence. Dressed in spotless white from head to foot (currently fashionable attire among even the young, matched tunic and leggings), he wandered over to the metal horse without looking at them. Then, slowly, he climbed on and steadied the animal's rocking with the toe tips of his white slippers.

He was facing them. Behind him, as backdrop, one of the quilted wall banners: a navy-blue one with a crimson phoenix in its center, wings outspread. Zoe couldn't help thinking that every detail of Paul's entrance and positioning had been planned beforehand. Or maybe it was that this quarterly ritual had so powerfully suffused them all that the need for planning was long since past. Anyhow, knowing it all to be nonsense, Zoe had to acknowledge that little pulses of electricity were moving along her spine. Like the time she had first quilted with the group.

Slowly, mesmerizingly slowly, Paul began to rock. And softly he began to preach the True Word. "When we were young," he said, "there was fire, and sky, and grass, and air, and creatures that weren't men. The human brain was plugged into this, the human brain was run on the batteries of fire and sky and all of it out there."

"Amen!" Luther interjected, without interrupting Paul's rhythm, but all Zoe could think was, The city still has creatures that aren't men: pigeons. But the rocking horse began to move faster, and as it picked up speed its rider's voice also acquired momentum, a rhythmic impetus of its own. As Paul spoke on, preached on, an "Amen!" or a "Yessir, brother!"

occasionally provided an audible asterisk to some especially strange or vehement assertion in his text. All of it part of the ritual. But then Zoe was caught up in it in a way that she could see herself being caught up. Very odd: she found herself seconding Paul's insane remarks with "Amen!" or "All praises!" or some other curiously heartfelt interjection that she *never* used. This increased as the rocking horse's careening grew more violent and as Paul's eyes, the horse going up and down, flashed like eerie strobes.

"Then before our lives was half over, they put us in our tombs. They said we was dead even though we could feel the juices flowin' through us and electricity jumpin' in our heads. Up went the tombs, though, up they went. It didn't matter what we felt, it didn't matter we was still plugged into the life outside our tombs, the air and fire and sky. Because with the tombs up, you really do start dyin', you really do start losin' the voltage you have flowin' back and forth between you and the outside. Just look at yourself, just look at all of us."—Could anything be more ridiculous than this reasoning?—"It's slippin' away, that current, that precious, precious juice. It's because our brains are plugged into the sun or the moon, one socket or the other, and now they've stuck us in a place where the current won't flow."

Even as she said "Yessir!" Zoe was thinking that he, Paul, must have been plugged into the moon: loony.

But in another way, an upside-down way, it made a kind of loony sense, too. Even though everybody knew the world had been going to hell in a handcar before the domes went up, it still made a loony kind of sense. Maybe, at a certain time in your life (which was already past for her), you learned how to pass judgment on others, even unfavorable ones, without condemning. Zoe was doing that now. She beheld the madly rocking Paul from two utterly opposed perspectives and had no desire to reconcile them. In fact, the reconciliation happened, was happening, without her willing it to. As it always had for her, since Rabon's death. It was the old binocular phenomenon at work on a philosophical rather than a physical plane. Long ago it had occurred in Helen, too, the Phoenix "mediator," and just as Helen's little black goggles brought the physical world into focus for her, this double vision Zoe was now experiencing brought the two galloping Pauls—the demoniac one and the human one—into the compass of her understanding and merged them. Since this had happened before for her, why was she surprised?

". . . And the key to not-dying, and preserving the body too, is the brain. That's where we all are. We have to plug ourselves into the sun again, the sun and the moon. No one can do that unless he is resurrected from the tomb we were put in even before our lives were half over. . . ."

The horse was rocking frenetically, and Paul's voice was swooping into each repetitive sentence with a lean, measured hysteria. The bracelet on Zoe's wrist seemed to be singing. She looked at the biomonitor cabinet beside the orpianoogla and saw the oscilloscope attuned both to Paul's brain waves and his heartbeat sending a shower of pale comets back and forth, back and forth, across its screen. The other six windows were vividly pulsing, too, and she wondered if someone downstairs was taking note of this activity. Well, they were certainly all alive: very much alive.

Now Paul's eyes had rolled back in his head and the rocking horse had carried him into a country of either uninterrupted childhood or eternally stalled ripeness. He was alone in there, with just his brain and the concupiscent wavelets washing back from his body. Still preaching, too. Still ranting. Until, finally, the last word came out.

Only then did Paul slump forward across the neck of his aluminum steed, spent. Or dead maybe.

Zoe stood up—sprang up, rather. Amazingly, the other Phoenix—Toodles, Helen, Jerry, and Parthena—were applauding. Luther exempted himself from this demonstration in order to catch Paul before he slid off the still rocking horse and broke his head open.

"That the bes' one he manage in a long time," Parthena said.

Since the applause continued, Zoe, feeling foolish, joined in too. And while they all clapped (did sermons always end like this, the congregation joining in a spontaneous ovation?), Luther carried Paul over to the biomonitor cabinet, laid him out, and administered oxygen from the metal bottle he had earlier taken out of the closet. After which the wraithlike cowboy lifted his head a bit and acknowledged their applause with a wan grin. Then Luther put him to bed.

"You have to let him hear you," Toodles said. "Otherwise the old bastard thinks you didn't like it."

But he wasn't much good for three days after the sermon. He stayed in the common room, sleeping or staring at the ceiling. Zoe sat with him on the first night and let him sip soup through a flexible straw. In a few minutes he waved the bowl away, and Zoe, thinking he wanted to sleep, got up to leave. Paul reached out for her wrist and missed. She saw it, though, and turned back to him. His hand patted the bed: *Sit down.* So she lowered herself into the easy chair there and took his liver-spotted hand in her own. For an hour she sat there and held it. Then the long, raw lips opened and he said, "I'm afraid, Zoe."

"Sometimes," she said carefully, "I am, too." Now and again she was, she had to admit it.

The mouth remained open, the Weimaraner eyes glazed. Then Paul ran his tongue around his long lips. "Well," he said, "you can get in bed with me if you want to."

And closed his eyes. And went to sleep.

12. *somewhere over the broomstick*

It had never been in doubt. Maybe a little, just a little, in jeopardy the first night when the menfolk insulted Toodles. Or maybe a bit uncertain with Paul, until after his rocking-horse oration and subsequent collapse. But never really perilously in doubt.

So when Luther came up to the rooftop on that evening at the end of Winter and said, "You're in, Zoe, you're in," her joy was contained, genuine but contained. You don't shout Hooray! until the wedding's over or the spacemen have got home safely. Zoe embraced Luther. Downstairs, she embraced the others.

On the morning after the group's decision, they had the covenant ceremony in the hostel quadrangle. Leland Tanner presided. Day 1 of Spring, 2040, New Calendar designation.

"All right," Mr. Leland said. "Each septigamoklan has its own covenant procedure, Zoe, since any way that it chooses to ratify its bond is legal in the eyes of the Human Development Commission. The Phoenix ceremony owes its origin to an idea of Parthena's." He looked at the group. They were all standing on a section of the artificial lawn surrounded by tubbed ginkgo trees. A table with refreshments was visible in the nearest arbor. "That's right, isn't it?"

"That right," Parthena said.

And then, of all crazy things, Mr. Leland brought a broom out from behind his back. He laid it on the wiry turf at his feet and backed up a few steps. "OK," he said. "What you all do now is join hands and step over the broomstick together." He reconsidered. "Maybe we better do it in two groups of three, Zoe, you making the fourth each time. Any objections?"

"No," Parthena said. "So long as she cross it in the same direction both times, so none of it get undone."

OK. That's the way they did it. Zoe went first with Helen, Toodles, and Luther, then a second go-round with Parthena, Paul, and Jerry. Jerry had to drive his wheelchair over one end of the broom handle.

"I pronounce you," Mr. Leland said, "all seven of you, married in the Phoenix. Six of you for a second time, one of you for the first." He took them all over to the arbor and passed out drinks. "Viva the Phoenix."

Zoe drank. They all drank. Toasts went around the group several times. It was all very fitting that when you were sold down the river, into freedom, you got married by jumping over a broomstick. How else should you do it? No other way at all. No other way at all.

Paul and Toodles, the oldest and the second youngest in the family, died in 2042. A year later Luther died. In 2047, two days short of her eightieth birthday, Helen died. In this same year Dr. Leland Tanner resigned his position at the Human Development Tower; he protested uninformed interference in a study that was then twelve years old. Upon his departure from the Geriatrics Hostel his programs were discontinued, the remaining members of the ten septigamoklans separated. In 2048 Jeremy Zitelman died in the hostel's nursing ward. Parthena and Zoe, by the time of his death, had been returned to their "surviving families," Parthena to a surfaceside Bondville tenement, Zoe to the Level 1 cubicle of Sanders and Melanie Noble. Oddly enough, these two last members of the Phoenix died within twelve hours of each other on a Summer day in 2050, after brief illnesses. Until a month or two before their deaths, they met each other once a week in a small restaurant on West Peachtree, where they divided a single vegetable dinner between them and exchanged stories about their grandchildren. Parthena, in fact, was twice a *great*-grandmother.

After the broomstick-jumping ceremony in the garden court Mr. Leland took Zoe aside and said that someone wanted to talk to her in the room that he had once called an "air-lock." His horsy face had a tic in one taut cheek, and his hands kept rubbing themselves against each other in front of his bright blue tunic. "I told him to wait until we were finished out here, Zoe. And he agreed."

Why this mystery? Her mind was other places. "Who is it?"

"Your son-in-law."

She went into the air-lock, the decompression chamber, whatever you wanted to call it, and found Sanders ensconced in one corner of the sofa playing with the lint on his socks. When he saw her he got up, clumsily, with a funereal expression on his face. He looked like somebody had been stuffing his mouth with the same sort of lint he'd been picking off his socks: bloated jowls, vaguely fuzzy lips. She just stared at him until he had worked his mouth around so that it could speak.

"Lannie lost the baby," he said.

So, after Lannie got out of the hospital, she spent a week in their Level 3 cubicle helping out until her daughter could do for herself. When that week was over, she returned to her new family in the Geriatrics Hostel. But before she left she pulled Sanders aside and said, "I've got some advice for you, something for you to tell Lannie too. Will you do it?"

Sanders looked at his feet. "OK, Zoe."

"Tell her," Zoe said, "to try again."

*The recent wave of nostalgia for the 1950s inspired some good movies
(American Grafitti; The Buddy Holly Story), some dreadful movies
(Grease; American Hot Wax), a few mediocre television series (Happy
Days; Laverne and Shirley), and a lot of revivals of old rock music as
played by older rock musicians; fueled the comeback of short haircuts and
T-shirts; saved the word "cool" from extinction; and opened the
floodgates on a torrent of cheap sociological speculation. However, the
fifties mystique has seldom been examined by an eye as cool, perceptive,
and unsentimental as that possessed by new writer James P. Girard, who
here gives us a very offbeat kind of time-travel story.*

JAMES P. GIRARD
September Song

I had just finished a solo jump, an easy one, and I was feeling nice and
loose and sleepy; so I didn't jump home all at once. Instead, I turned off
the radio and cruised out of Indianapolis, going west on US 40, even
entertaining the notion of just driving all the way back to Wichita before
jumping home, to enjoy the pleasant summer of 1966 or at least the late-
summer thunderstorm that was building up to the west. But when the
wet-wind smell turned into real raindrops against the windshield, I
thought about driving that dark highway in the rain and turned the radio
back on, and it barely had time to say:

> *Wouldn't it be nice if we were older,*
> *then we wouldn't have to wait so long*

And then I was jumped so fast that it might only have been my mind,
running on ahead, that supplied the last couple of words. I was in
Wichita, 1954, and the radio said:

> *Got one in 1970, Blue. Southern*
> *California. We jumped you home so*
> *you could pick up your assistants.*
> *Could be a rough one.*

I was sitting at the intersection of Kellogg and Rock Road, still heading
west but waiting for a red light. I knew it was home because there was no
Howard Johnson's—or much of anything else—between me and the lights

of the city a couple of miles ahead. The only structure of any size was a 1954 drive-in, catty-corner from me, where they were showing *The Day the Earth Stood Still*. When the light changed, I laid down a little rubber to excite the kids.

I guessed it was about nine or ten at night. The radio wasn't saying anything for a while. I reached down under the dashboard and gave it a slap.

"Come on. Let me have it."

Of course, it didn't work. It always irritates me that they take so long getting their messages together or whatever it is they're doing, and they won't let me listen to music in the meantime. I sighed and unbuttoned my shirt, letting the air from the window vent cool my chest. There was a wind moving around, with a touch of rain in it, and it made me feel sleepy. The car grumbled on into nighttime city lights, past the VA center and the cemetery and on toward the place where they'd be building the viaduct in a couple of years.

Finally, the radio said:

> *We've got one female alien, traveling with a group of natives, some kind of diabolists or sadists. The usual late sixties stuff. Nobody'll miss any of them, if you can't get the alien alone. The Oracle recommends anytime between 5:00 P.M. and midnight, December 20, 1970, at 5234 Loma Linda Drive, West Covina. That gives you . . . oh, two months, easy, before the next loop. Okay?*

"Okay. Great. Anything else?"

But the radio just said:

> *Well, I give you all my money,*
> *but you just don't treat me right.*

Which was fine with me. One of the things I liked best about the home time they gave me—and even most of the working time, up to the mid-eighties, anyway—was the music. I opened the glove compartment and flicked on the finder.

It led me further into the west side, over the river, and then south on Seneca, to where there was a little industrial area, crosscut by railroad tracks, to the west of the city prison farm. The homing beam was pretty strong; so I checked at Calvin's Hamburger Haven and at a couple of liquor stores, but Chug and Harley weren't in their usual haunts. At last I just cruised, quartering the area, until I turned down a narrow gravel road running beside some tracks between two low buildings, and the finder went ape. Curious, I cut the lights and turned off the radio and the finder and then rode the brake, letting the car inch forward slowly into the darkness until my eyes adjusted enough to see some movement in one of the loading docks across the tracks from me. Then I killed the engine and got out of the car, crossing the tracks as quietly as possible.

It was my "assistants," all right, and they had somebody down in a corner of the dock. Whoever it was was struggling, but none of them was making any sounds beyond occasional grunts and heavy breathing. As I drew nearer, some gravel crunched under one of my boots and Harley whirled around, a blade blossoming out of his fist in the same motion.

"It's me," I said.

He peered for a moment and then relaxed.

"Hey, Blue. Great." He spoke in a loud whisper. "Come hold her legs for me while I get my pants undone."

I put a hand on the edge of the dock and vaulted up. It looked as though the girl had a cast on one arm. Chug had a hand over her mouth and was twisting the cast up toward her chin with the other, using it to pin her good arm against her chest. It must have hurt, but she was still kicking at Harley with her bare legs, her skirt already pushed up around her waist. He was on his knees, trying to open his pants and hold her legs at the same time. As he turned back toward her from talking to me, one of her legs got loose and struck his hand, knocking the knife loose. He went scuttling after it.

"Grab her legs," Chug whispered.

All things being equal, I would have waited for them to finish, but there was no way I could help them. My touching her would have defeated their whole purpose. Instead, I said: "The Oracle is calling."

They both let go of the girl at once and began getting to their feet, their clumsiness suddenly vanishing. Standing, they looked at me in silence, waiting.

"The car's across the tracks," I said. "Wait for me."

They nodded and jumped down off the dock. Harley gave a puzzled glance back at the girl, as if he'd never seen her before. She was lying still with her eyes closed, breathing in sobs through her mouth, clutching at her cast with her good arm. I watched her for a moment, trying to decide whether she'd be a problem. If Chug and Harley got in serious trouble with the law, it would mean either relocating them—in time as well as space—or finding new helpers. It was an inconvenience either way.

She opened her eyes and returned my gaze, apparently in control of herself. Her body tensed slightly, as if gathering strength for another struggle. She couldn't have been more than twelve, but I'd killed younger. I'd just about made up my mind to finish her off, and I had even reached out with one hand, to touch her, but instead of drawing away, as women usually do, she reached her good hand toward me, apparently unafraid, as if she thought I were offering to help her to her feet. It startled me so that I jerked my hand back, as if from some unfamiliar instinct, and her hand fell on my leather sleeve. Gripping my arm, she pulled herself up and then used her good arm to smooth her skirt down around her legs. Neither of us said anything. After a moment she nodded once, quickly, and then jumped off the end of the dock, landing like a cat on bent legs, and disappeared into the dark. I frowned to myself, feeling foolish, and then jumped down myself and headed for the car.

When I started the engine, the radio said:

At Royal Cleaners we know how, yes, we know how to clean.

And I let the car roll on down the dark road, fixing in my mind a parking lot I knew of, outside a liquor store near the state fairgrounds in Pomona, California, counting back carefully in time from the occasion when I'd been there last, to make sure I wouldn't catch up with my earlier self and close the loop. Time is flexible enough to tolerate a lot of paradoxes, but multiple selves is not one of them. The later self disappears, merges perhaps; no one knows what it feels like, and no one much wants to find out. After a moment, I hit the farthest-right radio button, and the radio said:

And the Mississippi River
runs like molasses in the summertime.

I listened to the music for a while, letting the engine idle, watching the traffic on the freeway beyond the far fence of the parking lot, and getting my bearings, thinking how to get from Pomona to where I wanted to go—not jumping, just driving like anyone else. Chug and Harley waited in the backseat. The radio told me it was 7:30 P.M.

"I'm after a single female alien," I told my helpers at last. "She's with a group of natives who might try to defend her."

"Armed?" Harley asked.

I shrugged.

"You've been to 1970 before. It might be anything from broadswords to machine guns. Most likely, they'll have blades of some kind, with maybe a handgun or two. Possibly clubs and chains—that kind of thing."

Chug and Harley busied themselves, checking all the little lethal things they carried, while I put the car in gear and headed for the freeway. It was a cool night—not like spring in Wichita, but like December in Los Angeles: not enough wind and cooling as it darkened. Everything looked pretty much as I remembered it. I have what I guess is a nervous habit of checking things out, to make sure the times haven't changed on me. Part of the reason is the danger of looping. I can jump only to within a couple of weeks of times and places I've been to before, unless the Oracle jumps me; so I try to visualize times and places in some detail, to avoid overshooting. Also, I used to worry about jumping clear to another track, though I've been told it's impossible. When I was new to the job, I worried about knocking off one of my own ancestors, until the Oracle convinced me it wouldn't matter. I'd still be me; I'd just be living in a track that hadn't (or wouldn't) produce me. I used to think about these things, until it started keeping me up nights and giving me headaches, and I decided just to put in my (subjective) time and let the Oracle worry about keeping track of all the other kinds.

I came down off the West Covina exit and then had to cruise for a while to find Loma Linda Drive. Number 5234 turned out to be the usual fake Spanish mission with the semicircular drive in front. There were no lights on in the front windows, but one of them harbored a faint glow, as if there were lights on somewhere deeper inside. We crossed the front yard on foot, cutting an arc of the driveway, and found a walkway leading to a gate in the tall wooden fence that hid the backyard.

Inside the fence was nothing but a concrete walkway, surrounding a swimming pool. A big square of light from the patio doors floated on the water, making everything else seem darker. Chug stumbled over something, and we paused to look. It was a dog, a German shepherd, with its throat cut, though there was hardly any blood on the concrete where it lay.

"Vampires?" Harley asked.

I shrugged. After 1965, in Southern California, anything was possible.

"Dig that," Chug said, surprising me. He rarely spoke, in either persona.

There was something hanging from the diving board, at the darkest end of the pool. Harley got out the infrared scope and zoomed it in for us so that we wouldn't have to cross in front of the patio doors. It was a girl, naked, apparently dead, hung up literally by her thumbs, the rope looped over the board. It wasn't a high board; her feet dangled in the water. She looked to be covered with blood, as if it had been painted on her, over every bit of skin. I scanned to the poolside behind her and spotted a yellow plastic bucket, stained with something dark.

"That's where the dog's blood went," I said.

We moved toward the patio doors, keeping as much in shadow as possible. When we could see inside, we stopped.

It was one of those scenes you have to spend some time sorting out before you know what you're looking at. The first thing that caught my eye was the writing on the opposite wall: PIGS PIGGIES DIE. It was written in some kind of blood, and there appeared to be a lot more available. There was a guy strung up by his wrists in a doorway at one corner of the room, with a barbecue fork sticking in one side, though the wound it had made didn't seem large enough to account for the blood soaking his swimming trunks. Other than that, I could make out half a dozen freaks, three guys and three girls. The girls all carried big, heavy-looking knives, with tape wrapped around the handles; the guys had pieces of stiff wire—maybe car radio antennae—and were using them to slash at something lying on the floor behind a sofa. I kept an eye on the girls, who were in a little group to one side of the room, apparently giggling over something they'd found in the desk there.

I told Harley to cover the patio door, and Chug and I went back along the side of the house until we found a side door which led through the kitchen into a little hallway that ran back to the den. I stood in the darkness there while Chug went looking for the third entrance, the one where the guy in the swimming suit was tied up. From where I stood I could see what was behind the sofa: another guy in a swimming suit, his head hidden by a blood-soaked terry-cloth shirt. He looked like red meat, as if his skin had been stripped off. I could also see what I'd missed before—a seventh freak and a fourth victim. The freak was a big, smelly-looking guy with fly-away hair, dressed in a black jacket like mine, except that his was greasy and its sleeves were torn off. His victim, wearing only the bottom half of her swimsuit, was kneeling in a corner next to the patio door, while the freak stood in front of her, legs spread, with his hands in front of him, apparently attempting to get a blowjob. It was a lost cause; the woman looked as if she were trying very hard to go catatonic and was about three-quarters of the way there. Her head was bent rigidly sideways, her face all closed up, as if she were trying to seal out the whole world—not just from her eyes and mouth, but from her pores.

I was more interested in the three chicks with the knives, since one of them had to be my alien. There was no way to tell which one from that distance; all the aliens I've ever met have seemed perfectly human. And I suspect they are. My guess is that they're only alien in the sense that they're on the other side—the "bad guys." I don't care, one way or the other; I took the job because I liked the idea of living in a time when you can go outside without a mask on, and you can have a room all to yourself' not because I'm some kind of hero.

I saw one of the girls do a double take toward the door where Chug would be appearing. She took a step backward and yelled: "Donny!"

Everyone stopped to see what was happening, and I took the opportunity to step into the room, beckoning to Harley at the same time.

The would-be mouth-rapist, whom I took to be Donny, came whirling out of the corner with his erection in one hand and a fancy, red switchblade in the other, sticking straight up in his fist, the way you hold a bouquet. Behind him, I now saw a single trickle of blood running down the cheek of the woman.

There was a funny little moment of silence while everyone stared at Chug, who had his own blade drawn, holding it as if he knew how to use it. Donny stuffed himself back into his pants with his free hand, keeping the switchblade out in front of him. The girls were between him and Chug, and one of them had gone into a semicrouch, her knife raised above her shoulder like a spear. Chug glanced her way, somehow refocusing his whole body in her direction, and she took a small step backward.

I cleared my throat.

"What the fuck . . . ?" Donny began, but then one of the guys with radio aerials nodded toward Harley, who had come in soundlessly through the patio doors, closing them behind him. Donny glanced that way and then licked his lips indecisively.

I had them pegged as power-trippers, not fighters, the kind who are at their best against unarmed straights. The late sixties and the early seventies were full of them, which is why I recruited Chug and Harley from the fifties. Already most of them were giving little looks here and there, not at one another, but at the windows and doors.

"You guys Angels?" Donny asked at last.

"Ghosts," I said. It looked as if some of them were so caught up in their own horror show that they were ready to believe it. Donny looked at me the way you look at an unfriendly dog, wondering whether to brazen it out or risk a hand trying to make friends.

"Look," he said, "we got no hassle with you dudes. We ought to be on the same side, against the pigs." He glanced around at his group's handiwork, maybe taking courage from the gore. "Besides," he added hopefully, "we got you seven to three."

I made a little motion to Chug, who made a little underhand motion of his own. Donny, startled, dropped his knife and held out both hands, like someone trying to catch a baseball but afraid of it, and Chug's blade went between them somehow and buried itself in his belly. He jerked backward, making only a little, unvocalized sound, as if the wind had been knocked out of him, and then he sat down heavily, clutching at the knife with both hands, gave a little moan, and fell sideways, fainting before dying.

The girl who had held up her knife before made a lunge toward Chug but stopped when she saw he already had another blade out.

"You three can go," I said to the guys with the aerials. They didn't even glance at the three girls, who drew closer to one another as if suddenly understanding our intentions. The guys edged past Harley and out the patio doors, and in the little silence that followed, we all heard their bare footfalls padding away on the concrete before disappearing into grass and nighttime.

I stepped toward the girls, Chug and Harley closing in on either side to hem them in. They backed up against the wall, stiff and wary, trying to get a psychic consensus, maybe, on whether to yield or fight.

"Drop the knives," Chug told them, and two of them did so at once. The third glared at him and then threw the knife down nearly at his feet.

"It's not what you think," I told them when I was within touching distance. "I'm from the Oracle." None of them gave any visible reaction. I held out one hand toward them, the fingers slightly spread. "Touch my hand," I told them, "and you can leave."

Two of them watched me suspiciously; the third stared at my hand. I moved it only slightly in her direction, and she trembled faintly but did not flinch.

"Why?" one of the others asked huskily. "What's the catch?"

"No catch. I get off on it; that's all. Call it a power thing. Touch my hand and you can go."

Two of them glanced at one another and then reached out hesitantly. The third pushed one of them toward me and made a break toward the nearest door, but Chug intercepted her, spinning her around to face me, then holding her in an armlock.

"I'm no threat to the Oracle," she screamed. "I just wanted to get away." They always say something like that, if they say anything. I touched her cheek with the tips of my fingers, and Chug let her fall.

The other girls were on their knees now, staring at her, then at me. The alien's last words had been in a language no one would speak for a couple of thousand years.

"Go on," I told them. They went.

I sent Chug and Harley back to the car and then took a last look around. Everyone looked dead except the woman in the corner, who had retreated into some other world. I left everything the way it was and went out the patio doors. As I was going along the path beside the house, someone standing in the shadow of the house next-door said: "Hello, Blue."

I stopped, suspending judgment for a moment, and waited for her to come out in the open. When she did, I had a fleeting moment of recognition but then couldn't fix it in my mind. I had thought at first she must be someone from the Oracle's time, but I knew that wasn't where I'd seen her before. She wasn't especially good-looking—too thin for my tastes—but she wore her hair long, in the current style. She had on a simple yellow dress, not quite knee-length, which must have seemed nearly out of place in Southern California, 1970.

"I'm a friend," she said. "An old friend. I knew you more than ten years ago, in the late fifties." She hardly looked old enough for that to be true; I guessed that she was twenty-six or twenty-seven.

"If that's true," I said, "then this is our first meeting, as far as I'm concerned."

She shook her head, giving a tiny smile.

"Not quite, You met me about two hours ago, by your time. You saved me from your . . . friends." She nodded toward the front drive, reminding me that I ought to be getting out before anyone investigated what had been going on.

"You were a child," I said. "Anyway, I don't have any friends, old or otherwise. Chug and Harley work for me."

"I was your friend," she insisted. "I showed you how to touch people without killing them."

I'm hard to shock, but that came close. I nearly smiled, though I'm unaccustomed to doing so.

"That's not possible. It's beyond my control. The price I pay for living in these times."

"You think it's impossible," she said. "But it's not. You do control it. They gave you a triggering mechanism that you use unconsciously, but you can override it."

There was a low whistle from the front yard, a query from Harley. I gave an answering whistle, temporizing. I had thought I was immune to desire in the ordinary sense, but what she said—the possibilities it raised—had touched something inside me. I frowned.

"I never went for kids," I said.

She reddened.

"We weren't lovers. We were friends. You took care of me."

That was a role I had trouble imagining for myself. I held out a hand to her.

"Prove it," I said.

She came toward me but didn't touch me.

"Close your eyes," she said, "and think of things you like. Think of a thunderstorm."

When she told me to close my eyes, it fleetingly crossed my mind that she might be an unusually clever alien, looking to take me out, but the mention of thunderstorms hooked me. I loved thunderstorms; I get a kick out of walking in them—partly because they're deadly back where I come from originally. An alien who didn't know me would have been more likely to think they terrified me. I closed my eyes and thought of a time when I'd walked ten blocks in a rainstorm. I remembered the way the warm water had hung in my sweater, making it heavy and only gradually turning cold against my skin. Something warm and soft touched against my hand.

I opened my eyes to see her hand resting on top of mine. She gave me a nervous smile and said: "Keep thinking good thoughts. Think of Buddy Holly."

Another score. Holly was one of my favorites, but his whole career lay within the home time I hadn't lived through yet, and no one had ever made a film of him performing. One of the things I was looking forward to was seeing him in person. I thought of him singing "Rave On," one of my favorites. I pictured stills I had seen of Holly and the Crickets, and I tried to imagine, as I had sometimes before, how he would look in front of an audience of screaming teenagers—a skinny, funny-looking guy with glasses.

"Now that you know it's possible, you'll be able to do it when you want to," she said. I felt her hand still against mine, still warm. It was something I hadn't felt since . . . when? Maybe never.

"Why?" I asked. "Is it so you won't have to teach me the first time, back in the fifties?" I felt dizzy, as if slightly high.

She shook her head.

"I spent a long time looking for you," she said. "Back then, I mean. And then it took a while to make friends. We had only about three years together. You disappeared at the end of 1959."

I nodded.

"Retired back home." It wasn't something I was looking forward to.

"You thought there might be a way to make more time for us," she said, "if we could get together outside the fifties."

I nodded, already thinking of a couple of possibilities.

"But why wait ten years?" I asked. "There were lots of times you could have intercepted me during the sixties."

She reddened again.

"I wanted our ages to be closer together," she said.

I nodded, thinking of the Poni-Tails' song "Born Too Late." What would it be like to wait ten years for someone you loved, knowing he might kill you without a word? I couldn't imagine.

"I can't imagine falling in love with anyone," I told her bluntly.

She looked at the ground, still flushed.

"I know," she said. "You aren't like that."

Another whistle came from the front yard, and then I heard the distant sound of sirens.

"We've got to split," I told her. "And . . ."

"And you're not sure yet."

I nodded.

"I'll go to the end of the block and wait for fifteen minutes," she said.

"If you haven't come back by then, I'll know you decided not to."

I nodded again and turned away from her. Going across the front yard, I rubbed at the back of my hand, where it still seemed to tingle from her touch. Chug and Harley were waiting in the backseat.

I left the lights off until we were several blocks away, and then I turned the radio on, too, and it said:

> *Just be nice to the gentlemen, Fancy,*
> *and they'll be nice to you.*

I reached toward the jump button, thinking of 1954 but then changed my mind, unaccountably reluctant to go home yet, to get back in touch with the Oracle. Instead, I did something you're never supposed to do: I punched the button without thinking of anything at all, and the radio said:

> *Saddest thing in the whole wide world*
> *is to see your baby with another girl.*

And we were moving slowly through rush-hour traffic in a cold city that might have been Milwaukee or Omaha or Dayton, and it occurred to me that if she was telling the truth, there was no need to go back for her; she had already shown me how to touch people, and I wondered why she hadn't thought of that, and then I wondered if she had, and I frowned and punched again, and the radio said:

> *They said they found my high-school ring*
> *clutched in your fingers tight.*

And there was snow all over the hills, and a hawk circled overhead, scanning for movement in all the white below, and salt rattled against the bottom of the car, and I thought of the things I could do if I could really touch people: swim at the Joyland pool, play basketball at the Downtown Y, stand in lines at the movies, go dancing . . . and Harley asked:

"What's going on?"

And I didn't say anything, just punched again, and the radio said:

> *She loved me so long*
> *and she loved me so hard*
> *I finally passed out*
> *in her front yard.*

And it was hot nighttime, and there was an ocean salt smell in the car, reminding me of a time in Baltimore when I'd touched the forehead of a blind beggar, and he'd rolled past me into the street, and two small black boys had appeared from nowhere to pick up the coins rolling and bouncing from his cup, and that reminded me of something else—the time the Oracle had jumped me to 1933, to cover for another agent who would have looped there, and I pushed the button with a purpose this time, and the radio didn't say anything, and there was rain running straight down, cold and windless, filling up the Portland streets, and most of the stores were locked and boarded, and I thought, *We could have seven years of this, and then the forties, but I'd never get to see Buddy Holly after all, because the Oracle would take the car back.* And then I remembered that she—what was her name?—would loop in the early forties, anyway, whenever she was born, and I frowned and punched again, and the radio said:

> *But it's all right now;*
> *in fact, it's a gas.*

And heat washed through the car like an electric pulse, in a place that might have been West Texas or hell, and I thought of the other extreme, the farthest forward I'd ever been, except for my native time, where we could live together for the rest of our lives, or at least until our oxygen ran out, and I shook my head and thought of a thunderstorm—not any particular one—remembering her touch, and I punched, and the radio said:

> *And these few precious days*
> *I'll share with you.*

And I sat straight up in my seat, trying to see through the black water running on the windshield, convinced for an instant I'd jumped into my early home time, but then I realized I hadn't looped, and I wondered if I'd gotten into another track, after all, though I figured it was just someone playing a golden oldie: and then I knew it was, becaused the announcer came on, and then the news, to say that Spiro Agnew had resigned, and I thought that the easiest thing to do after all would be to go home, to 1954 and find the girl and make what I could of those six years, even though—let's face it—I'd rather spend the time with the woman. And then I suddenly saw how I could do it, and I punched again, and the radio said:

> *Wouldn't it be nice to be together*
> *In the kind of world where we belong?*

And I pulled off the side of the road, somewhere on US-40 west of Indianapolis, with a rainstorm gathering ahead, and I told Chug and Harley to climb out, and as soon as they had, I punched again, and the radio crackled with late-night white noise, and I turned off the engine and got out, waiting for my eyes to adjust to the dark; and in a moment I saw her, running toward me, and I waited until she was near enough to touch, and I stepped out to the edge of the railroad track, blocking her path, and she stopped, startled, and then frowned when she saw who I was and gave a glance backward, and I smiled and said: "By the way, what's your name?"

And she stared at me for a moment and then said: "Angela."

And I reached a hand out to her once again, saying: "I'm sorry, Angela."

And she took the hand nearly without hesitating, and nothing happened for a moment, and then I made myself think a certain way I hadn't even known I could before . . . and it hurt.

I put her body in the backseat and sealed the windows and vents and turned on the oxygen, and punched again, and the radio crackled in protest but didn't say anything, and I put on my mask and gloves and got out into the fog that never goes away and laid her body down on the beach by the ocean that nothing lived in anymore, and I touched her again, on the forehead, feeling a way I'd never felt before, and got back in and punched again, and the radio said:

Love the one you're with.

And I had to take a minute to unseal the car and flush it out and take off the mask and gloves, and then I cruised around the back way, avoiding Loma Linda Drive, and came up behind her at the corner; and when she saw me she came running out, and I reached over and pushed the door open, and as soon as she was in I punched again, and we were back in the alley alongside the railroad tracks, but it was graying into morning, and Don McNeill was on the radio, and she asked: "Where are we?"

"June 1954."

She gave me a startled look.

"But I haven't looped?"

I shook my head.

"I took care of it."

She accepted that for the moment, though I knew I'd have to tell her sometime exactly how I'd done it. But not yet.

"Out," I said, and when we were both out, I found a long piece of scrap metal and reached it back through the window, and the radio started to say:

Blue? Where . . .

And I was standing there with Angela, with half a piece of scrap metal in my hand.

"I just resigned," I said. "And that's company property."

"You sent it back?"

"Not exactly. I sent it to Riverside Park in December 1959. You can live straight through, now, but I'll loop in 1960. Maybe I'll think of more options by then, if the Oracle doesn't have some way of grabbing the car during a jump."

She nodded and took hold of my hand, and she stayed alive, and I felt as good as I had in a long time. It occurred to me that I might be an alien now, and there might be somebody like me coming around to touch me one of these days—although I had a hunch that the Oracle might be inclined to leave me alone, rather than expose more agents to the knowledge which Angela had given me.

She was looking around now, recognizing the place from her childhood, though that had been in a different track.

"Hey, this could be fun," she said.

I nodded and put an arm around her, enjoying the feel of freedom to do that small a thing.

"You're lucky," I told her. "You get to see Buddy Holly twice."

Contact with alien beings is often envisioned today in cool, cerebral terms: radio messages and mathematical codes whispering out through the light-years to remote civilizations we will never encounter in the flesh. Here Nebula-winner Gregory Benford—who has emerged as one of SF's most powerful writers with books like In the Ocean of Night *(Dell),* The Stars in Shroud *(Berkley/Putnam), and, in collaboration with Gordon Eklund,* If the Stars Are Gods, *(Berkley)—gives us instead the gritty, concrete* actuality *of alien contact: the touch of its flesh on yours, the heat of its massive body, its smell, the sight of nerves and muscles working under its waxen and glossy skin, the pressure and tight enclosure of its surrounding bulk, the effort to make contact with that distant—perhaps cool, perhaps cerebral, perhaps not—intelligence that is at the hot and fleshy core of every living creature.*

GREGORY BENFORD
In Alien Flesh

I

—green surf lapping, chilling—

Reginri's hand jerked convulsively on the sheets. His eyes were closed.

—silver coins gliding and turning in the speckled sky, eclipsing the sun—

The sheets were a clinging swamp. He twisted in their grip.

—a chiming song, tinkling cool rivulets washing his skin—

He opened his eyes.

A yellow blade of afternoon sunlight hung in the room, dust motes swimming through it. He panted in shallow gasps. Belej was standing beside the bed.

"They came again, didn't they?" she said, almost whispering.

"Ye . . . yes." His throat was tight and dry.

"This can't go *on*, darling. We thought you could sleep better in the daytime, with everyone out in the fields, but—"

"Got to get out of here," he mumbled. He rolled out of bed and pulled on his black work suit. Belej stood silent, blinking rapidly, chewing at her lower lip. Reginri fastened his boots and slammed out of the room. His steps thumped hollowly on the planking. She listened to them hurry down the hallway. They paused; the airless silence returned. Then the outer door creaked, banged shut.

She hurried after him.

She caught up near the rim of the canyon, a hundred meters from the log buildings. He looked at her. He scratched at his matted hair and hunched his shoulders forward.

"That one was pretty bad," he said woodenly.

"If they keep on getting worse . . ."

"They won't."

"We hope. But we don't know that. If I understood what they're about . . ."

"I can't quite describe it. They're different each time. The *feeling* seems the same, even though . . ." Some warmth had returned to his voice. "It's hard."

Belej sat down near the canyon edge. She looked up at him. Her eyebrows knitted together above large dark eyes. "All right," she said, her mood shifting suddenly, an edge coming into her voice. "One, I don't know what these nightmares are about. Two, I don't know where they come from. That horrible expedition you went on, I suppose, but you're not even clear about that. Three, I don't know why you insisted on joining their dirty expedition in the—"

"I told you, dammit. I had to go."

"You wanted the extra money," Belej said flatly. She cupped her chin in a tiny hand.

"It wasn't *extra* money, it was *any* money." He glowered at the jagged canyon below them. Her calm, accusing manner irritated him.

"You're a pod cutter. You could have found work."

"The season was bad. This was last year, remember. Rates weren't good."

"But you had heard about this Sasuke and Leo, what people said about them—"

"Vanleo, that's the name. Not Leo."

"Well, whatever. You didn't have to work for them."

"No, of course not," he said savagely. "I could've busted my ass on a field-hopper in planting season, twelve hours a day for thirty units pay, max. And when I got tired of that, or broke a leg, maybe I could've signed on to mold circuitry like a drone." He picked up a stone and flung it far over the canyon edge. "A great life."

Belej paused a long moment. At the far angular end of the canyon a pink mist seeped between the highest peaks and began spilling downward, gathering speed. Zeta Reticuli still rode high in the mottled blue sky; but a chill was sweeping up from the canyon. The wind carried an acrid tang.

He wrinkled his nose. Within an hour they would have to move inside. The faint reddish haze would thicken. It was good for the plant life of northern Persenuae, but to human lungs the fog was an itching irritant.

Belej sighed. "Still," she said softly, "you weren't forced to go. If you had known it would be so—"

"Yes," he said, and something turned in his stomach. "If anybody had known."

II

At first it was not the Drongheda that he found disquieting. It was the beach itself and, most of all, the waves.

They lapped at his feet with a slow, sucking energy, undermining the coarse sand beneath his boots. They began as little ripples that marched in from the gray horizon and slowly hissed up the black beach. Reginri watched one curl into greenish foam further out; the tide was falling.

"Why are they so slow?" he said.

Sasuke looked up from the carry-pouches. "What?"

"Why do the waves take so long?"

Sasuke stopped for a moment and studied the ponderous swell, flecked with yellow waterweed. An occasional large wave broke and splashed on the sharp lava rocks further out. "I never thought about it," Sasuke said. "Guess it's the lower gravity."

"Uh-hum." Reginri shrugged.

A skimmer fish broke water and snapped at something in the air. Somehow, the small matter of the waves unnerved him. He stretched restlessly in his skinsuit.

"I guess the low-gee sim doesn't prepare you for everything," he said. Sasuke didn't hear; he was folding out the tappers, coils and other gear.

Reginri could put it off no longer. He fished out his binocs and looked at the Drongheda.

At first it seemed like a smooth brown rock, water-worn and timeless. And the reports were correct: it moved landward. It rose like an immense blister on the rippled sea. He squinted, trying to see the dark circle of the pithole. There, yes, a shadowed blur ringed with dappled red. At the center, darker, lay his entranceway. It looked impossibly small.

He lowered the binocs, blinking. Zeta Reticuli burned low on the flat horizon, a fierce orange point that sliced through this planet's thin air.

"God, I could do with a burn," Reginri said.

"None of that, you'll need your wits in there," Sasuke said stiffly. "Anyway, there's no smoking blowby in these suits."

"Right." Reginri wondered if the goddamned money was worth all this. Back on Persenuae—he glanced up into the purpling sky and found it, a pearly glimmer nestling in closer to Zeta—it had seemed a good bet, a fast and easy bit of money, a kind of scientific outing with a tang of adventure. Better than agriwork, anyway. A far better payoff than anything else he could get with his limited training, a smattering of electronics and fabrication techniques. He even knew some math, though not enough to matter. And it didn't make any difference in this job, Sasuke had told him, even if math was the whole point of this thing.

He smiled to himself. An odd thought, that squiggles on the page were a commercial item, something people on Earth would send a ramscoop full of microelectronics and bioengineered cells in exchange for—

"Some help here, eh?" Sasuke said roughly.

"Sorry."

Reginri knelt and helped the man spool out the tapper lines, checking the connectors. Safely up the beach, beyond the first pale line of sand dunes, lay the packaged electronics gear and the crew, already in place, who would monitor while he and Vanleo were inside.

As the two men unwound the cables, unsnarling the lines and checking the backup attachments, Reginri glanced occasionally at the Drongheda. It was immense, far larger than he had imagined. The 3Ds simply didn't convey the massive feel of the thing. It wallowed in the shallows, now no more than two hundred meters away.

"It's stopped moving," he said.

"Sure. It'll be there for days, by all odds." Sasuke spoke without looking up. He inserted his diagnostic probe at each socket, watching the meters intently. He was methodical, sure of himself—quite the right sort of man to handle the technical end, Reginri thought.

"That's the point, isn't it? I mean, the thing is going to stay put."

"Sure."

"So you say. It isn't going to roll over while we're in there, because it never has."

Sasuke stopped working and scowled. Through his helmet bubble, Reginri could see the man's lips pressed tight together. "You fellows always get the shakes on the beach. It never fails. Last crew I had out here, they were crapping in their pants from the minute we sighted a Drongheda."

"Easy enough for you to say. You're not going in."

"I've been in, mister. You haven't. Do what we say, what Vanleo and I tell you, and you'll be all right."

"Is that what you told the last guy who worked with you?"

Sasuke looked up sharply. "Kaufmann? You talked to him?"

"No. A friend of mine knows him."

"Your friend keeps bad company."

"Sure, me included."

"I meant—"

"Kaufmann didn't quit for no reason, you know."

"He was a coward," Sasuke said precisely.

"The way he put it, he just wasn't fool enough to keep working this thing the way you want. With this equipment."

"There isn't any other way."

Reginri motioned seaward. "You could put something automated inside. Plant a sensor."

"That will transmit out through thirty meters of animal fat? Through all that meat? Reliably? With a high bit rate? Ha!"

Reginri paused. He knew it wasn't smart to push Sasuke this way, but the rumors he had heard from Kaufmann made him uneasy. He glanced back toward the lifeless land. Down the beach, Vanleo had stopped to inspect something, kneeling on the hard-packed sand. Studying a rock, probably—nothing alive scuttled or crawled on this beach.

Reginri shrugged. "I can see that, but why do we have to stay in so long? Why not just go in, plant the tappers and get out?"

"They won't stay in place. If the Drongheda moves even a little, they'll pop out."

"Don't make 'em so damned delicate."

"Mister, you can't patch in with spiked nails. That's a neural terminus point you're going after, not a statphone connection."

"So, I have to mother it through? Sit there up in that huge gut and sweat it out?"

"You're getting paid for it," Sasuke said in clipped tones.

"Maybe not enough."

"Look, if you're going to bellyache—"

Reginri shrugged. "Okay, I'm not a pro at this. I came mostly to see the Drongheda anyway. But once you look at it, that electronics rig of yours seems pretty inadequate. And if that thing out there decides to give me a squeeze—"

"It won't. Never has."

A short, clipped bark came over the earphones. It was Vanleo's laugh, ringing hollow in their helmets. Vanleo approached, striding smoothly along the water line. "It hasn't happened, so it won't? Bad logic. Simply because a series has many terms does not mean it is infinite. Nor that it converges."

Reginri smiled warmly, glad that the other man was back. There was a remorseless quality about Sasuke that set his teeth on edge.

"Friend Sasuke, don't conceal what we both know from this boy." Vanleo clapped Sasuke on the back jovially. "The Drongheda are a cipher. Brilliant, mysterious, vast intellects—and, it is presumptuous to pretend we understand anything about them. All we are able to follow is their mathematics—perhaps that is all they wish us to see." A brilliant smile creased his face.

Vanleo turned and silently studied the cables that played out from the dunes and into the surf.

"Looks okay," he said. "Tide's going out."

He turned abruptly and stared into Reginri's eyes. "Got your nerve back now, boy? I was listening on suit audio."

Reginri shuffled uneasily. Sasuke was irritating, but at least he knew how to deal with the man. Vanleo, though . . . somehow Vanleo's steady, intent gaze unsettled him. Reginri glanced out at the Drongheda and felt a welling dread. On impulse he turned to Vanleo and said, "I think I'll stay on the beach."

Vanleo's face froze. Sasuke made a rough spitting sound and began, "Another goddamned—" but Vanleo cut him off with a brusque motion of his hand.

"What do you mean?" Vanleo said mildly.

"I . . . I don't feel so good about going inside."

"Oh. I see."

"I mean, I don't know if that thing isn't going to . . . well, it's the first time I did this, and . . ."

"I see."

"Tell you what. I'll go out with you two, sure. I'll stay in the water and keep the cables from getting snarled—you know, the job you were going to do. That'll give me a chance to get used to the work. Then, next time . . ."

"That might be years from now."

"Well, that's right, but . . ."

"You're endangering the success of the entire expedition."

"I'm not experienced. What if . . ." Reginri paused. Vanleo had logic on his side, he knew. This was the first Drongheda they had been able to reach in over two years. Many of them drifted down the ragged coast, hugging the shallows. But most stayed only a day or two. This was the first in a long while that had moored itself offshore in a low, sheltered shoal. The satellite scan had picked it up, noted its regular pattern of movements that followed the tides. So Vanleo got the signal, alerted Reginri and the stand-by crew, and they lifted in a fast booster from Persenuae . . .

"A boot in the ass is what he needs," Sasuke said abruptly.

Vanleo shook his head. "I think not," he said.

The comtempt in Sasuke's voice stiffened Reginri's resolve. "I'm not going in."

"Oh?" Vanleo smiled.

"Sue me for breach of contract when we get back to Persenuae, if you want. I'm not doing it."·

"Oh, we'll do much more than that," Vanleo said casually. "We'll transfer the financial loss of this expedition to your shoulders. There's no question it's your fault."

"I—"

"So you'll never draw full wages again, *ever*, Vanleo continued calmly.

Reginri moved his feet restlessly. There was a feeling of careful, controlled assurance in Vanleo that gave his words added weight. And behind the certainty of those eyes Reginri glimpsed something else.

"I don't know . . ." He breathed deeply, trying to clear his head. "Guess I got rattled a little, there."

He hesitated and then snorted self-deprecatingly. "I guess, I guess I'll be all right."

Sasuke nodded, holding his tongue. Vanleo smiled heartily. "Fine. Fine. We'll just forget this little incident, then, eh?" Abruptly he turned and walked down the beach. His steps were firm, almost jaunty.

III

An air squirrel glided in on the gathering afternoon winds. It swung out over the lip of the canyon, chattering nervously, and then coasted back to the security of the hotbush. The two humans watched it leisurely strip a seed pod and nibble away.

"I don't understand why you didn't quit then," Belej said at last. "Right then. On the beach. A lawsuit wouldn't stick, not with other crewmen around to fill in for you."

Reginri looked at her blankly. "Impossible."

"Why? You'd seen that thing. You could see it was dangerous."

"I knew that before we left Persenuae."

"But you hadn't *seen* it."

"So what? I'd signed a contract."

Belej tossed her head impatiently. "I remember you saying to me it was a kind of big fish. That's all you said that night before you left. You could argue that you hadn't understood the danger . . ."

Reginri grimaced. "Not a fish. A mammal."

"No difference. Like some other fish back on Earth, you told me."

"Like the humpback and the blue and the fin and the sperm whales," he said slowly. "Before men killed them off, they started to suspect the blues might be intelligent."

"Whales weren't mathematicians, though, were they?" she said lightly.

"We'll never know, now."

Belej leaned back into the matted brownish grass. Strands of black hair blew gently in the wind. "That Leo lied to you about that thing, the fish, didn't he?"

"How?"

"Telling you it wasn't dangerous."

He sat upright in the grass and hugged his knees. "He gave me some scientific papers. I didn't read most of them—hell, they were clogged with names I didn't know, funny terms. That's what you never understood, Belej. We don't know much about Drongheda. Just that they've got lungs and a spine and come ashore every few years. Why they do even that, or what makes them intelligent—Vanleo spent thirty years on that. You've got to give him credit—"

"For dragging you into it. Ha!"

"The Drongheda never harmed anybody. Their eyes don't seem to register us. They probably don't even know we're there, and Vanleo's simple-minded attempts to communicate failed. He—"

"If a well-meaning, blind giant rolls over on you," she said, "you're still dead."

Reginri snorted derisively. "The Drongheda balance on ventral flippers. That's how they keep upright in the shallows. Whales couldn't do that, or—"

"You're not listening to me!" She gave him an exasperated glance.

"I'm telling you what happened."

"Go ahead, then. We can't stay out here much longer."

He peered out at the wrinkled canyon walls. Lime-green fruit trees dotted the burnished rocks. The thickening pink haze was slowly creeping across the canyon floor, obscuring details. The airborne life that colored the clouds would coat the leathery trees and trigger the slow rhythms of seasonal life. Part of the sluggish, inevitable workings of Persenuae, he thought.

"Mist looks pretty heavy," he agreed. He glanced back at the log cabins that were the communal living quarters. They blended into the matted grasses.

"Tell me," she said insistently.

"Well, I . . ."

"You keep waking me up with nightmares about it. I deserve to know. It's changed our lives together. I—"

He sighed. This was going to be difficult. "All right."

IV

Vanleo gave Reginri a clap on the shoulder and the three men set to work. Each took a spool of cable and walked backward, carrying it, into the surf. Reginri carefully watched the others and followed, letting the cable play out smoothly. He was so intent upon the work that he hardly noticed the enveloping wet that swirled about him. His oxygen pellet carrier was a dead awkward weight at his back, but once up to his waist in the lapping water, maneuvering was easier, and he could concentrate on something other than keeping his balance.

The sea bottom was smooth and clear, laced with metallic filaments of dull silver. Not metal, though; this was a planet with strangely few heavy elements. Maybe that was why land life had never taken hold here, and the island continents sprinkled amid the ocean were bleak, dusty deserts. More probably, the fact that this chilled world was small and further from the sun made it too hostile a place for land life. Persenuae, nearer in toward Zeta, thrived with both native and imported species, but this world had only sea creatures. A curious planet, this; a theoretical meeting point somewhere between the classic patterns of Earth and Mars. Large enough for percolating volcanoes, and thus oceans, but with an unbreathable air curiously high in carbon dioxide and low in oxygen. Maybe the wheel of evolution had simply not turned far enough here, and someday the small fish—or even the Drongheda itself—would evolve upward, onto the land.

But maybe the Drongheda *was* evolving, in intelligence, Reginri thought. The things seemed content to swim in the great oceans, spinning crystalline-mathematical puzzles for their own amusement. And for some reason they had responded when Vanleo first jabbed a probing electronic feeler into a neural nexus. The creatures spilled out realms of mathematical art that, Earthward, kept thousands working to decipher it—to rummage among a tapestry of cold theorems, tangled referents, seeking the quick axioms that lead to new corridors, silent pools of geometry and the intricate pyramiding of lines and angles, encasing a jungle of numbers.

"Watch it!" Sasuke sang out.

Reginri braced himself and a wave broke over him, splashing green foam against his faceplate.

"Riptide running here," Vanleo called. "Should taper off soon."

Reginri stood firm against the flow, keeping his knees loose and flexible for balance. Through his boots he felt the gritty slide of sand against smoothed rock. The cable spool was almost played out.

He turned to maneuver, and suddenly to the side he saw an immense brown wall. It loomed high, far above the gray waves breaking at its base. Reginri's chest tightened as he turned to study the Drongheda.

Its hide wall was delicately speckled in gold and green. The dorsal vents were black slashes that curved up the side, forming deep oily valleys.

Reginri cradled the cable spool under one arm and gingerly reached out to touch it. He pushed at it several times experimentally. It gave slightly with a soft, rubbery resistance.

"Watch the flukes!" Vanleo called. Reginri turned and saw a long black flipper break water fifty meters away. It languidly brushed the surface with a booming whack audible through his helmet and then submerged.

"He's just settling down, I expect," Vanleo called reassuringly. "They sometimes do that."

Reginri frowned at the water where the fluke had emerged. Deep currents welled up and rippled the surface.

"Let's have your cable," Sasuke said, "Reel it over here. I've got the mooring shaft sunk in."

Reginri spun out the rest of his spool and had some left when he reached Sasuke. Vanleo was holding a long tube pointed straight down into the water. He pulled a trigger and there was a muffled clap Reginri could hear over suit radio. He realized Vanleo was firing bolts into the ocean rock to secure their cable and connectors. Sasuke held out his hands and Reginri gave him the cable spool.

It was easier to stand here; the Drongheda screened them from most of the waves, and the undercurrents had ebbed. For a while Reginri stood uselessly by, watching the two men secure connections and mount the tapper lines. Sasuke at last waved him over, and as Reginri turned his back, they fitted the lines into his backpack.

Nervously, Reginri watched the Drongheda for signs of motion, but there were none. The ventral grooves formed an intricate ribbed pattern along the creature's side, and it was some moments before he thought to look upward and find the pithole. It was a red-rimmed socket, darker than the dappled brown around it. The ventral grooves formed an elaborate helix around the pithole, then arced away and down the body toward a curious mottled patch, about the same size as the pithole.

"What's that?" Reginri said, pointing at the patch.

"Don't know," Vanleo said. "Seems softer than the rest of the hide, but it's not a hole. All the Drongheda have 'em."

"Looks like a welt or something."

"Ummm," Vanleo murmured, distracted. "We'd better boost you up in a minute. I'm going to go around to the other side. There's another pithole exposed there, a little further up from the water line. I'll go in that way."

"How do I get up?"

"Spikes," Sasuke murmured. "It's shallow enough here."

It took several minutes to attach the climbing spikes to Reginri's boots. He leaned against the Drongheda for support and tried to mentally compose himself for what was to come. The sea welled around him, lapping warmly against his skinsuit. He felt a jittery sense of anticipation.

"Up you go," Sasuke said. "Kneel on my shoulders and get the spikes in solid before you put any weight on them. Do what we said, once you're inside, and you'll be all right."

V

Vanleo steadied him as he climbed onto Sasuke's back. It took some moments before Reginri could punch the climbing spikes into the thick, crinkled hide.

He was thankful for the low gravity. He pulled himself up easily, once he got the knack of it, and it took only a few moments to climb the ten meters to the edge of the pithole. Once there, he paused to rest.

"Not so hard as I thought," he said lightly.

"Good boy." Vanleo waved up at him. "Just keep steady and you'll be perfectly all right. We'll give you a signal on the com-line when you're to come out. This one won't be more than an hour, probably."

Reginri balanced himself on the lip of the pithole and took several deep breaths, tasting the oily air. In the distance gray waves broke into surf. The Drongheda rose like a bubble from the wrinkled sea. A bank of fog was rolling down the coastline. In it a shadowy shape floated. Reginri slitted his eyes to see better, but the fog wreathed the object and blurred its outline. Another Drongheda? He looked again but the form melted away in the white mist.

"Hurry it up," Sasuke called from below. "We won't move until you're in."

Reginri turned on the fleshy ledge beneath him and pulled at the dark blubbery folds that rimmed the pithole. He noticed that there were fine, gleaming threads all round the entrance. A mouth? An anus? Vanleo said not; the scientists who came to study the Drongheda had traced its digestive tract in crude fashion. But they had no idea what the pithole was for. It was precisely to find that out that Vanleo first went into one. Now it was Vanleo's theory that the pithole was the Drongheda's method of communication, since why else would the neural connections be so close to the surface inside? Perhaps, deep in the murky ocean, the Drongheda spoke to each other through these pitholes, rather than singing, like whales. Men had found no bioacoustic signature in the schools of Drongheda they had observed, but that meant very little.

Reginri pushed inward, through the iris of spongy flesh, and was at once immersed in darkness. His suit light clicked on. He lay in a sheath of meat with perhaps two hand spans of clearance on each side. The tunnel yawned ahead, absorbing the weak light. He gathered his knees and pushed upward against the slight grade.

"Electronics crew reports good contact with your tapper lines. This com okay?" Sasuke's voice came thin and high in Reginri's ear.

"Seems to be. Goddamned close in here."

"Sometimes it's smaller near the opening," Vanleo put in. "You shouldn't have too much climbing to do—most pitholes run pretty horizontal, when the Drongheda is holding steady like this."

"It's so tight. Going to be tough, crawling uphill," Reginri said, an uncertain waver in his voice.

"Don't worry about that. Just keep moving and look for the neural points." Vanleo paused. "Fish out the contacts for your tappers, will? I just got a call from the technicians, they want to check the connection."

"Sure." Reginri felt at his belly. "I don't seem to find . . ."

"They're right there, just like in training," Sasuke said sharply. "Pull'em out of their clips."

"Oh, yeah." Reginri fumbled for a moment and found the two metallic cylinders. They popped free of the suit and he nosed them together. "There."

"All right, all right, they're getting the trace," Vanleo said. "Looks like you're all set."

"Right, about time," Sasuke said. "Let's get moving."

"We're going around to the other side. So let us know if you see anything." Reginri could hear Vanleo's breath coming faster. "Quite a pull in this tide. Ah, there's the other pithole."

The two men continued to talk, getting Vanleo's equipment ready. Reginri turned his attention to his surroundings and wriggled upward, grunting. He worked steadily, pulling against the pulpy stuff. Here and there scaly folds wrinkled the walls, overlapping and making handholds. The waxen membranes reflected back none of his suit light. He dug in his heels and pushed, slipping on patches of filmy pink liquid that collected in the trough of the tunnel.

At first the passageway flared out slightly, giving him better purchase. He made good progress and settled down into a rhythm of pushing and turning. He worked his way around a vast bluish muscle that was laced by orange lines.

Even through his skinsuit he could feel a pulsing warmth come from it. The Dronbgheda had an internal temperature fifteen degrees Centigrade below the human's, but still an oppressive dull heat seeped through to him.

Something black lay ahead. He reached out and touched something rubbery that seemed to block the pithole. His suit light showed a milky pink barrier. He wormed around and felt at the edges of the stuff. Off to the left there was a smaller opening. He turned, flexed his legs and twisted his way into the new passage. Vanleo had told him the pithole might change direction and that when it did he was probably getting close to a nexus. Reginri hoped so.

VI

"Everything going well?" Vanleo's voice came distantly.

"Think so," Reginri wheezed. "I'm at the lip. Going inside now." There came the muffled sounds of a man working, and Reginri mentally blocked them out, concentrating on where he was.

The walls here gleamed like glazed, aging meat. His fingers could not dig into it. He wriggled with his hips and worked forward a few centimeters. He made his body flex, thrust, flex, thrust—he set up the rhythm and relaxed into it, moving forward slightly. The texture of the walls coarsened and he made better progress. Every few moments he stopped and checked the threads for the com-line and the tappers that trailed behind him, reeling out on spools at this side.

He could hear Sasuke muttering to himself, but he was unable to concentrate on anything but the waxen walls around him. The passage narrowed again, and ahead he could see more scaly folds. But these were different, dusted with a shimmering pale powder.

Reginri felt his heart beat faster. He kicked forward and reached out a hand to one of the encrusted folds. The delicate frosting glistened in his suit lamp. Here the meat was glassy, and deep within it he could see a complex interweaving network of veins and arteries, shot through with silvery threads.

It had to be a nexus; the pictures they had shown him were very much like this. It was not in a small pocket the way Vanleo said it would be, but that didn't matter. Vanleo himself had remarked that there seemed no systematic way the nodes were distributed. Indeed, they appeared to migrate to different positions inside the pithole, so that a team returning a few days later could not find the nodules they had tapped before.

Reginri felt a swelling excitement. He carefully thumbed on the electronic components set into his waist. Their low hum reassured him that everything was in order. He barked a short description of his find into his suit mike, and Vanleo responded in monosyllables. The other man seemed to be busy with something else, but Reginri was too occupied to wonder what it might be. He unplugged his tapper cylinders and worked them upward from his waist, his elbows poking into the pulpy membranes around him. Their needle points gleamed softly in the light as he turned them over, inspecting. Everything seemed all right.

He inched along and found the spot where the frosting seemed most dense. Carefully, bracing his hands against each other, he jabbed first one and then the other needle into the waxen flesh. It puckered around the needles.

He spoke quickly into his suit mike asking if the signals were coming through. There came an answering yes, some chatter from the technician back in the sand dunes, and then the line fell silent again.

Along the tapper lines were flowing the signals they had come to get. Long years of experiment had—as far as men could tell—established the recognition codes the technicians used to tell the Drongheda they had returned. Now, if the Drongheda responded, some convoluted electrical pulses would course through the lines and into the recording instruments ashore.

Reginri relaxed. He had done as much as he could. The rest depended on the technicians, the electronics, the lightning microsecond blur of information transfer between the machines and the Drongheda. Somewhere above or below him were flukes, ventral fins, slitted recesses, a baleen filter mouth through which a billion small fish lives had passed, all a part of this vast thing. Somewhere, layered in fat and wedged amid huge organs, there was a mind.

Reginri wondered how this had come about. Swimming through deep murky currents, somehow nature had evolved this thing that knew algebra, calculus, Riemannian metrics, Tchevychef subtleties—all as part of itself, as a fine-grained piece of the same language it shared with men.

Reginri felt a sudden impulse. There was an emergency piece clipped near his waist, for use when the tapper lines snarled or developed intermittent shorts. He wriggled around until his back was flush with the floor of the pithole and then reached down for it. With one hand he kept the needles impacted into the flesh above his head; with the other he extracted the thin, flat wedge of plastic and metal that he needed. From it sprouted tiny wires. He braced himself against the tunnel walls and flipped the wires into the emergency recesses in the tapper cylinders. Everything seemed secure; he rolled onto his back and fumbled at the rear of his helmet for the emergency wiring. By attaching the cabling, he could hook directly into a small fraction of the Drongheda's output. It wouldn't interfere with the direct tapping process. Maybe the men back in the sand dunes wouldn't even know he had done it.

He made the connection. Just before he flipped his suit com-line over to the emergency cable, he thought he felt a slight sway beneath him. The movement passed. He flipped the switch. And felt—

—Bursting light that lanced through him, drummed a staccato rhythm of speckled green—

—Twisting lines that meshed and wove into perspectives, triangles warped into strange saddle-pointed envelopes, coiling into new soundless shapes—

—A latticework of shrill sound, ringing at edges of geometrical flatness—

—Thick, rich foam that lapped against weathered stone towers, precisely turning under an ellipsoid orange sun—

—Miniatured light that groaned and spun softly, curving into moisture that beaded on a coppery matrix of wire—

—A webbing of sticky strands, lifting him

—A welling current

—Upward, toward the watery light—

Reginri snatched at the cable, yanking it out of the socket. His hand jerked up to cover his face and struck his helmet. He panted, gasping.

He closed his eyes and for a long moment thought of nothing, let his mind drift, let himself recoil from the experience.

There had been mathematics there, and much else. Rhomboids, acute intersections in veiled dimensions, many-sided twisted sculptures, warped perspectives, polyhedrons of glowing fire.

But so much more—he would have drowned in it.

There was no interruption of chatter through his earphone. Apparently the electronics men had never noticed the interception. He breathed deeply and renewed his grip on the tapper needles. He closed his eyes and rested for long moments. The experience had turned him inside out for a brief flicker of time. But now he could breathe easily again. His heart had stopped thumping wildly in his chest. The torrent of images began to recede. His mind had been filled, overloaded with more than he could fathom.

He wondered how much the electronics really caught. Perhaps, transferring all this to cold ferrite memory, the emotional thrust was lost. It was not surprising that the only element men could decipher was the mathematics. Counting, lines and curves, the smooth sheen of geometry—they were abstractions, things that could be common to any reasoning mind. No wonder the Drongheda sent mostly mathematics through this neural passage; it was all that men could follow.

After a time it occurred to Reginri that perhaps Vanleo wanted it this way. Maybe he eavesdropped on the lines. The other man might seek this experience; it certainly had an intensity unmatched by drugs or the pallid electronic core-tapping in the sensoriums. Was Vanleo addicted? Why else risk failure? Why reject automated tapping and crawl in here—particularly since the right conditions came so seldom?

But it made no sense. If Vanleo had Drongheda tapes, he could play them back at leisure. So . . . maybe the man was fascinated by the creatures themselves, not only the mathematics. Perhaps the challenge of going inside, the feel of it, was what Vanleo liked.

Grotesque, yes . . . but maybe that was it.

VII

He felt a tremor. The needles wobbled in his hand.

"Hey!" he shouted. The tube flexed under him.

"Something's happening in here. You guys—"

In midsentence the 'com-line went dead. Reginri automatically switched over to emergency, but there was no signal there either. He glanced at the tapper lines. The red phosphor glow at their ends had gone dead; they were not receiving power.

He wriggled around and looked down toward his feet. The tapper lines and the com cable snaked away into darkness with no breaks visible. If there was a flaw in the line, it was further away.

Reginri snapped the tapper line heads back into his suit. As he did so, the flesh around him oozed languidly, compressing. There was a tilting sense of motion, a turning—

"*Frange* it! Get me—" then he remembered the line was dead. His lips pressed together.

He would have to get out on his own.

He dug in with his heels and tried to pull himself backward. A scaly bump scraped against his side. He pulled harder and came free, sliding a few centimeters back. The passage seemed tilted slightly downward. He put his hands out to push and saw something wet run over his fingers. The slimy fluid that filled the trough of the pithole was trickling toward him. Reginri pushed back energetically, getting a better purchase in the pulpy floor.

He worked steadily and made some progress. A long, slow undulation began and the walls clenched about him. He felt something squeeze at his legs, then his waist, then his chest and head. The tightening had a slow, certain rhythm.

He breathed faster, tasting an acrid smell. He heard only his own breath, amplified in the helmet.

He wriggled backward. His boot struck something and he felt the smooth lip of a turning in the passage. He remembered this, but the angle seemed wrong. The Drongheda must be shifting and moving, turning the pithole.

He forked his feet into the new passageway and quickly slipped through it.

This way was easier; he slid down the slick sides and felt a wave of relief. Further along, if the tunnel widened, he might even be able to turn around and go headfirst.

His foot touched something that resisted softly. He felt around with both boots, gradually letting his weight settle on the thing. It seemed to have a brittle surface, pebbled. He carefully followed the outline of it around the walls of the hole until he had satisfied himself that there was no opening.

The passage was blocked.

His mind raced. The air seemed to gain a weight of its own, thick and sour in his helmet. He stamped his boots down, hoping to break whatever it was. The surface stayed firm.

Reginri felt his mind go numb. He was trapped. The com-line was dead, probably snipped off by this thing at his feet.

He felt the walls around him clench and stretch again, a massive hand squeezing the life from him. The pithole sides were only centimeters from his helmet. As he watched, a slow ripple passed through the membrane, ropes of yellow fat visible beneath the surface.

"Get me out!" Reginri kicked wildly. He thrashed against the slimy walls, using elbows and knees to gouge. The yielding pressure remained, cloaking him.

"Out! Out!" Reginri viciously slammed his fists into the flesh. His vision blurred. Small dark points floated before him. He pounded mechanically, his breath coming in short gasps. He cried for help. And he knew he was going to die.

Rage burst out of him. He beat at the enveloping smoothness. The gathering tightness in him boiled up, curling his lips into a grimace. His helmet filled with a bitter taste. He shouted again and again, battering at the Drongheda, cursing it. His muscles began to ache.

And slowly, slowly the burning anger melted. He blinked away the sweat in his eyes. His vision cleared. The blind, pointless energy drained away. He began to think again.

Sasuke. Vanleo. Two-faced bastards. They'd known this job was dangerous. The incident on the beach was a charade. When he showed doubts they'd bullied and threatened him immediately. They'd probably had to do it before, to other men. It was all planned.

He took a long, slow breath and looked up. Above him in the tunnel of darkness, the strands of the tapping lines and the com cable dangled.

One set of lines.

They led upward, on a slant, the way he had come.

It took a moment for the fact to strike him. If he had been backing down the way he came, the lines should be snarled behind him.

He pushed against the glazed sides and looked down his chest. There were no tapper lines near his legs.

That meant the lines did not come up through whatever was blocking his way. No, they came only from above. Which meant that he had taken some wrong side passage. Somehow a hole had opened in the side of the pithole and he had followed it blindly.

He gathered himself and thrust upward, striving for purchase. He struggled up the incline, and dug in with his toes. Another long ripple passed through the tube. The steady hand of gravity forced him down, but he slowly worked his way forward. Sweat stung his eyes.

After a few minutes his hands found the lip, and he quickly hoisted himself over it, into the horizontal tunnel above.

He found a tangle of lines and tugged at them. They gave with a slight resistance. This was the way out, he was sure of it. He began wriggling forward, and suddenly the world tilted, stretched, lifted him high. Let him drop.

He smashed against the pulpy side and lost his breath. The tube flexed again, rising up in front of him and dropping away behind. He dug his hands in and held on. The pithole arched, coiling, and squeezed him. Spongy flesh pressed at his head and he involuntarily held his breath. His faceplate was wrapped in it, and his world became fine-veined, purple, marbled with lacy fat.

Slowly, slowly the pressure ebbed away. He felt a dull aching in his side. There was a subdued tremor beneath him. As soon as he gained maneuvering room, he crawled urgently forward, kicking viciously. The lines led him forward.

The passage flared outward and he increased his speed. He kept up a steady pace of pulling hands, gouging elbows, thrusting knees and toes. The weight around him seemed bent upon expelling, imparting momentum, ejecting. So it seemed, as the flesh tightened behind him and opened before.

He tried the helmet microphone again but it was still inert. He thought he recognized a vast bulging bluish muscle that, on his way in, had been in the wall. Now it formed a bump in the floor. He scrambled over its slickness and continued on.

He was so intent upon motion and momentum that he did not recognize the end. Suddenly the walls converged again and he looked around frantically for another exit. There was none. Then he noticed the rings of cartilage and stringy muscle. He pushed at the knotted surface. It gave, then relaxed even more. He shoved forward and abruptly was halfway out, suspended over the churning water.

VIII

The muscled iris gripped him loosely about the waist. Puffing steadily, he stopped to rest.

He squinted up at the forgiving sun. Around him was a harshly lit world of soundless motion. Currents swirled meters below. He could feel the brown hillside of the Drongheda shift slowly. He turned to see—

The Drongheda was splitting in two.

But no, no—

The bulge was another Drongheda close by moving. At the same moment another silent motion caught his eye. Below, Vanleo struggled through the darkening water, waving. Pale mist shrouded the sea.

Reginri worked his way out and onto the narrow rim of the pithole. He took a grip at it and lowered himself partway down toward the water. Arms extended, he let go and fell with a splash into the ocean. He kept his balance and lurched away awkwardly on legs of cotton.

Vanleo reached out a steadying hand. The man motioned at the back of his helmet. Reginri frowned, puzzled, and then realized he was motioning toward the emergency com cable. He unspooled his own cable and plugged it into the shoulder socket on Vanleo's skinsuit.

"—damned lucky. Didn't think I'd see you again. But it's *fantastic*, come see it."

"What? I got—"

"I understand them now. I know what they're here for. It's not just communication, I don't think that, but that's part of it too. They've—"

"Stop babbling. What happened?"

"I went in," Vanleo said, regaining his breath. "Or started to. We didn't notice that another Drongheda had surfaced, was moving into the shallows."

"I saw it. I didn't think—"

"I climbed up to the second pithole before I saw. I was busy with the cables, you know. You were getting good traces and I wanted to—"

"Let's get away, come on." The vast bulks above them were moving.

"No, no, come see. I think my guess is right, these shallows are a natural shelter for them. If they have any enemies in the sea, large fish or something, their enemies can't follow them here into the shallows. So they come here to, to mate and to communicate. They must be terribly lonely, if they can't talk to each other in the oceans. So they have to come here to do it. I—"

Reginri studied the man and saw that he was ablaze with his inner vision. The damned fool loved these beasts, cared about them, had devoted a life to them and their goddamned mathematics.

"Where's Sasuke?"

"—and it's all so natural. I mean, humans communicate and make love, and those are two separate acts. They don't blend together. But the Drongheda—they have it all. They're like, like . . ."

The man pulled at Reginri's shoulder, leading him around the long curve of the Drongheda. Two immense burnished hillsides grew out of the shadowed sea. Zeta was setting, and in profile Reginri could see a long dexterous tentacle curling into the air. It came from the mottled patches, like welts, he had seen before.

"They extend through those spots, you see. Those are their sensors, what they use to complete the contact. And—I can't prove it, but I'm sure—that is when the genetic material is passed between them. The mating period. At the same time they exchange information, converse. That's what we're getting on the tappers, their stored knowledge fed out. They think we're another of their own, that must be it. I don't understand all of it, but—"

"Where's Sasuke?"

"—but the first one, the one you were inside, recognized the difference as soon as the second Drongheda approached. They moved together and the second one extruded that tentacle. Then—"

Reginri shook the other man roughly. "Shut up! Sasuke—"

Vanleo stopped, dazed, and looked at Reginri. "I've been telling you. It's a great discovery, the first real step we've taken in this field. We'll understand so much *more* once this is fully explored."

Reginri hit him in the shoulder.

Vanleo staggered. The glassy, pinched look of his eyes faded. He began to lift his arms.

Reginri drove his gloved fist into Vanleo's faceplate. Vanleo toppled backward. The ocean swallowed him. Reginri stepped back, blinking.

Vanleo's helmet appeared as he struggled up. A wave foamed over him. He stumbled, turned, saw Reginri.

Reginri moved toward him. "No. No," Vanleo said weakly.

If you're not going to tell me—"

"But I, I am." Vanleo gasped, leaned forward until he could brace his hands on his knees.

"There wasn't time. The second one came up on us so, so fast."

"Yeah?"

"I was about ready to go inside. When I saw the second one moving in, you know, the only time in thirty years, I knew it was important. I climbed down to observe. But we needed the data, so Sasuke went in for me. With the tapper cables."

Vanleo panted. His face was ashen.

"When the tentacles went in, it filled the pithole exactly. Tight. There was no room left," he said. "Sasuke . . . was there. Inside."

Reginri froze, stunned. A wave swirled around him and he slipped. The waters tumbled him backward. Dazed, he regained his footing on the slick rocks and began stumbling blindly toward the bleak shore, toward humanity. The ocean lapped around him, ceaseless and unending.

IX

Belej sat motionless, unmindful of the chill. "Oh my God," she said.

"That was it," he murmured. He stared off into the canyon. Zeta

Reticuli sent slanting rays into the layered reddening mists. Air squirrels darted among the shifting shadows.

"He's crazy," Belej said simply. "That Leo is crazy."

"Well . . ." Reginri began. Then he rocked forward stiffly and stood up. Swirls of reddish cloud were crawling up the canyon face toward them. He pointed. "That stuff is coming in faster than I thought." He coughed. "We'd better get inside."

Belej nodded and came to her feet. She brushed the twisted brown grass from her legs and turned to him.

"Now that you've told me," she said softly, "I think you ought to put it from your mind."

"It's hard. I . . ."

"I know. I know. But you can push it far away from you, forget it happened. That's the best way."

"Well, maybe."

"Believe me. You've changed since this happened to you. I can feel it."

"Feel what?"

"You. You're different. I feel a barrier between us."

"I wonder," he said slowly.

She put her hand on his arm and stepped closer, an old, familiar gesture. He stood watching the reddening haze swallowing the precise lines of the rocks below.

"I want that screen between us to dissolve. You made your contribution, earned your pay. Those damned people understand the Drongheda now—"

He made a wry, rasping laugh. "We'll never grasp the Drongheda. What we get in those neural circuits are mirrors of what we want. Of what we are. We can't sense anything totally alien."

"But—"

"Vanleo saw mathematics because he went after it. So did I, at first. Later . . ."

He stopped. A sudden breeze made him shiver. He clenched his fists. Clenched. Clenched.

How could he tell her? He woke in the night, sweating, tangled in the bedclothes, muttering incoherently . . . but they were not nightmares, not precisely.

Something else. Something intermediate.

"Forget those things," Belej said soothingly. Reginri leaned closer to her and caught the sweet musk of her, the dry crackling scent of her hair. He had always loved that.

She frowned up at him. Her eyes shifted intently from his mouth to his eyes and then back again, trying to read his expression. "It will only trouble you to recall it. I—I'm sorry I asked you to tell it. But remember—" she took both his hands in hers—"you'll never go back there again. It can be . . ."

Something made him look beyond her. At the gathering fog.

And at once he sensed the shrouded abyss open below him. Sweeping him in. Gathering him up. Into—

—*a thick red foam lapping against weathered granite towers*—

—*an ellipisodal sun spinning soundlessly over a silvered, warping planet*—

—*watery light*—

—*cloying strands, sticky, a fine-spun coppery matrix that enfolded him, warming*—

—*glossy sheen of polyhedra, wedged together, mass upon mass*—

—*smooth bands of moisture playing lightly over his quilted skin*—

—*a blistering light shines through him, sets his bones to humming resonance*—

—*pressing*—

—*coiling*—

Beckoning. Beckoning.

When the moment had passed, Reginri blinked and felt a salty stinging in his eyes. Every day the tug was stronger, the incandescent images sharper. This must be what Vanleo felt, he was sure of it. They came to him now even during the day. Again and again, the grainy texture altering with time . . .

He reached out and enfolded Belej in his arms.

"But I must," he said in a rasping whisper. "Vanleo called today. He . . . I'm going. I'm going back."

He heard her quick intake of breath, felt her stiffen in his arms.

His attention was diverted by the reddening fog. It cloaked half the world and still it came on.

There was something ominous about it and something inviting as well. He watched as it engulfed trees nearby. He studied it intently, judging the distance. The looming presence was quite close now. But he was sure it would be all right.

Gene Wolfe's name does not usually show up on those invidious lists of the Ten Best SF Writers that are sometimes released by reckless or foolhardy critics, but SF authorities as diverse in their tastes as Damon Knight, Terry Carr, Algis Budrys, and Harlan Ellison have all indicated on occasion that Wolfe would show up on their lists if they chose to release such, and not anywhere close to the bottom either. Carr even went so far as to say that when he is asked who the best SF writer today is "the name that comes to mind more than any other is Gene Wolfe." That is an opinion that will startle most, delight many, and dismay some, but I agree wholeheartedly with Carr—at his best, writing at the top of his powers on a subject that moves and interests him, Gene Wolfe may well be the best SF writer working today.

His novel The Fifth Head of Cerberus *(Ace) is a recognized classic, and in its original form is probably the single best novella of the seventies, to date. His* The Devil in a Forest *(Ace) is one of the most perfect evocations of the medieval world I have ever read. His novel* Peace *(Harper & Row), ostensibly a book about the mundane life of a frozen-orange-juice manufacturer, contains enough magic and genuine wonder for a dozen sword-and-sorcery novels. And his new tetralogy,* The Book of the New Sun *(the first volume of which,* The Shadow of the Torturer, *is forthcoming from Pocket Books), may set a new standard for science-fantasy.*

"Seven American Nights," a top Nebula finalist this year, is also Wolfe at his evocative best, creating a ruined and haunted America of the future, an America whose topsoil washes away to stain the sea yellow even while its people starve in squalor, a sinisterly beautiful America of shattered cities and broken people, a country dreaming of the past even as it bleeds.

GENE WOLFE
Seven American Nights

ESTEEMED AND LEARNED MADAME:

As I last wrote you, it appears to me likely that your son Nadan (may Allah preserve him!) has left the old capital and traveled—of his own will or another's—north into the region about the Bay of Delaware. My conjecture is now confirmed by the discovery in those regions of the notebook I enclose. It is not of American manufacture, as you see; and though it holds only the records of a single week, several suggestive items therein provide us new reason to hope.

I have photocopied the contents to guide me in my investigations; but I am alert to the probability that you, Madame, with your superior knowledge of the young man we seek, may discover implications I have overlooked. Should that be the case, I urge you to write me at once.

Though I hesitate to mention it in connection with so encouraging a finding, your most recently due remission has not yet arrived. I assume that this tardiness results from the procrastination of the mails, which is here truly abominable. I must warn you, however, that I shall be forced to discontinue the search unless funds sufficient for my expenses are forthcoming before the advent of winter.

With inexpressible respect,
Hassan Kerbelai

Here I am at last! After twelve mortal days aboard the *Princess Fatimah*—twelve days of cold and ennui—twelve days of bad food and throbbing engines—the joy of being on land again is like the delight a condemned man must feel when a letter from the shah snatches him from beneath the very blade of death. America! America! Dull days are no more! They say that everyone who comes here either loves or hates you, America—by Allah I love you now!

Having begun this record at last, I find I do not know where to begin. I had been reading travel diaries before I left home; and so when I saw you, O Book, lying so square and thick in your stall in the bazaar—why should I not have adventures too, and write a book like Osman Aga's? Few come to this sad country at the world's edge after all, and most who do land farther up the coast.

And that gives me the clue I was looking for—how to begin. America began for me as colored water. When I went out on deck yesterday morning, the ocean had changed from green to yellow. I had never heard of such a thing before, neither in my reading, nor in my talks with Uncle Mirza, who was here thirty years ago. I am afraid I behaved like the greatest fool imaginable, running about the ship babbling, and looking over the side every few minutes to make certain the rich mustard color was still there and would not vanish the way things do in dreams when we try to point them out to someone else. The steward told me he knew. Golam Gassem the grain merchant (whom I had tried to avoid meeting for the entire trip until that moment) said, "Yes, yes," and turned away in a fashion that showed he had been avoiding me too, and that it was going to take more of a miracle than yellow water to change his feelings.

One of the few native Americans in first class came out just then: Mister—as the style is here—Tallman, husband of the lovely Madam Tallman, who really deserves such a tall man as myself. (Whether her husband chose that name in self-derision, or in the hope that it would erase others' memory of his infirmity; or whether it was his father's, and is merely one of the countless ironies of fate, I do not know. There was something wrong with his back.) As if I had not made enough spectacle of myself already, I took this Mr. Tallman by the sleeve and told him to look over the side, explaining that the sea had turned yellow. I am afraid Mr. Tallman turned white himself instead, and turned something else too—his back—looking as though he would have struck me if he dared. It was comic enough, I suppose—I heard some of the other passengers chuckling about it afterward—but I don't believe I have seen such hatred in a human face before. Just then the captain came strolling up, and I—considerably deflated but not flattened yet, and thinking that he had not overheard Mr. Tallman and me—mentioned for the final time that day that the water had turned yellow. "I know," the captain said. "It's his country" (here he jerked his head in the direction of the pitiful Mr. Tallman), "bleeding to death."

Here it is evening again, and I see that I stopped writing last night before I had so much as described my first sight of the coast. Well, so be it. At home it is midnight, or nearly, and the life of the cafés is at its height. How I wish that I were there now, with you, Yasmin, not webbed among these red- and purple-clad strangers, who mob their own streets like an invading army, and duck into their houses like rats into their holes. But you, Yasmin, or Mother, or whoever may read this, will want to know of my day—only you are sometimes to think of me as I am now, bent over an old, scarred table in a decayed room with two beds, listening to the hastening feet in the streets outside.

I slept late this morning; I suppose I was more tired from the voyage than I realized. By the time I woke, the whole of the city was alive around me, with vendors crying fish and fruits under my shuttered window, and the great wooden wains the Americans call *trucks* rumbling over the broken concrete on their wide iron wheels, bringing up goods from the ships in the Potomac anchorage. One sees very odd teams here, Yasmin. When I went to get my breakfast (one must go outside to reach the lobby and dining room in these American hotels, which I would think would be very inconvenient in bad weather) I saw one of these *trucks* with two oxen, a horse, and a mule in the traces, which would have made you laugh. The drivers crack their whips all the time.

The first impression one gets of America is that it is not as poor as one has been told. It is only later that it becomes apparent how much has been handed down from the previous century. The streets here are paved, but they are old and broken. There are fine, though decayed, buildings everywhere (this hotel is one—the Inn of Holidays, it is called), more modern in appearance than the ones we see at home, where for so long traditional architecture was enforced by law. We are on Maine Street, and when I had finished my breakfast (it was very good, and very cheap by our standards, though I am told it is impossible to get anything out of season here) I asked the manager where I should go to see the sights of the city. He is a short and phenomenally ugly man, something of a hunchback as so many of them are. "'There are no tours," he said. "Not any more."

I told him that I simply wanted to wander about by myself, and perhaps sketch a bit.

"You can do that. North for the buildings, south for the theater, west for the park. Do you plan to go to the park, Mr. Jaffarzadeh?"

"I haven't decided yet."

"You should hire at least two securities if you go to the park—I can recommend an agency."

"I have my pistol."

"You'll need more than that, sir."

Naturally, I decided then and there that I would go to the park, and alone. But I have determined not to spend this, the sole, small coin of adventure this land has provided me so far, before I discover what else it may offer to enrich my existence.

Accordingly, I set off for the north when I left the hotel. I have not, thus far, seen this city, or any American city, by night. What they might be like if these people thronged the streets then, as we do, I cannot imagine. Even by clearest day, there is the impression of carnival, of some mad circus whose performance began a hundred or more years ago and has not ended yet.

At first it seemed that only every fourth or fifth person suffered some trace of the genetic damage that destroyed the old America, but as I grew more accustomed to the streets, and thus less quick to dismiss as Americans and no more the unhappy old woman who wanted me to buy flowers and the boy who dashed shrieking between the wheels of a *truck*, and began instead to look at them as human beings—in other words, just as I would look at some chance-met person on one of our own streets—I saw that there was hardly a soul not marked in some way. These deformities, though they are individually hideous, in combination with the bright, ragged clothing so common here, give the meanest assemblage the character of a pageant. I sauntered along, hardly out of earshot of one group of street musicians before encountering another, and in a few strides passed a man so tall that he was taller seated on a low step than I standing; a bearded dwarf with a withered arm; and a woman whose face had been divided by some devil into halves, one large-eyed and idiotically despairing, the other squinting and sneering.

There can be no question about it—Yasmin must not read this. I have been sitting here for an hour at least, staring at the flame of the candle. Sitting and listening to something that from time to time beats against the steel shutters that close the window of this room. The truth is that I am paralyzed by a fear that entered me—I do not know from whence—yesterday, and has been growing ever since.

Everyone knows that these Americans were once the most skilled creators of consciousness-altering substances the world has ever seen. The same knowledge that permitted them to forge the chemicals that destroyed them, so that they might have bread that never staled, innumerable poisons for vermin, and a host of unnatural materials for every purpose, also contrived synthetic alkaloids that produced endless feverish imaginings.

Surely some, at least, of these skills remain. Or if they do not, then some of the substances themselves, preserved for eighty or a hundred years in hidden cabinets, and no doubt growing more dangerous as the world forgets them. I think that someone on the ship may have administered some such drug to me.

That is out at last! I felt so much better at having written it—it took a great deal of effort—that I took several turns about this room. Now that I have written it down, I do not believe it at all.

Still, last night I dreamed of that bread, of which I first read in the little schoolroom of Uncle Mirza's country house. It was no complex, towering "literary" dream such as I have sometimes had, and embroidered, and boasted of afterward over coffee. Just the vision of a loaf of soft white bread lying on a plate in the center of a small table: bread that retained the fragrance of the oven (surely one of the most delicious in the world) though it was smeared with gray mold. Why would the Americans wish such a thing? Yet all the historians agree that they did, just as they wished their own corpses to appear living forever.

It is only this country, with its colorful, fetid streets, deformed people, and harsh, alien language, that makes me feel as drugged and dreaming as I do. Praise Allah that I can speak Farsi to you, O Book. Will you believe that I have taken out every article of clothing I have, just to read the makers' labels? Will *I* believe it, for that matter, when I read this at home?

The public buildings to the north—once the great center, as I understand it, of political activity—offer a severe contrast to the streets of the still-occupied areas. In the latter, the old buildings are in the last stages of decay, or have been repaired by makeshift and inappropriate means; but they seethe with the life of those who depend upon such commercial activity as the port yet provides, and with those who depend on them, and so on. The monumental buildings, because they were constructed of the most imperishable materials, appear almost whole, though there are a few fallen columns and sagging porticos, and in several places small trees (mostly the sad *carpinus caroliniana*, I believe) have rooted in the crevices of walls. Still, if it is true, as has been written, that Time's beard is gray not with the passage of years but with the dust of ruined cities, it is here that he trails it. These imposing shells are no more than that. They were built, it would seem, to be cooled and ventilated by machinery. Many are windowless, their interiors now no more than sunless caves, reeking of decay; into these I did not venture. Others had had fixed windows that once were mere walls of glass; and a few of these remained, so that I was able to sketch their construction. Most, however, are destroyed. Time's beard has swept away their very shards.

Though these old buildings (with one or two exceptions) are deserted, I encountered several beggars. They seemed to be Americans whose deformities preclude their doing useful work, and one cannot help but feel sorry for them, though their appearance is often as distasteful as their importunities. They offered to show me the former residence of their Padshah, and as an excuse to give them a few coins I accompanied them, making them first pledge to leave me when I had seen it.

The structure they pointed out to me was situated at the end of a long avenue lined with impressive buildings; so I suppose they must have been correct in thinking it once important. Hardly more than the foundation, some rubble, and one ruined wing remain now, and it cannot have been originally of an enduring construction. No doubt it was actually a summer palace or something of that kind. The beggars have now forgotten its very name, and call it merely "the white house."

When they had guided me to this relic, I pretended that I wanted to make drawings, and they left as they had promised. In five or ten minutes, however, one particularly enterprising fellow returned. He had no lower jaw, so that I had quite a bit of difficulty in understanding him at first; but after we had shouted back and forth a good deal—I telling him to depart and threatening to kill him on the spot, and he protesting—I realized that he was forced to make the sound of d for b, n for m, and t for p; and after that we got along better.

I will not attempt to render his speech phonetically, but he said that since I had been so generous, he wished to show me a great secret— something foreigners like myself did not even realize existed.

"Clean water," I suggested.

"No, no. A great, great secret, Captain. You think all this is dead." He waved a misshapen hand at the desolated structures that surrounded us.

"Indeed I do."

"One still lives. You would like to see it? I will guide. Don't worry about the others—they're afraid of me. I will drive them away."

"If you are leading me into some kind of ambush, I warn you, you will be the first to suffer."

He looked at me very seriously for a moment, and a man seemed to stare from the eyes in that ruined face, so that I felt a twinge of real sympathy. "See there? The big building to the south, on Pennsylvania? Captain, my father's father's father was chief of a department" ("detartnent") "there. I would not betray you."

From what I have read of this country's policies in the days of his father's father's father, that was little enough reassurance, but I followed him.

We went diagonally across several blocks, passing through two ruined buildings. There were human bones in both, and remembering his boast, I asked him if they had belonged to the workers there.

"No, no." He tapped his chest again—a habitual gesture, I suppose—and scooping up a skull from the floor held it beside his own head so that I could see that it exhibited cranial deformities much like his own. "We sleep here, to be shut behind strong walls from the things that come at night. We die here, mostly in wintertime. No one buries us."

"You should bury each other," I said.

He tossed down the skull, which shattered on the terrazzo floor, waking a thousand dismal echoes. "No shovel, and few are strong. But come with me."

At first sight the building to which he led me looked more decayed than many of the ruins. One of its spires had fallen, and the bricks lay in the street. Yet when I looked again, I saw that there must be something in what he said. The broken windows had been closed with ironwork at least as well made as the shutters that protect my room here; and the door, though old and weathered, was tightly shut, and looked strong.

"This is the museum," my guide told me. "The only part left, almost, of the Silent City that still lives in the old way. Would you like to see inside?"

I told him that I doubted that we would be able to enter.

"Wonderful machines." He pulled at my sleeve. "You *see* in, Captain. Come."

We followed the building's walls around several corners, and at last entered a sort of alcove at the rear. Here there was a grill set in the weed-grown ground, and the beggar gestured toward it proudly. I made him stand some distance off, then knelt as he had indicated to look through the grill.

There was a window of unshattered glass beyond the grill. It was very soiled now, but I could see through into the basement of the building, and there, just as the beggar had said, stood an orderly array of complex mechanisms.

I stared for some time, trying to gain some notion of their purpose; and at length an old American appeared among them, peering at one and then another, and whisking the shining bars and gears with a rag.

The beggar had crept closer as I watched. He pointed at the old man, and said, "Still come from north and south to study here. Someday we are great again." Then I thought of my own lovely country, whose eclipse—though without genetic damage—lasted twenty-three hundred years. And I gave him money, and told him that, yes, I was certain America would be great again someday, and left him, and returned here.

I have opened the shutters so that I can look across the city to the obelisk and catch the light of the dying sun. Its fields and valleys of fire do not seem more alien to me, or more threatening, than this strange, despondent land. Yet I know that we are all one—the beggar, the old man moving among the machines of a dead age, those machines themselves, the sun, and I. A century ago, when this was a thriving city, the philosophers used to speculate on the reason that each neutron and proton and electron exhibited the same mass as all the others of its kind. Now we know that there is only one particle of each variety, moving backward and forward in time, an electron when it travels as we do, a positron when its temporal displacement is retrograde, the same few particles appearing billions of billions of times to make up a single object, and the same few particles forming all the objects, so that we are all the sketches, as it were, of the same set of pastels.

I have gone out to eat. There is a good restaurant not far from the hotel, better even than the dining room here. When I came back the manager told me that there is to be a play tonight at the theater, and assured me that because it is so close to his hotel (in truth, he is very proud of this theater, and no doubt its proximity to his hotel is the only circumstance that permits the hotel to remain open) I will be in no danger if I go without an escort. To tell the truth, I am a little ashamed that I did not hire a boat today to take me across the channel to the park; so now I will attend the play, and dare the night streets.

Here I am again, returned to this too-large, too-bare, uncarpeted room, which is already beginning to seem a second home, with no adventures to retail from the dangerous benighted streets. The truth is that the theater is hardly more than a hundred paces to the south. I kept my hand on the butt of my pistol and walked along with a great many other people (mostly Americans) who were also going to the theater, and felt something of a fool.

The building is as old as those in the Silent City, I should think; but it has been kept in some repair. There was more of a feeling of gaiety (though to me it was largely an alien gaiety) among the audience than we have at home, and less of the atmosphere of what I may call the sacredness of Art. By that I knew that the drama really is sacred here, as the colorful clothes of the populace make clear in any case. An exaggerated and solemn respect always indicates a loss of faith.

Having recently come from my dinner, I ignored the stands in the lobby at which the Americans—who seem to eat constantly when they can afford it—were selecting various cold meats and pastries, and took my place in the theater proper. I was hardly in my seat before a pipe-puffing old gentleman, an American, desired me to move in order that he might reach his own. I stood up gladly, of course, and greeted him as "Grandfather," as our own politeness (if not theirs) demands. But while he was settling himself and I was still standing beside him, I caught a glimpse of his face from the exact angle at which I had seen it this afternoon, and recognized him as the old man I had watched through the grill.

Here was a difficult situation. I wanted very much to draw him into conversation, but I could not well confess that I had been spying on him. I puzzled over the question until the lights were extinguished and the play began.

It was Vidal's *Visit to a Small Planet*, one of the classics of the old American theater, a play I have often read about but never (until now) seen performed. I would have liked it much better if it had been done with the costumes and settings of its proper period; unhappily, the director had chosen to "modernize" the entire affair, just as we sometimes present *Rustam Beg* as if Rustam had been a hero of the war just past. General Powers was a contemporary American soldier with the mannerisms of a cowardly bandit, Spelding a publisher of libelous broadsheets, and so on. The only characters that gave me much pleasure were the limping spaceman, Kreton, and the ingenue, Ellen Spelding, played as and by a radiantly beautiful American blonde.

All through the first act my mind had been returning (particularly during Spelding's speeches) to the problem of the old man beside me. By the time the curtain fell, I had decided that the best way to start a conversation might be to offer to fetch him a kebab—or whatever he might want—from the lobby, since his threadbare appearance suggested that he might be ready enough to be treated, and the weakness of his legs would provide an admirable excuse. I tried the gambit as soon as the flambeaux were relit, and it worked as well as I could have wished. When I returned with a paper tray of sandwiches and bitter drinks, he remarked to me quite spontaneously that he had noticed me flexing my right hand during the performance.

"Yes," I said, "I had been writing a good deal before I came here."

That set him off, and he began to discourse, frequently with a great deal more detail than I could comprehend, on the topic of writing machines. At last I halted the flow with some question that must have revealed that I knew less of the subject than he had supposed. "Have you ever," he asked me, "carved a letter in a potato, and moistened it with a stamp pad, and used it to imprint paper?"

"As a child, yes. We use a turnip, but no doubt the principle is the same."

"Exactly; and the principle is that of extended abstraction. I ask you—on the lowest level, what is communication?"

"Talking, I suppose."

His shrill laugh rose above the hubbub of the audience. "Not at all! Smell" (here he gripped my arm), "smell is the essence of communication. Look at that word *essence* itself. When you smell another human being, you take chemicals from his body into your own, analyze them, and from the analysis you accurately deduce his emotional state. You do it so constantly and so automatically that you are largely unconscious of it, and say simply, 'He seemed frightened,' or 'He was angry.' You see?"

I nodded, interested in spite of myself.

"When you speak, you are telling another how you would smell if you smelled as you should and if he could smell you properly from where he stands. It is almost certain that speech was not developed until the glaciations that terminated the Pliocene stimulated mankind to develop fire, and the frequent inhalation of wood smoke had dulled the olfactory organs."

"I see."

"No, you hear—unless you are by chance reading my lips, which in this din would be a useful accomplishment." He took an enormous bite of his sandwich, spilling pink meat that had surely come from no natural animal. "When you write, you are telling the other how you would speak if he could hear you, and when you print with your turnip, you are telling him how you would write. You will notice that we have already reached the third level of abstraction."

I nodded again.

"It used to be believed that only a limited number K of levels of abstraction were possible before the original matter disappeared altogether—some very interesting mathematical work was done about seventy years ago in an attempt to derive a generalized expression for K for various systems. Now we know that the number can be infinite if the array represents an open curve, and that closed curves are also possible."

"I don't understand."

"You are young and handsome—very fine looking, with your wide shoulders and black mustache; let us suppose a young woman loves you. If you and I and she were crouched now on the limb of a tree, you would scent her desire. Today, perhaps she tells you of that desire. But it is also possible, is it not, that she may write you of her desire?"

Remembering Yasmin's letters, I assented.

"But suppose those letters are perfumed—a musky, sweet perfume. You understand? A closed curve—the perfume is not the odor of her body, but an artificial simulation of it. It may not be what she feels, but it is what she tells you she feels. Your real love is for a whale, a male deer, and a bed of roses." He was about to say more, but the curtain went up for the second act.

I found that act both more enjoyable, and more painful, than the first. The opening scene, in which Kreton (soon joined by Ellen) reads the mind of the family cat, was exceptionally effective. The concealed orchestra furnished music to indicate cat thoughts; I wish I knew the identity of the composer, but my playbill does not provide the information. The bedroom wall became a shadow screen, where we saw silhouettes of cats catching birds, and then, when Ellen tickled the real cat's belly, making love. As I have said, Kreton and Ellen were the play's best characters. The juxtaposition of Ellen's willowy beauty and high-spirited näiveté, and Kreton's clear desire for her illuminated perfectly the Paphian difficulties that would confront a powerful telepath, were such persons to exist.

On the other hand, Kreton's summoning of the presidents, which closes the act, was as objectionable as it could possibly have been made. The foreign ruler conjured up by error was played as a Turk, and as broadly as possible. I confess to feeling some prejudice against that bloodthirsty race myself, but what was done was indefensible. When the president of the World Council appeared, he was portrayed as an American.

By the end of that scene I was in no very good mood. I think that I have not yet shaken off the fatigues of the crossing; and they, combined with a fairly strenuous day spent prowling around the ruins of the Silent City, had left me now in that state in which the smallest irritation takes on the dimensions of a mortal insult. The old curator beside me discerned my irascibility, but mistook the reason for it, and began to apologize for the state of the American stage, saying that all the performers of talent emigrated as soon as they gained recognition, and returned only when they had failed on the eastern shore of the Atlantic.

"No, no," I said. "Kreton and the girl are very fine, and the rest of the cast is at least adequate."

He seemed not to have heard me. "They pick them up wherever they can—they choose them for their faces. When they have appeared in three plays, they call themselves actors. At the Smithsonian—I am employed there, perhaps I've already mentioned it—we have tapes of real theater:

Laurence Olivier, Orson Welles, Katharine Cornell. Spelding is a barber, or at least he was. He used to put his chair under the old Kennedy statue and shave the passersby. Ellen is a trollop, and Powers a drayman. That lame fellow Kreton used to snare sailors for a singing house on Portland Street."

His disparagement of his own national culture embarrassed me, though it put me in a better mood. (I have noticed that the two often go together—perhaps I am secretly humiliated to find that people of no great importance can affect my interior state with a few words or some mean service.) I took my leave of him and went to the confectioner's stand in the lobby. The Americans have a very pretty custom of duplicating the speckled eggs of wild birds in marzipan, and I bought a box of these—not only because I wanted to try them myself, but because I felt certain they would prove a treat for the old man, who must seldom have enough money to afford luxuries of that kind. I was quite correct—he ate them eagerly. But when I sampled one, I found its odor (as though I were eating artificial violets) so unpleasant that I did not take another.

"We were speaking of writing," the old man said. "The closed curve and the open curve. I did not have time to make the point that both could be achieved mechanically; but the monograph I am now developing turns upon that very question, and it happens that I have examples with me. First the closed curve. In the days when our president was among the world's ten most powerful men—the reality of the Paul Laurent you see on the stage there—each president received hundreds of requests every day for his signature. To have granted them would have taken hours of his time. To have refused them would have raised a brigade of enemies."

"What did they do?"

"They called upon the resources of science. That science devised the machine that wrote this."

From within his clean, worn coat he drew a folded sheet of paper. I opened it and saw that it was covered with the text of what appeared to be a public address, written in a childish scrawl. Mentally attempting to review the list of the American presidents I had seen in some digest of world history long ago, I asked whose hand it was.

"The machine's. Whose hand is being imitated here is one of the things I am attempting to discover."

In the dim light of the theater it was almost impossible to make out the faded script, but I caught the word *Sardinia*. "Surely, by correlating the contents to historical events it should be possible to date it quite accurately."

The old man shook his head. "The text itself was composed by another machine to achieve some national psychological effect. It is not probable that it bears any real relationship to the issues of its day. But now look here." He drew out a second sheet, and unfolded it for me. So far as I could see, it was completely blank. I was still staring at it when the curtain went up.

As Kreton moved his toy aircraft across the stage, the old man took a final egg and turned away to watch the play. There was still half a carton left, and I, thinking that he might want more later, and afraid that they might be spilled from my lap and lost underfoot, closed the box and slipped it into the side pocket of my jacket.

The special effects for the landing of the second spaceship were well done; but there was something else in the third act that gave me as much pleasure as the cat scene in the second. The final curtain hinges on the device our poets call *the Peri's asphodel*, a trick so shopworn now that it is acceptable only if it can be presented in some new light. The one used here was to have John—Ellen's lover—find Kreton's handkerchief and, remarking that it seemed perfumed, bury his nose in it. For an instant, the shadow wall used at the beginning of the second act was illuminated again to graphically (or I should say, pornographically) present Ellen's desire, conveying to the audience that John had, for that moment, shared the telepathic abilities of Kreton, whom all of them had now entirely forgotten.

The device was extremely effective, and left me feeling that I had by no means wasted my evening. I joined the general applause as the cast appeared to take their bows; then, as I was turning to leave, I noticed that the old man appeared very ill. I asked if he were all right, and he confessed ruefully that he had eaten too much, and thanked me again for my kindness—which must at that time have taken a great deal of resolution.

I helped him out of the theater, and when I saw that he had no transportation but his feet, told him I would take him home. He thanked me again, and informed me that he had a room at the museum.

Thus the half-block walk from the theater to my hotel was transformed into a journey of three or four kilometers, taken by moonlight, much of it through rubble-strewn avenues of the deserted parts of the city.

During the day I had hardly glanced at the stark skeleton of the old highway. Tonight, when we walked beneath its ruined overpasses, they seemed inexpressibly ancient and sinister. It occurred to me then that there may be a time-flaw, such as astronomers report from space, somewhere in the Atlantic. How is it that this western shore is more antiquated in the remains of a civilization not yet a century dead than we are in the shadow of Darius? May it not be that every ship that plows that sea moves through ten thousand years?

For the past hour—I find I cannot sleep—I have been debating whether to make this entry. But what good is a travel journal, if one does not enter everything? I will revise it on the trip home, and present a cleansed copy for my mother and Yasmin to read.

It appears that the scholars at the museum have no income but that derived from the sale of treasures gleaned from the past; and I bought a vial of what is supposed to be the greatest creation of the old hallucinatory chemists from the woman who helped me get the old man into bed. It is—it was—about half the height of my smallest finger. Very probably it was alcohol and nothing more, though I paid a substantial price.

I was sorry I had bought it before I left, and still more sorry when I arrived here; but at the time it seemed that this would be my only opportunity, and I could think of nothing but to seize the adventure. After I have swallowed the drug I will be able to speak with authority about these things for the remainder of my life.

Here is what I have done. I have soaked the porous sugar of one of the eggs with the fluid. The moisture will soon dry up. The drug—if there is a drug—will remain. Then I will rattle the eggs together in an empty drawer, and each day, beginning tomorrow night, I will eat one egg.

I am writing today before I go down to breakfast, partly because I suspect that the hotel does not serve so early. Today I intend to visit the park on the other side of the channel. If it is as dangerous as they say, it is very likely I will not return to make an entry tonight. If I do return—well, I will plan for that when I am here again.

After I had blown out my candle last night I could not sleep, though I was tired to the bone. Perhaps it was only the excitement of the long walk back from the museum; but I could not free my mind from the image of Ellen. My wandering thoughts associated her with the eggs, and I imagined myself Kreton, sitting up in bed with the cat on my lap. In my daydream (I was not asleep) Ellen brought me my breakfast on a tray, and the breakfast consisted of the six candy eggs.

When my mind had exhausted ifself with this kind of imagery, I decided to have the manager procure a girl for me so that I could rid myself of the accumulated tensions of the voyage. After about an hour during which I sat up reading, he arrived with three; and when he had given me a glimpse of them through the half-open door, he slipped inside and shut it behind him, leaving them standing in the corridor. I told him I had only asked for one.

"I know, Mr. Jaffarzadeh, I know. But I thought you might like to have a choice."

None of them—from the glimpse I had had—resembled Ellen; but I thanked him for his thoughtfulness and suggested that he bring them in.

"I wanted to tell you first, sir, that you must allow me to set the price with them—I can get them for much less than you, sir, because they know they cannot deceive me, and they must depend on me to bring them to my guests in the future." He named a sum that was in fact quite trivial.

"That will be fine," I said. "Bring them in."

He bowed and smiled, making his pinched and miserly face as pleasant as possible and reminding me very much of a picture I had once seen of an imp summoned before the court of Suleiman. "But first, sir, I wished to inform you that if you would like all three—together—you may have them for the price of two. And should you desire only two of the three, you may have them for one and one half the price of one. All are very lovely, and I thought you might want to consider it."

"Very well, I have considered it. Show them in."

"I will light another candle," he said, bustling about the room. "There is no charge, sir, for candles at the rate you're paying. I can put the girls on your bill as well. They'll be down as room service—you understand,

I'm sure."

When the second candle was burning and he had positioned it to his liking on the nightstand between the two beds, he opened the door and waved in the girls, saying, "I'll go now. Take what you like and send out the others." (I feel certain this was a stratagem—he felt I would have difficulty in getting any to leave, and so would have to pay for all three.)

Yasmin must never see this—that is decided. It is not just that this entire incident would disturb her greatly, but because of what happened next. I was sitting on the bed nearest the door, hoping to decide quickly which of the three most resembled the girl who had played Ellen. The first was too short, with a wan, pinched face. The second was tall and blond, but plump. The third, who seemed to stumble as she entered, exactly resembled Yasmin.

For a few seconds I actually believed it was she. Science has so accustomed us to devising and accepting theories to account for the facts we observe, however fantastic, that our minds must begin their manufacture before we are aware of it. Yasmin had grown lonely for me. She had booked passage a few days after my own departure, or perhaps had flown, daring the notorious American landing facilities. Arriving here, she had made inquiries at the consulate, and was approaching my door as the manager lit his candle, and not knowing what was taking place had entered with prostitutes he had engaged.

It was all moonshine, of course. I jumped to my feet and held up the candle, and saw that the third girl, though she had Yasmin's large, dark eyes and rounded little chin, was not she. For all her night-black hair and delicate features, she was indisputably an American; and as she came toward me (encouraged, no doubt, because she had attracted my attention) I saw that like Kreton in the play she had a club foot.

As you see, I returned alive from the park after all. Tonight before I retire I will eat an egg; but first I will briefly set down my experiences.

The park lies on the opposite side of the Washington Channel, between the city and the river. It can be reached by land only at the north end. Not choosing to walk so far and return, I hired a little boat with a tattered red sail to carry me to the southern tip, which is called Hains Point. Here there was a fountain, I am told, in the old times; but nothing remains of it now.

We had clear, sunny spring weather, and made our way over exhilarating swells of wave with nothing of the deadly wallowing that oppressed me so much aboard the *Princess Fatimah*. I sat in the bow and watched the rolling greenery of the park on one side of the channel and the ruins of the old fort on the other, while an elderly man handled the tiller, and his thin, sun-browned granddaughter, aged about eleven, worked the sail.

When we rounded the point, the old man told me that for very little more he would take me across to Arlington to see the remains of what is supposed to be the largest building of the country's antiquity. I refused, determined to save that experience for another time, and we landed where a part of the ancient concrete coping remained intact.

The tracks of old roads run up either shore; but I decided to avoid them, and made my way up the center, keeping to the highest ground in so far as I could. Once, no doubt, the whole area was devoted to pleasure. Very little remains, however, of the pavilions and statuary that must have dotted the ground. There are little, worn-away hills that may once have been rockeries but are now covered with soil, and many stagnant pools. In a score of places I saw the burrows of the famous giant American rats, though I never saw the animals themselves. To judge from the holes, their size has not been exaggerated—there were several I could have entered with ease.

The wild dogs, against which I had been warned by both the hotel manager and the old boatman, began to follow me after I had walked about a kilometer north. They are short-haired, and typically blotched with black and brown flecked with white. I would say their average weight was about twenty-five kilos. With their erect ears and alert, intelligent faces they did not seem particularly dangerous; but I soon noticed that whichever way I turned, the ones in back of me edged nearer. I sat on a stone with my back to a pool and made several quick sketches of them, then decided to try my pistol. They did not seem to know what it was, so I was able to center the red aiming laser very nicely on one big fellow's chest before I pressed the stud for a high energy pulse.

For a long time afterward, I heard the melancholy howling of these dogs behind me. Perhaps they were mourning their fallen leader. Twice I came across rusting machines that may have been used to take invalids through the gardens in such fair weather as I myself experienced today. Uncle Mirza says I am a good colorist, but I despair of ever matching the green-haunted blacks with which the declining sun painted the park.

I met no one until I had almost reached the piers of the abandoned railway bridge. Then four or five Americans who pretended to beg surrounded me. The dogs, who as I understand it live mostly upon the refuse cast up by the river, were more honest in their intentions and cleaner in their persons. If these people had been like the pitiful creatures I had met in the Silent City, I would have thrown them a few coins; but they were more or less able-bodied men and women who could have worked, and chose instead to rob. I told them that I had been forced to kill a fellow countryman of theirs (not mentioning that he was a dog) who had assaulted me; and asked where I could report the matter to the police. At that they backed off, and permitted me to walk around the northern end of the channel in peace, though not without a thousand savage looks. I returned here without further incident, tired and very well satisfied with my day.

I have eaten one of the eggs! I confess I found it difficult to take the first taste; but marshaling my resolution was like pushing at a wall of glass—all at once the resistance snapped, and I picked the thing up and swallowed it in a few bites. It was piercingly sweet, but there was no other flavor. Now we will see. This is more frightening than the park by far.

Nothing seemed to be happening, so I went out to dinner. It was twilight, and the carnival spirit of the streets was more marked than ever—colored lights above all the shops, and music from the rooftops where the wealthier natives have private gardens. I have been eating mostly at the hotel, but was told of a "good" American-style restaurant not too far south on Maine Street.

It was just as described—people sitting on padded benches in alcoves. The table tops are of a substance like fine-grained, greasy, artificial stone. They looked very old. I had the Number One Dinner—buff-colored fish soup with the pasty American bread on the side, followed by a sandwich of ground meat and raw vegetables doused with a tomato sauce and served on a soft, oily roll. To tell the truth, I did not much enjoy the meal; but it seems a sort of duty to sample more of the American food than I have thus far.

I am very tempted to end the account of my day here, and in fact I laid down this pen when I had written *thus far*, and made myself ready for bed. Still, what good is a dishonest record? I will let no one see this—just keep it to read over after I get home.

Returning to the hotel from the restaurant, I passed the theater. The thought of seeing Ellen again was irresistible; I bought a ticket and went inside. It was not until I was in my seat that I realized that the bill had changed.

The new play was *Mary Rose.* I saw it done by an English company several years ago, with great authenticity; and it struck me that (like Mary herself) it had far outlived its time. The American production was as inauthentic as the other had been correct. For that reason, it retained—or I should have said it had acquired—a good deal of interest.

Americans are superstitious about the interior of their country, not its coasts, so Mary Rose's island had been shifted to one of the huge central lakes. The highlander, Cameron, had accordingly become a Canadian, played by General Powers' former aide. The Speldings had become the Morelands, and the Morelands had become Americans. Kreton was Harry, the knife-throwing wounded soldier; and my Ellen had become Mary Rose.

The role suited her so well that I imagined the play had been selected as a vehicle for her. Her height emphasized the character's unnatural immaturity, and her slenderness, and the vulnerability of her pale complexion, would have told us, I think, if the play had not, that she had been victimized unaware. More important than any of these things was a wild and innocent affinity for the supernatural, which she projected to perfection. It was that quality alone (as I now understood) that had made us believe on the preceding night that Kreton's spaceship might land in the Speldings' rose garden—he would have been drawn to Ellen, though he had never seen her. Now it made Mary Rose's disappearances and reappearances plausible and even likely; it was as likely that unseen spirits lusted for Mary Rose as that Lieutenant Blake (previously John Randolf) loved her.

Indeed it was more likely. And I had no sooner realized that, than the whole mystery of *Mary Rose*—which had seemed at once inexplicable and banal when I had seen it well played in Teheran—lay clear before me. We of the audience were the envious and greedy spirits. If the Morelands could not see that one wall of their comfortable drawing room was but a sea of dark faces, if Cameron had never noticed that we were the backdrop of his island, the fault was theirs. By rights then, Mary Rose should have been drawn to us when she vanished. At the end of the second act I began to look for her, and in the beginning of the third I found her, standing silent and unobserved behind the last row of seats. I was only four rows from the stage, but I slipped out of my place as unobtrusively as I could, and crept up the aisle toward her.

I was too late. Before I had gone halfway, it was nearly time for her entrance at the end of the scene. I watched the rest of the play from the back of the theater, but she never returned.

Same night. I am having a good deal of trouble sleeping, though while I was on the ship I slept nine hours a night, and was off as soon as my head touched the pillow.

The truth is that while I lay in bed tonight I recalled the old curator's remark that the actresses were all prostitutes. If it is true and not simply an expression of hatred for younger people whose bodies are still attractive, then I have been a fool to moan over the thought of Mary Rose and Ellen when I might have had the girl herself.

Her name is Ardis Dahl—I just looked it up in the playbill. I am going to the manager's office to consult the city directory there.

Writing before breakfast. Found the manager's office locked last night. It was after two. I put my shoulder against the door and got it open easily enough. (There was no metal socket for the bolt such as we have at home—just a hole mortised in the frame.) The directory listed several Dahls in the city, but since it was nearly eight years out of date it did not inspire a great deal of confidence. I reflected, however, that in a backwater like this people were not likely to move about so much as we do at home, and that if it were not still of some utility, the manager would not be likely to retain it; so I selected the one that appeared from its address to be nearest the theater, and set out.

The streets were completely deserted. I remember thinking that I was now doing what I had previously been so afraid to do, having been frightened of the city by reading. How ridiculous to suppose that robbers would be afoot now, when no one else was. What would they do, stand for hours at the empty corners?

The moon was full and high in the southern sky, showering the street with the lambent white fluid of its light. If it had not been for the sharp, unclean odor so characteristic of American residential areas, I might have thought myself walking through an illustration from some old book of wonder tales, or an actor in a children's pantomime, so bewitched by the scenery that he has forgotten the audience.

(In writing that—which to tell the truth I did not think of at the time, but only now, as I sat here at my table—I realized that that is in fact what must happen to the American girl I have been in the habit of calling Ellen but must now learn to call Ardis. She could never perform as she does if it were not that in some part of her mind her stage became her reality.)

The shadows about my feet were a century old, tracing faithfully the courses they had determined long before New Tabriz came to jewel the lunar face with its sapphire. Webbed with thoughts of her—my Ellen, my Mary Rose, my Ardis!—and with the magic of that pale light that commands all the tides, I was elevated to a degree I cannot well describe.

Then I was seized by the thought that everything I felt might be no more than the effect of the drug.

At once, like someone who falls from a tower and clutches at the very wisps of air, I tried to return myself to reality. I bit the interiors of my cheeks until the blood filled my mouth, and struck the unfeeling wall of the nearest building with my fist. In a moment the pain sobered me. For a quarter hour or more I stood at the curbside, spitting into the gutter and trying to clean and bandage my knuckles with strips torn from my handkerchief. A thousand times I thought what a sight I would be if I did in fact succeed in seeing Ellen, and I comforted myself with the thought that if she were indeed a prostitute it would not matter to her—I could offer her a few additional rials and all would be well.

Yet that thought was not really much comfort. Even when a woman sells her body, a man flatters himself that she would not do so quite so readily were he not who he is. At the very moment I drooled blood into the street, I was congratulating myself on the strong, square face so many have admired; and wondering how I should apologize if in kissing her I smeared her mouth with red.

Perhaps it was some faint sound that brought me to myself; perhaps it was only the consciousness of being watched. I drew my pistol and turned this way and that, but saw nothing.

Yet the feeling endured. I began to walk again; and if there was any sense of unreality remaining, it was no longer the unearthly exultation I had felt earlier. After a few steps I stopped and listened. A dry sound of rattling and scraping had followed me. It too stopped now.

I was nearing the address I had taken from the directory. I confess my mind was filled with fancies in which I was rescued by Ellen herself, who in the end should be more frightened than I, but who would risk her lovely person to save mine. Yet I knew these *were* but fancies, and the thing pursuing me was not, though it crossed my mind more than once that it might be some *druj* made to seem visible and palpable to me.

Another block, and I had reached the address. It was a house no different from those on either side—built of the rubble of buildings that were older still, three-storied, heavy-doored, and almost without windows. There was a bookshop on the ground floor (to judge by an old sign) with living quarters above it. I crossed the street to see it better, and stood, wrapped again in my dreams, staring at the single thread of yellow light that showed between the shutters of a gable window.

As I watched that light, the feeling of being watched myself grew upon me. Time passed, slipping through the waist of the universe's great hourglass like the eroded soil of this continent slipping down her rivers to the seas. At last my fear and desire—desire for Ellen, fear of whatever it was that glared at me with invisible eyes—drove me to the door of the house. I hammered the wood with the butt of my pistol, though I knew how unlikely it was that any American would answer a knock at such a time of night, and when I had knocked several times, I heard slow steps from within.

The door creaked open until it was caught by a chain. I saw a gray-haired man, fully dressed, holding an old-fashioned, long-barreled gun. Behind him a woman lifted a stub of smoking candle to let him see; and though she was clearly much older than Ellen, and was marked, moreover, by the deformities so prevalent here, there was a certain nobility in her features and a certain beauty as well, so that I was reminded of the fallen statue that is said to have stood on an island farther north, and which I have seen pictured.

I told the man that I was a traveler—true enough!—and that I had just arrived by boat from Arlington and had no place to stay, and so had walked into the city until I had noticed the light of his window. I would pay, I said, a silver rial if they would only give me a bed for the night and breakfast in the morning, and I showed them the coin. My plan was to become a guest in the house so that I might discover whether Ellen was indeed one of the inhabitants; if she were, it would have been an easy matter to prolong my stay.

The woman tried to whisper in her husband's ear, but save for a look of nervous irritation he ignored her. "I don't dare let a stranger in." From his voice I might have been a lion, and his gun a trainer's chair. "Not with no one here but my wife and myself."

"I see," I told him. "I quite understand your position."

"You might try the house on the corner," he said, shutting the door, "but don't tell them Dahl sent you." I heard the heavy bar dropped into place at the final word.

I turned away—and then by the mercy of Allah who is indeed compassionate happened to glance back one last time at the thread of yellow between the shutters of that high window. A flicker of scarlet higher still caught my attention, perhaps only because the light of the setting moon now bathed the rooftop from a new angle. I think the creature I glimpsed there had been waiting to leap upon me from behind, but when our eyes met it launched itself toward me. I had barely time to lift my pistol before it struck me and slammed me to the broken pavement of the street.

For a brief period I think I lost consciousness. If my shot had not killed the thing as it fell, I would not be sitting here writing this journal this morning. After half a minute or so I came to myself enough to thrust its weight away, stand up, and rub my bruises. No one had come to my aid; but neither had anyone rushed from the surrounding houses to kill and rob me. I was as alone with the creature that lay dead at my feet as I had been when I only stood watching the window in the house from which it had sprung.

After I found my pistol and assured myself that it was still in working order, I dragged the thing to a spot of moonlight. When I glimpsed it on the roof, it had seemed a feral dog, like the one I had shot in the park. When it lay dead before me, I had thought it a human being. In the moonlight I saw it was neither, or perhaps both. There was a blunt muzzle; and the height of the skull above the eyes, which anthropologists say is the surest badge of humanity and speech, had been stunted until it was not greater than I have seen in a macaque. Yet the arms and shoulders and pelvis—even a few filthy rags of clothing—all bespoke mankind. It was a female, with small, flattened breasts still apparent on either side of the burn channel.

At least ten years ago I read about such things in Osman Aga's *Mystery Beyond the Sun's Setting;* but it was very different to stand shivering on a deserted street corner of the old capital and examine the thing in the flesh. By Osman Aga's account (which no one, I think, but a few old women has ever believed) these creatures were in truth human beings—or at least the descendants of human beings. In the last century, when the famine gripped their country and the irreversible damage done to the chromosomal structures of the people had already become apparent, some few turned to the eating of human flesh. No doubt the corpses of the famine supplied their food at first; and no doubt those who ate of them congratulated themselves that by so doing they had escaped the effects of the enzymes that were then still used to bring slaughter animals to maturity in a matter of months. What they failed to realize was that the bodies of the human beings they ate had accumulated far more of these unnatural substances than were ever found in the flesh of the short-lived cattle. From them, according to *Mystery Beyond the Sun's Setting*, rose such creatures as the thing I had killed.

But Osman Aga has never been believed. So far as I know, he is a mere popular writer, with a reputation for glorifying Caspian resorts in recompense for free lodging, and for indulging in absurd expeditions to breed more books and publicize the ones he has already written—crossing the desert on a camel and the Alps on an elephant—and no one else has ever, to my knowledge, reported such things from this continent. The ruined cities filled with rats and rabid bats, and the terrible whirling dust storms of the interior, have been enough for other travel writers. Now I am sorry I did not contrive a way to cut off the thing's head; I feel sure its skull would have been of interest to science.

As soon as I had written the preceding paragraph, I realized that there might still be a chance to do what I had failed to do last night. I went to the kitchen, and for a small bribe was able to secure a large, sharp knife, which I concealed beneath my jacket.

It was still early as I ran down the street, and for a few minutes I had high hopes that the thing's body might still be lying where I had left it; but my efforts were all for nothing. It was gone, and there was no sign of its presence—no blood, no scar from my beam on the house. I poked into alleys and waste cans. Nothing. At last I came back to the hotel for breakfast, and I have now (it is mid-morning) returned to my room to make my plans for the day.

Very well. I failed to meet Ellen last night—I shall not fail today. I am going to buy another ticket for the play, and tonight I will not take my seat, but wait behind the last row where I saw her standing. If she comes to watch at the end of the second act as she did last night, I will be there to compliment her on her performance and present her with some gift. If she does not come, I will make my way backstage—from what I have seen of these Americans, a quarter rial should get me anywhere, but I am willing to loosen a few teeth if I must.

What absurd creatures we are! I have just reread what I wrote this morning, and I might as well have been writing of the philosophic speculations of the Congress of Birds or the affairs of the demons in Dom-daniel, or any other subject on which neither I nor anyone else knows or can know a thing. O Book, you have heard what I supposed would occur, now let me tell you what actually took place.

I set out as I had planned to procure a gift for Ellen. On the advice of the hotel manager, I followed Maine Street north until I reached the wide avenue that passes close by the obelisk. Around the base of this still imposing monument is held a perpetual fair in which the merchants use the stone blocks fallen from the upper part of the structure as tables. What remains of the shaft is still, I should say, upwards of one hundred meters high; but it is said to have formerly stood three or four times that height. Much of the fallen material has been carted away to build private homes.

There seems to be no logic to the prices in this country, save for the general rule that foodstuffs are cheap and imported machinery—cameras and the like—costly. Textiles are expensive, which no doubt explains why so many of the people wear ragged clothes that they mend and dye in an effort to make them look new. Certain kinds of jewelry are quite reasonable; others sell for much higher prices than they would in Teheran. Rings of silver or white gold set, usually, with a single modest diamond, may be had in great numbers for such low prices that I was tempted into buying a few to take home as an investment. Yet I saw bracelets that would have sold at home for no more than half a rial, for which the seller asked ten times that much. There were many interesting antiques, all of which are alleged to have been dug from the ruined cities of the interior at the cost of someone's life. When I had talked to five or six vendors of such items, I was able to believe that I knew how the country was depopulated.

After a good deal of this pleasant, wordy shopping, during which I spent very little, I selected a bracelet made of old coins—many of them silver—as my gift to Ellen. I reasoned that women always like jewelry, and that such a showy piece might be of service to an actress in playing some part or other, and that the coins must have a good deal of intrinsic value. Whether she will like it or not—if she ever receives it—I do not know; it is still in the pocket of my jacket.

When the shadow of the obelisk had grown long, I returned here to the hotel and had a good dinner of lamb and rice, and retired to groom myself for the evening. The five remaining candy eggs stood staring at me from the top of my dresser. I remembered my resolve, and took one. Quite suddenly I was struck by the conviction that the demon I believed I had killed the night before had been no more than a phantom engendered by the action of the drug.

What if I had been firing my pistol at mere empty air? That seemed a terrible thought—indeed it seems so to me still. A worse one is that the drug really may have rendered visible—as some say those ancient preparations were intended to—a real but spiritual being. If such things in fact walk what we take to be unoccupied rooms and rooftops, and the empty streets of night, it would explain many sudden deaths and diseases, and perhaps the sudden changes for the worse we sometimes see in others and others in us, and even the birth of evil men. This morning I called the thing a *druj*; it may be true.

Yet if the drug had been in the egg I ate last night, then the egg I held was harmless. Concentrating on that thought, I forced myself to eat it all, then stretched myself upon the bed to wait.

Very briefly I slept and dreamed. Ellen was bending over me, caressing me with a soft, long-fingered hand. It was only for an instant, but sufficient to make me hope that dreams are prophecies.

If the drug was in the egg I consumed, that dream was its only result. I got up and washed, and changed my clothes, sprinkling my fresh shirt liberally with our Pamir rosewater, which I have observed the Americans hold in high regard. Making certain my ticket and pistol were both in place, I left for the theater.

The play was still *Mary Rose*. I intentionally entered late (after Harry and Mrs. Otery had been talking for several minutes), then lingered at the back of the last row as though I were too polite to disturb the audience by taking my seat. Mrs. Otery made her exit; Harry pulled his knife from the wood of the packing case and threw it again, and when the mists of the past had marched across the stage, Harry was gone, and Moreland and the parson were chatting to the tune of Mrs. Moreland's knitting needles. Mary Rose would be on stage soon. My hope that she would come out to watch the opening scene had come to nothing; I would have to wait until she vanished at the end of Act II before I could expect to see her.

I was looking for a vacant seat when I became conscious of someone standing near me. In the dim light I could tell little except that he was rather slender, and a few centimeters shorter than I.

Finding no seat, I moved back a step or two. The newcomer touched my arm and asked in a whisper if I could light his cigarette. I had already seen that it was customary to smoke in the theaters here, and I had fallen into the habit of carrying matches to light the candles in my room. The flare of the flame showed the narrow eyes and high cheekbones of Harry—or as I preferred to think of him, Kreton. Taken somewhat aback, I murmured some inane remark about the excellence of his performance.

"Did you like it? It is the least of all parts—I pull the curtain to open the show, then pull it again to tell everyone it's time to go home."

Several people in the audience were looking angrily at us, so we retreated to a point at the head of the aisle that was at least legally in the lobby, where I told him I had seen him in *Visit to a Small Planet* as well.

"Now *there* is a play. The character—as I am sure you saw—is good and bad at once. He is benign, he is mischievous, he is hellish."

"You carried it off wonderfully well, I thought."

"Thank you. This turkey here—do you know how many roles it has?"

"Well, there's yourself, Mrs. Otery, Mr. Amy—"

"No, no." He touched my arm to stop me. "I mean *roles*, parts that require real acting. There's one—the girl. She gets to skip about the stage as an eighteen-year-old whose brain atrophied at ten; and at least half what she does is wasted on the audience because they don't realize what's wrong with her until Act I is almost over."

"She's wonderful," I said. "I mean Mlle. Dahl."

Kreton nodded and drew on his cigarette. "She is a very competent ingenue, though it would be better if she weren't quite so tall."

"Do you think there's any chance that she might come out here—as you did?"

"Ah," he said, and looked me up and down.

For a moment I could have sworn that the telepathic ability he was credited with in *Visit to a Small Planet* was no fiction; nevertheless, I repeated my question: "Is it probable or not?"

"There's no reason to get angry—no, it's not likely. Is that enough payment for your match?"

"She vanishes at the end of the second act, and doesn't come on stage again until near the close of the third."

Kreton smiled. "You've read the play?"

"I was here last night. She must be off for nearly forty minutes, including the intermission."

"That's right. But she won't be here. It's true she goes out front sometimes—as I did myself tonight—but I happen to know she has company backstage."

"Might I ask who?"

"You might. It's even possible I might answer. You're Moslem, I suppose—do you drink?"

"I'm not a *strict* Moslem; but no, I don't. I'll buy you a drink gladly though, if you want one, and have coffee with you while you drink it."

We left by a side door and elbowed our way through the crowd in the street. A flight of narrow and dirty steps descending from the sidewalk led us to a cellar tavern that had all the atmosphere of a private club. There was a bar with a picture (now much dimmed by dirt and smoke) of the cast of a play I did not recognize behind it, three tables, and a few alcoves. Kreton and I slipped into one of these and ordered from a barman with a misshapen head. I suppose I must have stared at him, because Kreton said, "I sprained my ankle stepping out of a saucer, and now I am a convalescent soldier. Should we make up something for him too? Can't we just say the potter is angry sometimes?"

"The potter?" I asked.

" 'None answered this; but after Silence spake/A Vessel of a more ungainly Make:/They sneer at me for leaning all awry;/What! Did the Hand then of the Potter shake?' "

I shook my head. "I've never heard that; but you're right, he looks as though his head had been shaped in clay, then knocked in on one side while it was still wet."

"This is a republic of hideousness as you have no doubt already seen. Our national symbol is supposed to be an extinct eagle; it is in fact the nightmare."

"I find it a very beautiful country," I said. "Though I confess that many of your people are unsightly. Still there are the ruins, and you have such skies as we never see at home."

"Our chimneys have been filled with wind for a long time."

"That may be for the best. Blue skies are better than most of the things made in factories."

"And not all our people are unsightly," Kreton murmured.

"Oh no. Mlle. Dahl—"

"I had myself in mind."

I saw that he was baiting me, but I said, "No, you aren't hideous—in fact, I would call you handsome in an exotic way. Unfortunately, my tastes run more toward Mlle. Dahl."

"Call her Ardis—she won't mind."

The barman brought Kreton a glass of green liqueur, and me a cup of the weak, bitter American coffee.

"You were going to tell me who she is entertaining."

"Behind the scenes." Kreton smiled. "I just thought of that—I've used the phrase a thousand times, as I suppose everyone has. This time it happens to be literally correct, and its birth is suddenly made plain, like Oedipus's. No, I don't think I promised I would tell you that—though I suppose I said I might. Aren't there other things you would really rather know? The secret hidden beneath Mount Rushmore, or how you might meet her yourself?"

"I will give you twenty rials to introduce me to her, with some assurance that something will come of the introduction. No one need ever find out."

Kreton laughed. "Believe me, I would be more likely to boast of my profit than keep it secret—though I would probably have to divide my fee with the lady to fulfill the guarantee."

"You'll do it then?"

He shook his head, still laughing. "I only pretend to be corrupt; it goes with this face. Come backstage after the show tonight, and I'll see that you meet Ardis. You're very wealthy, I presume, and if you're not, we'll say you are anyway. What are you doing here?"

"Studying your art and architecture."

"Great reputation in your own country, no doubt?"

"I am a pupil of Akhon Mirza Ahmak; he has a great reputation, surely.

He even came here, thirty years ago, to examine the miniatures in your National Gallery of Art."

"Pupil of Akhon Mirza Ahmak, pupil of Akhon Mirza Ahmak," Kreton muttered to himself. "That is very good—I must remember it. But now"—he glanced at the old clock behind the bar—"it's time we got back. I'll have to freshen my makeup before I go on in the last act. Would you prefer to wait in the theater, or just come around to the stage door when the play's over? I'll give you a card that will get you in."

"I'll wait in the theater," I said, feeling that would offer less chance for mishap; also because I wanted to see Ellen play the ghost again.

"Come along then—I have a key for that side door."

I rose to go with him, and he threw an arm about my shoulder that I felt it would be impolite to thrust away. I could feel his hand, as cold as a dead man's, through my clothing, and was reminded unpleasantly of the twisted hands of the beggar in the Silent City.

We were going up the narrow stairs when I felt a gentle touch inside my jacket. My first thought was that he had seen the outline of my pistol, and meant to take it and shoot me. I gripped his wrist and shouted something—I do not remember what. Bound together and struggling, we staggered up the steps and into the street.

In a few seconds we were the center of a mob—some taking his side, some mine, most only urging us to fight, or asking each other what the disturbance was. My pocket sketchpad, which he must have thought held money, fell to the ground between us. Just then the American police arrived—not by air as the police would have come at home, but astride shaggy, hulking horses, and swinging whips. The crowd scattered at the first crackling arc from the lashes, and in a few seconds they had beaten Kreton to the ground. Even at the time I could not help thinking what a terrible thing it must be to be one of these people, whose police are so quick to prefer any prosperous-looking foreigner to one of their own citizens.

They asked me what had happened (my questioner even dismounted to show his respect for me), and I explained that Kreton had tried to rob me, but that I did not want him punished. The truth was that seeing him sprawled unconscious with a burn across his face had put an end to any resentment I might have felt toward him; out of pity, I would gladly have given him the few rials I carried. They told me that if he had attempted to rob me he must be charged, and that if I would not accuse him they would do so themselves.

I then said that Kreton was a friend; and that on reflection I felt certain that what he had attempted had been intended as a prank. (In maintaining this I was considerably handicapped by not knowing his real name, which I had read on the playbill but forgotten, so that I was forced to refer to him as "this poor man.")

At last the policeman said, "We can't leave him on the street, so we'll have to bring him in. How will it look if there's no complaint?"

Then I understood that they were afraid of what their superiors might say if it became know that they had beaten him unconscious when no charge was made against him; and when I became aware that if I would not press charges, the charges they would bring themselves would be far more serious—assault or attempted murder—I agreed to do what they wished, and signed a form alleging the theft of my sketchbook.

When they had gone at last, carrying the unfortunate Kreton across a saddlebow, I tried to reenter the theater. The side door through which we had left was locked, and though I would gladly have paid the price of another ticket, the box office was closed. Seeing that there was nothing further to be done, I returned here, telling myself that my introduction to Ellen, if it ever came, would have to wait for another day.

Very truly it is written that we walk by paths that are always turning. In recording these several pages I have managed to restrain my enthusiasm, though when I described my waiting at the back of the theater for Ardis, and again when I recounted how Kreton had promised to introduce me to her, I was forced for minutes at a time to lay down my pen and walk about the room singing and whistling, and—to reveal everything—jumping over the beds! But now I can conceal no longer. I have seen her! I have touched her hand; I am to see her again tomorrow; and there is every hope that she will become my mistress!

I had undressed and laid myself on the bed (thinking to bring this journal up to date in the morning) and had even fallen into the first doze of sleep, when there was a knock at the door. I slipped into my robe and pressed the release.

It was the only time in my life that for even an instant I thought I might be dreaming—actually asleep—when in truth I was up and awake.

How feeble it is to write that she is more beautiful in person than she appears on the stage. It is true, and yet it is a supreme irrelevance. I have seen more beautiful women—indeed Yasmin is, I suppose, by the formal standards of art, more lovely. It is not Ardis' beauty that draws me to her—the hair like gold, the translucent skin that then still showed traces of the bluish makeup she had worn as a ghost, the flashing eyes like the clear, clean skies of America. It is something deeper than that; something that would remain if all that were somehow taken away. No doubt she has habits that would disgust me in someone else, and the vanity that is said to be so common in her profession, and yet I would do anything to possess her.

Enough of this. What is it but empty boasting, now that I am on the point of winning her?

She stood in my doorway. I have been trying to think how I can express what I felt then. It was as though some tall flower, a lily perhaps, had left the garden and come to tap at my door, a thing that had never happened before in all the history of the world, and would never happen again.

"You are Nadan Jaffarzadeh?"

I admitted that I was, and shamefacedly, twenty seconds too late, moved out of her way.

She entered, but instead of taking the chair I indicated, turned to face me; her blue eyes seemed as large as the colored eggs on the dresser, and they were filled with a melting hope. "You are the man, then, that Bobby

O'Keene tried to rob tonight."

I nodded.

"I know you—I mean, I know your face. This is insane. You came to *Visit* on the last night and brought your father, and then to *Mary Rose* on the first night, and sat in the third or fourth row. I thought you were an American, and when the police told me your name I imagined some greasy fat man with gestures. Why on earth would Bobby want to steal from *you*?"

"Perhaps he needed the money."

She threw back her head and laughed. I had heard her laugh in *Mary Rose* when Simon was asking her father for her hand; but that had held a note of childishness that (however well suited to the part) detracted from its beauty. This laugh was the merriment of houris sliding down a rainbow. "I'm sure he did. He always needs money. You're sure, though, that he meant to rob you? You couldn't have . . ."

She saw my expression and let the question trail away. The truth is that I was disappointed that I could not oblige her, and at last I said, "If you want me to be mistaken, Ardis, then I was mistaken. He only bumped against me on the steps, perhaps, and tried to catch my sketchbook when it fell."

She smiled, and her face was the sun smiling upon roses. "You would say that for me? And you know my name?"

"From the program. I came to the theater to see you—and that was not my father, who it grieves me to say is long dead, but only an old man, an American, whom I had met that day."

"You brought him sandwiches at the first intermission—I was watching you through the peephole in the curtain. You must be a very thoughtful person."

"Do you watch everyone in the audience so carefully?"

She blushed at that, and for a moment could not meet my eyes.

"But you will forgive Bobby, and tell the police that you want them to let him go? You must love the theater, Mr. Jef— Jaff—"

"You've forgotten my name already. It is Jaffarzadeh, a very commonplace name in my country."

"I hadn't forgotten it—only how to pronounce it. You see, when I came here I had learned it without knowing who you were, and so I had no trouble with it. Now you're a real person to me and I can't say it as an actress should." She seemed to notice the chair behind her for the first time, and sat down.

I sat opposite her. "I'm afraid I know very little about the theater."

"We are trying to keep it alive here, Mr. Jaffar, and—"

"Jaffarzadeh. Call me Nadan—then you won't have so many syllables to trip over."

She took my hand in hers, and I knew quite well that the gesture was as studied as a salaam and that she felt she was playing me like a fish; but I was beside myself with delight. To be played by *her*! To have *her* eager to cultivate my affection! And the fish will pull her in yet—wait and see!

"I will," she said, "Nadan. And though you may know little of the theater, you feel as I do—as we do—or you would not come. It has been such a long struggle; all the history of the stage is a struggle, the gasping of a beautiful child born at the point of death. The moralists, censorship and oppression, technology, and now poverty have all tried to destroy her. Only we, the actors and audiences, have kept her alive. We have been doing well here in Washington, Nadan."

"Very well indeed," I said. "Both the productions I have seen have been excellent."

"But only for the past two seasons. When I joined the company it had nearly fallen apart. We revived it—Bobby and Paul and I. We could do it because we cared, and because we were able to find a few naturally talented people who can take direction. Bobby is the best of us—he can walk away with any part that calls for a touch of the sinister . . ."

She seemed to run out of breath. I said, "I don't think there will be any trouble about getting him free."

"Thank God. We're getting the theater on its feet again now. We're attracting new people, and we've built up a following—people who come to see every production. There's even some money ahead at last. But *Mary Rose* is supposed to run another two weeks, and after that we're doing *Faust*, with Bobby as Mephistopheles. We've simply no one who can take his place, no one who can come close to him."

"I'm sure the police will release him if I ask them to."

"They *must*. We have to have him tomorrow night. Bill—someone you don't know—tried to go on for him in the third act tonight. It was just ghastly. In Iran you're very polite; that's what I've heard."

"We enjoy thinking so."

"We're not. We never were; and as . . ."

Her voice trailed away, but a wave of one slender arm evoked everything—the cracked plaster walls became as air, and the decayed city, the ruined continent, entered the room with us. "I understand," I said.

"They—we—were betrayed. In our souls we have never been sure by whom. When we feel cheated we are ready to kill; and maybe we feel cheated all the time."

She slumped in her chair, and I realized, as I should have long before, how exhausted she was. She had given a performance that had ended in disaster, then had been forced to plead with the police for my name and address, and at last had come here from the station house, very probably on foot. I asked when I could obtain O'Keene's release.

"We can go tomorrow morning, if you'll do it."

"You wish to come too?"

She nodded, smoothed her skirt, and stood. "I'll have to know. I'll come for you about nine, if that's all right."

"If you'll wait outside for me to dress, I'll take you home."

"That's not necessary."

"It will only take a moment," I said.

The blue eyes held something pleading again. "You're going to come in with me—that's what you're thinking, I know. You have two beds here—bigger, cleaner beds than the one I have in my little apartment; if I were to ask you to push them together, would you still take me home afterward?"

It was as though I were dreaming indeed—a dream in which everything I wanted—the cosmos purified—delivered itself to me. I said, "You won't have to leave at all—you can spend the night with me. Then we can breakfast together before we go to release your friend."

She laughed again, lifting that exquisite head. "There are a hundred things at home I need. Do you think I'd have breakfast with you without my cosmetics, and in these dirty clothes?"

"Then I will take you home—yes, though you lived in Kasvin. Or on Mount Kaf."

She smiled. "Get dressed, then. I'll wait outside, and I'll show you my apartment; perhaps you won't want to come back here afterward."

She went out, her wooden-soled American shoes clicking on the bare floor, and I threw on trousers, shirt, and jacket, and jammed my feet into my boots. When I opened the door, she was gone. I rushed to the barred window at the end of the corridor, and was in time to see her disappear down a side street. A last swirl of her skirt in a gust of night wind, and she had vanished into the velvet dark.

For a long time I stood there looking out over the ruinous buildings. I was not angry—I do not think I could be angry with her. I was, though here it is hard to tell the truth, in some way glad. Not because I feared the embrace of love—I have no doubt of my ability to suffice any woman who can be sated by man—but because an easy exchange of my cooperation for her person would have failed to satisfy my need for romance, for adventure of a certain type, in which danger and love are twined like coupling serpents. Ardis, my Ellen, will provide that, surely, as neither Yasmin nor the pitiful wanton who was her double could. I sense that the world is opening for me only now; that I am being born; that that corridor was the birth canal, and that Ardis in leaving me was drawing me out toward her.

When I returned to my own door, I noticed a bit of paper on the floor before it. I transcribe it exactly here, though I cannot transmit its scent of lilacs.

> *You are a most attractive man and I want very much to stretch the truth and tell you you can have me freely when Bobby is free but I won't sell myself etc. Really I will sell myself for Bobby but I have other fish to fry tonight. I'll see you in the morning and if you can get Bobby out or even try hard you'll have (real) love from the vanishing*
>
> *Mary Rose*

Morning. Woke early and ate here at the hotel as usual, finishing about eight. Writing this journal will give me something to do while I wait for Ardis. Had an American breakfast today, the first time I have risked one. Flakes of pastry dough toasted crisp and drenched with cream, and with it strudel and the usual American coffee. Most natives have spiced pork in one form or another, which I cannot bring myself to try; but several of the people around me were having egg dishes and oven-warmed bread, which I will sample tomorrow.

I had a very unpleasant dream last night; I have been trying to put it out of my mind ever since I woke. It was dark, and I was under an open sky with Ardis, walking over ground much rougher than anything I saw in the park on the farther side of the channel. One of the hideous creatures I shot night before last was pursuing us—or rather, lurking about us, for it appeared first to the left of us, then to the right, silhouetted against the night sky. Each time we saw it, Ardis grasped my arm and urged me to shoot, but the little indicator light on my pistol was glowing red to show that there was not enough charge left for a shot. All very silly, of course, but I am going to buy a fresh powerpack as soon as I have the opportunity.

It is late afternoon—after six—but we have not had dinner yet. I am just out of the tub, and sit here naked, with today's candy egg laid (pinker than even I) beside this book on my table. Ardis and I had a sorry, weary time of it, and I have come back here to make myself presentable. At seven we will meet for dinner; the curtain goes up at eight, so it can't be a long one, but I am going backstage to watch the play from the wings, where I will be able to talk to her when she isn't performing.

I just took a bite of the egg—no unusual taste, nothing but an unpleasant sweetness. The more I reflect on it, the more inclined I am to believe that the drug was in the first I ate. No doubt the monster I saw had been lurking in my brain since I read *Mysteries*, and the drug freed it. True, there were bloodstains on my clothes (the Peri's asphodel!) but they could as easily have come from my cheek, which is still sore. I have had my experience, and all I have left is my candy. I am almost tempted to throw out the rest. Another bite.

Still twenty minutes before I must dress and go for Ardis—she showed me where she lives, only a few doors from the theater. To work then.

Ardis was a trifle late this morning, but came as she had promised. I asked where we were to go to free Kreton, and when she told me—a still-living building at the eastern end of the Silent City—I hired one of the rickety American caleches to drive us there. Like most of them, it was drawn by a starved horse; but we made good time.

The American police are organized on a peculiar system. The national secret police (officially, the Federated Enquiry Divisions) are in a tutorial position to all the others, having power to review their decisions, promote, demote, and discipline, and as the ultimate reward, enroll personnel from the other organizations. In addition they maintain a uniformed force of their own. Thus when an American has been arrested by uniformed police, his friends can seldom learn whether he has been taken by the local police, by the F.E.D. uniformed national force, or by members of the F.E.D. secret police posing as either of the foregoing.

Since I had known nothing of these distinctions previously, I had no way of guessing which of the three had O'Keene; but the local police to whom Ardis had spoken the night before had given her to understand that he had been taken by them. She explained all this to me as we rattled along, then added that we were now going to the F.E.D. Building to secure his release. I must have looked as confused as I felt at this, because she added, "Part of it is a station for the Washington Police Department—they rent the space from the F.E.D."

My own impression (when we arrived) was that they did no such thing—that the entire apparatus was no more real than one of the scenes in Ardis' theater, and that all the men and women to whom we spoke were in fact agents of the secret police, wielding ten times the authority they pretended to possess, and going through a solemn ritual of deception. As Ardis and I moved from office to office, explaining our simple errand, I came to think that she felt as I did, and that she had refrained from expressing these feelings to me in the cab not only because of the danger, the fear that I might betray her or the driver be a spy, but because she was ashamed of her nation, and eager to make it appear to me, a foreigner, that her government was less devious and meretricious than is actually the case.

If this is so—and in that windowless warren of stone I was certain it was—then the very explanation she proffered in the cab (which I have given in its proper place) differentiating clearly between local police, uniformed F.E.D. police, and secret police, was no more than a children's fable, concealing an actuality less forthright and more convoluted.

Our questioners were courteous to me, much less so to Ardis, and (so it seemed to me) obsessed by the idea that something more lay behind the simple incident we described over and over again—so much so in fact that I came to believe it myself. I have neither time nor patience enough to describe all these interviews, but I will attempt to give a sample of one.

We went into a small, windowless office crowded between two others that appeared empty. A middle-aged American woman was seated behind a metal desk. She appeared normal and reasonably attractive until she spoke; then her scarred gums showed that she had once had two or three times the proper number of teeth—forty or fifty, I suppose, in each jaw—and that the dental surgeon who had extracted the supernumerary ones had not always, perhaps, selected those he suffered to remain as wisely as he might. She asked, "How is it outside? The weather? You see, I don't know, sitting in here all day."

Ardis said, "Very nice."

"Do you like it, *Hajji?* Have you had a pleasant stay in our great country?"

"I don't think it has rained since I've been here."

She seemed to take the remark as a covert accusation. "You came too late for the rains, I'm afraid. This is a very fertile area, however. Some of our oldest coins show heads of wheat. Have you seen them?" She pushed a small copper coin across the desk, and I pretended to examine it. There are one or two like it in the bracelet I bought for Ardis, and which I still have not presented to her. "I must apologize on behalf of the District for what happened to you," the woman continued. "We are making every effort to control crime. You have not been victimized before this?"

I shook my head, half suffocated in that airless office, and said I had not been.

"And now you are here." She shuffled the papers she held, then pretended to read from one of them. "You are here to secure the release of the thief who assaulted you. A very commendable act of magnanimity. May I ask why you brought this young woman with you? She does not seem to be mentioned in any of these reports."

I explained that Ardis was a co-worker of O'Keene's, and that she had interceded for him.

"Then it is you, Ms. Dahl, who are really interested in securing this prisoner's release. Are you related to him?"

And so on.

At the conclusion of each interview we were told either that the matter was completely out of the hands of the person to whom we had just spent half an hour or an hour talking, that it was necessary to obtain a clearance from someone else, or that an additional deposition had to be made. About two o'clock we were sent to the other side of the river—into what my guidebooks insist is an entirely different jurisdiction—to visit a penal facility. There we were forced to look for Kreton among five hundred or so miserable prisoners, all of whom stank and had lice. Not finding him, we returned to the F.E.D. Building past the half-overturned and yet still brooding figure called the Seated Man, and the ruins and beggars of the Silent City, for another round of interrogations. By five, when we were told to leave, we were both exhausted, though Ardis seemed surprisingly hopeful. When I left her at the door of her building a few minutes ago, I asked her what they would do tonight without Kreton.

"Without Harry, you mean." She smiled. "The best we can, I suppose, if we must. At least Paul will have someone ready to stand in for him tonight."

We shall see how well it goes.

I have picked up this pen and replaced it on the table ten times at least. It seems very likely that I should destroy this journal instead of continuing with it, were I wise; but I have discovered a hiding place for it which I think will be secure.

When I came back from Ardis' apartment tonight there were only two candy eggs remaining. I am certain—absolutely certain—that three were left when I went to meet Ardis. I am almost equally sure that after I had finished making the entry in this book, I put it, as I always do, at the left side of the drawer. It was on the right side.

It is possible that all this is merely the doing of the maid who cleans the room. She might easily have supposed that a single candy egg would not be missed, and have shifted this book while cleaning the drawer, or peeped inside out of curiosity.

I will assume the worst, however. An agent sent to investigate my room might be equipped to photograph these pages—but he might not, and it is not likely that he himself would have a reading knowledge of Farsi. Now I have gone through the book and eliminated all the passages relating to my reason for visiting this leprous country. Before I leave this room tomorrow I will arrange indicators—hairs and other objects whose positions I shall carefully record—that will tell me if the room has been searched again.

Now I may as well set down the events of the evening, which were truly extraordinary enough.

I met Ardis as we had planned, and she directed me to a small restaurant not far from her apartment. We had no sooner seated ourselves than two heavy-looking men entered. At no time could I see plainly the face of either, but it appeared to me that one was the American I had met aboard the *Princess Fatimah* and that the other was the grain dealer I had so assiduously avoided there, Golam Gassem. It is impossible, I think, for my divine Ardis ever to look less than beautiful; but she came as near to it then as the laws of nature permit—the blood drained from her face, her mouth opened slightly, and for a moment she appeared to be a lovely corpse. I began to ask what the trouble was, but before I could utter a word she touched my lips to silence me, and then, having somewhat regained her composure, said, "They have not seen us. I am leaving now. Follow me as though we were finished eating." She stood, feigned to pat her lips with a napkin (so that the lower half of her face was hidden) and walked out into the street.

I followed her, and found her laughing not three doors away from the entrance to the restaurant. The change in her could not have been more startling if she had been released from an enchantment. "It is so funny," she said. "Though it wasn't then. Come on, we'd better go; you can feed me after the show."

I asked her what those men were to her.

"Friends," she said, still laughing.

"If they are friends, why were you so anxious that they not see you? Were you afraid they would make us late?" I knew that such a trivial explanation could not be true, but I wanted to leave her a means of evading the question if she did not want to confide in me.

She shook her head. "No, no. I didn't want either to think I did not trust him. I'll tell you more later, if you want to involve yourself in our little charade."

"With all my heart."

She smiled at that—that sun-drenched smile for which I would gladly have entered a lion pit. In a few more steps we were at the rear entrance to the theater, and there was no time to say more. She opened the door, and I heard Kreton arguing with a woman I later learned was the wardrobe mistress. "You are free," I said, and he turned to look at me.

"Yes. Thanks to you, I think. And I do thank you."

Ardis gazed on him as though he were a child saved from drowning. "Poor Bobby. Was it very bad?"

"It was frightening, that's all. I was afraid I'd never get out. Do you know Terry is gone?"

She shook her head, and said, "What do you mean?" but I was certain—and here I am not exaggerating or coloring the facts, though I confess I have occasionally done so elsewhere in this chronicle—that she had known it before he spoke.

"He simply isn't here. Paul is running around like a lunatic. I hear you missed me last night."

"God, yes," Ardis said, and darted off too swiftly for me to follow.

Kreton took my arm. I expected him to apologize for having tried to rob me, but he said, "You've met her, I see."

"She persuaded me to drop the charges against you."

"Whatever it was you offered me—twenty rials? I'm morally entitled to it, but I won't claim it. Come and see me when you're ready for something more wholesome—and meanwhile, how do you like her?"

"That is something for me to tell her," I said, "not you."

Ardis returned as I spoke, bringing with her a balding black man with a mustache. "Paul, this is Nadan. His English is very good—not so British as most of them. He'll do, don't you think?"

"He'll have to—you're sure he'll do it?"

"He'll love it," Ardis said positively, and disappeared again.

It seemed that "Terry" was the actor who played Mary Rose's husband and lover, Simon; and I—who had never acted in so much as a school play—was to be pressed into the part. It was about half an hour before curtain time, so I had all of fifty minutes to learn my lines before my entrance at the end of the first act.

Paul, the director, warned me that if my name were used, the audience would be hostile; and since the character (in the version of the play they were presenting) was supposed to be an American, they would see errors where none existed. A moment later, while I was still in frantic rehearsal, I heard him saying, "The part of Şimon Blake will be taken by Ned Jefferson."

The act of stepping onto the stage for the first time was really the worst part of the entire affair. Fortunately I had the advantage of playing a nervous young man come to ask for the hand of his sweetheart, so that my shaky laughter and stammer became "acting."

My second scene—with Mary Rose and Cameron on the magic island—ought by rights to have been much more difficult than the first. I had had only the intermission in which to study my lines, and the scene called for pessimistic apprehension rather than mere anxiety. But all the speeches were short, and Paul had been able by that time to get them lettered on large sheets of paper, which he and the stage manager held up in the wings. Several times I was forced to extemporize, but though I forgot the playwright's words, I never lost my sense of the *trend* of the play, and was always able to contrive something to which Ardis and Cameron could adapt their replies.

In comparison to the first and second acts, my brief appearance in the third was a holiday; yet I have seldom been so exhausted as I was tonight when the stage darkened for Ardis' final confrontation with Kreton, and Cameron and I, and the middle-aged people who had played the Morelands were able to creep away.

We had to remain in costume until we had taken our bows, and it was nearly midnight before Ardis and I got something to eat at the same small, dirty bar outside which Kreton had tried to rob me. Over the steaming plates she asked me if I had enjoyed acting, and I had to nod.

"I thought you would. Under all that solidity you're a very dramatic person, I think."

I admitted it was true, and tried to explain why I feel that what I call *the romance of life* is the only thing worth seeking. She did not understand me, and so I passed it off as the result of having been brought up on the *Shah Namah*, of which I found she had never heard.

We went to her apartment. I was determined to take her by force if necessary—not because I would have enjoyed brutalizing her, but because I felt she would inevitably think my love far less than it was if I permitted her to put me off a second time. She showed me about her quarters (two small rooms in great disorder), then, after we had lifted into place the heavy bar that is the sigil of every American dwelling, put her arms about me. Her breath was fragrant with the arrack I had bought for her a few minutes before. I feel sure now that for the rest of my life that scent will recall this evening to me.

When we parted, I began to unloose the laces that closed her blouse, and she at once pinched out the candle. I pleaded that she was thus depriving me of half the joy I might have had of her love; but she would not permit me to relight it, and our caresses and the embraces of our couplings were exchanged in perfect darkness. I was in ecstasy. To have seen her, I would have blinded myself; yet nothing could have increased my delight.

When we separated for the last time, both spent utterly, and she left to wash, I sought for matches. First in the drawer of the unsteady little table beside the bed, then among the disorder of my own clothes, which I had dropped to the floor and we had kicked about. I found some eventually, but could not find the candle—Ardis, I think, had hidden it. I struck a match; but she had covered herself with a robe. I said, "Am I never to see you?"

"You will see me tomorrow. You're going to take me boating, and we'll picnic by the water, under the cherry trees. Tomorrow night the theater will be closed for Easter, and you can take me to a party. But now you are going home, and I am going to sleep." When I was dressed and standing in her doorway, I asked her if she loved me; but she stopped my mouth with a kiss.

I have already written about the rest—returning to find two eggs instead of three, and this book moved. I will not write of that again. But I have just—between this paragraph and the last—read over what I wrote earlier tonight, and it seems to me that one sentence should have had more weight than I gave it: when I said that in my role as Simon I never lost the *trend* of the play.

What the fabled secret buried by the old Americans beneath their carved mountain may be I do not know; but I believe that if it is some key to the world of human life, it must be some form of that. Every great man, I am sure, consciously or not, in those terms or others, has grasped that secret—save that in the play that is our life we can grapple that trend and draw it to left or right if we have the will.

So I am doing now. If the taking of the egg was not significant, yet I will make it so—indeed I already have, when I infused one egg with the drug. If the scheme in which Ardis is entangled—with Golam Gassem and Mr. Tallman if it be they—is not some affair of statecraft and dark treasure, yet I will make it so before the end. If our love is not a great love, destined to live forever in the hearts of the young and the mouths of the poets, it will be so before the end.

Once again I am here; and in all truth I am beginning to wonder if I do not write this journal only to read it. No man was ever happier than I am now—so happy, indeed, that I was sorely tempted not to taste either of the two eggs that remain. What if the drug, in place of hallucination, self-knowledge, and euphoria, brings permanent and despairing madness? Yet I have eaten it nonetheless, swallowing the whole sweet lump in a few bites. I would rather risk whatever may come than think myself a coward. With equanimity I await the effects.

The fact is that I am too happy for all the Faustian determination I penned last night. (How odd that *Faust* will be the company's next production. Kreton will be Mephistopheles of course—Ardis said as much, and it would be certain in any case. Ardis herself will be Margaret. But who will play the Doctor?) Yet now, when all the teeth-gritting, table-pounding determination is gone, I know that I will carry out the essentials of the *plan* more surely than ever—with the ease, in fact, of an accomplished violinist sawing out some simple tune while his mind roves elsewhere. I have been looking at the ruins of the Jeff (as they call it), and it has turned my mind again to the fate of the old Americans. How often they, who chose their leaders for superficial appearances of strength, wisdom, and resolution, must have elected them only because they were as fatigued as I was last night.

I had meant to buy a hamper of delicacies, and call for Ardis about one, but she came for me at eleven with a little basket already packed. We walked north along the bank of the channel until we reached the ruins of the old tomb to which I have already referred, and the nearly circular artificial lake the Americans call the Basin. It is rimmed with flowering trees—old and gnarled, but very beautiful in their robes of white blossom. For some little American coin we were given command of a bright blue boat with a sail twice or three times the size of my handkerchief, in which to dare the halcyon waters of the lake.

When we were well away from the people on shore, Ardis asked me, rather suddenly, if I intended to spend all my time in America here in Washington.

I told her that my original plan had been to stay here no more than a week, then make my way up the coast to Philadelphia and the other ancient cities before I returned home; but that now that I had met her I would stay here forever if she wished it.

"Haven't you ever wanted to see the interior? This strip of beach we live on is kept half alive by the ocean and the trade that crosses it; but a hundred miles inland lies the wreck of our entire civilization, waiting to be plundered."

"Then why doesn't someone plunder it?" I asked.

"They do. A year never passes without someone bringing some great prize out—but it is so large . . ." I could see her looking beyond the lake and the fragrant trees. "So large that whole cities are lost in it. There was an arch of gold at the entrance to St. Louis—no one knows what became of it. Denver, the Mile High City, was nested in silver mines; no one can find them now."

"Many of the old maps must still be in existence."

Ardis nodded slowly, and I sensed that she wanted to say more than she had. For a few seconds there was no sound but the water lapping against the side of the boat.

"I remember having seen some in the museum in Teheran—not only our maps, but some of your own from a hundred years ago."

"The courses of the rivers have changed," she said. "And when they have not, no one can be sure of it."

"Many buildings must still be standing, as they are here, in the Silent City."

"That was built of stone—more solidly than anything else in the country. But yes, some, many, are still there."

."Then it would be possible to fly in, land somewhere, and pillage them."

"There are many dangers, and so much rubble to look through that anyone might search for a lifetime and only scratch the surface."

I saw that talking of all this only made her unhappy, and tried to change the subject. "Didn't you say that I could escort you to a party tonight? What will that be like?"

"Nadan, I have to trust someone. You've never met my father, but he lives close to the hotel where you are staying, and has a shop where he sells old books and maps." (So I had visited the right house—almost—after all!) "When he was younger, he wanted to go into the interior. He made three or four trips, but never got farther than the Appalachian foothills. Eventually he married my mother and didn't feel any longer that he could take the risks . . ."

"I understand."

"The things he had sought to guide him to the wealth of the past became his stock in trade. Even today, people who live farther inland bring him old papers; he buys them and resells them. Some of those people are only a step better than the ones who dig up the cemeteries for the wedding rings of the dead women."

I recalled the rings I had bought in the shadow of the broken obelisk, and shuddered, though I do not believe Ardis observed it.

"I said that some of them were hardly better than the grave robbers. The truth is that some are worse—there are people in the interior who are no longer people. Our bodies are poisoned—you know that, don't you?

All of us Americans. They have adapted—that's what Father says—but they are no longer human. He made his peace with them long ago, and he trades with them still."

"You don't have to tell me this."

"Yes I do—I must. Would you go into the interior, if I went with you? The government will try to stop us if they learn of it, and to confiscate anything we find."

I assured her with every oath I could remember that with her beside me I would cross the continent on foot if need be.

"I told you about my father. I said that he sells the maps and records they bring him. What I did not tell you is that he reads them first. He has never given up, you see, in his heart."

"He has made a discovery?" I asked.

"He's made many—hundreds. Bobby and I have used them. You remember those men in the restaurant? Bobby went to each of them with a map and some of the old letters. He's persuaded them to help finance an expedition into the interior, and made each of them believe that we'll help him cheat the other—that keeps them from combining to cheat us, you see."

"And you want me to go with you?" I was beside myself with joy.

"We weren't going to go at all—Bobby was going to take the money, and go to Baghdad or Marrakesh, and take me with him.But, Nadan," here she leaned forward, I remember, and took my hands in hers, "there really is a secret. There are many, but one better—more likely to be true, more likely to yield truly immense wealth than all the others. I know you would share fairly with me. We'll divide everything, and I'll go back to Teheran with you."

I know that I have never been more happy in my life than I was then, in that silly boat. We sat together in the stern, nearly sinking it, under the combined shade of the tiny sail and Ardis' big straw hat, and kissed and stroked one another until we would have been pilloried a dozen times in Iran.

At last, when I could bear no more unconsummated love, we ate the sandwiches Ardis had brought, and drank some warmish, fruit-flavored beverage, and returned to shore.

When I took her home a few minutes ago, I very strongly urged her to let me come upstairs with her; I was on fire for her, sick to impale her upon my flesh and pour myself into her as some mad god before the coming of the Prophet might have poured his golden blood into the sea. She would not permit it—I think because she feared that her apartment could not be darkened enough to suit her modesty. I am determined that I will yet see her.

I have bathed and shaved to be ready for the party, and as there is still time I will insert here a description of the procession we passed on the way back from the lake. As you see, I have not yet completely abandoned the thought of a book of travels.

A very old man—I suppose a priest—carried a cross on a long pole, using it as a staff, and almost as a crutch. A much younger one, fat and sweating, walked backward before him swinging a smoking censer. Two robed boys carrying large candles preceded them, and they were followed by more robed children, singing, who fought with nudges and pinches when they felt the fat man was not watching them.

Like everyone else, I have seen this kind of thing done much better in Rome; but I was more affected by what I saw here. When the old priest was born, the greatness of America must have been a thing of such recent memory that few can have realized it had passed forever; and the entire procession—from the flickering candles in clear sunshine, to the dead leader lifted up, to his inattentive, bickering followers behind—seemed to me to incarnate the philosophy and the dilemma of these people. So I felt, at least, until I saw that they watched it as uncomprehendingly as they might if they themselves were only travelers abroad, and I realized that its ritualized plea for life renewed was more foreign to them than to me.

It is very late—three, my watch says.

I resolved again not to write in this book. To burn it or tear it to pieces, or to give it to some beggar; but now I am writing once again because I cannot sleep. The room reeks of my vomit, though I have thrown open the shutters and let in the night.

How could I have loved that? (And yet a few moments ago, when I tried to sleep, visions of Ellen pursued me back to wakefulness.)

The party was a masque, and Ardis had obtained a costume for me—a fantastic gilded armor from the wardrobe of the theater. She wore the robes of an Egyptian princess, and a domino. At midnight we lifted our masks and kissed, and in my heart I swore that tonight the mask of darkness would be lifted too.

When we left, I carried with me the bottle we had brought, still nearly half full; and before she pinched out the candle I persuaded her to pour out a final drink for us to share when the first frenzy of our desire was past. She—it—did as I asked, and set it on the little table near the bed. A long time afterward, when we lay gasping side by side, I found my pistol with one groping hand and fired the beam into the wide-bellied glass. Instantly it filled with blue fire from the burning alcohol. Ardis screamed, and sprang up.

I ask myself now how I could have loved; but then, how could I in one week have come so near to loving this corpse-country? Its eagle is dead—Ardis is the proper symbol of its rule.

One hope, one very small hope remains. It is possible that what I saw tonight is only an illusion, induced by the egg. I know now that the thing I killed before Ardis' father's house was real, and between this paragraph and the last I have eaten the last egg. If hallucinations now begin, I will know that what I saw by the light of the blazing arrack was in truth a thing with which I have lain, and in one way or another will see to it that I never return to corrupt the clean wombs of the women of our enduring race. I might seek to claim the miniatures of our heritage after all, and allow the guards to kill me—but what if I were to succeed? I am not fit to touch them. Perhaps the best end for me would be to travel alone into this maggot-riddled continent; in that way I will die at fit hands.

Later. Kreton is walking in the hall outside my door, and the tread of his twisted black shoe jars the building like an earthquake. I heard the word *police* as though it were thunder. My dead Ardis, very small and bright, has stepped out of the candle-flame, and there is a hairy face coming through the window.

The old woman closed the notebook. The younger woman, who had been reading over her shoulder, moved to the other side of the small table and seated herself on a cushion, her feet politely positioned so that the soles could not be seen. "He is alive then," she said.

The older woman remained silent, her gray head bowed over the notebook, which she held in both hands.

"He is certainly imprisoned, or ill; otherwise he would have been in touch with us." The younger woman paused, smoothing the fabric of her chador with her right hand, while the left toyed with the gem simulator she wore on a thin chain. "It is possible that he has already tried, but his letters have miscarried."

"You think this is his writing?" the older woman asked, opening the notebook at random. When the younger did not answer she added, "Perhaps. Perhaps."

Honorable Mentions—1978

Aldiss, Brian W., "A Chinese Perspective," *Anticipations*.
———, "The Small Stones of Tu Fu," *IASFM*, November-December.
———, "Three Ways," *F & SF*, April.
Anderson, Poul, "Hunter's Moon," *Analog*, November.
Bear, Greg, "Mandala," *New Dimensions 8*.
Benford, Gregory, "Nooncoming," *Universe 8*.
———, "Old Woman by the Road," *Destinies 1*.
———, "Starswarmer," *Analog*, September.
———, and Marc Laidlaw, "Hiss of Dragon," *Omni*, December.
Bischoff, David F., "In Medias Res," *Fantastic*, April.
Bishop, Michael, "Within the Walls of Tyre," *Weirdbook 13*.
———, and Strete, Craig, "Three Dream Woman," *New Dimensions 8*.
Blum, Christopher E., "Joy Ride," *Galileo 9*.
Bova, Ben, "The Last Decision," *Stellar 4*.
Boyd, J.P., "The First Star," *IASFM*, November-December.
Bryant, Edward, "Stone," *F & SF*, February.
Brennan, Herbie, "Time Lord," *F & SF*, January.
Broxon, Mildred Downey, "Singularity," *IASFM*, May-June.
Buckley, Bob, "The Runners," *Analog*, April.
Budrys, Algis, "The Nuptial Flight of Warbirds," *Analog*, May.
Cadigan, Patricia, "Death from Exposure," *Shayol 2*.
Card, Orson Scott, "Follower," *Analog*, February.

Carr, Terry, "Virra," *F & SF*, October.
Carver, Jeffrey A., "Seastate Zero," *F & SF*, October.
Cassutt, Michael, "Hunting," *Universe 8*.
Cherryh, C.J., "Cassandra," *F & SF*, October.
Clement, Hal, "Seasoning," *IASFM*, September-October.
Cross, Ronald Anthony, "The Birds are Free," *Orbit 20*.
Crowley, John, "Where Spirits Gat Them Home," *Shadows*.
Dann, Jack, "A Quiet Revolution for Death," *New Dimensions 8*.
Davidson, Avram, "A Good Night's Sleep," *F & SF*, August.
———, "The Redward Edward Papers," *The Redward Edward Papers*.
Disch, Thomas M., "Chanson Perpetuelle," *Immortal*.
———, "The Man Who Had No Idea, "*F & SF*, October.
Donaldson, Stephen R., "The Lady in White," *F & SF*, February.
Drake, David, "Caught in the Crossfire," *Chrysalis 2*.
Eisenstein, Phyllis, "In Answer to Your Call," *F & SF*, January.
Ellison, Harlan, "Opium," *Shayol 2*.
———, "The Man Who Was Heavily into Revenge," *Analog*, August.
Felice, Cynthia, "David and Lindy," *Universe 8*.
Gaither, Donald, "Wolf Tracks," *IASFM*, May-June.
Garrett, Randall, "Polly Plus," *IASFM*, May-June.
Grant, Charles L., "Caesar, Now Be Still," *F & SF*, September.
Gunn, Eileen, "What Are Friends For?" *Amazing*, November.
Hogan, James P., "Assassin," *Stellar 4*.
Ing, Dean, "Devil You Don't Know," *Analog*, January.
———, "Very Proper Charlies," *Destinies 1*.
Kelly, James Patrick, "Death Therapy," *F & SF*, July.
Kennedy, John, "Nova in a Bottle," *Galileo 6*.
Kennedy, Leigh, "Whale Song," *Omni*, November.
Kessel, John, "The Incredible Living Man," *Galileo 10*.
Killough, Lee, "A House Divided," *F & SF*, June.
King, Stephen, "The Gunslinger," *F & SF*, October.
———, "Nona," *Shadows*.
———, "Night of the Tiger," *F & SF*, October.
Lafferty, R.A., "Splinters," *Shadows*.
Lee, Tanith, "Winter White," *Best Horror Stories*.
Le Guin, Ursula K., "The Eye of the Heron," *Millennial Women*.
Leiber, Fritz, "Black Glass," *Andromeda 3*.
Lynn, Elizabeth A., "Jubilee's Story," *Millennial Women*.
Martin, George R.R., "Call Him Moses," *Analog*, February.
Monteleone, Thomas F., "Where All the Songs Are Sad," *Shadows*.
Moore, Raylyn, "The Ark Among the Flags," *F & SF*, May.
Nelson, R. Faraday, "Nightfall on the Dead Sea," *F & SF*, September.
Niven, Larry, "Cautionary Tale," *IASFM*, July-August.
———, "Flare Time," *Andromeda 3*.
Olonoff, Neil, "Indian Summer," *Unearth*, Summer.
Priest, Christopher, "The Cremation," *Andromeda 3*.
———,"The Watched," *F & SF*, April.
Pohl, Frederik, "The Way It Was," *Viva*, February.

Reamy, Tom, "Insects in Amber," *F* & *SF*, January.
———, "Waiting for Billy Starr," *Shayol 2*.
Roberts, Keith, "Ariadne Potts," *F* & *SF*, April.
Sargent, Pamela, "The Novella Race," *Orbit 20*.
———, "The Renewal," *Immortal*.
Sarowitz, Tony, "A Child of Penzance," *IASFM*, May-June.
Schenck, Hilbert, "The Morphology of the Kirkham Wreck," *F* & *SF*, *September*.
Sheffield, Charles, "Fixed Price War," *Analog*, May.
———, "The Treasure of Odirex," *Fantastic*, July.
Smith, Cordwainer, "The Queen of the Afternoon," *Galaxy*, April.
Sturgeon, Theodore, "Time Warp," *Omni*, October.
Tiptree, James Jr., "We Who Stole the Dream," *Stellar 4*.
Tuttle, Lisa, "A Piece of Rope," *Shayol 1*.
Vance, Jack, "The Secret," *The Many Worlds of Jack Vance*.
Vinge, Joan D., "Phoenix in the Ashes," *Millennial Women*.
Wallace, William, "The Mare," *Shayol 2*.
Wilhelm, Kate, "Moongate," *Orbit 20*.
Wolfe, Gene, "The Doctor of Death Island," *Immortal*.
Yolen, Jane, "The Tree's Wife," *F* & *SF*, June.
Zelazny, Roger, "Stand Pat, Ruby Stone," *Destinies 1*.